PRAISE FOR SIMON WOOD

"Simon Wood's *The One That Got Away* turns the serial-killer convention upside down in a genuinely suspenseful novel."

—Charlaine Harris, author of *The Day Shift*

"Wood is a master at ratcheting up the suspense—he starts strong on page 1 and doesn't let up until the final sentence. Wood is at the top of his game . . ."

—Allison Brennan, *New York Times* bestselling author of *Notorious*

"Wrenchingly intense—the talented Simon Wood goes psychologically dark and deeply disturbing. For those who like their thrillers twisty, shocking, and relentless."

—Hank Phillippi Ryan, Agatha, Anthony, Macavity, and Mary Higgins Clark award–winning author of *Truth Be Told*

"This author is a master at taking a simple situation and making it suspenseful."

—*Midwest Book Review*

"The tension is unbearable, and it gets worse as the pages fly by."

—*I Love a Mystery*

DECEPTIVE
PRACTICES

OTHER TITLES BY SIMON WOOD

DECEPTIVE
PRACTICES

SIMON
WOOD

Published by Thomas & Mercer, Seattle

www.apub.com

Amazon, the Amazon logo, and Thomas & Mercer are trademarks of Amazon.com, Inc., or its affiliates.

ISBN-13: 9781503940383
ISBN-10: 1503940381

Cover design by Jason Blackburn

Printed in the United States of America

For Royston. Miss you every day, buddy.

CHAPTER ONE

Rain streaked the Audi's windshield, obscuring Olivia's view. She didn't care. It hid the betrayal taking place across the street.

"You bastard, Richard," she murmured. "How could you?"

On the stoop of a house, her husband was in the arms of a woman she had never met. He held her in a tight embrace and kissed her with a passion Olivia hadn't seen from him in years.

Olivia didn't see what was so damn special about this woman. She was no supermodel, just blonde, trim, and willing. It wasn't like she was even young. Olivia guessed she was maybe five years younger at the most.

I have everything she has. The thought burned her. She knew that wasn't true. She was carrying a few extra pounds that hadn't been there when she'd married Richard eight years ago, but that was nothing an extra visit to the gym every week and a touch of dieting couldn't cure. In a matter of months, she could be sporting the same figure as Richard's piece of ass.

But looks weren't the problem. While it was easy to blame everything on them, she knew Richard's cheating was due to more than her appearance. Even through the tears and rain, Olivia saw one other distinct difference between her and her husband's mistress. The woman brimmed with excitement and lust. It had been a long time since Olivia had felt that way. Somewhere along the line, their life had become routine. Clocks could be set by it. When they had sex. When they went to eat out. When they saw their friends. The crackle of spontaneity had fizzled out at some point, and Olivia couldn't put her finger on when. The wipers pulsed, refreshing her view of the treachery.

She closed her eyes and wished for the bliss of ignorance so she could go along believing in her idyllic, suburban existence. She wished she hadn't seen the cracks in her life appear over the last few months. Richard always seemed to have an excuse not to be around her. He spent most of his time at work or at the athletic club. Yes, their lovemaking had dropped off since the early days of their marriage, but even she'd noticed their recent lack of sex play. Richard was always tired. Now she knew why. God, she'd been so dumb.

Finally, Richard pulled away from his mistress. He gazed lovingly into the woman's eyes and said something to her, then kissed her quickly on the mouth and trotted through the rain to his Mercedes sedan. He waved to her as he slipped behind the wheel. His mistress didn't step back inside. She watched him, standing barefoot on the cold concrete path, the rain soaking into her silk robe.

Love, Olivia thought. *He loves her.* Something sharp embedded itself into Olivia's heart. She pressed a hand to her chest and massaged the pain, but it wouldn't go away.

Richard got as far as firing up the engine before his little tramp called out to him. He killed the engine, and she disappeared inside the house. A moment later, she reemerged with his duffel bag.

His damn squash bag. It had been the smoking gun that had led Olivia here, to their love nest. Squash was Richard's game. He played every Tuesday and Thursday. Olivia was terrible at the game and never joined him. Last Thursday, he'd left his bag behind. She, being the dutiful wife, had run it over to the athletic club. Richard wasn't there, and no one had seen him in weeks. Although the truth had scratched at the base of her brain, she'd given him a chance to come clean. When he came home, she asked, "How'd the game go?"

"Great. I wiped the floor with Jerry."

He had kissed her. His hair was wet and slicked back from showering, and he smelled fresh and clean—like he always did after his matches.

"You forgot your bag."

"Yeah," he said with the merest of hesitations. "I begged and borrowed everything I needed from the guys."

The lies came so easily practiced. He hadn't even grappled for a deception. It was there, close at hand.

She'd caught him in a lie, but what kind of lie? Adultery had crossed her mind, but so had a dozen other possibilities. She saw no point in accusing him. All she had were suspicions. Throwing those in his face would drive the truth even further underground. But if she followed him and caught him in the act, then she robbed him of any chance to lie.

It had been stunningly easy to catch Richard. She knew the squash games were his cover. She'd simply waited outside of his office for him to leave. She had expected a long night of following her husband from place to place. Instead, he'd simply driven here to this house. He'd been in there two hours. It wasn't hard to imagine what he was doing. She could have run up to the door and kicked it in, but she hadn't had the heart. Discovering the truth had left her in misery.

The mistress scampered along the path with Richard's duffel in hand. He hopped from the car and met her halfway. He took the bag and cast it to the ground, then gathered her up in his arms, and the kissing started all over again.

Olivia felt sick. They were so blinded by their fun and games that they didn't even notice her parked across the street. Didn't they have any shame? Didn't they consider for one moment they'd be discovered?

The answer had to be no. God, she'd love to see their faces if she walked right up to them. Then they'd be sorry. Then they'd show some shame.

A sob leaked out of her and echoed off the confines of the car's cabin. The sound of it shocked her. It was the sound of her marriage ending.

It was time to bring the curtain down on this charade. Time to make the scene. Time for the ugly accusations and denials. She reached for her keys in the ignition, but instead of pulling them out, she hesitated.

Where was her victory in all this? Sure, she held the moral high ground. She was the jilted wife. But that was a hollow trophy.

She ran her thumb and forefinger over the comforting feel of her car key. An ugly thought developed in her head, one filled with revenge and hate and rage. She could run them down. They wouldn't know what hit them. They wouldn't even see it coming. She could do it. No one could stop her.

Her cell burst into song in the cup holder next to her. Clare's name appeared on the small display. Her sister was the only person who knew she was out here. If Olivia could have turned to anyone else, she would have. Their relationship was one bound by family guilt and obligation, which usually revolved around her bailing out her sister in some form or another. But for all that, Clare still ranked as the closest thing to a friend Olivia had. There was no one else she could turn to for support. When there was no one else, you turned to family, for better or worse.

Despite their tenuous relationship, Clare had stepped up and offered to join her tonight, but Olivia wanted to be alone for this. She couldn't face anyone witnessing the worst night of her life, even though Clare knew the pain of a broken marriage. At least her husband had the decency to run off. She picked up the phone.

"Is it a squash night?" Sarcasm weighed down Clare's question.

"He's cheating."

"Christ, I should have known, but I didn't want it to be true. I thought Richard was better than that. Do you know her?"

"No."

"Where are you?"

"In Walnut Creek. Outside her place. She lives only twenty minutes away. Very convenient."

"Saves on the gas, I suppose."

"They're outside on the street, kissing. They don't care who sees them."

"What are you going to do?"

"Run them down."

"That's not what I meant, Liv."

It was what Olivia meant. She didn't know where the idea had come from, but now that it was there, she'd warmed to it. What was the point of exposing the cheating couple? Who did it benefit? Not her. Her marriage was in tatters, and calling them out didn't solve anything. Worse still, Richard benefited. He had *her* to turn to. What did Olivia have? Nothing but a busted marriage and pain to look forward to. They deserved some pain too. If they wanted to be together, so be it, but there was a price to be paid.

She twisted the key in the ignition, and the engine burst to life. The sound failed to alert the lovers, who were too selfish to care about their surroundings. It would be so gratifying to hear their bones break against the car's unforgiving aluminum body.

"They haven't spotted me. I'm across the street in my car." She dragged the gearshift into drive. "I could take my foot off the brake and plow right over them."

Fear crept into Clare's voice. "Hey, that's dangerous talk, Liv."

"Who cares? They deserve it."

"You don't want to do that, Liv. They're the ones who've screwed up. If you hurt them, you're the one who gets into trouble. Not them."

Richard tightened his lover's embrace to the point that he lifted his mistress off the ground.

Clare was making sense, but who cared? Olivia's life was imploding, and it wasn't fair. Her foot trembled on the brake pedal, and the car inched forward.

"So they should get away with it?"

"No. I'm not saying that."

"It doesn't matter what happens. They get what they want—each other. I still lose. This way, at least there's some payback."

"I'm coming out there."

"No. Don't."

"This isn't you, Liv. Now me on the other hand, we both know I'm the stupid one when it comes to this crap. Not you. You're the smart one."

"I don't want to be smart. I'm sick of doing the right thing."

"Don't give them the satisfaction."

"Who gives a shit?"

"I do."

Her sister's concern cut her in two. Olivia needed it, but it hurt so much.

"You want payback?"

"Yes." The word came out exhausted and defeated.

"Then I can provide it. Forget them for now. Come to my place. You can have your payback. You just have to do it right. I can make it happen." Clare paused. "Are you listening, Liv?"

Olivia was.

CHAPTER TWO

It didn't take long to make the short journey from Walnut Creek to Martinez. As Olivia pulled into her sister's trailer park, another weight dropped onto her shoulders. She never liked coming here. It reminded her of an upbringing she'd left behind. Olivia had worked hard to escape the gravitational pull of trailer parks and crappy apartment complexes that her sister remained mired in. Clare was older than Olivia by three years, but she was reckless. If there was a way of screwing up a good situation, Clare would find it. Her behavior had always forced Olivia to be the responsible one.

Olivia stopped in front of the trailer. Clare had the door to her double-wide open before Olivia reached it. Her sister was small, not much over five feet and slight, which made her look fragile. Despite the small age gap, Clare appeared much older than Olivia. Crow's-feet and laugh lines had etched her face prematurely, and her bleached hair washed out her fine features.

"Oh, Liv. I'm so sorry," she said, pulling Olivia into a hug.

"Me too."

"C'mon, inside."

Clare sat Olivia down on the sofa in the same spot she'd sat last week when she'd poured out her fears and suspicions about Richard. It should have felt like a problem halved, but it felt more like a problem doubled. Speaking her fears out loud had only intensified the shame and embarrassment.

"I still can't believe he cheated," Olivia said.

"I can."

"What the hell is that supposed to mean?"

"He's a guy. It was just a matter of time. They all get bored, and obviously you didn't do enough to keep his dick from wandering."

"Thanks for the moral support, Sis."

"What do you want me to do, hold your hand and tell you it's all going to be okay?"

"A bit of sisterly love would be nice."

"Okay, okay, it probably feels like the end of the world right now, but it's not. You'll get through this. I did, and you will."

Clare knew this road well. Her ex-husband had taken off six years ago, leaving his debts and commitments for her to honor. It was probably why she had such a rosy image of men.

"I suppose that's the best I'm going to get."

"Yep."

Her sister grabbed a bottle of vodka from the refrigerator and two glasses from a kitchen cabinet, then went to pour them each a drink. Olivia put her hand up. Alcohol and self-pity were an ugly combination. Her refusal didn't stop Clare from pouring herself one.

Clare raised her glass. "Here's to the single life."

"Oh God, don't say that. I can't stand the thought of another failed marriage."

Olivia had once joked that Mark had been her starter husband. She'd married him straight out of high school. Playing grown-up had proved too hard for him. Two years into their marriage, he wrapped his

Trans Am around a tree. His blood-alcohol level had been through the roof at the time.

"I thought Richard was different."

"Everyone thinks that. The women of this family really know how to pick their men," Clare said with a smile. "But we Lyndon girls survive."

Survival had never sounded so depressing.

"How long do you think it's been going on?" Clare asked.

"A couple of months? A year? God knows."

"How do you feel?"

Olivia jumped to her feet and stormed away from her sister. There was no avoiding the question. In the trailer's limited space, she quickly ran out of real estate. "How do you think? Sad. Betrayed. Angry. Confused."

Olivia's words bounced off Clare. She sat, just sipping her vodka. "What do you want?"

"Want? I want tonight never to have happened. I want Richard to have stayed faithful. I want my marriage not to be on the rocks. What do these questions have to do with anything? I thought you said you could help me."

"I can, but I need you to answer my question first."

Olivia waved her hands dismissively. She brushed by her sister and grabbed her purse. "Look, I don't have time for this. I need to get home. I have a marriage to end."

"That's fine. Go. But one last question."

Olivia wasn't interested and kept heading for the door.

"Would you have really run Richard down?"

The question stopped Olivia and neutralized the rage boiling up inside her. She hated to admit it, but the answer was yes. Maybe her conscience would have stepped in at some point, but she knew in her heart of hearts that if Clare had told her to do it instead of talking her off the ledge, she would have done it.

"Sit down, Liv. We need to talk."

Olivia did as she was told.

"Do you want to patch things up with Richard?"

"It's not for me to patch anything. He's the one who broke a good thing."

Clare raised a hand. "Okay, are you interested in him making up for his mistake?"

"I don't know. A part of me says yes. I love Richard, but I'm not sure I can forgive him, and worse, I'm not sure I can trust him. There's nothing to say he won't do this again."

Clare refilled her glass, then looked at her drink. The sight of it seemed to disappoint her, and she put it next to the vodka bottle.

"Clare, please tell me what any of this has to do with the call. I understand if you were only talking me down, and I appreciate it. I could have done something really stupid tonight, and you stopped me. But if that's it, then I need to go."

"I'm trying to gauge how you feel. I want you to answer my first question."

"Which was what?"

"What do you want? Forget reconciliation. Forget divorce. Think about your emotions. How do you feel, and what do you want?"

It wasn't hard to answer. When she peeled everything back to the core, the answer was plain and simple. "I want to hurt Richard as much as he hurt me."

"That can be arranged."

Clare's answer stunned Olivia into silence. The only sound in the room was the growling air conditioner. "What does that mean?"

"There are people who can make him pay for what he's done to you."

"What are you talking about?"

"Infidelity Limited. They offer a discreet service that deals with infidelity issues."

"What do they do?"

Clare hesitated, just for a second, but that was enough. The hesitation told Olivia exactly what Infidelity Limited did to the adulterous men.

"Richard hurt you," Clare said, "and Infidelity Limited can hurt him back, in the way you wanted to tonight."

"They'll run him down?"

"No. They'll give him a beating."

"I can't have them do that. That's crazy."

"Liv, less than an hour ago, you were talking about wiping those two out. This is a safer option."

Yes, she'd come close to running Richard down, but that had been in the heat of the moment. Sending someone after him was a premeditated act of violence. "How do you know about these people?"

"I hired them to deal with Nick."

"You had Nick beaten up? Is that why he left you?"

"Yes. I'm not proud of what I did, but it had to be done. You have to understand that. If I hadn't done it, things would have been worse. He was flushing our lives down the toilet. He was spending money we didn't have. He knocked over a 7-Eleven; did you know that? I needed someone to scare him straight, so he would shape up or ship out. He chose to ship out."

Olivia's cell rang, making both of them jump. She pulled out the phone. It was Richard, calling from home. She frowned and answered the call.

"Hey, babe," Richard said. "Where are you? I thought you were staying in tonight."

Richard calling her "babe" after what he'd done tonight grated against every one of her nerve endings. She pushed her disgust to one side and injected a cheerful tone into her voice. "I'm at Clare's."

"What's gone wrong this time—money or men?"

His derision would have been justified yesterday. Not tonight. Piety only worked for the pious.

"Family is family," she replied.

"That's why I love you."

Each word of that lie burned her flesh through to the bone. Her grip on the phone turned into a stranglehold. "I'm going to stay here tonight. I'll come home in the morning."

"Okay. Call me if you need anything."

Did she detect a note of joy in his voice? The wife wasn't coming home, so he could run back to his slut for the night. She put the thought from her mind. There was no point in torturing herself. There'd be plenty of time for that in the coming weeks and months.

"I will. See you tomorrow," she said and hung up. "You asked me what I want to do, Clare? I want you to call Infidelity Limited."

CHAPTER THREE

Olivia sat, watching the shoppers at the Sunvalley Mall drift by her. There weren't many on a Friday morning. She felt conspicuous, as if everyone knew why she was there.

She checked her watch. Infidelity Limited was late. She'd kept up her end of the bargain. She'd arrived at the Starbucks precisely at noon, bought a coffee, and taken a table in the outdoor area. It was now 12:40, and she couldn't keep nursing her cold coffee for much longer. She couldn't believe she'd burned a vacation day on this shambles.

Clare had set up the meeting. It had taken a couple of days of calls through various intermediaries to get the word that they wanted to meet Olivia. Olivia understood the need for all the precautions, but it did nothing for her nerves. Her resolve was shrinking with every passing minute. Was she really going to have Richard beaten up?

The precautions had initially given her confidence, because they meant these people knew what they were doing. Now, she wasn't so sure. Being forty minutes late and counting didn't say much for their professionalism. In the meantime, Richard was still running around on her. Only last night he'd had another "squash night."

God, what am I doing? she thought. How had she gotten herself into this position?

She checked her watch again. She'd give Infidelity Limited until the top of the hour. If they hadn't contacted her by then, she was going. Screw them, and screw Richard. She'd go home, confront him, and tell him to get out. It wasn't like he didn't have somewhere to go.

A woman leaving the Starbucks interrupted Olivia from her thoughts. The woman crouched down, then dropped a napkin on the table. "Excuse me. I think you dropped this."

Olivia thanked the woman absently and picked up the paper napkin. She rolled it around in her hand for a minute before noticing the writing.

WOMEN'S RESTROOMS. UPPER LEVEL. NEXT TO PENNEY'S. NOW.

Olivia looked up. The woman who'd given her the napkin was long gone. Not that Olivia would recognize her. She hadn't even looked at her.

It didn't matter now. She'd been given her signal.

She left the coffee on the table, grabbed her purse, and rode the escalator to the upper level. The women's restroom was in a corner next to one of the main entrances into the mall. Her heart was beating rabbit fast when she pushed open the door to the ladies' room.

Two women were at the sinks, washing their hands and chatting. They didn't react to Olivia's arrival.

Were these women her contacts? Was she supposed to introduce herself? The napkin hadn't said.

The door to the handicapped stall opened, and a severe-looking woman with broad shoulders stood in the doorway. She put her finger to her lips and waved Olivia over.

Olivia glanced at the two women at the sinks to see if they'd caught the exchange. They hadn't, so Olivia joined the woman in the oversized stall and closed the door.

The woman was in her fifties. She was big in all her proportions. She weighed at least 250 pounds and stood close to six feet tall. Her hands were large and coarse. Her nails were unpainted, chipped, and split. She looked more than capable of dishing out a beating on Richard.

Olivia started to speak, but the woman raised a finger to silence her. When the two women at the sinks left, the woman said, "Okay. Strip."

"What?"

"We don't have time for questions. Strip."

"No."

"Look, you play by our rules or not at all. We don't take chances when it comes to this kind of work. We don't know who you are. You could be a cop for all we know. So you strip. Okay?"

Olivia nodded. The woman took Olivia's purse and rifled through it as Olivia kicked off her shoes and stripped down to her underwear. She guessed humiliation was part of their business too. They wanted to prove who was in charge.

The woman made a turn-around gesture and picked through Olivia's hair before checking her body for hidden devices. Then she turned her attention to Olivia's clothes, inspecting them for micro cameras, wires, and God knew what else. The inspection was conducted in silence, while other women entered and left the restroom unaware of the events going on inside the handicapped stall.

When the woman was done, she nodded to Olivia, and Olivia put her clothes back on.

The woman listened to make sure they were alone before opening the stall door. "I'll leave first. You wait two minutes; then you leave. Thank you for your cooperation. We'll be in touch."

Olivia grabbed the woman's arm. "Hey, wait a minute. What's going on here? I thought we had an arrangement."

The woman jabbed Olivia in the stomach. Suddenly, Olivia couldn't breathe. She sucked in air, but it didn't seem to find its way into her lungs. The woman guided her onto the toilet.

"What did I tell you about following the rules? If you want our help, you'll do as you're told."

Olivia nodded, still struggling for breath.

"I'm leaving now. Don't let me catch you tailing me."

Olivia nodded again, and the woman let herself out.

Olivia waited the two minutes before leaving the restroom. The woman was nowhere to be seen.

She'd had enough of this crap. Getting back at Richard wasn't worth this. A good divorce lawyer was what she needed.

She headed back to her car. Every time she took a step, she felt the woman's fingers where she'd poked Olivia under her rib cage.

They'd get in touch with her? No, she'd get in touch with them. She'd have Clare tell them thanks but no thanks. They had rules, and so did she. She had the right to choose, and she chose no.

As she walked through the parking garage, a Chrysler 300 stopped in front of her. The passenger window slid down, and a bald man craned his head to see her better.

"Get in," he said.

She froze.

"C'mon, Olivia. I don't have all day. You called us. Not the other way around."

Olivia glanced around before getting into the car.

He hit the gas the second she had her seat belt on.

"Apologies for the cloak-and-dagger act, but we can't take any chances. It's for your protection as well as ours. None of our clients will ever feel any pain if we do our due diligence."

Olivia rubbed her aching stomach. "Has anyone told the woman in the bathroom about that policy?"

The man laughed. "Dolores mentioned she had to use some force. She's a trip, isn't she?"

Yeah, you can say that again, Olivia thought.

"She gets a little overzealous from time to time. Jail time will do that to you. Her heart is in the right place. I'm Roy, by the way. I'm your case officer."

Like Dolores, Roy was in his fifties and had an ex-football-player look to him. He was broad shouldered and muscled despite some extra weight. He wore a Rolex and an ugly pinkie ring on his right hand.

Roy left the parking garage and joined the freeway, heading south toward San Jose. A trickle of fear seeped into her. There was no escape. She was this man's prisoner.

"If you're so concerned with security, why did you and Dolores let me see your faces?"

"I want you to see my face. It's important that you know me. It's easy for someone to sell out a faceless organization, but it's not so easy when you know the people you're doing business with. Knowing me will keep you honest."

"I don't think us being friends would stop me from selling you out."

"I didn't say we'd be friends. Look at me, Olivia. Take a good look. I want you to see the kind of man I am because just by looking at me, I think you can imagine the kind of pain I can inflict on a person."

Olivia didn't have to imagine too hard. He possessed the strength and size to fell the biggest of men. She'd already noticed the scar tissue built up over his knuckles. Now, she wondered how much of that scar tissue had been a result of people who'd tried to screw him and Infidelity Limited over.

"Make no mistake; I won't go to jail for you, Olivia. If you do anything to compromise my business, I will come after you. I know what you look like. I know where you live. I can get to you at any time. I'm more than well equipped. Do I make myself clear?"

Olivia started to speak, but her mouth had gone dry, and her voice cracked. She cleared her throat. "Crystal clear."

Roy smiled, the warmth returning to his face. "Do you have the consultation fee? I hate to ask for it, but with all the precautions I have to take, people need to be paid."

Olivia handed him an envelope from her purse, containing $500 in cash. He didn't check the envelope's contents; he simply dropped it in the door pocket.

"How much do you know about us?" Roy asked.

"Only what Clare told me. You take care of cheating spouses."

"That's how Infidelity Limited started out. If a wife found out her husband was cheating and she wanted a little payback, we provided the fists to do that. A little Old Testament, I'll grant you, but we were scratching an itch. We've come a long way since then. Cheating spouses are only one part of the business. We deal with wayward kids, abusive parents and spouses, stalkers, and people with addictions. If there's someone in your life causing you pain and grief, we can take care of it. And I don't want you thinking that we're nothing more than a bunch of thugs who go around whaling on people. We tailor our approach to your specific situation. For example, cheating spouses get treated differently than a stalker. Vengeance might be the overriding desire in cases of infidelity, whereas safety is the primary concern when it comes to stalkers. Making that stalker leave town will be our primary aim."

It was odd to listen to Roy speak about Infidelity Limited in such lofty terms, like they were some philanthropic organization and not a criminal enterprise. She couldn't decide if it was a method for desensitizing their clients to the violence or legitimizing their existence to themselves.

"The reason I'm telling you all this is we can't do our job if you don't tell us what you want to gain from our intervention. What are your needs here?"

It was a good question that she had trouble answering.

Roy picked up on her hesitancy. "Why don't you tell me a little about the situation? Your husband is having an affair, right?"

"Yes."

"How long's it been going on for?"

"I don't know. I found out for sure a week ago last Thursday, but I think it's been going on some time."

"Who's the woman?"

"I don't know her, but I know where she lives."

"Why don't you tell me how you feel about your husband's cheating?"

"I feel like a failure."

Roy smiled. "And a host of other things, I bet."

Olivia smiled back. "Yes."

"I've become a little bit of an amateur therapist with this job. I've heard it and seen it all. Everybody's story is different, but also the same. The big question is, do you want revenge?"

"He hurt me, and I want to hurt him back. If I scream at him, tell him what a shit he's been, demand answers, and do all the things he expects, I doubt he'll get the message. He might understand all this if you did something to him. That's what I'm telling myself anyway."

"That makes sense and is very fair under the circumstances. Do you want him back? It will dictate how I go about *educating* Richard on his mistake."

Educating. She liked that. Never had she equated violence with education, but maybe that was why her life was in the toilet.

"I don't know. Part of me says no. He betrayed me, and it's over. But part of me says yes. I know this is stupid, but I still love him. We've had a lot of good years together, and I would hate to write them off. To be honest, it's all too raw. I don't know what I want. I don't even know what's possible. I think I might take him back under the right circumstances, but I'd want to see real contrition."

"I might be able to turn him around. I've managed it with others, but there are no guarantees. People will only reform if they want to. He won't appreciate our intervention. At least, he certainly won't in the short term. Just know that the action Infidelity Limited takes could push him further away."

She was prepared for that eventuality. Saying it with flowers worked. Saying it with fists probably didn't. A failed marriage would hurt, but she'd accept it if it happened.

"How safe am I from reprisals?" she asked.

"It all depends. Do you think Richard will be violent?"

"No, but what's stopping him from calling the police? He'll know that I orchestrated this."

"The honest answer is there's nothing stopping him. But you don't have anything to fear. No one we've dealt with is thinking about the police after we've visited them. Either they're walking the wrong side of the law themselves and wouldn't welcome any police involvement or they don't want the world to know their spouse caught them cheating and they caught a beating for it."

If there was one thing Richard valued, it was his reputation. If push came to literal shove, he'd keep quiet.

"Got any questions for me?"

"Are you married, Roy?"

He showed her his ringless left hand. "Not married, but I have a woman in my life who is very special to me."

"Ever cheated on her or anyone else?"

"No. Never."

"How'd you get into all this?"

"A friend needed someone bigger and stronger than her to send a message, and I was that person. I saw how I could do the same for others, so I started Infidelity Limited. Let's get you back to your car."

Roy turned the car around at the next exit. On the way back, he made small talk. After a while, Olivia noticed he always kept to generalities, never divulging anything personal about himself. Precautions again. She didn't let it bother her. She was growing to like Roy despite what he did.

"I don't think I have to tell you that you can't breathe a word of our arrangement to anyone. I know your sister is a previous client, but I don't even want you discussing this with her. We have a doctor-patient-style arrangement here. Your sister doesn't tell you about her arrangement, and you don't tell her about yours. Infidelity Limited operates and survives under a veil of secrecy. Is that understood?"

Olivia nodded.

"How would you like me to proceed?" Roy asked.

Two days ago she would have told Roy to go ahead. Now she wasn't so sure. Infidelity Limited scared her. They were slick and capable. Their clandestine display this morning demonstrated their relative ease at this kind of work. She could only imagine how efficiently they'd take care of Richard. Strangely, she would have felt more comfortable around a less competent group. It would even up the playing field. Richard stood a chance against thugs but not against the likes of Roy.

"If you want time to think about it, that's not a problem," Roy said. "Prudence is a good thing. This isn't a decision to be taken lightly. There's no going back once you start down this road. If you're hoping for reconciliation, it might not be an option once we get going. In the meantime, there's something for you in the glove box."

Olivia opened it and removed a cell phone.

"If you want to get in contact with me, use that phone and only that phone. It's disposable and totally untraceable. My number is programmed into it. It will be live for two weeks only. After that, the number will go dead, and I'll assume you don't wish to go any further. Understood?"

Olivia eyed Roy and nodded.

He scared her, but not physically. She wasn't scared of him. She was scared of herself. Roy had held up a mirror, and she hadn't liked her reflection. She considered herself as red-blooded as the next person, but like most people, she came equipped with an inhibitor switch that prevented her baser side from taking over. It had almost failed her outside the mistress's house, but she had held herself back from running over Richard and his piece of ass. Meeting with Infidelity Limited underlined how far she'd floated into the deep end. Desperate people, not her, hired thugs to solve their problems. She owed Roy a debt of gratitude. He'd helped her come to her senses. There was a right way and a wrong way to solve problems, and she'd come a decision away from making a regrettable choice.

She shook her head. What was wrong with her? What had made her think Infidelity Limited was the solution to her problems? The answer wasn't a what, but a who. Infidelity Limited was such a Clare thing to do. Poor decisions were her sister's MO. She didn't blame Clare for bringing in the likes of Roy to deal with Nick. Nick wasn't the kind of guy to see sense, so telling him not to piss his life away was never going to work. It would have taken someone beating the living crap out of him before he made a life change.

But it was wrong for her to pin everything on Clare. Her sister had been trying to help, trying to stop her from doing a monumentally stupid thing. She'd lost her head when options were still open to her. Yes, Clare had led her to Infidelity Limited, but she didn't have to employ them.

The fault belonged to one person and one person alone—Richard. He was the one who'd cheated. He'd hurt her so badly that she'd considered inflicting physical harm on him.

Yes, he deserved to be punished, but Infidelity Limited wasn't the answer. Counseling or a divorce lawyer was. She needed to do what she should have done last Thursday—confront him. Put the onus on him. What happened next between them rested on his shoulders, not hers. If he wanted to end the affair and make a concerted effort to repair the damage, so be it. She'd help him make up for his mistake. If he wanted his mistress and not her, screw him, and she'd see him in court.

The thought of divorce threw her back to the night she discovered Richard cheating. Divorce did nothing to punish him. It only gave him what he wanted—an out. It would cost him financially, but California was a no-fault-divorce state, so there was no punitive cost for what he'd done to her. He'd get to keep his half and move on. She'd have her assets but no victory. No pound of flesh.

Roy glanced over at her. "Everything okay? You've gone a bit quiet on me."

"Yeah. Fine."

He nodded and turned back to his driving.

Why did she have to do the right thing, when everyone else could be reckless? That single thought seared her to the core. God knew Clare never suffered any consequences. Even Richard had his mistress and nothing significant was going to happen to him because of it. If it was okay for them, then why couldn't it be okay for her? For once in her life, she wasn't going to be the grown-up; she wasn't going to do the right thing, the better thing. She was going to take her hands off the wheel and let fate do the driving and not worry about what happened next.

Roy eased the Chrysler off I-680 and drove back to the mall's parking lot. He found an empty parking stall and stopped the car. He turned in his seat. "It's been a pleasure meeting you, Olivia. I do wish it had been under better circumstances. Take the cell phone, and think about your next step. Give me a call with whatever you decide. Like I said, I'll keep the line open for the next two weeks."

"I don't need two weeks."

"No?"

"I want you to go ahead," she said after a moment.

"You realize there's no going back?"

"I do."

"And you're sure? Please don't feel pressured."

She lifted her gaze from the burner cell phone and looked Roy in the eyes. "I want to do this."

"Good. We need to make arrangements. I'll need two thousand for the job, in cash and in advance. There's no follow-up after it's done. We do it; then you don't hear from us again and vice versa. Okay?"

"Okay. Good."

"That's the easy part. I'll also need a complete rundown of Richard's movements on a daily basis—where he goes and who he meets. I want the names and addresses of his place of work and regular hangouts, and that includes his mistress's place."

"Are you going to involve her?"

"Not unless you want me to."

"No, I don't want that."

"Okay, in this kind of work, we have to move fast and usually at the spur of the moment. When a good opportunity presents itself, we go for it. Make sense?"

"Yes."

"What's the make and model of his car and the license plate number?"

She told him.

"I also need a couple of good head shots of Richard. I don't want to make any mistakes when it comes to identification. Yes?"

She nodded.

He reached over and grabbed the cell phone from the glove box. "When you have all the information and the money ready, call me."

She nodded again. The ability to speak seemed to have deserted her now that she'd made the decision.

"Don't worry, Olivia. You'll feel a lot better when this is done."

CHAPTER FOUR

Roy stood on the ninth floor of an office building with "For Lease" signs on every floor, gazing out at downtown San Jose. Power still fed the dormant building, and fluorescent light spilled into the night. It was a futile beacon serving to entice potential renters to move in. He'd selected this location because vacant lots and derelict warehouses tended to unsettle most of his clientele. Office buildings provided familiar and friendly places to meet.

He'd arrived early, primarily to get the lay of the land in case his client tried to get cute. This way, he could also take in the world and get a little silence. He made a very nice living at Infidelity Limited, but it wasn't an easy one. He was always in motion—meeting clients, wrangling people, twisting arms, and breaking legs. Whenever he could, he grabbed some peace and quiet. And he got it here. It was refreshing, watching the world through soundproofed glazing. Out there, people were living their lives, raising families, and doing the best they could. He'd never meet those people because he made his bed with the desperate and the angry. It was why he was meeting Brian Townsend here today.

His cell phone burst into song. He removed it from his pocket and eyed the tiny display. "Hello, Olivia. How are you?"

"I'm fine."

Over the years, Roy had gotten good at reading potential clients. He knew within a minute who would fold and who'd go all in. He'd known Olivia would go all in. He saw it in her eyes and the way she held herself. Some might see her as just a rich wife, but only if they concentrated on the superficial—the clothes, the platinum credit cards, the house, and the car. If you really looked at Olivia and saw through the consumerism, you would see a woman who'd lived. She was soft around the edges now, but she hadn't always been that way. Roy had a background check under way, but he knew it would come back with the news that she'd clawed her way up to where she found herself now. She was too self-aware not to be a woman who'd experienced the harsher side of life. Someone might have gotten the better of her once, but it wouldn't happen twice.

It had been a few days since he'd met her. "Do you have everything for me?"

"Yes, I've got everything I think you'll need and the money."

"Good. We'll meet for the exchange. I'll call you. Be ready to meet me the second I call. Can you do that?"

"Yes."

Her response came out flustered, which was just the way he wanted. He couldn't let her have any time to think. She might be the client, but he called the shots. He often put his clients in a threatening position, hit them with rapid-fire demands, or kept them unsure of the schedule to put them permanently on their back foot. This forced them to be forever reacting to the situation, robbing them of the ability to compose their own plans. Manipulation ensured his personal safety and the safety of the business.

Roy's two-way radio squawked on a table.

"I'll be in touch, Olivia," he said and hung up before she could ask any further questions.

He grabbed the radio and keyed the mic. "Yeah?"

"Townsend's on his way," Carrington, one of his trusted freelancers, said. "ETA two minutes."

"Is he being a good boy?"

"Looks like it."

"Okay. When he gets here, you can take off."

"Don't you want me to stick around?"

Even if he'd only half managed to whip Townsend into a nervous state, the guy still posed no threat to him. "No, you're done for the night."

He put the radio down and switched off the office lights before grabbing a pair of binoculars. He went to the window and watched for Townsend's arrival.

A minute later, Townsend's SUV pulled into the parking lot. Roy focused the binoculars on the vehicle. Townsend emerged looking suitably sheepish, shooting furtive glances in all directions. The man was off-kilter, but was he following instructions?

"Where is it, Brian?"

Townsend scurried around to the rear of the car, popped the tailgate, and jerked a briefcase from the trunk.

"Good boy."

Roy watched Townsend until he entered the building. He flicked the lights back on and waited at the elevators in the hallway. The "Up" arrow lit up, and a minute later the elevator doors slid open. Townsend stepped off. He was frighteningly pale.

"This way, Brian," Roy said, nodding to the open office. "I'm all ready for you in here." Roy pointed to an abandoned conference table in the middle of the office.

Townsend stopped in the doorway. "I brought the money. Now where's . . ." He stalled midsentence. "Where is it? Where's my stuff?"

Interesting, Roy thought. Townsend couldn't bring himself to say "the murder weapon" or "the evidence." The world was a squeamish place.

"Not so fast, Brian. You're not buying a burger at a drive-through. This is serious business. If you want to make sure nothing goes wrong, we have to go through this carefully." Roy patted the table. "Now come in."

Beads of sweat ran down Townsend's face when he shook his head. He licked his lips with a dry tongue. Roy guessed Townsend would be close to dehydration by the time this meeting was over.

"Show me yours, and I'll show you mine," Roy said with a smile, and Townsend put his briefcase on the table.

Roy let the briefcase sit there. "You've behaved yourself, Brian, haven't you?"

"Yes. I've done exactly as you've told me."

"That's good, because I wouldn't want to learn you'd gotten into bed with the cops. They might pretend to be your friends, but I guarantee they don't give a shit about you. You have only one friend in the world, and that's me."

"Some friend you are."

Roy put a hand to his heart. "Oh, Brian, I'm hurt."

Townsend's face creased into disgust. "I haven't been to the cops."

"But they've been to you."

"Only because you took it too far."

Roy shrugged. "These things happen. You knew the risks going in."

"These things happen? You killed my wife."

Laura Townsend had been a serial adulterer. She'd been running around on Townsend for most of their eighteen-year marriage. Townsend had put up with the running around until he discovered that his daughter wasn't his. He wanted his wife to be taught a lesson, and Roy was true to his word.

In some ways, Roy didn't fault Laura for her philandering. Townsend was hardly a man to keep the fire alive. Roy had spent two weeks shadowing her. She was vivacious in every sense of the word. She'd been keeping two men on the go.

"Don't tell me you aren't secretly pleased by what we did."

Townsend ran a trembling hand across his mouth. "Christ, I wish I'd never met you people."

"I think we're getting a little off track. Is that my money?"

"Yes."

"Then let's see it."

Townsend opened up the briefcase, and what looked to be the $200,000 Roy had requested spilled onto the table. "That's it. That's everything I have."

If Townsend was hoping for sympathy, he wasn't getting it. Instead, Roy picked up a banded pack of bills and counted. Townsend paced as Roy went through all twenty packs. Good to his word, Townsend had brought the $200,000. Not a dollar more or less. No explosive dye packs or GPS trackers. He was playing by the rules.

"Satisfied?" Townsend asked.

"Very."

Townsend swiped at the money with the back of his hand, sending it flying. A pack of bills bounced off Roy's legs. "Well then."

"Watch your tone, Brian. I'm being courteous to you, and I expect the same in return."

Townsend sneered. "Forgive my bad manners. Under the circumstances, I'm not in the mood for your bullshit."

Townsend was growing some balls. Roy needed to watch that. He might develop a hero complex, and that needed to be nipped in the bud. Roy popped the locks on an aluminum briefcase and opened it. Before touching any of the contents, he snapped on a pair of gloves. He removed a carving knife with blood dried on the blade and tossed it on the table. It skittered across the table's smooth surface, coming to a halt in front of Townsend.

Townsend tried to say something, but his words died in his throat.

Roy had thought the introduction of the murder weapon might have that effect.

Townsend clutched his stomach and pressed a hand against the table to keep upright. "I never wanted this."

"Whether you wanted it or not, you got it."

Suddenly, Townsend backed away from the knife that had been used to kill his wife as if it were a smoking stick of dynamite. "The cops think I killed her."

"And you did."

"I didn't."

"You might not have had your hand wrapped around the knife, but you paid us to hurt your wife—and hurt her we did."

Townsend bumped into a support column and slid down onto his butt. He put his hands to his head, stared into the carpeting, and shook his head. "What have I done?"

Roy examined Townsend. His body language screamed defeat. If the cops scooped him up now, he'd spill his guts at the first question.

"I haven't brought everything," Roy said. "I still have her dress and jewelry."

That snapped Townsend back into the here and now. "No. We agreed on everything. That's what the money is for. That's not right."

"I know, but I'm keeping those things. My people have been monitoring the situation, and the sharks are circling, Brian. The cops are preparing an arrest warrant, and Infidelity Limited can't be implicated, so we've taken precautions. In the event of your arrest, the police will find vital physical evidence. The evidence will negate any attempts you make to implicate us. Is that clear?"

"No," Townsend said.

Roy wasn't sure if his answer was in response to the question or an act of defiance. "Yes. You need to prepare yourself for the fact that the police will arrest you and there's nothing you can do to stop it."

Roy didn't bother telling Townsend he'd been feeding the murder investigation information from the moment it became clear that Townsend was a liability. This happened from time to time. Clients came to Infidelity Limited spitting fire and baying blood but found their raw emotion and righteous indignation withered on the vine when faced with the harsh realities of bloody vengeance. It was understandable. Not everyone had the stomach for the consequences. Brian Townsend was one such person. Roy had seen the cracks in Townsend's resolve after Townsend gave him the green light to go after his cheating wife. As a precaution, Roy had put a surveillance team on him. Townsend had made cryptic calls to a lawyer buddy and tried to warn his wife. Every rule Roy had given him, he set about breaking. At that point, Roy had made the decision to burn Townsend before he could burn Infidelity Limited.

"What do I do? Can you help me?"

Roy contained a smile. He liked it when they played into his hands. "You can run, of course. I can help you with that, but there are no guarantees. Besides, it'll cost money to set you up with a new identity in a new location. Do you have any more money?"

It was a cruel question on Roy's part. They both knew the answer to that. All the money Townsend had in the world sat on the table between them. Townsend eyed his dirty cash. So close yet so out of reach. His gaze fell away, and he shook his head.

"You can try running on your own. I doubt you'd get far. Living off the radar is damn near impossible."

"Stop. Just stop. You've made your point. I'll turn myself in to the cops."

"You do have another option. It's very doable and comes at no extra charge."

"What is it?"

There was no hope in Townsend's eyes. He'd surrendered. That was good. He was just where Roy wanted him.

Roy reached inside his briefcase and produced a gun. The .38-caliber revolver was one of many unregistered weapons he had available to him. He put it on the table in front of Townsend.

"I think if you're truly honest with yourself, you know you won't do well in prison. I don't mean to be disparaging. Not many people do. That's why there are so many law-abiding people."

"Is it loaded?" Townsend asked.

"Yes."

Townsend picked up the weapon and examined it. Roy fought the urge to give instructions. They weren't necessary. Townsend would figure it out all by himself.

"This is my escape?" Townsend asked.

"If you want it."

Townsend aimed the gun at Roy.

Roy's pulse remained steady. He'd had a lot of guns aimed at him over the years. Very few people were capable of murder. Townsend wasn't one, or he would have taken care of his wife himself.

"And what is your escape?" Townsend asked.

"I just take my money and disappear."

"And what if I change that for you?"

"You can, but you won't. You want someone to blame. I get that. But remember, you came to me. You wanted this, and it didn't work out for you the way you had hoped. Killing me won't rid you of your guilt for your part in this."

"My wife is dead."

"I know."

"I didn't want that."

"No one ever does."

Townsend's grip tightened on the .38, but Roy saw no conviction in his eyes. "I should kill you."

"But you won't."

Townsend let his arm go slack. "Get out. I'm tired of you and your theories."

Roy nodded. He piled the cash back into the briefcase and walked out. While he waited for the elevator to arrive, he listened to Townsend sob, spew self-incriminating rhetoric, and call out his wife's name. Just as the elevator doors opened, the gun went off.

Roy let the elevator go and returned to the office. He staged the scene a little better to make it more conducive to a suicide. He took everything he and Townsend had brought to the office building—the travel case, the binoculars—leaving only the incriminating evidence and the gun.

On the ride down to the lobby, he called home.

"Is it done?" Beth asked.

"Yes. I have the money, and Townsend's body will be discovered by security in the morning. Another piece of good news is that Olivia Shaw is ready to go. There's a lot more mileage with her than with Townsend."

"Then make all the necessary arrangements."

"Already on it. See you tomorrow."

CHAPTER FIVE

Olivia listened to the prerecorded voice telling her to leave a message again. She threw the cell phone across the room. It hit the sofa and bounced onto the floor.

"Goddamn you, Roy."

She hadn't heard anything from Infidelity Limited since she'd paid them the two grand. Every time she tried to get in touch, she got the same message. Roy had assured her that she'd see results in a few days, and there'd been nothing. It had been two weeks. Infidelity Limited was a scam. She was convinced of it.

In the meantime, she'd been forced to watch Richard carry on as normal. That was the worst part of this farce—the knowing. When she'd lived in ignorance, it was fine. But now, to know for sure that her husband was cheating and have to pretend she was as dumb as he believed her to be was excruciating.

Since it was his Thursday night "squash game," she grabbed her car keys and peeled out of the garage. If Infidelity Limited wasn't going to do its job, then she would. She cut across town to *her* place.

Her. She would like to know her name. It was one of those things that she hoped Infidelity Limited would find out for her. She was tired of thinking of her as *that bitch, that slut, that tramp.*

She pulled up in front of the house. The place was in darkness, and Richard's car wasn't parked outside. Tonight's festivities were happening elsewhere.

She climbed from the car, leaving the engine running. A tingle ran through her when she set foot on the woman's property. This was the source of her misery. She went up to the door and pressed the doorbell. When no one answered, she banged on the door and yelled Richard's name. Still nothing.

Wrong again, she thought. *Wrong place. Wrong time.* Tears welled up and spilled down her face. They burned a path across her flushed cheeks. She felt like kicking in the door, but what was the point? She returned to her car and got behind the wheel.

She sat there for a moment, contemplating her next move. Go home. Richard would eventually return to her. He always did. It was so passive. And that was her problem. She had taken a backseat to her problems. She never used to, but somehow she'd fallen into lazy ways. What was she going to do now? She could trawl the streets for them, but she wouldn't find them. If she couldn't take her frustrations out on Richard and his slut, someone else would have to do, and she knew just the person—Clare. She'd put her in touch with Infidelity Limited. She had some explaining to do.

She turned the car around and drove to Martinez. With her foot down, she made the journey in minutes. She turned the corner onto the narrow road where Clare's trailer sat. A pickup blocked Clare's aging Honda Civic in its carport. The pickup's driver, a heavily built, balding guy, circled the trailer like a hungry animal with a whiff of prey in its nostrils.

Olivia pulled up alongside the pickup.

The driver circled back around to the front of the trailer and thumped on the door with a fist. "C'mon, Clare. I know you're in there. Get your ass out here."

Olivia jumped from the car. "Hey, what do you think you're doing?"

The guy jerked out a hand to stop her from coming any closer. "If you're here to collect too, you get paid after I do. Okay?"

Olivia groaned inside. Clare and money. Two things that failed to stay in each other's company for more than a fleeting moment. She brushed the driver aside to get to the front door.

"Clare, it's me. Open up."

"Yeah, Clare, do as the lady says and bring cash."

She flashed the jerk a look of irritation.

"What?" he said. "And don't think you're going to get my money out of her."

"I'm her sister, asshole. If you want your money, you'll back off and let me deal with this."

The pickup driver frowned, but said nothing. Olivia knew she could push the guy without any fear of retaliation. If he wanted to leave with his money, he'd have to sit on his pride awhile.

The lock on the trailer door snapped back, and Clare peeked out. The driver stepped forward, but Olivia stopped his advance with a look.

"Can I come in?" Olivia asked her sister.

Clare nodded.

"You wait there," Olivia told the pickup driver. "You'll get your money."

Clare opened up the door, and Olivia slipped inside. Clare relatched the door, then ushered Olivia into the living room.

"What's going on?" Olivia asked. "Who is that guy?"

Clare dropped onto the sofa. "He's a friend of a friend. I owe him money."

Friends of Clare's friends were usually in the money-lending business. Olivia pictured some astronomical interest rate racking up by the minute.

"What happened to the five hundred I gave you the other week?" Olivia asked.

"What do you think, Liv? Food. Expenses."

"So how much do you owe this guy?"

"Three grand or so."

"Three thousand? How can you get that far behind, Clare?"

"Liv, don't start. Bills are piling up. The Honda's transmission needed fixing. I was behind on the rent. It all adds up."

"You've been gambling again, haven't you?"

"Jesus. I knew you'd say that. No, I haven't been gambling."

Olivia knew her sister too well. Clare thought she could make money the easy way, by winning it instead of earning it. One lucky streak and she'd be living the good life. Olivia had helped her sister curb her gambling problem, but not kick it. The loan shark outside now made perfect sense.

"Oh, Clare. Why do you always do this?"

"Don't give me that. It's easy for you to make your money troubles go away with a snap of your fingers, but it doesn't work that way for the rest of us."

Olivia didn't bother telling her sister that her ability to pay her way came from constructing a lifestyle that could weather financial storms. It was an old argument between them that neither of them ever saw eye to eye on. She knew what was coming next in this familiar argument. She was the rich sister. She'd be asked to bail out her sibling with a loan that would never be repaid because she could afford to lose a few grand here and there. Family ties. Sometimes the knots really bound. She wasn't about to go through the dog and pony show again and went to the door.

"What are you doing?" Clare demanded.

"Getting rid of this guy."

Olivia opened the door. The pickup owner was leaning against Clare's Honda. He pushed himself off when she appeared.

"How much do you need to go away?" she asked.

"Thirty-one hundred."

Olivia pulled out her checkbook from her purse.

"This is a cash-only transaction."

"You see that Audi next to your piece of crap? That's mine. Does it look like I can't cover thirty-one hundred?"

"How do I know it's not leased?"

"You don't, but that's not the issue here. You get a check. You get my name and address. You know exactly where to find me if it doesn't clear."

She let the pickup driver mull that one over for a minute.

"Okay," he said. "I'll take a check, but I want any cash you have."

"I'll give you the hundred in cash."

The guy frowned and held out his hand.

Olivia wrote out the check, leaving the payee line blank, and held it out with the cash. When the pickup driver grabbed it, Olivia held on to her end. "If Clare runs up a debt, I don't want to find you banging on her door. You come to me. Got it?"

The pickup driver grinned and looked her up and down. "Sure thing. You must be the smart sister."

She released her grip on the check and slammed the trailer door in his face.

Problem solved. She'd dealt with Clare's problems effectively and efficiently. How come she couldn't do the same for herself?

Olivia had surprised herself with her display. She hadn't shown her tough side in a long while. Maybe her current problems were bringing it out. Since she'd met Richard, life had been good to her, but it had made her soft. Richard's cheating and Infidelity Limited's ineffectiveness were helping her find some muscle memory.

"Thanks, Liv."

"Do you still need cash?" she asked, because she knew the request would be coming.

"Maybe another five hundred."

Olivia wrote a check for a thousand. Clare thanked her again and reached for it, but Olivia kept it just out of her reach. "I can't keep doing this, Clare. You really need to sort out your finances."

"Did you want something, or did you come here to lecture?"

Olivia saw them heading toward an argument she didn't want. She sat down on the sofa across from Clare. "It's about Infidelity Limited."

"Did they take care of Richard?"

Olivia shook her head. "Nothing's happened since I paid Roy. He never answers the phone or returns my messages, and I have no other way of getting in touch. Meanwhile, Richard is out there banging his tramp and I have to sit back and take it."

"I wouldn't worry. Sometimes these things take time. They'll do their job."

"Will they? How do I know this isn't some scam and they haven't made off with my money, never to be seen again?"

"They helped me, didn't they?"

Did they? It suddenly occurred to Olivia that the Infidelity Limited scam could be of Clare's devising. She always needed money, and Olivia always played the part of the surrogate ATM. Last year, Clare's gambling debt had topped ten grand. Richard had cleared her debts with one proviso—no more bailouts. Other than the occasional handout here and there, Olivia had held strong. So Infidelity Limited could be Clare's way of squeezing another couple of thousand out of her. Olivia dropped the thought as quickly as it had come. Clare had hustled her from time to time, and it wouldn't be the first time she'd invented something to get a few dollars out of her sister, but the interactions with Roy were far too convoluted and complex for this to be one of Clare's schemes.

"How long after you paid before they got to Nick?"

"A few days."

"It's been nearly two weeks and nothing."

"They have to be careful when it comes to Richard. Nick is a scum-bag who hung around with scumbags. If someone got to him, no one cared. Richard is different. If he walks into the office with a broken nose, people are going to ask questions."

It was a good point. "I want to know what they're doing. You got in touch with them before. Can you do it again?"

"Sure. I guess."

"Can you give me the number?"

"Let me talk to them first. They're cagey. They don't like it when people exchange information."

A nervous, sheepish tone had crept into Clare's voice. Was she truly scared of Infidelity Limited's retribution? Roy had told her not to talk to her sister or anyone else about their arrangement. She knew the man was capable of violence, but would he use it on his clients?

"Okay. You do it."

Clare smiled. "Good. Now go home. Don't worry. They'll come through."

They'd better, she thought.

Clare saw Olivia out to her car. They hugged, and Clare kissed Olivia on the cheek. "Just take it easy. I love you, Sis. I'll call when I hear something."

Olivia drove home. When she arrived, the empty garage said Richard was still out banging his slut, but the sight of a dark-blue sedan parked out front distracted her from her ugly thoughts. She stopped her car inside the garage, and a man and a woman emerged from the vehicle. They didn't look like a couple. He was in his fifties, rail thin and balding, with what hair he did have close-cropped. The woman was younger, midthirties, with an athletic figure that a tailored jacket over jeans helped accentuate. The gun she wore on her hip ruined the perfect flow of the jacket.

Cops, Olivia thought. She knew it before the man produced his ID. She waited for them on the threshold of the garage.

"Mrs. Shaw?" the man asked.

"Yes."

"I'm Detective Mike Finz, and this is Detective Madeleine Lyon. We're from the Concord Police Department."

"Is something wrong?"

"Could we go inside? It's about your husband," Finz said.

This was Roy's doing. She knew it without asking. He'd finally followed through on his promise, but police weren't a good sign. This was supposed to be a private beating. Cops weren't supposed to be part of the equation. Had Richard gone to them? He would know who was behind his assault. She had to play along for now.

"Has something happened?" The note of panic in her voice was real.

Olivia read something on the woman's face. It was pity. Why would these cops pity her? It was just a beating, right? Beatings didn't warrant the kind of sorrow this woman was showing.

"Something's happened, hasn't it? Something bad. Please tell me."

"We really should take this inside," Finz said.

"I'm not going anywhere until you tell me what's happened to my husband."

Finz exchanged a brief look with Lyon before she said, "I'm sorry to inform you that your husband has been killed."

CHAPTER SIX

Olivia hadn't realized she was falling until she felt the sharp pain of her knees striking the concrete garage floor. Lyon and Finz caught her before she fell on her face. They spoke to her, but all she heard was white noise.

"No, no, no, no," she moaned.

Richard was dead. That wasn't meant to happen. It was just supposed to be a beating. Just a lesson to remind him he couldn't cheat. How had it turned into this? What had Roy done? Worse, what had she done?

Lyon and Finz gathered Olivia up and led her inside the house.

"I'm going to be sick," she said.

The detectives got her to the guest bathroom. Olivia dropped in front of the toilet. She retched until intense dots of light burned in her vision, but failed to bring anything up. Every phantom hurl felt as if her internal organs were being crushed. It was a relief when the retching passed. She stayed hunched over the bowl, sucking in ragged breaths and inhaling the sharp scent of the toilet-bowl cleaner. She'd never liked that odor, but it helped bring her back to the real world.

Lyon stroked Olivia's back. "Just take a deep breath. It's going to be okay."

Was it? Olivia couldn't see how. "I'm so sorry."

"It's okay," Lyon said. "Don't worry about it. These things happen."

"I hate to come across as callous," Finz said, "but we need to ask you some questions."

Olivia nodded.

They sat her down in the living room. Finz brought her a glass of water, and a few sips helped settle her stomach.

"What happened?" Olivia asked.

"It looks as if Richard was the victim of a mugging gone wrong," Finz said.

Olivia felt the color drain from her face. No, not a mugging gone wrong, a beating gone wrong. Roy or whomever he'd sent to work Richard over had gone too far.

She noticed Finz and Lyon staring at her, studying her. What did they see? A grieving wife or the person responsible for Richard's murder? Her shock and dismay were real. She hoped they would camouflage her guilt.

A tremor started in her hands and spread throughout her body until she was shaking from head to toe. The manifestation stunned her. She was so detached from it. The shakes seemed to be happening a million miles away, and any attempts to quell them were well beyond her reach. The water in the glass slopped onto her knees. She clasped her hands tightly around the glass to exert some form of control over herself. The attempt failed. Her clasped hands bounced on her trembling legs.

She noticed them staring at her.

"I can't seem to stop."

Lyon pressed a surprisingly strong hand on Olivia's forearm, which helped mute the shaking. She took the glass from Olivia and set it down on the table before edging closer to her on the couch. Then Finz leaned forward, invading her space. Olivia didn't like how they were crowding her. She wanted to tell them to give her room, but that would look suspicious, as if she couldn't deal with being under their scrutiny. She had to stick it out. At this point, she had nothing to worry about. She wasn't a suspect. Only doing something stupid would change that.

"Is there someone you'd like us to call?" Lyon asked.

Infidelity Limited sprang immediately to Olivia's mind. She needed to talk to Roy and find out what had gone wrong. "There's my sister, but I'm not sure I want to trouble her with this."

"Don't be silly. You need family at a time like this."

Olivia regretted mentioning Clare the second she did it. She didn't want Clare brought into this until they'd had time to get their stories straight, but it would be a mistake to labor the point.

"You're right," Olivia said.

Lyon brought out a cell from her pocket. "What's her number?"

Olivia gave the detective the number, and Lyon punched it in. "Can I talk to her? I want this coming from me." Olivia didn't want Clare blurting out something or coming to the wrong conclusion. She hated all the second-guessing she was having to do, but she had little choice. Trying to outthink the cops was going to be in her future for a considerable time.

Lyon smiled and handed the phone over.

The second Clare answered the call, Olivia spoke. She couldn't give Clare the chance to say the wrong thing. "Clare, Richard's been murdered."

Clare was silent. This was good. Olivia needed her speechless. Words could and would sink them.

"The police are with me now," Olivia said. "Can you come over?"

"Yes. Of course. Where are you?"

"At home."

"I'm on my way."

Olivia handed the cell phone back to Lyon.

"Does she live far away?" Lyon asked.

"No. Martinez."

"That's good."

Olivia needed space from these two. She stood and picked up a framed photo from the mantel. It had been taken in the Bahamas a few years ago, when things were good between them. It was a snapshot of Richard squinting into the sun, leaning against a low wall with the ocean behind him. It was a typical vacation picture, but it somehow summed up Richard, her husband, his essence. She held it to her chest.

"Did he suffer?"

"Olivia, you don't need to know," Lyon said.

"Yes, I do." It was part of her punishment.

"He was severely beaten," Finz answered.

While she'd been bitching to Clare about Infidelity Limited, Richard had been dying. Was that fate or twisted karma? It didn't bear contemplating.

Olivia replaced the photo on the mantel and pressed her hand to Richard's image before retaking her seat next to Lyon.

"Can you tell me where your husband was tonight?" Madeleine Lyon asked.

Banging his mistress, she thought, but kept to her cover story. She guessed the investigation would unearth Richard's affair, but she couldn't be the one to tell them about it. They had to find that nugget all by themselves. "Yes, he was at the Crow Canyon Athletic Club in San Ramon. Do you know it?"

"We'll find it," Finz said.

"He plays in their squash league on Tuesday and Thursday nights. I don't know if tonight was his practice night or a league game."

"That's okay."

"Does he usually come straight home after a game?" Lyon asked.

"Yes, but sometimes he goes out for dinner with his teammates. Look, I don't understand. Did this happen at the club?"

"No, his body was discovered on Shary Court in Concord. It's a commercial district not far from the BART maintenance yard," Finz said. "Would he have any reason for being there? Is that close to where he works?"

Olivia shook her head. "No. I can't think of a reason why he'd be there. He works for an ad agency in San Francisco."

"I see. And what do you do?"

"I'm a Realtor. My office is here in Walnut Creek."

"Where were you tonight, Mrs. Shaw? We had to wait for quite a while for you to come home."

Was that an accusation? Maybe all this concern for the grieving widow was merely window dressing. Or was her guilt getting to her? She couldn't be sure about their suspicions, but they couldn't have any firm beliefs about her involvement, not yet. She hadn't given them any cause to suspect her. She had to play it cool. "I was at my sister's."

"When was the last time you saw your husband?"

"This morning when he left for work."

"Did your husband have any enemies?" Lyon asked.

"No. He's a good man." The present tense. It no longer applied. "He was a good man. There's no one out there who'd want to harm him."

Her answer had been reflexive. Each word came crashing back at her. Yes, he was a good man, but there was one person out there who wanted him to come to harm—her. She broke down under the weight of what she'd done and burst into uncontrollable sobs.

Lyon told Olivia it was all going to be okay. Olivia wished she believed that.

"I'm sorry that we have to ask these questions," Finz said. "But they will help us catch the person responsible for this. Anything you know could help us."

"I don't know anything. I wish I did, but I don't. I . . . I can't even believe this is happening. I'm still expecting him to walk through the door."

"I understand."

"What happens now? Can I see him?"

Lyon frowned as if in pain. "It's better that you don't."

"His body will be released after the autopsy, probably after the weekend. The coroner will contact you about arrangements. You'll be able to see him then, but I urge you not to. Everyone wants to make their last farewells, but it's better you remember him the way you saw him this morning," Finz said. "Rest assured, we will find your husband's killer."

"How can you be sure?"

"I will personally be investigating this case, and Detective Lyon and the rest of the detective unit will be supporting me. This isn't San Francisco or Oakland. Homicides are rare here. We have the time to pursue your husband's case until we have the culprit in custody. The killer was messy and unsophisticated. That means he was careless. Careless people leave a trail. It's only a matter of time."

Finz's little speech was supposed to instill confidence, but it did the opposite. Roy had given her the impression that his people were smart, a crack team of professionals who knew how to do their job and slip away unnoticed. Finz was describing an incompetent. Someone either had panicked or couldn't turn off the violence. And if Finz caught that person, it would lead him to Infidelity Limited, and Roy would place this murder at her feet.

"That's good to know," Olivia replied.

"I hate to ask, but I have to cover all the bases. Did your husband have any vices—drugs, alcohol, gambling? Was he in debt to anyone?"

If Richard was hiding a mistress under her nose, could he have hidden something else from her? She'd followed him around for a few days and hadn't seen anything else, but that didn't mean anything.

"No, Richard didn't have any vices," she answered. "We are very ordinary people, leading very ordinary lives."

The significance of what she'd said sank in. They'd been ordinary people, existing at the top of society's bell curve, but somehow they'd gone off the rails. Richard had lived a secret life, and she consorted with gangsters who beat people up. They were hardly ordinary anymore.

"Can you tell me more about Richard?" Lyon asked. "For instance, how long have you two been married? How did you meet?"

Olivia smiled despite the situation. "Eight years. We met over a flat tire. I was coming home from work, and I picked up a flat on Highway 24. It was raining, and I was getting soaked. He stopped to help."

"How very chivalrous."

"It would have been if he knew how to change a tire. He was no handyman."

The detectives laughed, and Olivia found herself laughing with them.

"Why'd he stop?" Finz asked.

"That's what I asked, and he said he stopped because he couldn't take his gaze off me. It was cute, but it didn't help me change the tire. So instead, I put on the spare while teaching him how to do it. As a thank-you, he took me out to dinner, and things went from there."

"And the rest is history," Lyon said.

Olivia didn't think Lyon realized the significance of her words. She was right. Their relationship was history. The future had been stolen away. The reminiscence had temporarily alleviated the pain, but that thought brought it all back and the tears with it.

"It's going to be okay," Lyon assured her. "You're going to survive this."

It was a nice idea, but she wasn't so sure.

"Mrs. Shaw, for us to proceed full steam ahead, I need your permission to access Richard's bank, credit card, and phone records. It's the twenty-first century, so you can't cough without leaving an official record of it somewhere," Finz said.

All their accounts were joint accounts. Saying no wasn't an option, and besides, she had nothing to fear. There was nothing in them that would connect her to Infidelity Limited.

"Sure. No problem. Do I have to sign a form or something?"

Finz smiled. "No. You just have to obtain them and hand them over to us. The last six months will be good."

"Is tomorrow okay?"

"That's fine, Mrs. Shaw," Finz said. "You wouldn't happen to know the code to Richard's cell phone, would you? We have his phone, but we're locked out."

"Yes, it's two-seven-two-seven. His high school football number repeated."

Finz smiled and jotted down the number.

"Do you have contact info for Richard's squash buddies? I'd like to talk to them," Finz said.

She reeled off the half a dozen or so names of the guys she'd met in the past. "Their info should be on his phone."

A cell phone rang. It took a moment before Olivia realized it belonged to her. The bland ringtone was coming from the cell Roy had given her.

She reached for her purse and knocked it off the table. Half its contents spilled onto the floor. Finz picked up the ringing phone and glanced at the postage stamp–sized screen before handing the cell to Olivia. Luckily, Roy's name hadn't come up on the caller ID, just the number and the words "cell phone." She pressed the key to ignore the call.

"No one important?" Finz asked.

"Under the circumstances, no."

Finz's attention went to something else on the ground. She followed his gaze to her other cell phone.

"You have two cell phones?" he asked. "That's unusual."

Olivia was saved from responding by Clare letting herself in through the front door. She swept in, calling Olivia's name.

"We're in the living room," Olivia answered.

Clare blew by Finz and Lyon and crushed Olivia in a hug. "I'm so sorry, Liv."

Being held felt good, and Olivia sagged, letting her sister take her weight.

Finz and Lyon got the message that their interview was over for now and stood. They excused themselves, and Olivia and Clare saw them out.

Olivia closed the door on the detectives. She shrugged off the weight of having to pretend and slumped against the door. She closed her eyes. She just needed a moment of clarity to decide what to do next, but there was no peace.

The clinking of glasses from the direction of the kitchen drew her back to her feet. In the kitchen she found Clare with a bottle of wine and two glasses. It was just like her sister to hit the booze when a clear head was needed. Clare pushed a glass over to her.

"What are we going to do?" Olivia asked.

"Nothing," Clare said.

Nothing was a dangerous proposition. Nothing was taking her hands off the wheel. Nothing put others in control. Nothing wasn't an option.

"The way I see it," Olivia said, "we have two options: tell the cops or—"

"No way," Clare blurted. "The second you mention your involvement, it's game over."

Olivia knew going to the cops was putting a gun to her head, but she recognized the value. "The longer we deceive them, the worse it will be. If we go to them now, we stand a chance. They can protect us. We can work out a deal."

"What deal, Liv? You had your husband killed. The only deal they'll give you is life in prison or the death sentence."

"Hey, I never wanted him killed."

Clare jerked a thumb in the direction of the recently departed detectives. "Do you think Cagney and Lacey will care? Anyway, it doesn't matter. We aren't going to the cops. What's the other option?"

"We talk to Roy. We need to find out what happened."

"And then what? Have his people turn themselves in? Liv, it doesn't work like that."

Leverage was the problem. Olivia didn't have anything she could use against Roy and Infidelity Limited. If she didn't give Finz and Lyon something to implicate him, she'd just be throwing herself under the bus. As it stood now, she had this fantastical story about a shadowy organization. They weren't going to believe that without names and faces. Roy had been right when he boasted about Infidelity Limited's ghostlike existence. Trying to sell Infidelity Limited as a defense was up there with the Twinkie defense. Screwed didn't begin to describe her position.

"We don't even know if Roy had anything to do with this," Clare said.

Christ. That was Clare for you. When the going got tough, deny the tough existed. No wonder she was always in a hole. Olivia might be in the hole with her, but she'd be damned if she'd keep on digging.

"Bullshit. Do you think the coincidence fairy just struck? Of course it was Roy. He called while the cops were here. That wasn't happenstance. He was calling to let us know something had gone wrong."

"You keep saying *us*."

Clare's remark was small, but the implications were huge. Olivia knew her sister well enough to know she was getting ready to bolt from her problems. She always did. It wasn't personal on her sister's part. It was instinct. Self-preservation came before everything else, including family. Clare wouldn't dodge her responsibilities this time. Olivia wouldn't let her.

"Whether you like it or not, Clare, you're involved."

Clare held up her hands. "I just put you in touch with Roy. That's it."

"That's more than enough. In the eyes of the law, you and I are just as guilty as the killer."

Olivia saw the panic in her sister's eyes. That wasn't good. Olivia couldn't afford to lose Clare to her fears. Olivia couldn't count on her sister when she felt insecure.

"I know it's not right. We need to work together to make it right, or as right as possible."

"What's that mean?"

Olivia was guilty. Even if she could show she had no part in Richard's murder, she was still guilty of hiring Infidelity Limited. God, she'd been stupid. She'd let emotion and a moment of weakness brush aside good judgment. Not that that was a defense.

"I have to go to the cops," Olivia said.

"Are you crazy?"

"No, not if I go to them with something proving we had nothing to do with the murder."

"How the hell are you going to do that?"

That was the hard part. "I don't know."

"Jesus, Liv. You're going to have to do better than that."

"I know."

"Screw it. Let's pack up everything we can and disappear."

Olivia was losing Clare again. She was after the simple solution that never existed. "How do we do that exactly?"

"I . . . I . . . I don't know, but it sounds a shitload better than your idea."

Clare had an answer, but it wasn't a good one. No one could disappear these days. They'd get picked up in a week, and that was being optimistic. Even if they could disappear, what kind of life would they live? No, Olivia wasn't going down that twisted road.

"C'mon, Liv. How are you going to save us? You're the smart one. You're the successful one. You have all the answers. It's time for you to come up with one."

"Clare, just stop. Give me a second."

Clare came back to the counter and swiped up her drink. "Well, you'll need to work faster than that if you expect me to stick around."

"I need to talk to Roy. He obviously tried to talk to me. I need to know what he has planned."

"That's your answer?"

"Yes. Do you think Roy wanted Richard killed? No, something went wrong. He won't want any part of that. He'll want to give up the people who did this as much as we do."

"Yeah, that's all well and good, but what if Roy was the one who killed Richard?"

It was a thought Olivia had already considered and feared. "There's only one way to find out."

Olivia retrieved the cell from her purse and dialed Roy's number.

The call rang and rang. He couldn't be far away from the phone. She doubted he'd want to apologize, but he'd want to talk to her.

"Shit. Voice mail."

Clare frowned.

"Roy, it's Olivia. Call me." She kept her tone calm. Roy wouldn't respond well to panic. If he thought she was going off the rails, he would be on the first plane to Rio. She ended the call.

"Liv, I don't like this. Infidelity Limited is an underground organization. You won't find them."

"Everybody can be found."

Olivia placed the phone on the kitchen table, and they waited for Roy to call back.

Half an hour passed without him returning the call. Olivia had visions of him buying his plane ticket. She called him back twice over the next two hours, and he still didn't answer. On the third call, her call went straight to voice mail.

"He's switched the phone off. I think we're screwed."

CHAPTER SEVEN

It had been a while since Finz had started his day with an autopsy. The Concord murder rate rarely reached the heady height of three in a calendar year, which made his job as the department's only homicide detective fairly light. Usually, his workload centered on robbery, felony assault, and domestic violence. That all changed with a murder. He headed the investigation, and the other detectives assisted, but as the lead detective, he did all the heavy lifting—like attending autopsies. He walked into the morgue just as Louise Hiller was about to start.

"Hey, Mike, long time no see," Hiller said.

"Well, our good citizens have been playing nice."

"Until now."

"Until now," he agreed.

Finz looked down at Richard Shaw. Last night, Mr. Shaw could barely be recognized as a result of his vicious beating. Washed and cleaned, the man could be seen through the wounds, but drained of color and life, he was no less dead.

Finz stood to one side while Hiller and her assistant worked with precision. He made his own notes as they worked. A complete coroner's report would take a while, thanks to the lab work. The autopsy didn't unearth anything he didn't already know. Richard Shaw had been bludgeoned to death with a blunt instrument. The shape of the wounds said the weapon had been something metal and small in diameter, ruling out a baseball bat but not a length of pipe or a tire iron. Defensive wounds, in the form of two broken fingers on his right hand and a fractured left radius, said he'd seen the attack coming. He'd clocked twenty-seven strikes to the head, neck, and chest. Two had been hard enough to split his skull open. The rest were products of hate or panic. Finz had been hoping that Shaw had gotten in a couple of his own hits before his attacker got the better of him, but it didn't look like it from the lack of trace on his hands. *Poor son of a bitch.*

The upshot was a fast and frenzied attack. That said two possible things about the killer. He was either a novice who didn't know when to stop or someone who liked inflicting pain and couldn't stop. Regardless of the motive, Finz would find Richard Shaw's murderer.

He left Hiller to finish up and walked out into the parking lot. It felt good to be outside again with the sun on his face. He sucked in a lungful of fresh air. Not that it was that fresh with Highway 4 below him, but anything beat the morgue's chilled air. He never got used to that numb and listless environment.

He climbed into his car and drove to Berkeley to meet with Allen Yager. Yager was a senior chemist working for Bayer and one of Shaw's squash buddies. Finz had made appointments to speak to all of them this morning.

He introduced himself at reception, and a lanky man in his forties, with a mess of brown curls, appeared a minute later.

Yager pumped Finz's hand. "Detective, I still can't believe Richard's dead. I'm waiting for him to leap out and tell me it's a joke."

"Sadly, that won't be happening. Is there somewhere we can talk?"

"Yes. Sorry. This way."

He led Finz into a small meeting room next to the reception area.

Finz pulled out his notebook and a digital recorder and put it on the table between them. "Okay if I record this?"

"No problem."

Finz pressed "Record." "How long have you known Richard Shaw?"

"Seven years or so. We met through the athletic club."

"Would you call yourself a close friend?"

"Pretty close."

"Were you aware of any problems in his life—money troubles, rifts with anyone, any incidents that occurred recently?"

Yager shook his head. "As far as I know, everything was good. I didn't know of any money troubles or enemies. That's why none of this makes any sense."

"What frame of mind was he in when you saw him last night?"

Yager produced a blank look. During the course of an interview, one question usually proved to be a change maker, and that one appeared to be it.

"According to Mrs. Shaw, Richard was playing his regular Thursday-night squash game at the club last night. Can you corroborate that?"

Yager squirmed.

"Are Thursday nights your regular league practice nights, Mr. Yager?"

"Yes."

"Were you there?"

"Yes."

"Was Mr. Shaw there?"

"No." His answer came out slow.

"Can you explain why?"

More squirming.

"Mr. Yager."

"Richard was seeing someone, okay?"

"What kind of someone?"

Yager threw up his arms. "What do you think? A woman. He was seeing a woman behind his wife's back."

Finz ignored the little outburst. Finally, Finz had his first chink in Richard Shaw's armor. Every victim he'd ever investigated started off as a paragon of virtue, but it was never long before he unearthed a vice or two. That was the problem with vices. They tended to be hard to control, and if not dealt with, they could get you killed.

"You know this for sure?" Finz asked.

"No, not for sure, but he dropped hints. Not that he needed to. It wasn't hard to read between the lines."

"How long had his affair been going on for?"

"I'd say around four months. That's how long he'd been skipping our club nights."

"Did you ever meet Richard's mistress, or did he tell you her name?"

Yager's face wrinkled at the word *mistress*. "No. Richard was careful."

"Did Mrs. Shaw know or suspect anything?"

"I don't think so. He'd been using the squash nights as cover for all those months, although that cover story could have been blown."

"What do you mean?"

"A few weeks ago, Olivia came rushing in with Richard's duffel bag that he'd forgotten and obviously found Richard wasn't around."

"What did you tell her?"

Yager squirmed again. "We told her that he hadn't been to the club in weeks."

"Did you tell Richard about the incident?"

"No way. If Richard wanted to run around on his wife, that was his problem. I wasn't getting sucked into his marital games."

"I think I have everything I need for the time being, Mr. Yager."

Finz played over his conversation with Yager on the way back to his car. He didn't think he'd bother interviewing Shaw's other squash buddies for the moment. He doubted they'd have anything more to contribute than Allen Yager. He had a new line of inquiry.

He popped the trunk and retrieved the personal belongings Richard Shaw had on him when he was killed. Louise Hiller had officially handed the pocket contents to him after the autopsy. He took the evidence bags and sat behind the wheel.

Shaw's iPhone was among the items. A mugger would have snatched the phone. It was a commodity, especially once it was cloned. But this wasn't a mugging gone bad. That story failed to hold water at first glance. The killer had not only skipped the phone, he'd also skipped the Omega watch, the wedding ring, and the Mercedes. No one killed just for a wallet.

What also put a nail through the heart of a mugging gone bad was the location. Shaw wasn't on his turf. He'd gone to meet someone, and that someone killed him.

He put on latex gloves, removed Shaw's iPhone, and switched it on. He unlocked the phone with the code Olivia Shaw had given him and scrolled through the incoming and outgoing call logs. Richard had received a call at nine fifteen the evening before. That was an hour before his body had been discovered.

Finz called the number on his cell. The phone went straight to voice mail. The owner of that phone had it switched off.

He scanned through the calls made on Tuesday and Thursday nights. The same number kept reappearing. It was also the number of the second-to-last call Shaw had received, and it belonged to Cassie Hill. He called her number.

"Miss Hill, I'm Detective Mike Finz from the Concord Police Department. I'm calling about Richard Shaw. I'm sorry to inform you that he's been murdered. I think we have a lot to talk about."

*   *   *

Finz stopped his car in front of Cassie Hill's house. He'd caught her at work, but she'd told him to meet her at her home. Her address was about the only thing he'd managed to get out of her before she'd broken down.

He walked up to the door and found it ajar. The sound of a woman sobbing greeted him.

"Miss Hill? It's Detective Finz."

"Yes."

Finz entered and closed the door after him. He found Cassie in the living room, slumped on the sofa, as if blown there by an explosion. Tragedy tended to have that effect on the survivors. He showed her his identification and sat down.

Cassie was an attractive blonde in her midthirties. At least Shaw hadn't pissed on his marriage with some bimbo barely out of high school.

It was easy to tell that Cassie lived alone. There was something about a single person's home that always gave it away. The decor was uncompromised and self-indulgent. At the same time, the furnishings were sparse. A sofa and armchair were plenty for a single person, but not enough for a family. People living alone rarely had pictures of themselves hanging on the wall. Few people were that vain. Instead, pictures of family, iconic movie posters, and prints by well-known artists covered the walls. All these telltale signs were true for Cassie.

"Miss Hill, I have a few questions for you."

"Please call me Cassie. I can't deal with formality right now."

Finz saw no point in pussyfooting around. "You were having an affair with him, correct?"

She managed a nod before bursting into sobs again.

He handed her a fresh Kleenex from the box on the coffee table, and she thanked him. "Could you tell me how the affair started?"

She dabbed her eyes, then pulled herself up straight. "Richard and I work together. We developed a close relationship that turned flirtatious. I don't even remember when. About five months ago, we were having drinks after work to celebrate a new account we'd just landed.

We shared a cab. When we arrived here, I invited him in, and it went on from there."

"You knew he was married?"

Cassie cut him a bitter look. "Yes, I knew. I'm not proud of myself. I never thought I'd be 'the other woman.' It just happened. Love is like that. It doesn't care about the situation or the damage it causes."

Neither does hate, Finz thought. "You say you loved Mr. Shaw. Was your relationship going to develop into something more formal?"

"Was Richard going to leave his wife for me, you mean?"

Finz nodded.

Cassie broke eye contact and stared at her hands. She touched her naked ring finger on her left hand. "We talked about it, but we hadn't decided on a timetable."

We or just him? Finz wondered. Cassie had everything to gain from Shaw's divorce, whereas Shaw would lose half his assets in that mess. Finz didn't know the victim well enough to know if he was stringing this woman along, but if he wanted to pull the trigger, he would have done it by now.

"Did his wife suspect anything?" he asked.

"No. Richard was very careful."

"Did Mr. Shaw ever mention why he was being unfaithful to his wife?"

Cassie's features tightened. "I'm not in the business of wrecking marriages."

"I never said you were. I have no opinion. I care about one thing, finding Richard Shaw's killer. So I ask again, did Mr. Shaw ever mention why he was being unfaithful to his wife?"

"He just fell out of love with her. He said they'd grown apart."

"Do you know of any other affairs?"

"No. Richard wasn't that kind of man."

"And there isn't an ex-boyfriend who wouldn't take too kindly to your seeing Mr. Shaw?"

"No." The single-word reply came out clipped and squeezed.

She was getting defensive. He could feel her walls rising up. It was time to come at her from a less antagonistic angle.

"As far as I can tell, you were the last person to see Mr. Shaw before his death. Could you walk me through your time with him?"

"It was a regular workday. We saw each other in the office, and we had lunch together. After work, he followed me here, and we did what we normally did when we were together."

"And nothing out of the ordinary happened during that time?"

She shook her head.

"No confrontations with anyone? Nobody acting suspicious around him?"

And another head shake.

"When did Mr. Shaw leave?"

"It was after nine. He left after he received the call."

Cassie had Finz's attention. "His cell phone history shows that he received a call at nine fifteen."

"That sounds right."

"Do you know who called him?"

"He said it was his wife."

CHAPTER EIGHT

Roy sat alone in the covered bleachers of the Marin County fairground. At this time of year, the fairground went unused during the day, making it quiet and secluded. It also had an absence of security systems and cameras. This was of vital importance during a postkill meeting. When it came to money exchanges and the disposal of physical evidence, anonymity mattered.

The van bringing John Proctor stopped at the entrance to the fairground, and he climbed out of the back, clutching a black Hefty bag. Roy hoped it was double bagged.

Proctor looked to the retreating van for his next instruction, but it reversed back out to the street. Roy saw the bewilderment on Proctor's face, so he called him on the burner cell he'd given him.

"John, I'm up in the bleachers. Come join me."

Proctor was a big guy, bear-like in his build. He wasn't someone most people would want to run into in a dark alley. He lumbered toward the bleachers. It wasn't a pretty sight. He was uncoordinated and clumsy with his movements. The Hefty bag bounced off his leg with every stride. Pound for pound, he and Roy appeared to be worthy opponents, but from a conscience perspective, Proctor was no match for Roy. Few people could deal with the guilt that came with taking a life. Roy was one of these few. He could more than handle the likes of John Proctor on any given day.

Proctor was out of breath by the time he reached Roy in the higher reaches of the bleachers. He held out the plastic bag to him. Roy stared at it for a long moment. He waited until Proctor's arm sagged under the weight before telling him to put it on the seat between them. Roy wanted Proctor to feel the weight of ownership of the murder weapon for as long as possible. He wanted the pressure of what Proctor had done to squeeze him into a tight ball. It made him docile, controllable, and dependent. Roy preferred for his clients to see him as God, with the will to save or destroy them.

"Is it all in there—murder weapon, clothes, shoes—everything?" Roy asked.

"Yes. Everything."

Roy pawed through the bag until he found the tire iron in a plastic bag. It was from Olivia's Audi. He'd stolen it a few days before the murder, when Olivia and Richard had left the house in Richard's car. The tire iron was a good item to take. It was something that made for an excellent weapon while also being something that was seldom needed and wouldn't be missed.

"I never should have gotten involved with you," Proctor said.

Proctor had come to Roy eighteen months ago to scare some sense into his ex-wife. She was being unreasonable when it came to visitation rights, child support, and alimony, despite being the one who'd cheated on him. No-fault divorce laws didn't mean they had to play fair. As the innocent party, Proctor had lost out, and he just wanted to level the score.

Sadly, leveling wasn't something people got when they employed Infidelity Limited. Nicole Proctor was killed. Proctor had gone to pieces when Roy explained the facts of life about Infidelity Limited's operations. Roy had thought Proctor would crumple under the inevitable police scrutiny, but he'd surprised him and survived the ordeal. He'd been lucky in one respect. Nicole's body hadn't been recovered, and her reputation as a loose woman helped support the cops' belief that she'd walked out on her family. Proctor got what he wanted, a fresh start with his kids, and Roy got what he wanted—Nicole's life insurance payout. Proctor had been a strong and confident man until Roy called him two weeks ago to tell him it was his turn to pay it forward.

"How are you feeling, John? You look like you've been through the wringer."

"I have."

"It's never easy being violent."

"No." Proctor's single-word answer seemed to come from a faraway place.

His clients required propping up at this phase of the operation. They were frightened, vulnerable, and needed someone to turn to. A friend. A father confessor. He was all of those things, despite being the one who'd placed them in that position. Their willingness to turn to him despite all he'd done to them never failed to surprise him. He wondered if there was a psychological term for it. It wasn't quite Stockholm syndrome. Maybe there was no term for it. Maybe he'd created something new.

"It's important that you keep it together. Would you like someone to talk to? Someone to help you through this? I can arrange something for you."

Proctor was silent for a moment before nodding. "I think that would be good."

It paid to have someone close to the clients. Proctor would keep his shit together as long as he felt supported. Roy had a defrocked therapist on retainer for these situations. "I'll set something up. Look, there's something else we need to discuss. You went a little crazy the other night with Richard. The crime scene reports showed a very messy and ugly affair."

Proctor's gaze fell to his hands. Hands that had claimed a life.

"That has placed a lot of scrutiny on this killing."

"I know. He fought back, and I panicked. I hit him again and again. I wanted to stop, but I just kept hitting him."

Proctor was on the verge of tears. It was time to back off. If Roy pushed him too hard, he'd shatter, and Roy didn't want that. Not if it could be avoided. He needed Proctor to hold it together for the sake of Infidelity Limited. He had to be coddled for now. Roy threw an arm around the man's shoulders.

"It's understandable, but I expected more from you. We handed you a very clean assignment that made it impossible for the police to investigate. You've handed me a very messy outcome that will require a lot of effort to sanitize."

"I'm sorry."

Roy brushed the apology away. "What's happened has happened. All we can do is work with what we've got, and luckily, we have plenty going for us, thanks to your diligent preparation."

"Really?" Hope entered Proctor's voice.

"Yes. The police have little to go on. While there's a crime scene, they don't have much in the way of physical evidence or witness accounts to move their investigation forward. See how well this operation works?"

Proctor nodded.

"You must have been a real mess after it was over."

"I was. I had blood all over me. There was so much blood."

Roy placed a hand on Proctor's thick shoulder. "I'm sure, but it's okay now. Those clothes are in the bag, yes?"

"Yes."

"Every stitch?"

"Underwear. Socks. Everything. You have it all."

"Good. I'll make sure it's disposed of."

That was a lie. It would all be rebagged, cataloged, and stored in a cooler back at the house to be produced at a later date if needed.

"What about your car?"

"I put down plastic and had it detailed afterward, just as you instructed."

"My people are going over it as we speak, just so that every speck of DNA is eradicated. We can't be too careful."

"We can't. Thanks."

"Naturally, we will be incurring costs that we'll have to recover from you."

"Roy, you can't."

Roy raised his hand to cut Proctor off. "I hadn't anticipated you getting so carried away. Remember, I'm cleaning up your mess. It's not fair that I should foot the cost, now is it?"

"No," Proctor said with a heavy note of defeat. "How much?"

"Five thousand."

Proctor opened his mouth to object, but nodded instead. "I'll get you the money."

"Good."

Proctor was silent for a moment before he said, "Now that I've done this for you, is it over?"

"Over?"

"Yes, over. I've paid you. I've killed for you. I don't want this to continue. I want it to be over."

Roy expected this request. It always came at this stage. "You've kept up your part of the bargain, and I respect that."

"Then I'm done."

"Well, not quite."

"Not quite? What more do you want from me?"

Roy held up his hand again. "Patience. That's all I ask. We're at a delicate stage. The police are still in the middle of their investigation. You'll be done when they are done. I don't think I have to remind you that if I go down, you go down with me."

"You said that if I brought you everything from last night, I could have the murder weapon and everything you had on Nicole's murder back. Because all this"—Proctor pointed at the plastic bag—"is what you hold over Richard Shaw's wife. That's the cycle. I've done my bit. Now it's your turn. Give me Nicole's things, please. You promised, Roy."

Proctor sounded like a child to Roy, gullible and overly trusting. Proctor was a weak man, and Roy had eroded his will over time to the point where good judgment was no longer part of his character. It was sad to witness, but Roy felt powerful for it.

"I said you could have it back when the police had dropped their investigation. That hasn't happened yet."

Proctor shook his head back and forth like an obstinate child. "That's not fair. You have everything, and I have nothing."

"Really? I don't think so. You have your kids, don't you?"

"Yes."

"Nicole is no longer a thorn in your side?"

"Yes, but—"

"Then there you have it. You have everything you wanted, while I have all the burden of risk. I have to balance some of it on you. That's only fair."

Proctor jumped to his feet. "No, Roy. I'm done. I'm out."

Roy kept his tone cool and measured. He'd already put the fear of God into Proctor. He wanted to appear reasonable and calm. It diffused any potential panic. If he was calm, then Proctor would be too. He couldn't look like a loose cannon. Making clients think he was out of control was a surefire way to send them running to the cops. "I say when you're done, John. Not you. Remember, I can turn you over to the police at any time."

"You can't. You wouldn't."

"Don't test me."

The threat shoved Proctor back into his seat. He sagged under the weight of his own guilt.

"Do I have to worry about you? Do I have to take steps?"

Proctor shook his head.

Roy believed him—for now. Proctor had something of value to protect, his kids. Anything his clients truly valued kept them in line. The ones that didn't have that were the ones to worry about. He stood and picked up the Hefty bag.

"I'm going now. You just hang out here. My people will be along to pick you up when they've finished with your car. I'll have one of my counselors get in touch too. Sound good?"

Proctor nodded halfheartedly.

"Hang in there, John. This'll all be over before you know it. You just have to be smart. You can be smart, can't you?"

CHAPTER NINE

Olivia woke up just after five in the morning. She tried to go back to sleep, but the bed seemed vast without Richard, and she didn't seem to possess the body heat to keep it warm. Clare had gone home in the early hours. Olivia knew her sister's patterns well. She wouldn't want to be around while Olivia dealt with the responsibilities that came with Richard's death.

She hadn't slept, not really. Every time she closed her eyes, she was either back in the car with Roy as he sold the virtues of Infidelity Limited or watching Richard in the arms of his mistress.

Padding through the house, she felt a Richard-sized hole. Normally, even when she had the house to herself, she felt his presence, but not now. He was never coming home, and that made the house a little colder, a little darker.

She got in the shower to make herself feel human again. In the kitchen, she made herself coffee and breakfast that she had no real intention of eating, but it helped pass the time before she got down to the real business of the day—ruining people's mornings by informing them of Richard's death.

She started with Richard's family, which was the most difficult. His parents had retired to Idaho years earlier. Her in-laws hadn't approved of their marriage, and Richard's murder seemed to justify their lack of faith. She withstood the veiled resentment from Richard's mother during the exchange. It took everything Olivia had not to mention her precious boy's infidelity, but it wasn't the time or the place. She had to focus on the big picture, and Richard's mom wasn't part of it. After notifying family, she called their friends and acquaintances. She listened to some cry, while others offered their love and support. It all felt like nails being drawn across a chalkboard. She couldn't deal with their pain or condolences. It wasn't what she deserved.

Richard's office came next. She psyched herself up to go through a second round of shock, dismay, and condolences, but she needn't have bothered. Finz had beaten her to the punch. He was certainly off and running with his investigation.

It was easier talking to the bank, the credit card companies, the life insurance company, their lawyer, and the various other forms of officialdom. They didn't know Richard or her, so their hollow sympathies had little effect on her.

By lunchtime she'd had enough. She got in the car and drove to the one place she wanted to be.

Shary Court was a dead-end street lined with businesses ranging from light engineering to a print-and-graphic-design outfit. She had to come here sooner or later. She had to see the place where Richard had died.

If the police had cordoned off a crime scene, there was no sign of it now. Vehicles lined the street, and everyone seemed to be going about their normal business. It was as if Richard's death had never happened. Almost. Not all traces of Richard's murder were so easily erased. Blood still remained on the sidewalk and wall. A bloodstain was a sad epitaph to memorialize Richard. The police had picked over the scene, probably bagged every grain of dirt and dropped trash, but there was only so much they could do about the blood. It looked as if someone had washed the area, but not scrubbed it. Only time would remove all remnants. She hoped time would take its time.

Someone had left a small bouquet of flowers. That was nice. She should do the same. She picked up the bouquet and looked for a card so she could thank the person who'd left them, but they hadn't left a note.

A man came out of the welding-and-fabrication shop that was the backdrop to Richard's murder. His face was screwed up into a grimace. She guessed there'd been more than a few tourists through here since last night. His expression softened at the sight of her. He must have recognized the pain on her face.

"Can I help you?" he asked.

Olivia returned the flowers to the sidewalk. "My husband died here last night."

"I'm sorry. My condolences. Would you like to come in? You're welcome to use the restroom or have a cup of coffee." He smiled. "I'll warn you. The coffee isn't great."

Olivia smiled back. "That's okay. I just wanted a moment here. I hope that's all right."

"Of course. Take your time. If you need anything, just come in. And if anyone gives you any trouble, let me know. The name's Tom."

"Thanks, Tom. I'm Olivia."

Tom disappeared back inside the building, and she wondered if he had left the flowers.

She peered down at the bloodstained sidewalk. Finz hadn't gone into detail, but the bloodstains told a story. One stain almost two feet across marked where Richard had fallen, but the dozens and dozens of rust-colored splatters covering a much-wider area must have been the result of the blows Richard had endured. She pictured him lying there after the killer had beaten him and left him to die. The thought caused a shiver.

This was her fault. She'd made the decision that had gotten Richard killed. Shame and guilt built up in her chest until they squeezed against her heart. She sucked in a breath to ease the pressure, but it stagnated in her lungs. Her guilt was suffocating her. It was a fitting end, dying here, in the same spot as her husband. She dropped to her knees and wept, pressing her hand to the largest bloodstain on the sidewalk. "Oh, Richard."

Gentle hands supported her shoulders. "Mrs. Shaw, it's okay. Take a breath."

It was Detective Finz. Compassion marked his expression.

If he only knew, she thought. For the first time, she felt like confessing. The consequences no longer mattered.

Tom burst through the doorway. "What's going on? You okay, Olivia?"

"I'm a cop. It's okay," Finz said.

Tom raised his hands and retreated back into the building.

Finz took out a handkerchief and handed it to Olivia. She wiped her eyes and blew her nose. When she had control of herself again, he helped her to her feet.

"You shouldn't have come here."

"I had to see where it happened."

Finz nodded his understanding. "Are you okay?"

"I think so. Thanks."

"Got a few minutes to answer some questions?"

"If you can answer some of mine."

"Sure. Let's chat in my car."

"No," Olivia said. They were standing in the shade of the buildings, and the coolness felt good. "I need the air."

"Okay," Finz said, "but let's put some distance between us and this spot."

Olivia didn't object, and she let him guide her to the end of the block. She looked back down the street. The high walls on both sides turned it into an urban canyon. It was faceless and anonymous. Anything could happen here unnoticed, especially at night.

"You said you have questions," Finz said.

She nodded. "What have you found out?"

"We're still at the early phase of the investigation."

Olivia recognized that was code for the cops had no leads.

"I did attend the autopsy this morning, so I have the coroner's preliminary findings."

Autopsy. The thought turned her stomach. It wasn't enough that Richard had been brutalized; he also had to suffer the indignity of being sliced up by the coroner.

"Your husband suffered repeated blows from a blunt instrument."

"Did he put up a fight?"

"I believe so. There are defensive wounds, so I believe he fought back as best he could. My working theory is that Richard came here to meet his attacker. It was more than likely someone he knew or at least trusted."

That can't be right, Olivia thought. *Infidelity Limited wouldn't have sent someone Richard knew.* "What makes you say that?"

"This location for a start. Richard had no reason to be here, so this was a planned rendezvous. That means Richard didn't view his attacker as a threat and let this person get close to him. Also, the struggle was limited to a small area."

"What do you mean?"

"I'll show you."

Finz walked her back down the street, past the bloodstains.

"Your husband was first struck here." Finz pointed. "His car was parked there, some two hundred feet away. This was a smart move. It isolated him from his vehicle. There was a struggle here. We found loose change scattered. The subsequent strikes took place over a distance of less than fifty feet. Your husband was trying to make it back to his car. Like I said, it's a working theory."

It was better than a working theory. It sounded like Infidelity Limited's MO. Despite the heat, Olivia's arms and legs had gone cold, and her fingertips tingled. Finz's perceptiveness scared her. Roy would have to work hard to stay one step ahead of him. The world caved in on itself, and a whining sound drowned out Finz's last words. The sunlight seemed to intensify, blinding her. She slapped a hand over her mouth as the nausea climbed up her throat.

"Are you okay?" Finz asked.

"Excuse me?"

"You've gone pale."

She touched her face. It was clammy. "I'm sorry. I thought I was ready to hear this."

"No, I'm sorry. I should have been more discreet. Let's get you out of the sun."

Finz guided her over to his car and sat her down in the passenger seat. He climbed into the driver's seat and gunned the engine. A wave of ice-cool air poured from the vents, pushing her nausea away.

"I have a couple more questions. Are you up for answering them?"

Olivia nodded.

"Are you sure that you don't know what Richard was doing out here?"

Didn't he like my first answer? she thought. Guilt had her looking for the damning question because she deserved to be damned for her part in all this. She had to be smart if she wanted to survive this. That meant taking every question at face value and answering it that way. She thought she was doing okay so far. "I don't have a clue."

"Don't worry. We'll get to the bottom of it. Who stands to financially benefit from your husband's death?"

It was a standard question. She knew better than to be upset by it. "Me, I suppose. There's a life insurance policy. Richard and I have a family trust. Essentially, we leave everything to each other. Richard did bequeath some things to his parents and his brother's children. That's about it."

"Okay. I had to ask."

"I understand."

Finz asked if he could walk Olivia back to her car.

"I have the bank and phone records you asked for." She pulled them out of her purse and handed them over. "I don't have Richard's cell phone records. His firm issued that to him."

"Not a problem. I met with Richard's employer this morning. They gave me access to his phone and e-mail. I wonder if I could borrow your home computer? It would only be for a few days."

"No problem."

"Good, I'll have someone drop by to get it. One other question. Do you know Cassie Hill?"

She wondered if that was Richard's mistress's name. "No. Why?"

"No reason. Her name cropped up. If I find out more, I'll let you know."

Had that been a gotcha question? It could have been one if she'd known Richard's mistress's name. If she was going to beat this, ignorance might very well be the thing that saved her. "Thank you."

Finz held the car door open for her, and she got in. The temperature inside the car had rocketed. She stuck the key in the ignition and powered all the windows down. Finz remained, holding the door. She smiled at him.

"One last thing. I'd like you to come in for a polygraph."

Olivia's smile dropped. "A polygraph?"

"Yeah, it's a formality. There's nothing to worry about. It's for your protection. When we apprehend a suspect, the defense will try to shift blame to those with something to gain from Richard's death. That's why we get a poly on record at the beginning. It tightens our case. I've taken one. All sworn officers do. It prevents anything from being used against us."

Was this a line he was spinning her? Did he suspect her? The spouse was always the first suspect when no obvious assailant was on hand. She couldn't be offended. She was involved.

She played back his questions. She felt an accusatory tone in his questioning. Maybe that was the paranoia talking. Roy had put her in this position, and the cops were zeroing in on her. It was only a matter of time before they worked it all out. And it would all come crashing down if she took that lie-detector test.

"Well, if you think it's for the best, I don't have any problems with it."

"That's great. I'll give you a call to set up a time. And Mrs. Shaw, don't worry. We'll find out who's responsible for your husband's murder."

Olivia was afraid of that.

CHAPTER TEN

It was evening before Olivia reached home. She was happy for any excuse to avoid dealing with the silence and emptiness of the place. After Finz left her, she'd visited a nondenominational church, which would conduct Richard's service. He hadn't been particularly religious, but she knew it was important to Richard's mother that his funeral follow tradition. And despite her own religious apathy, she wanted a formal ceremony for Richard. It seemed the right thing to do under the circumstances. She arranged everything with them, except for the date. The coroner had yet to release the body to the funeral home.

In the kitchen, she stared at the refrigerator's contents. She needed to eat, but none of it appealed. She had no hunger, so she took a leaf out of Clare's book and grabbed a bottle of wine. She took a big-bowled wineglass intended for a burgundy and filled it all the way to the top with a chardonnay. Somewhere a sommelier was frowning in disgust at her poor wine etiquette, but she didn't care. She wasn't drinking to enjoy. She was drinking to get wrecked.

Carrying the glass and bottle into the living room, she dropped onto the sofa, managing to slop only a little of the booze. She hammered back half the glass's contents before coming up for air.

She eyed her glass and raised it. "Here's to you, Olivia Shaw."

She had really screwed things up for herself. Her cheating husband was dead, and the cops were circling, all because she'd let her deadbeat sister talk her into hiring idiots to beat Richard up. So much for taking her hands off the wheel and letting fate do the driving. Fate had proved it couldn't drive for shit. Christ, how had she been so stupid? It figured that the one time she took a risk, did one thing that strayed from the straight and narrow, her husband ended up dead and she'd likely be facing a murder charge, which was inevitable since she'd obviously fail the polygraph.

"Pity party for one," she said, refilling her glass.

Yes, she was getting a little too self-indulgent for her liking. The problem was she just wanted someone to talk to, and the sad fact about it was there wasn't anyone. For all Clare's faults, she was Olivia's go-to person, but not for this. Clare had contributed to this mess, but she had rabbit blood in her veins. At the first sign of trouble, she ran, literally and figuratively. And Clare was looking for any reason not to face up to the situation they were in. Her earlier remark, which suggested this wasn't a shared problem but Olivia's problem only, said everything Olivia needed to know about Clare's state of mind.

Other friends really were few and far between. As she drained her wineglass, she picked through her mental Rolodex. Not a single name sprang to mind. Yes, she had friends, but surface-level ones only. It was stunning to her how many of them were friends through business, hobbies, or marriage. None of them were friends with deep and unshakable roots. She had stronger ties to people when she was a kid than she did now. Maybe that was the price of getting older. The more you spread yourself through the world, the more tenuous your personal connections became.

She dwelled on that thought through the remainder of the bottle and into the start of a pricey bottle of red Richard had been talked into buying at a Napa vineyard. To her it was just fuel for getting drunk.

Returning to the living room, she pulled out a couple of photo albums from the bookshelves and dropped to the floor with them. It had been ages since she'd looked at them. She flipped the pages, leafing through her life. She stopped at a photo of her, no more than four years old, sitting next to Clare with their mother behind them, her arms draped over their shoulders. There was no sign of her dad in the shot or in any of the images around that time. He'd yet to dump his family, but even when he was there, he wasn't. She had no memory of the photo. It looked like the Martinez Waterfront Park in the background. Not that it mattered where the photo had been taken.

She ran a finger over her mom's face. Her memory of her mom was that she was tired and older than her years, but she'd known her mom through the eyes of youth. Here in this picture, her mother looked young. And she was. In this shot, she was younger than Olivia was now. Despite having to raise Clare and her on minimum wage and being in a shitty marriage, she looked happy in this picture. Olivia smiled and turned the page.

Page after page, Olivia went from child to teen. Time was documented in school photos and snapshots of family occasions. While all the faces were familiar, names weren't. Time had robbed them of their identities, if not their antics.

She stopped at one particular picture. It was a group shot, with Clare and Nick, Mark and Brianna, and Andrew and her all sitting on the hood of Mark's Trans Am. She remembered it like it was yesterday. It was the summer straight after high school. She was eighteen, and anything was possible. They'd been a tight group, but time had pulled them apart. She'd lost touch with Bri within a year of this picture being taken, when Bri took off for college.

Time hadn't pulled Andrew and her apart, circumstances had. They'd been together at the time of this photo. He was fun, cool, and exciting, and she'd thought marriage was a possibility for them. Then Andrew had gone and ruined it. She'd found out he was dealing weed.

He was just cashing in on what a cousin of his was growing, but she'd had zero tolerance for drugs and anyone involved with them. Her father was a slave to his addiction. In his case, it was booze, but drugs were no different. She'd dumped Andrew on the spot. Mark had been her rebound, and she'd made the mistake of marrying him.

When she broke up with Andrew, he'd joined the army, and she hadn't seen him again until a few years ago. She was the real estate agent representing the buyer for a house Andrew was selling. God, they'd been so close. Out of everybody in the world, she trusted Andrew the most. She still had his number somewhere.

She clambered to her feet and dug her phone out from her purse. She scrolled through her contacts, and there was Andrew's info. She hit the icon next to his cell phone number.

He answered the call. The background noise said he was on the road. "Hello."

"Andrew, it's Olivia Shaw. Olivia Lyndon that was."

"Hey, Olivia. It's been a long time."

It had. Too long. What had she been thinking?

"What can I do for you?" His tone was cordial, as if he were talking to a client and not a friend. She'd screwed up.

"Nothing. Sorry, I shouldn't have called."

"Hey, it's okay. What do you need?"

She liked that. That was what friends said. It was the first time she'd heard that said by someone who meant it. "My husband was killed."

"I know. I saw the news. I'm sorry, Liv. How are you doing?"

It was a good question. She wasn't grieving. Guilt and fear were getting in the way. "About as well as you'd expect."

"You've got people around you, yes?"

Just the cops and Infidelity Limited, she thought. "Yes." She failed to sound convincing, even to her own ear. "I'm just calling people to let them know and invite them to the service."

"You okay, Liv? What's wrong? Tell me."

The simple answer was she didn't trust anyone else. She had friends, good people whom she genuinely liked, but they weren't the kind of people who helped find a killer. They enjoyed easy lives and had no comprehension of the trouble people could get themselves into. Andrew was different. They had grown up together and knew things about each other that they hadn't shared with anyone else. She hadn't known that kind of bond with anyone else. When it came to entrusting herself to someone with a lifeline, Andrew was the only person who made the list.

"I'd gotten a little maudlin, and I was thinking about the old days," she replied. "I wanted to talk to an old friend. I know it's stupid."

"It's not. Do you want me to come over? I'm happy to. Just give me your address."

Part of her wanted to hang up, but a larger part of her wanted Andrew to come over. She needed to talk to someone she could trust who wasn't involved in this mess.

"Yes, that would be great," she said and gave him her details.

*   *   *

Andrew arrived half an hour later. She'd left the door ajar for him, and he let himself in.

"Liv?"

"In the living room."

He stood in the doorway, dressed in work boots, jeans, and a short-sleeved shirt with "Macready Construction" embroidered on it. The years had been good to him. Very little gray marred his blond hair. He was still in shape, which she put down to the construction work. She thought he was better looking now in his forties, like her, than he had been back when they were kids. He'd burned away the puppy fat of youth she'd seen in that picture of them sitting on the Trans Am. His face had real definition now.

She got up from her chair and hugged him. The hug's familiarity transported her back to her teens. "It's great to see you. It's been a long time."

"Too long."

He released her. The warmth in his smile lifted a weight from her shoulders. She felt safe in his presence.

"I came straight over. Sorry to still be in my work gear."

"That's okay. Sit. Can I get you something to drink—wine, beer?"

"I'm driving, so a soda would be good."

She grabbed him a Diet Coke from the fridge. She handed him the can before sinking into the chair across from him. It was Richard's chair. She thought she felt his contours from years of repeated use.

"I'm really sorry about Richard," he said. "I really don't know what to say."

"You being here means a lot."

"It was the least I could do, Liv."

"I see you have your own company," she said, pointing to the company name on his shirt.

"Eight years now. I went into construction after getting out of the army and went out on my own a few years later."

"Married? Kids?"

"Was married. We broke up a few years ago. No kids."

"I'm sorry."

"No need to be. We just wanted different things. Enough about me. I'm here for you. Tell me what's happening."

She outlined the basic circumstances of Richard's death. She left out Richard's affair and Infidelity Limited.

"And you don't know why he was there and who he was meeting?"

"No," she lied.

"Do the cops have a suspect?"

"No. Possibly me."

Andrew jerked back from her answer. "You?"

"If there aren't any suspects, they look at the spouse. Isn't that always the way?"

"Yeah, but are they serious? What makes you think they're looking at you?"

"Is a polygraph serious enough? The detective in charge told me today he wanted me to take one."

"Who's the cop in charge?"

"Detective Mike Finz. Know him?"

He shook his head. "But I've done work for the Concord PD in the past. I can ask around and find out what kind of reputation he's got."

"No. Don't. If he's suspicious of me, I don't want to give him any reason to suspect me more."

"Did he say why he wanted you to take a polygraph?"

"For elimination purposes, essentially. He says it's routine and it helps strengthen their case against the defense."

"There you have it. I doubt he means anything by it. Even if he does, you'll ace it and he'll have to knuckle down and do his job."

In an ideal world, Andrew would be totally correct, but this wasn't an ideal world. She wouldn't ace the polygraph. If she took that test, it'd be game over and everything would come tumbling down. Finz would charge her, and she'd have no defense against it. She could point the finger at Infidelity Limited, but as Roy had proudly proclaimed in his sales pitch to her, Infidelity Limited was a ghost. It didn't exist beyond word of mouth, and no one talked. Even if she did talk, who would believe that something like Infidelity Limited could exist? There was no escape for her.

"I doubt the cops are going to railroad you, but you need to protect yourself. Do you have a lawyer?"

"No."

"Okay. Let me make a few calls and see if I can get one."

"I don't know. Guilty people get lawyers."

"No, smart people get lawyers. Look, your husband has been murdered. You need to mourn and make arrangements, so you should have someone who can act as an interface between you and the investigation."

"Will a lawyer be able to get me out of taking the polygraph?"

"Possibly, but you may not have a choice. Look, you weren't involved in Richard's death, so there's nothing to worry about. Even if this Finz likes you as the killer, a polygraph is going to punch a hole in his case."

Olivia was torn. Why had she called Andrew if it wasn't to have someone to confide in? She'd been a little drunk when she'd phoned him, but she'd sobered up in a hurry. She wasn't sure she should confide in him. The second she told him her secret, there was no going back. Someone outside of the Infidelity Limited circle would know, and there'd be no way of controlling the situation. She had no idea how Andrew would react. She couldn't prevent him from telling Finz what he knew. As much as she wanted to tell someone the truth, she had to treat Andrew the same as Finz and tell him nothing.

"I'm definitely going to check out this Finz character and see what his record looks like," Andrew said, breaking her train of thought. "Don't worry. He won't know that I checked him out. Are you okay for money for the funeral service?"

"Yes. We have money, and Richard had life insurance."

"Okay, but if you need some, I have it."

"Thanks, Andrew. I mean it."

"I've taken up too much of your time, so I'll go. I'm going to look into Richard's death. Anything I find out, I'll bring it to you—and the police." He smiled. "I won't do anything stupid and take care of it myself."

She didn't tell him not to. At the moment, Roy was playing hard to get, and he held all the power. She didn't know where to find him and had no way of stopping him from incriminating her. Worse still, she had nothing she could use against Roy and Infidelity Limited to protect herself. If Andrew turned something up that would lead her to them, it would even up the score.

Andrew checked his watch. "Call me anytime, Liv. I mean it. I'm here for you."

She saw him to the door. "We haven't seen each other in so long. Why are you doing all this?"

"Call it an apology. I let you down when we were together, and I never got to make it up to you. This is my chance. Us Martinez kids have to stick together. I've got your back, Liv."

CHAPTER ELEVEN

Roy arrived home after three days on the road. He smiled as he blew through the private gates leading up to his Santa Barbara house, like he always did. He loved this house. It was the place he'd always dreamed of owning and never thought he would. But this was the house that Infidelity Limited had built. Twenty years of profiteering off people's desperation and revenge had bought them the four-thousand-square-foot, two-story Spanish mission–style house sprawled over an acre of land. To the casual observer, the place might belong to a celebrity.

Roy parked in front of the house, and Luis emerged. Luis ran the house by himself, taking care of Beth and acting as Roy's eyes and ears when he was working. When Luis started working for them ten years ago, he'd only been a kid and Roy hadn't thought he'd last the week. He was just out of high school and fresh faced. The kid looked as if he didn't know his ass from his elbow when it came to how the world worked, but he was unflappable. Beth could drive Roy to distraction, but not Luis. Whatever tantrum Beth threw, he simply dealt with it without ever letting it get to him. But his greatest asset was his discretion. He'd take their secrets to the grave.

Luis took Roy's overnight bag. "Good trip?"

"Not bad. A few problems, but they're under control. How's Beth?"
Luis frowned.

"That good, huh? Where is she?"

"On the patio. I was just about to take her breakfast out to her."

"I'll do it."

Roy found the breakfast Luis had prepared for Beth on a tray in the kitchen—a spinach, onion, and mushroom omelet with coffee, juice, and toast. She'd only eat a fraction of it. He wondered how she survived, eating so little.

He carried the food out to the patio, where he saw the crew Luis had hired to take care of the landscaping. They worked at the far end of the property, away from the house—and Beth. She spooked them. She spooked everyone who'd ever worked for them. They'd stopped trying to employ a permanent household staff. Not many people could handle dealing with a person disfigured by fire.

Beth sat alone on the patio with the newspaper, looking small and frail. She ignored the paper in favor of the landscapers. Her fire-ravaged side faced Roy, although it was hard to tell. She always wore long sleeves, and her long, dark hair covered her face. Her hand and face gave a clue to the devastation she'd suffered. Like wax, her flesh looked as if it had melted and reset. Her disfigurement meant little to him. Her beauty was truly more than skin deep. He loved the woman he'd met all those years ago. She saw the real him. Where everyone saw nothing more than a pair of fists, she saw his potential, his intelligence. No one would have thought he could build an empire like Infidelity Limited, except her. Her physical and mental scars would never change that.

He set the tray down on the table and kissed her on the good side of her face. Though her looks didn't bother him, they bothered her. "It's good to see you."

"And you," she said without taking her gaze off the landscapers.

He noticed the ash on the concrete at her feet. It looked like the remains of one of her lace handkerchiefs. She'd been burning again.

He'd never understand why she liked to play with fire after what it had done to her. He let it go. It wasn't worth getting into an argument about, especially with the landscapers around.

He set the plate in front of her and poured himself a cup of coffee. "What a gorgeous morning. The air feels clean today."

Beth made no attempt to touch her breakfast. He picked up a fork and cut a piece for himself.

"How bad is the Olivia Shaw situation?" she asked.

It was good to see she was interested in work, but it was probably her way of avoiding a lecture on not eating.

"Proctor screwed up the hit. The cops are all over it now. There's no way of making that go away."

"Do the cops suspect anything?"

"Hard to say at this point. I don't think they suspect Olivia, but they will be looking to put someone's head on a spike."

Beth picked up her juice and sipped it.

"Do you want some of this omelet? It's good."

Instead, she produced her Zippo lighter. She rolled her thumb across the Zippo's wheel, and a flame popped into life. Roy had given up denying her a lighter long ago. It calmed her, even if she did burn something from time to time.

"So, we're vulnerable on this one?" she asked.

Roy put his fork down. "Yeah. But to Proctor's credit, he hasn't left the cops much in the way of leads, so I think we're in good shape there."

"How's he holding up?"

Roy had a ten-point scale when it came to their clients and their ability to deal with the situation. "I'd put him at a five. As long as the cops don't come knocking, that number won't go up."

"And if they do?"

"I don't think it's a concern."

"It's always a concern."

He detected a note of irritation in her voice. "Yes, we always need to be careful, but at the moment, there's nothing to cause concern."

It was a politician's answer and not one he favored, but as much as he had to manage their clients, he also had to manage Beth. She was ruthless. For her there were no shades of gray. She operated on a scorched-earth policy. At the first sign of trouble, she wanted all threats eliminated. His intervention had saved many lives over the years.

"And what about Olivia?"

"She's rattled, but I think she's got what it takes to go the distance on this one. I'd put her at a seven."

Beth passed her fingers over the flame. "I hear a but."

"Our vulnerability. The cops will need someone to hang the murder on. We can easily toss them Proctor, but his arrest would lead to some awkward questions. Olivia is a more natural choice. Cops always suspect the spouse. As loose ends go, Olivia's can be trimmed a lot easier. It would be a shame to do that, though."

Beth snapped the Zippo shut and grinned at him. The damaged half of her face failed to move, making the smile lopsided. "You like her, don't you?"

He developed a soft spot for their clients on occasion. From time to time, he'd relate to their plight. Olivia was one of those clients.

"It's not that I like her. It's that she's different. She's not like Proctor or her sister. There's no malice in Olivia. Her husband was running around on her, and she just wanted a little retribution. I get that—and I know you do too."

Beth went back to her juice. "How much can we get from her?"

When it came down to it, Infidelity Limited was a money business. As with any client, Roy had done his homework. When Clare reached out to him on Olivia's behalf, he'd squeezed a financial snapshot from her about her sister. What Olivia owned and how much she owed. He fleshed out the details by running a credit check and doing a dash of house breaking. He'd broken into Olivia's house prior to their first meeting to go through her hard-copy and electronic records. It hadn't taken much to work up a decent financial picture on her. If someone didn't pass muster on the money front, then he usually declined him or her as a client. Not all clients were judged on their net worth, however. If people possessed particular skills that might prove valuable down the road, they also got selected.

"There's four hundred and fifty grand in life insurance coming to her."

"So we can push her?"

"I think so."

"Push her all the way?"

Roy turned to the omelet to avoid answering. Beth was right. He did like Olivia, and as much as he wanted to go easy on her, he had a job to do.

"When the cops fail to come up with a suspect, they will turn on her," Beth said. "That means if we're going to get what we can from her, we have to fast-track her." She pushed her breakfast over to him, picked up the newspaper, and leafed through it.

"So how far do you want to take it with Olivia?" Roy asked.

Beth struck a flame with her Zippo and set fire to the newspaper. "I say we burn her up."

CHAPTER TWELVE

After a weekend of trying to accept her part in Richard's murder, Olivia started her week by going into work, but there was no way she could carry off a professional demeanor with Richard's murder looming over her. The fair thing to her clients was to palm them off onto the other Realtors at the agency. She arrived at nine and realized her mistake—an office full of people. She should have come in early to avoid them.

Everyone stopped what they were doing to engage her the moment she stepped inside. She suffered through the seemingly never-ending wave of condolences and ran the gauntlet of sympathetic hugs. Her colleagues offered their love and support. She found their concern cloying. Every expression of sympathy made her more uncomfortable. They ate away at her facade of the devastated wife. She cast them aside with a brave face and a simple thank-you. She asked for space and shut herself away in her office. Safe in the confines of the room, she relaxed. She spent the next hour shooting off e-mails to agents and leaving client files for them to pick up later before slipping out.

With that chore out of the way, it was time for the harder part—the funeral home.

Olivia had buried her dead before. There was her first husband, Mark, then her mother. For both occasions, she'd gone to Steele Funeral and Cremation in Oakland.

Leo Steele welcomed her upon her arrival. His hair had turned totally silver in the decade since she'd last come to him.

"Mrs. Shaw, I'm so sorry for your loss. Come into my office, and we can discuss your husband."

Steele was sympathetic and professional. He explained he'd taken charge of Richard's body this morning when the coroner had released it. Olivia hoped the coroner's swift release of Richard's remains was a good sign. Surely, if they truly suspected her, they wouldn't have turned the body over to her already.

"Will this be an open-casket service?"

She shook her head. Olivia knew Richard's mother would want an open casket so she could say good-bye to her only son, but Olivia couldn't do that. She couldn't face him, no matter how good the cosmetic cover-up. She'd see through the makeup to the violence she had instigated.

"Are you sure? I know it may not be something you want now, but it's something many people regret afterward. We have a very skilled staff. He'll look as you remember him. Mourners will be able to pay their respects to the Richard they knew and loved."

"No. Open casket wasn't something Richard wanted," she lied.

Steele nodded his understanding. He proceeded to go over the series of events leading up to the funeral next week and how he'd coordinate with the church she'd selected. She did her best to listen, but her thoughts turned to Finz. The polygraph was all she could think about. It was a bullet she couldn't dodge. If she refused, Finz would demand to know why. And if she took the test, Finz wouldn't have to ask why. Her reasons would be written out before her. She could be overthinking this. Finz probably meant what he'd said; it was a formality. That said, she'd never known anyone to be polygraphed who wasn't a suspect. She was so screwed.

"Mrs. Shaw?"

"Sorry. Yes."

"I just asked if you have any questions."

"No. I don't think so."

"Well, if you do, call me anytime."

She smiled. "I will."

Steele tactfully presented her with an invoice, and she wrote him a check.

She squinted against the sunlight when she walked outside. It was quite a contrast to the muted lighting inside the funeral home.

Her cell phone rang in her purse. Reflexively, she reached for it, but paused when she realized it was the one Roy had given her. She hadn't expected to hear from him again. She pulled out the phone and answered it.

"We need to talk," he said.

She hurried across the street to her car and shut herself inside. "You killed Richard. Why?"

"Meet me at the top of Mount Diablo now."

Before she could say any more, Roy hung up.

She cursed under her breath. Roy was manipulating her, pulling her strings because he could. But as much as he might shove her around, it didn't change the ugly fact that he'd screwed up. Killing Richard bound them tightly together. If Finz put two and two together, and she felt he would, they'd both go down for this. She bottled her frustration and gunned the engine.

It didn't take long to reach Mount Diablo's summit. Her car labored on the winding road that led to the four-thousand-foot peak. The road came to an end at a turnaround and a small parking lot in front of the Summit Visitor Center and Museum. Despite Roy telling her to be here, she didn't find him waiting for her. If their previous meeting was anything to go by, his absence was part of his vetting process. That meant someone else was watching her before giving him the okay. She was coming to realize these were the typical fun and games of dealing with Infidelity Limited. She parked in one of the vacant stalls and switched the engine off.

Mount Diablo was a smart choice. The parking lot was deserted, except for one other car. Not surprising. There weren't going to be many day hikers on a weekday morning. With just a single road going to the top, Roy had a clear view of anyone coming up the mountain. That would satiate his paranoia for security. If Olivia had turned to the cops, they'd have no way of proceeding unseen.

Giving her zero notice also negated any chance of her turning to someone for help. Roy really knew how to isolate his clients. If she wanted the upper hand, that would have to change.

She wondered what stunt Roy would pull this time. Was he going to parachute in? Come four-wheeling out from the trees? He seemed to like impressing everyone with Infidelity Limited's slick operation, but he had nothing to be proud of right now. It would be hard to act so high and mighty when he'd screwed everything up.

After thirty minutes, Roy rolled up in his Chrysler and parked two stalls over from her. He climbed from his car and gestured to her to join him.

Something inside her snapped. The sight of him coolly waving at her like nothing serious had happened infuriated her. The man had killed Richard, and she was tired of playing his childish games. She burst from her car and charged at him.

Surprise lit up his face, and his shock inspired her. It was about time he experienced a fraction of what she had been going through. She slammed into him, driving him back against the vehicle. She caught him across the jaw with her fist. The blow was good enough to pop one of her knuckles, but caused little more than a jerk of his head.

"You bastard! He's dead, and it's all your fault."

He smothered her in a tight hug that stopped her from landing any further punches and rocked her gently. "I know. I know," he cooed. "It shouldn't have happened, but it did, and we have to deal with it now. Don't we?"

The rage left her as quickly as it had arrived. Her body sagged, but Roy's grip kept her from falling to the ground. She sobbed in his arms, while he told her everything would be okay.

How can it ever be okay? she thought. Roy couldn't bring Richard back to life.

Roy guided her around the Chrysler and placed her in the passenger seat. He got behind the wheel. "Let's find somewhere a little more private."

He reversed out of his parking spot and drove the short distance down to the summit's overflow parking lot. Despite it only being a couple of hundred yards from the top, it might as well have been a million miles away in its seclusion.

"Out, please," he said when he parked.

Out of reflex, Olivia did as she was told. "Where are we going?"

Roy slipped an arm through hers and maneuvered her to the restrooms. He pushed the door to the men's room open and sent her ahead of him, then snapped the lock shut on the door.

She didn't have to ask what was happening next and began unbuttoning her blouse.

Roy held up a hand. "That won't be necessary."

He flicked her arms up and ran his hands down her sides, stomach, and back. He dropped to his knees, lifted her skirt, and repeated the move up and down each leg. The pat-down was intimate but not degrading, unlike the one Dolores had dished out at the mall.

Why hadn't he asked her to undress? Was it out of chivalry or out of trust? Dolores's pat-down had seemed to have more to do with setting a tone and stating the balance of power than a security screen. So why not now? If anything, he should have amped up the security. It was a turning point for both of them. The deal had gone south in the worst way. Maybe due diligence went out the window when there was a murder to cover up.

"Thank you, Olivia. There are picnic tables outside. Let's enjoy them."

She wanted to scream. How could he be treating this like a casual get-together when Richard was dead?

She followed him out to the picnic tables and sat across from him. A chill breeze swept over them.

"How are you, Olivia?"

Her rage flared. "How do you think? You killed my husband. I should turn you into the cops."

Roy smiled at her with the kind of smile adults reserved for children when they were humoring them. "But you won't."

"No."

"Because it will incriminate you," he said. "Have you talked to the police?"

"Of course I have. They came to my house."

Roy nodded. "I do apologize for that. We are very discreet, but when something goes wrong, then there are limits to what can be done, because the police are bound to be involved."

"Is that supposed to make me feel better? Because it doesn't. I have to submit to a polygraph next week."

Olivia caught a flicker of concern in Roy's expression. He should be concerned, because she was. She didn't have a clue what she would be asked, but one of the questions had to be: Did you kill your husband?

"I wouldn't sweat that too much. Do the police suspect your involvement?"

"How would I know? It's not like they would tell me."

"That's true. At the same time, there's not a lot you can admit to knowing either."

Does he really think that? she wondered. He might have said it for her benefit, but it sounded more like self-delusion.

"I thought you ran a well-oiled machine. How are you going to clear up this mess?" she demanded. "You were supposed to hurt Richard. Nothing else. What went wrong?"

"Nothing."

Olivia snorted her contempt. "You're going to stick to that story?"

"Yes."

She felt her grip on her temper slip. "You killed Richard. That wasn't in the plan."

"Yes, it was. Our only mistake was that Richard was found. Ideally, he would have simply disappeared."

"What?"

His patronizing smile was back, and for the first time, it was merited. She felt like a child. She didn't understand what was going on, and it scared her. A chill spread through her body.

"It's facts-of-life time, Olivia. You hired us to kill Richard. We never planned to let him go with just a beating."

"Oh, Jesus."

"I wasn't entirely honest with you about Infidelity Limited's mission. It would be nice if a firm of vigilantes dealt out a slice of street justice on our loved ones, but sadly that's a pipe dream. The ease with which intelligent people fall for the simplest of scams never fails to astound me."

Yes, Olivia had been gullible. She couldn't believe she'd been so dumb. Roy had set her up, and she'd walked face-first into his trap. The only excuse she could use in her defense was she'd been in a vulnerable place. He'd caught her in a moment of weakness, when she'd been angry with Richard and willing to believe in anything for a shot at revenge. Because of that, Richard had paid the price.

"Now you're in a nasty predicament. Your husband has been murdered, and you're the person who commissioned the hit."

"Don't twist the truth."

"I'm not. I'm telling you how it will look to the cops. Your husband was killed. You paid money for it to happen."

"I didn't order his death."

"It doesn't matter, Olivia. They won't believe you. A prosecutor will be able to prove premeditation. A good defense lawyer might be able to knock it down to second-degree murder, but at the end of the day, the facts are the facts."

"These aren't facts."

"They are whatever I say they are. Evidence can be interpreted in a number of ways. It's just a matter of what information is fed to the police. You withdrew money that you can't account for, and your husband subsequently died a violent death. That doesn't look good for you. It wouldn't take much for these details to be forwarded to the cops."

Olivia felt a sense of dread settle over her like a damp blanket. It forced a shiver from her. "What is it you want?"

Roy smiled. "Don't be like that."

Roy was revealing his true self now. A coldhearted killer had replaced the big-fisted thug with a heart of gold she'd first met.

"The important thing is that I can help you get out of this situation, but it is going to be expensive."

She contained her contempt. "How expensive?"

"One hundred thousand expensive."

So this had been the scheme all along—to extort money out of her. It was a despicable plan, and it would fail. Maybe the threat of going to jail frightened most people, but it didn't frighten her. She kept her wits about her, and she saw a big hole in Roy's business model. Incriminating her was incriminating himself.

"Why should I give you the money?" she demanded. "If I go down for Richard's murder, you go down with me."

"Really? How?"

"You killed him. His blood is on your hands."

"Is it? Are you sure? Prove it." He cut her off before she could answer. "Who am I, Olivia? Where do I live? Where do I do business? How do we contact each other? You have an untraceable cell phone number. That won't help you find me. If you want to see how ridiculous the whole idea of Infidelity Limited is, just try telling the cops about it. Even if they do believe you and try to investigate, they won't find anything. I'm a ghost. And no one believes in ghosts. Especially cops."

During Roy's initial pitch, he'd sold her on the virtue that Infidelity Limited's quasi existence protected her. If they couldn't be found, she couldn't be blamed. Really, that feature only protected him and his organization.

Olivia tried her best not to appear alarmed by the revelation. Roy was trying to scare her. If she kept calm, she stood a chance of escaping this. "There'll be physical evidence. There's no such thing as a perfect crime."

"I keep telling you that I didn't kill Richard."

"Okay, you sent someone to kill Richard. It doesn't matter. When the cops catch him, he'll roll over on Infidelity Limited to save his own neck."

Roy shook his head. "You're still not getting it, Olivia. There is no team of killers working on my behalf. I've never once taken a life. Maybe I should explain how all this works. I want more than just your money. I need you to do something for me. For Infidelity Limited to operate cleanly, for me that is, I have to be the middleman, taking no part in the procedure. I can't have a tangible connection to the killer, the same way I can't have a tangible connection to you. You wanted to beat some sense into your husband and wanted some plausible deniability. That's great. I arranged for someone to be your fists. What happens when the next person comes to me and wants the same done to their spouse? I'm going to need someone to beat that spouse's head in. That's where you come in, Olivia. This is where you get your hands dirty."

Olivia tasted bile at the back of her throat. "You want me to kill someone for you?"

"Yes. It's the way this works. If you kill your husband, the cops will catch you. If you kill someone else's spouse or loved one, there's no connection. Where's the logic? There is none, and an investigation falls apart. It's a system of bait and switch."

"Oh my God."

"I know it's hard to accept, but think of all this as a murderous version of pay it forward. You won't know when I'll need you, but one day you'll receive a call, and I will give you a name, a place, a time, and a date, and you will kill the target. You won't know the person, and you won't know why, but you will kill them. If you don't, vital information will get back to the cops about Richard's murder. Have I made myself clear?"

CHAPTER THIRTEEN

Roy left Olivia in the parking lot. She traipsed up the road back to her car and fell into the driver's seat, leaving the door open. She struggled to see a way out. Instead of solutions, she saw her ruin. If she confessed everything to Finz, she would incriminate herself. If she followed Roy's instructions, she would become a murderer. And then what? If she went through with it, she was bound to screw up and get arrested. Coming up with the $100,000 for Roy was going to draw attention. It would look exactly like what it was—a payoff. She was screwed. She was going down for this one way or another.

"How did you get yourself into this?" she murmured.

Clare. That was how. Her sister knew how these people operated. Roy had no doubt put her through the same treatment. How could her own flesh and blood have done this to her, knowing how Infidelity Limited worked?

A second thought crashed into the back of that one. If Clare was one of Infidelity Limited's clients, did that mean she had killed someone for them?

"Are you okay?"

A hiker peered in at her. She hadn't noticed him approach.

"Yes. Yes, I'm fine." She smiled a brittle smile. "Just thinking, that's all."

The hiker didn't appear convinced. "As long as you're okay."

"I am. Thanks," she said with a better smile.

She closed the door and eased out of her parking stall, then accelerated away, with the hiker still watching her. The second she was out of sight, she pulled out her cell phone and punched in Clare's number.

"Where are you?" she asked as soon as Clare picked up.

"And hello to you too."

"I don't have time for this, Clare. Where are you?"

"At work, where do you think?"

Clare worked at a Target in Pleasant Hill. "Tell them you've got a family emergency. I need to see you now."

"I can't just cut and run."

"Do it, Clare. I helped you. Now it's your turn to help me."

"What's going on?"

"Roy."

Silence followed for a second. "Okay. Where?"

"Your place."

Clare's Honda was parked in front of the trailer when Olivia rolled up. Olivia didn't bother knocking and let herself in. Clare spun around, a glass filled with vodka in her hand. That glass all but admitted her part in Roy's scheme. Olivia closed in on her sister.

"I suppose Roy pulled back the curtain to show you what you've really won," Clare said.

Olivia nodded.

"How much did he ask for to keep this quiet?"

Quiet wasn't how Olivia would have described it, seeing as Richard's murder was in the hands of the police. "A hundred thousand."

Clare whistled. "Roy's prices have gone up. He only took me for five grand."

Olivia had wondered how much he'd strong-armed out of Clare. Clare hadn't come begging for money when Nick went missing, so it had to have been something manageable.

"Business must be good if he's tagging you for six figures."

The big payout told her something about Roy. Either he knew his clients' ability to pay or he'd sought out bigger fish over the years. The latter seemed the most likely. Big risks deserved big rewards. So in the six years since Clare had hired Infidelity Limited, the business model had developed into something more complex. That meant it was an organization bigger than just Roy and Dolores. A sinking feeling pulled at Olivia. Infidelity Limited had her outgunned and outmanned. Ideas of escaping this mess looked remote.

"It's a trip, isn't it?" Clare said.

"So you knew this would happen?"

Clare dipped her finger in the vodka glass, then rubbed it around the ring until the glass sang. "Oh, yeah."

It hurt to hear her admit this. "If you knew the score, why'd you do it to me, Clare? After all I've done for you, how could you screw me like this?"

The words slapped Clare across the face. She straightened up. "After all you've done for me? What have you done? You throw me a bone when I need one because it makes you feel superior. That's about it. You've never really helped me."

"It's not my job to support you. You're a grown woman."

"It's not easy, y'know. Not everyone lands on their feet or is as lucky as you. It would have been nice if you'd shared that luck with your sister. I'm not looking for you to support me, but if you'd set me up with a home, a car, and a little self-respect, I could have turned my life around. But that didn't work for you. You needed the poor relation to make you feel good."

"You know that isn't true."

"Do I?"

Is that how Clare really sees things between us? It wasn't Clare's hurtful words that saddened her. It was the simplistic view of her life and the naive belief that it could magically work out if only someone else would pay for it. To Clare, Olivia had achieved all she had through dumb luck. She saw none of the work and discipline it had taken Olivia to get the things she wanted out of life. He sister's opinions were those of a child and not a grown woman, and that was the saddest part of all.

"What happens now?" Olivia asked.

"Nothing—for the moment. Infidelity Limited plays the long game. You might not hear from them for years. Then one day they'll have a job for you, and they'll expect you to do it."

"Is that what happened to you?"

"I don't want to talk about it."

"Clare, the time for being coy is over. You have to be up-front with me."

"No, I don't. Roy's number one rule is you don't talk. You keep your mouth shut, bury it deep, and pretend it never happened."

That worked for Clare and probably for most of Infidelity Limited's clientele, but not for Olivia. She needed the truth. It was the only way of finding the edges of this mess. "Have they called you?"

Clare's grip on her glass intensified until her knuckles turned white. "Olivia, I'm not telling you. Move on. Ask me something else."

"Have you killed for them?"

"No!"

Clare barked the answer. It hung in the air, seemingly taking form between them. Neither of them spoke until it dissipated.

"I haven't killed anyone. Not yet. I've been lucky. Roy hasn't called."

"Jesus."

"It's why I recommended them to you, because they never follow through. It was just a stick he used to keep people in line."

Olivia couldn't decide if Clare was monumentally naive or crazy. "What are you talking about? They killed Richard. They killed Nick. What makes you think they aren't going to get you to kill someone for them?"

"That's not true. Nick isn't dead."

"What are you talking about?"

"I don't know for sure that Nick is dead. His body was never found. I just had Roy's word for it. It was a scare tactic to keep me quiet."

"But Richard is dead. Doesn't that tell you something?"

Clare shook her head slowly, as if her neck were turning on a rusted joint. She could delude herself about past events, but not now, not with Richard's murder.

"Nick's dead, isn't he?" Olivia prodded.

"Olivia, just because your husband is dead doesn't mean mine is."

Olivia couldn't trust her sister. If Clare could lie to herself on this point, then she wasn't reliable on any point. It was time to get help.

CHAPTER FOURTEEN

Olivia stopped behind Andrew's pickup in front of the San Pablo address he'd given her when she'd called him. The street looked cramped, consisting of small homes on small lots. The two-story house he had built was a fresh addition in size and architecture, but it overwhelmed the tiny lot it sat upon.

The front door was open, and she walked inside. She expected a construction site, but the place looked finished. Walls were painted. Plastic sheeting protected new carpeting.

"Andrew, it's me, Olivia."

"In the kitchen."

She found him hunched over a countertop, filling out paperwork.

"You work alone?"

"No. This one is done and sold. My crew is working on another project. I just came here to do the final walk-through with city inspectors." He held up a sheet of paper. "I have my certificate of occupancy so I should be able to close the sale now. So what do you think?"

As new homes went, it was nothing fancy, but it pleased her. She liked the smell of fresh paint and new carpets. She felt the potential from the never-occupied rooms. A family would turn this house into a home when they moved in. "I like it. Think you'll end up building developments?"

He shook his head. "I don't need the stress. I make a good living from doing this, so I'm happy."

Olivia couldn't remember the last time she'd been happy. Work and commitments had taken priority over the last few years, at the expense of enjoying life.

He looked up from his paperwork and pushed it to one side. "But you're not here to talk about my business."

"No."

"What's up?"

"I need your help."

"Sure. What do you need?"

"I need you to promise you won't breathe a word of this to anyone."

Andrew put down his pen and rounded the countertop. "Liv, what's happened?"

She backed up a step, putting her hands out. "Promise, Andrew."

"I promise," he said. "Just tell me what's going on."

Stay or go. Stay or go. Those were her only choices. So much was at risk that walking out made sense, but out of everyone she ever knew, she trusted Andrew. He'd done some stupid things when they were kids, but he always stood by his friends. She was gambling on that trait. Still, it was a big risk. Sure, they'd been close twenty years ago, but now they were just strangers with a past. He wouldn't be the person he was back then. Lord knew she wasn't. That was the gamble. She was out of options, so she rolled the dice.

"I'm in trouble with the police."

"Why?" he said with trepidation in his voice.

"It has to do with Richard's murder. I'm involved."

There was no sudden rush to hug her this time. Instead, Andrew just stood there. "What did you do?"

She saw the shock and panic in his eyes. Bombshells had that effect on people. She did her best to allay his fears. "Richard was cheating on me. I wanted to strike out, so I hired some people to work him over. They killed him instead. It's a scam, and now they're framing me."

"Look," Andrew said after a long pause, "I don't really see how I can help you."

"I need a friend and a sounding board."

"As your friend, I'd recommend that you go to the police."

"I need more than that."

"Liv, I don't know."

She felt him backing away. "Let me tell you what's going on. You can go to the police if you want to, but please hear me out."

She watched his emotions play over his face as he debated with himself. Eventually, he shook his head and went to the front door. She thought he was going to tell her to get out, but instead, he closed and locked the door. He sat down in the middle of the living room floor and pointed to a spot opposite him. "I'll listen, but you'd better tell me before I change my mind."

She sat down and told him the entire story this time, leaving nothing out. This wasn't a time to hold back. If Andrew was going to help her, he needed all the facts. It felt good to unburden herself of everything that had happened since she'd discovered Richard's infidelity.

When she was finished, he took her hand and held it in his. "Wow, I don't know what to say."

"I know. It's a train wreck."

"I don't think it could be any worse if you tried. It's good to see that Clare still has a talent for sucking people into mayhem. What do you think I can do to help?"

"You were in the army. I thought you'd be able to help me track these people down."

"I think you have me confused with Special Forces. I was just an army grunt. Look, like I said before, the best advice I can give you is to go to the police."

"If I do that, I'll take the fall for Richard's murder. These people have set me up, and I need to prove it."

"Then find a good lawyer who'll negotiate you a deal. There's no way you're coming out of this clean, Liv. You hired them to assault Richard."

"I know and I accept that, but Infidelity Limited is preying on people. That's why I need your help. I can't do this alone. This is how they win. They have numbers. Their victims don't."

"What do you want to happen?"

"I want to expose them, find out who killed Richard, and set the cops on them."

Andrew was silent for a long moment. "You realize Richard's killer is someone in your position, right? Someone who had their arm twisted into killing for Infidelity Limited."

She did. She didn't like it, but this had to be done. She was in a predicament where it was either her or them. "Richard's killer had the chance to break the cycle, and he didn't. I feel sorry for him, but not for what he did."

"He might not have had a choice."

"And neither do I. That's why I need someone on my side."

"Do you realize how hard this is going to be? It will take more than tracking them down and pointing the finger at them, then expecting the cops to swoop in to save the day."

She was under no illusion that getting out of this wouldn't be messy. Andrew was probably right. She stood little chance of coming away clean, but if she took down Roy that would at least be something.

"I'm assuming Roy was telling you the truth when he told you he was untouchable. If so, Infidelity Limited will be very good at setting itself up in the shadows, and there will be nothing to tie these guys to.

Even if you record a phone call, you've got nothing to back it up, and you're still criminally involved."

"So what are you suggesting—give up?"

"No. What I'm saying is if you're hoping to get yourself off the hook and put Roy on it, then you're not going to have the luxury of playing by the law."

"So I'll have to break a few laws to set them up?"

"At the very least. Liv, if you want to get Roy off your back, then you're going to have to bring down Infidelity Limited."

"Which means?"

"Which means you're going to have to follow their instructions and learn everything you can about their operation."

"But they want me to kill someone."

Andrew shrugged. "Then you need to play along and stall for time. We have to get the evidence to turn them over to the cops before they can throw you under the bus. I think our first step should be to question Clare more thoroughly."

"'Our' first step? Does that mean you'll help me?"

Andrew's expression remained grim. "Yes. I don't know how much I can help, but I'll do all I can."

"Are you sure? If we fail, you'll be in Roy's crosshairs too."

"I know what I'm signing up for."

The world had turned into a series of dead ends put up by Roy and Finz. For the first time, Olivia saw an exit. She grabbed his hands. "Thank you."

"Don't thank me yet. You don't have a lot going for you."

"Except for Clare."

"Right. She's our way in. We need to know everything she knows about these people. She's been through this already and can warn us of what's coming. The more we know in advance, the better we can protect ourselves. Knowing Clare, she's going to be resistant. That might mean scaring her. Are you okay with that?"

She was. Clare had set her up. Richard would still be alive and she wouldn't be in this mess if it wasn't for Clare. She had no problems putting the fear of God into her sister. "We need to be careful, because Roy told me I couldn't tell anyone about this. If he finds out that you're involved, I have no idea what he'll do."

"Then we'll be careful," Andrew said. "Let's go."

They rode in Olivia's Audi. While she drove, he scanned the road for Roy or anyone else from Infidelity Limited. No one was following them.

"The problem I have right now is my upcoming polygraph," Olivia said.

"When is it?"

"In a few days. They haven't set a date. There's no way I can pass a lie-detector test with what I know."

"All I know is that there's only one foolproof way to pass a lie-detector test."

"And what's that?"

"Tell the truth."

"Then I'm screwed."

"No, you're not. A poly is a crude test. It works off a yes-or-no questioning system, which limits what you can be asked."

"Yes, but when they ask me if I killed Richard, it's game over."

"So you killed Richard?"

"No, someone at Infidelity Limited did, but I—"

Andrew held up his hand. "You're overcomplicating things. Answer the question you're asked. Did you kill Richard?"

"No."

"Do you know who killed Richard? And I mean do you know, by name, the person who killed Richard?"

"No, I don't."

Olivia understood Andrew's point. If she took the questions at face value and didn't read more into them, she could answer any of their questions honestly. She knew that a client from Infidelity Limited had killed Richard, but she didn't know his or her identity. Finz could only ask in generalities. Unless he was onto Infidelity Limited, those generalities would be her safe harbor.

"Did you pay to have your husband killed?" Andrew asked.

"No."

"Now you're getting it. You just have to believe in your answers. Remember, you didn't kill your husband, you don't know the identity of the perpetrator, and you didn't pay for him to be murdered."

It wasn't the perfect defense, but she thought she could pull it off. In her mind, she ran through the polygraph questions she'd likely be asked. She answered them, noting any anxiety. It was there, but if she practiced and desensitized herself to their impact, she might just fool the lie detector. "Okay, I think I can do this."

"There are supposed ways of deceiving polygraphs too. It'll be good for us to know them for extra insurance, so I'll research them," Andrew said.

"Thanks. I'd be lost without your help."

"It's easy to help when the problem isn't your own."

They arrived at Clare's trailer. Her Honda wasn't parked out front.

"She can't be gone," Olivia said in disbelief. "I left her here just before I came to see you."

They tried her door. Clare didn't answer.

"Where is she?" Andrew asked.

"I have no idea."

CHAPTER FIFTEEN

Sixteen. Conventional blackjack strategy dictated that Clare should stand. She didn't care about convention. She hadn't been counting cards, but she had paid attention, and a lot of face cards had been coming out of the dealer's shoe over the last few hands. She liked her chances and tapped the baize for another card.

The dealer dealt a five of hearts next to her nine of diamonds and seven of clubs.

"Twenty-one. Nicely played."

"Thanks, Chuck."

She knew Chuck, like most of the dealers, from her numerous visits to Cache Creek Casino. Chuck had been around for years, and it was a pleasure to watch him deftly send the cards flying across the table.

She was fortunate that there were half a dozen Indian casinos within a couple of hours' drive of the Bay Area. She liked Cache Creek the best and came often. It was only an hour away, and the cards treated her well here. Well, that wasn't quite true. She didn't lose as much here. The three grand she'd been into Gault for was due to a bad night at Thunder Valley.

"You rode your luck there," the guy two seats over from her said with admiration and raised his whiskey glass. He'd just busted with a twenty-three, attempting the same move.

She smiled at her fellow gambler. "You'll get it next time. Luck goes around the table."

Chuck finished doling out the cards. No one else made twenty-one, except for the dealer. Luck had gone the way of the house. She got to keep her chips while the dealer relieved everyone else of theirs. At least she'd broken even on that hand. That was more than she got to do outside of the casino. Her cards in the game of life were never good enough. Out there, she always came up short.

She was doing pretty well tonight. She was only $200 down on the grand that Olivia had given her. She'd been $250 up about five hands ago. She'd get it back. She was in for a good night. She felt it.

Olivia would disagree. She would say Clare was pissing her money away. It wasn't Olivia's money anyway. Not once she'd handed it over to her.

Clare wondered if her sister had seen through the lies about why she owed money when Gault had come collecting. Probably. Clare hated that her life was so transparent.

Screw you, Olivia. She hated how she allowed her sister to make her feel guilty about going to a casino. She was a grown woman, and she could do what she wanted.

It wasn't like Olivia's life was so fantastic. Richard had cheated on her—probably because she was so damn uptight. And now he was dead. Killed by Infidelity Limited. *Whose fault was that, Olivia?*

Guilt stabbed her between the ribs. The blame was partly hers. She'd known what Infidelity Limited was capable of.

Stop, she told herself. She'd come here to put a wall between her and her life. People always complained about the absence of windows and clocks in casinos. That was something she liked. Casinos were special places that existed outside of time and space. She always removed her watch as she entered. She didn't need to know the time. She released a breath to calm herself and focus. Her head needed to be in the game.

She let her fifty-dollar bet ride, and the gambling gods rewarded her with a blackjack. Now that was more like it. All thoughts of Olivia and Infidelity Limited faded into the background.

The shoe signaled it was down to the dregs, and Chuck took the used cards from the discard pile and put them into the auto shuffler.

While he reloaded the shoe, Clare looked around. Cache Creek was pretty busy tonight, shoulder-to-shoulder stuff. All the minimum-bet tables were full. It was the same story at the twenty-five-dollar table she was playing at. No sign of a global recession here. But that was always the way. People might not have a pot to piss in, but they'd use what they had for a chance of winning big.

Chuck dealt out fresh cards. She did well over the next three hands, winning two. Her confidence rose, and she upped her bets to seventy-five a hand.

He dealt her a pair of aces, and she split, putting seventy-five on each. She felt her heart race at the thought of a couple of face cards coming her way. They didn't come. She busted out on one hand and stood on seventeen on the other. Chuck dealt himself a nineteen, cleaning her out.

"That was mean, Chuck."

"It's the cards, Clare. Not me."

Chuck's cards continued to be mean for the next half an hour. She lost two hands for every one she won. Within the next hour, she was down $800 and chasing her luck instead of riding it. It was time to stop, but she just couldn't summon the will to pick up her chips and leave. She could have stemmed her chip bleed by dropping down to the twenty-five-dollar minimum bets, but how could she possibly win back what she'd lost at that rate?

Diana came up behind Chuck and tapped him on the shoulder. Diana was Asian, pretty, and one of the newer dealers.

"My time is done here," Chuck said and showed his hands. "Good luck, everyone."

"Shit," Clare murmured. She hated when dealers switched out. She felt the rapport built between the gambler and dealer. It was comfortable. Warm. The table went cold for her when a new dealer rotated in.

"Good evening, guys," Diana said. "I hope everyone is well."

Diana received a chorus of yeses.

Clare decided to give Diana a chance. Chuck had been dealing her cold cards for the last twenty minutes. Maybe Diana would change that.

She didn't.

Clare left the table with under a hundred in chips.

She wandered the casino floor. She couldn't leave now. She still felt a big win was within her grasp, and she wouldn't be denied. She'd come up big tonight, as long as she could get her hands on some more seed money.

Chuck waved to her as he came the other way with a soda in his hand. "Hey, Clare, why the long face?"

She held up her chips.

"Yeah, I saw your luck change."

"And I need it to change back."

"Have you tried Gault? He's in tonight. He'll front you the money. He knows you're good for it."

Gault made a living loan-sharking at all the Indian casinos. The last thing she needed was to be on the hook to him again after she'd just gotten herself free of him. "Is Mitch or Two Step in tonight?"

Chuck shook his head. "I've only seen Gault. He's over by the dollar slots if you want him. Anyway, I have to get back to it."

She watched Chuck leave, then looked at her chips again. Tonight was her night. She believed it. She cursed under her breath and went in search of Gault.

She found him playing the slots, just as Chuck had said. He grinned as she approached. "Can't get enough of me, eh, Clare? How much do you need?"

She hated that he knew what she was there for. "A grand."

"Things going that bad, eh?"

She felt her temperature rise, but kept it in check. Gault liked to get vindictive when he felt dissed. "Can I get it?"

"Sure, you can. Follow me into my office."

He led her outside into the parking lot. They sandwiched themselves between a couple of cars that belonged to neither of them. He brought out a thick roll of bills and peeled off hundreds with slow, deliberate speed.

"You know my rates, and I know where you live, so I don't want any hassles when it comes to collecting this time. Do I make myself understood, Clare?"

"You assume I'm going to lose."

Gault laughed. "Spoken like a true gambler."

His laughter followed her into the casino.

She didn't return to blackjack, in favor of the three-card poker tables. She liked blackjack, but it was a slow grind of a game. Three-card poker offered her the chance of greater reward, but naturally at a higher risk. She sat down and played.

She played hard and well, but her thousand only lasted her an hour.

Gault came over when she had lost two-thirds of her money. He watched her like a vulture watched a dying man. As soon as she stepped away from the table, he sidled up to her.

"Where now, Clare?"

"Home." The word tasted bitter on her tongue. It was supposed to be a winning night. "I know when it's time to admit defeat."

"You know the clock is ticking on that money?"

"Of course."

She didn't slow her pace and kept heading toward the exit. Gault kept in step. "The thing that worries me is how and when I'll get my money back. You're becoming a bigger and bigger risk."

"You'll get it back, plus interest."

"Oh, I like the determined tone, but"—he gripped her arm, his fingers biting into her flesh—"I need to know if you can get the cash."

"Don't you worry. I know how to get you the money."

CHAPTER SIXTEEN

"Wake up, Olivia," Andrew said. "She's back."

Olivia jerked awake. She grabbed the steering wheel and hauled herself up in her seat. She'd dozed off at some point without realizing it. She checked the Audi's dashboard clock. It was after one in the morning. Olivia hadn't expected Clare to be this late. What the hell was she doing out when she had work tomorrow? Then again, she was talking about Clare. Sensible wasn't in her vocabulary.

Clare stopped her car under the carport and climbed out.

They'd parked a few units over from Clare's to give them anonymity. They didn't want her bolting if she saw Olivia's car parked in front of her place. The second Clare emerged from her car, the two of them moved in.

"Olivia?" Clare said, but she was looking at Andrew.

"Where the hell have you been?" Olivia demanded. She wondered if Clare had run to Roy, but the stink of cigarettes and booze wafting off her sister told her Clare had been drowning her sorrows at some dive.

"Hey, I don't have to answer to you."

"I think we should take this inside," Andrew said.

"Take what inside? And who are you?" The security light on Clare's trailer clicked on to illuminate the three of them. "Andrew?"

"Yeah, it's me."

"I didn't know you two were still in touch after all these years."

Clare unlocked the door and let them in. She dropped onto her sofa and eyed both of them with a sneer. "What's he doing here?"

"I told him what's going on."

Clare snorted and shook her head. "Fan-fucking-tastic, Liv. Bring a stranger into all this."

"He's not a stranger."

"I'm here to help," Andrew said.

"Awesome. A clueless dope to the rescue." Clare jumped up from her seat, brushed by Olivia, and grabbed the vodka bottle from the fridge.

"Don't you think it's a little late for that?" Olivia said.

Clare shot her an ugly look. Olivia held up her hands in surrender. She wasn't going to fight over this issue. She needed Clare's cooperation, and it didn't matter if she had a drink in her hand.

Clare returned to the sofa with the vodka and a single glass. Obviously, she wasn't in the mood for sharing.

Olivia expected this reaction from Clare. She knew the fact that she'd brought Andrew would scare Clare, but also offend her. She would see this act of Olivia putting her faith in someone else as a sign that Olivia didn't trust her. And the truth was, Clare would be right.

Olivia and Andrew followed Clare to the living room and sat on the sofa opposite.

"We want to ask you about Infidelity Limited," Olivia said.

"Why?"

"We need to find a chink in their armor so that we can get to them."

"We're not supposed to talk about them, and definitely not supposed to involve anyone else. Why'd you drag Andrew into this? You don't get it, do you? They are professionals. They don't have chinks in their armor. Your best defense is to do what they say. It's not to talk about them, and it's not to bring in outsiders. What the hell do you think he can do to help?"

"Right now, I need all the friends and help I can get. Roy thrives on his victims suffering in silence and alone. As a group, we stand a chance against him. That includes you. It's why we're here."

Clare sneered at Olivia, poured herself a drink, and sank half of it before saying, "What do you two geniuses want to know?"

"I'm guessing that Infidelity Limited doesn't openly advertise their services," Andrew said. "How did you learn about them?"

"It's a referral system. Someone introduces you, and you introduce someone."

So Infidelity Limited was a verbal pyramid scheme. Pyramid schemes were effective, but they had an inherent weakness. The pyramid always tracked back to a single person. Roy would be at its pinnacle. All they had to do was find the path back to Roy. The only problem was the number of layers between them and Roy. Clare was a client six years ago. How many other people had been suckered in since then? It could be dozens, or it could be hundreds.

"What's the incentive to refer someone? Do they give you money?" Andrew asked.

Clare smacked her glass down on the table, sending her drink splashing over her hand and the table. "Christ, do you think I took money from these people after all they've done?"

"No. Sorry," Andrew said. "I'm just trying to understand how they get you to refer someone when you know they're going to screw them over."

"It's the same incentive they use for everything—fear. They make someone disappear, then they tell you they'll implicate you. They tell you to kill someone, and if you say you won't do it, they tell you they'll implicate you. They tell you to find another sucker, or they'll implicate you. Once you invite these people into your life, they put a gun to your head, and they never take it away."

Olivia was beginning to know all too well the element of fear Infidelity Limited employed. She felt the pressure of their weapon against the back of her head, but unlike Clare, she wanted to turn it on them. It was her only escape.

She felt for her sister. Infidelity Limited had tortured Clare for years. Like all great torturers, the likelihood of them making good on their threats wasn't constant. It didn't need to be. It just had to linger in the shadows, ready to emerge at any time. All the sympathy Olivia had for her sister went only so far. It was hard to reconcile the fact that Clare had put her in harm's way to save herself.

"Who introduced you?" Olivia asked.

"A friend. Or so I thought."

"What's this person's name?" Andrew asked.

"Maxine Groves."

"Are you still in contact?" Olivia asked.

"What do you think? No."

"Can you get in contact with her?"

"Yes, but why?"

"Currently, we have no leverage over Infidelity Limited, so we have to get some," Andrew said. "Everyone knows a bit about Roy. If we talk to enough of his victims, it'll help us build a big enough picture to track him down."

Clare barked a derisive little laugh. "You're crazy. Do you know how many people there are like us? Do you honestly think you can find them all?"

Olivia didn't. Roy had done a great job of insulating himself. There was no way of knowing how many people he had drawn into his web of deception and lies. Trawling through Infidelity Limited's client base seemed like a lost cause before they even started.

"No, but we have to try," Olivia said.

"You're wasting your time."

"Maybe so, but will you help us?" Andrew asked.

"If you pay me."

The demand stunned Olivia. For a second, she thought she'd misheard.

"I have valuable information. It comes at a price."

Disgust poured through Olivia. Clare had nerve, asking her for money after she'd screwed her in typical Clare fashion. Like usual, Clare had dug herself a hole and was trying to solve it by dragging others in after her. Olivia glared at her sister, but Clare didn't flinch under the heat of it. She was serious about her money.

"How much?" Andrew asked.

"Not much. Five hundred."

"Don't waste your breath on her," Olivia said. "Clare, you're responsible for me being in this position. You threw me to these sharks, and now you want me to pay you for your help? What the hell?"

"You said you'd try to help me, Liv. This is the help I need."

Olivia shook her head. Her sister was unbelievable. She had the blinkers on, and all that she could see was whatever she needed to fix her own problems and screw everyone else.

"Money won't help you," Olivia said. "You need to take some responsibility. I'll help you make that happen. Do the right thing for once. Do right by me for once. Because if you lose me, there's no one else who'll drag your sorry ass out of the fire next time you screw up."

Clare just continued to glare at Olivia.

"C'mon, we're done," Olivia told Andrew.

They'd gotten as far as the door when Clare stopped them. "I'll go to Detective Finz," she said. "I'll tell him everything."

How could Clare threaten her with that? Her older sister had raised a lot of feelings in Olivia during their lifetime. Few were positive. Anger, disappointment, and frustration were the go-to trio. She'd never felt contempt for her own flesh and blood like she did at that moment. It was all she could do not to beat the life from Clare.

The threat kept Olivia in place. If she knew one thing about Clare, it was her sister's weak resolve. Yes, Clare was weak enough to run to the cops. But she was just as weak when it came to the follow-through. It was easy for her to toss out threats but hard for her to follow up on them. Clare knew the consequences for herself if she went to Finz. The threat was hollow—or so Olivia hoped.

"Okay, let's all calm down," Andrew said. "I know everyone is frightened, but if we keep our heads, we'll be fine."

"You need money that badly, Clare?" Olivia said.

Clare raised her glass in a mocking toast. "Always."

"Look, I've got a hundred," Andrew said, reaching for his wallet.

Olivia clamped a hand over his forearm. "We're not paying her. She won't go to the police because she's an accessory."

"You willing to take that risk, Sister?"

"Clare, you owe me. You know it. I know it. You got me into this, and you can get me out of this. Call the person who referred you, and set up a meeting."

Olivia walked out of Clare's trailer, hoping she'd read her sister right and that Clare would do right by her.

CHAPTER SEVENTEEN

The million-dollar view of the bay couldn't make up for the stink coming off the marsh. It turned what could have been a luxury-home development into low-income housing with a fancy name that didn't fool anyone. This part of unincorporated Contra Costa County wasn't helped by its neighbors—a juvenile offenders' detention center on one side and a metal-finishing outfit on the other.

Andrew was working today, so Olivia had come out here alone. After grilling Clare last night, they'd agreed that if Olivia was going to go after Infidelity Limited, she needed to know what she was dealing with, and that meant knowing how much of what Clare had said was true and how much was bullshit.

It had been a while since Olivia had driven out this way. There'd been no reason, since Nick had disappeared. Nick came from a large family, but they were scattered across the country. His sister, Mandy, remained close to home.

If anyone knew where Nick was, it was Mandy. Olivia hoped Mandy would put her in touch with him, because she had to find out whether Clare had lied to her about him. She prayed to God that Infidelity Limited hadn't killed him.

Olivia pulled up in front of a cheaply constructed, unimaginative, wood frame house. The same design continued for the length of the street. Bars covered windows, and a security door strong enough to stop a charging bull protected the front door. A waist-high chain-link fence surrounded the weed-ravaged front yard. Kids' toys strewn across the path welcomed her as she walked up to the front door.

Before Olivia reached it, Mandy pushed open the screen. She sneered and said, "Olivia, long time no see."

Mandy was Nick's younger sister. She was close to ten years younger than Olivia, but she looked older. She'd been a good-looking woman, but her beauty was ruined by too much drinking, a crappy diet, and a bad dose of life. Olivia guessed this would have been her own outcome if she hadn't fought to escape her upbringing, then felt bad for thinking that way. Money and a career didn't make her better than Mandy, and her recent moral judgments sure as hell didn't make her an angel.

"What do you want?" Mandy demanded.

"Nick. Have you seen him? I need to get in touch with him."

"Why? Does Clare want him back?"

Mandy was doing nothing to hide her hostility. Olivia expected this treatment. Mandy idolized her older brother for reasons Olivia never understood.

"No," Olivia replied.

"If Clare wants something, then she should come ask for it herself instead of sending her fancy sister with the low-rent past. Does she think that your Audi will impress me? It doesn't. It's pathetic."

"It's nothing like that."

Mandy had yet to invite Olivia in, and her doorstep tantrum was drawing street flies as neighbors stopped to watch the social drama play out.

"Can I come in?"

"No, I don't want your family stinking up my home, no matter how much Dior you slather on."

"Mandy, please."

"This is about money, isn't it? Clare needs money again."

"No. What are you talking about?"

Mandy screwed up her face in disgust. "C'mon, drop the innocent act. Everybody knows your sister can't stay away from the blackjack tables. If she's not pissing money away at Cache Creek, it's Thunder Valley. That's if any of them will have her these days, with her credit score. No one minds the interest as long as someone can pay."

A smug smile showed off all Mandy's premature age lines.

So Clare's gambling was common knowledge. Olivia wondered how many people her sister had been hitting up for money in addition to her and how much of a debt she'd run up.

"Where's Nick, Mandy?" Olivia asked before she got sidetracked. "I just need to get in touch with him."

"Give me one good reason why I should tell you."

Olivia hadn't wanted to tell Mandy about Richard, but it was the only way to end the stalemate. "My husband was killed. Clare wanted him to come to the funeral."

The sucker punch delivered the knockout blow Olivia hoped for, wiping the stubborn grin from Mandy's face. Olivia relied on the shock to prevent Mandy from examining the situation too closely. Why, after six years, would Clare want Nick around for support?

"When?" Mandy asked.

"Last week. Look, do you have a number for Nick?"

"Was your husband the guy clubbed to death?"

"Yes."

"I'm sorry. That's horrible," Mandy said with little compassion, "but I don't have a number."

"Then how do you get in contact with him?"

"I don't. I haven't heard from my brother since he took off."

"What about his friends? Don't they keep in touch?"

"Your dead husband was his closest friend."

"Richard?"

"No, Mark." Mandy suddenly smirked. "Two dead husbands. You're a real black widow, Olivia."

And if Nick was dead, Olivia and Clare had three dead husbands between them. She asked Mandy to get in touch if she heard from him and drove off.

Nick was dead. Olivia knew it. Clare could delude herself and deny it. It was easy when you didn't have a body left on the sidewalk. Olivia glanced in her rearview mirror and caught Mandy staring at her. She'd been clinging to the hope that Nick was alive and staying away because he despised Clare. That hope was on life support now. She could see Nick disappearing, but he would have kept in touch with Mandy.

What have you done, Sis? Olivia thought.

Her cell rang in the car. It was Finz.

"Hi, Mrs. Shaw, I wanted to set up a time for that polygraph appointment."

She winced.

"How are you fixed for the day after tomorrow, Thursday, say one o'clock?"

"I am in the middle of funeral arrangements."

"I totally understand, and I apologize for that, but I promise it won't take long. An hour tops."

She couldn't see how she could avoid his request without making him suspicious. "Thursday at one, then."

"Thank you, Mrs. Shaw. See you then."

She groaned when she hung up. She'd hoped to have more time to practice.

"Did you kill your husband?" she asked herself. "No, I did not."

She joined the road and headed toward the freeway. A blue Explorer pulled onto the parkway a couple of hundred yards behind her. The sight of it unsettled her. It wasn't like Explorers were rare, but she could have sworn she'd seen the same SUV on the drive over. Was she being followed? If so, by whom? Roy? She was a liability to him if the police arrested her. If he was checking out everybody she was talking to, he'd find out that she was digging into Nick's disappearance. Shit. She was screwed if he found out what she was doing. Of course, Roy wasn't the only one with a reason to keep a close eye on her. This could be Finz. She didn't believe for one second that he wanted her to submit to a polygraph for routine purposes. She had a horrible feeling that he suspected she was involved in Richard's death.

The light ahead turned red. This caused a problem for the Explorer driver. With no cars between them, it forced him to stop behind her. She looked at him in her rearview mirror. The driver was neither Roy nor Finz, but that didn't mean anything. They'd both have people working for them.

Looking ahead, she caught a glimpse of herself in her mirror. "Are you losing it, girl?" she asked her reflection. "Only one way to find out."

The light turned green, and she and her Explorer shadow pulled forward. Instead of going through the next light, she turned left. The Explorer turned left too.

It was another strike against the man in the SUV, but not conclusive. They were on the through road to Pinole. He could be on his way there.

She turned right onto a residential street, and the Explorer did the same.

Either she was predicting this guy's drive home or he was following her. Her palms turned slick on the wheel, and she gripped it harder.

She slowed to a crawl, and the Explorer matched her speed, although he maintained his distance.

"Yeah, you're definitely following me, you son of a bitch."

She knew this neighborhood well, but she doubted he did. She took another left, knowing full well it was a cul-de-sac, and he turned in after her. His mistake made, he stopped the SUV at the mouth of the dead-end street.

Olivia jumped from her car and rushed him. His eyes widened in surprise.

She thumped a fist on the SUV's hood. "Who are you? What do you want?"

The man held his hands up. "Sorry. You've got it all wrong."

"Who sent you? Roy? Finz? Tell me."

He pointed at the back of her car.

Olivia didn't turn. She wouldn't let him distract her.

"Your plate. It's hanging off."

She glanced at the back of the Audi in disbelief. Her license plate was hanging at an angle, missing a mounting screw.

"I saw it hanging off, and I was just trying to let you know. The cops will ticket you for that."

Embarrassment flooded through her. "I'm sorry, but you should know better than to follow a woman like that. You could have honked or something."

"If I'd honked or flashed my lights, it would have been just as scary. I thought I would catch up to you at a stop sign or something and let you know."

She nodded. "Again, I'm sorry."

"You know what? Keep your apology, lady. This is why people don't help each other, because they always assume the worst." He jammed the Explorer into reverse and roared back onto the main street.

Olivia mumbled a curse under her breath. She was seeing monsters where there weren't any to find. Infidelity Limited was turning her into a basket case.

CHAPTER EIGHTEEN

Roy's basement served as Infidelity Limited's operations, which Beth had named the Vault. At over fifteen hundred square feet and fully finished, it served as home to everyone's dirty secrets, with the evidence to back it up. Roy lost himself down here for days at a time, updating his files and managing the physical evidence. He felt like a gardener tending to his land. An off-site location might be a safer bet, but Roy liked the facility he'd built under his home. It was secure and private.

Today was a housekeeping day. Roy had Olivia's file open on the computer as he wrote up Proctor's account of Richard Shaw's murder. If Proctor ever tried to throw him under the bus, the tire iron with Richard Shaw's blood and flesh welded to one end would make its way to the Concord police. The tire iron served a double purpose. When the time came to burn Olivia, it would be gifted to the cops with a supporting story that incriminated her. He closed the file.

"And that's you done, Mr. Proctor. For the moment."

He picked up the tire iron and carried it over to the bank of refrigerators that lined one wall. He rebagged it, transferring it from the Hefty bag Proctor had used to the wax-lined paper bag that helped preserve the blood evidence. The bag was tagged with its case-file number.

He just needed somewhere cool to keep the evidence safe. The blood evidence and DNA didn't have to be perfectly preserved. In fact, they needed to degrade. Five years from now, it wouldn't make sense for the cops to find the murder weapon with blood on it as fresh as the day of the murder.

Not everything went in the fridges. Nonbiological evidence, such as firearms, clothes, videotapes, and audio recordings, went in one of the storage cabinets lining the wall across from the fridges.

He placed the tire iron on its shelf inside refrigerator number sixteen. It was almost full. He couldn't believe he and Beth had filled sixteen units with the nooses to hang their clients for giving in to their baser emotions. That was the problem with people—as a breed, they were weak.

His cell rang. It was Carrington.

"What is it, Lou?"

"Olivia Shaw saw me. My cover is blown."

It wasn't like Carrington to screw up. "How?"

"She noticed me tailing her and led me into a cul-de-sac. It was a total sucker punch."

"Shit. Did she work out that you were connected to me?"

"No. I had tampered with her license plate and used that as the excuse for why I was following her. I made her think I was a misunderstood Good Samaritan. Do you want me to stay on her?"

"No. I'll make other arrangements. I'll be in touch with other work."

"Sorry, Roy."

Roy hung up. Olivia was quite a woman, and she would have to be squeezed as her punishment.

He crossed to the center of the room, which was filled with eight magnetic whiteboards on casters. Each board detailed an ongoing Infidelity Limited assignment. He went up to the board for Heather Moore-Marbach. She owned Moore Fitness, a chain of high-profile gyms up and down the West Coast. The whiteboard told her story. It had her picture and a head shot of her wife, Amy. It detailed both parties' lives and the problem. The most important detail was written at the top of the board in big, bold red letters—"Heather's net worth: $4 million." He couldn't wait to land this fish.

But who should he use to do the deed? He had about eight people who hadn't yet paid back their debt to Infidelity Limited, all of whom were dreading his call. Olivia was at the top of his list. She shouldn't have been yet, but with Richard's death having gone sideways, he needed to use her fast, before the cops got to her. He wrote Olivia's name on the board.

The intercom on his desk buzzed, and he answered. "Yes?"

"We've got a problem," Luis said.

"Shit. Be right there."

Roy opened the door to find Luis holding a sheer curtain in his hands. Roy took it. It was dry, but it reeked of the sharp stink of gasoline. He traced the smell to its source—the bottom hem. This was Beth's little trick. Soak the bottom edge of a curtain in gas or lighter fluid, then let it dry. Even though much of the gas would evaporate, it would still burn like a wildfire when she decided she wanted to watch something burn. They'd lost half the living room to this stunt last year.

"Where'd you find this?"

"In Beth's office."

"Does she know you've found it?"

"No. She hasn't come out of her bedroom this morning. I think she's having one of her dark days."

The last thing he needed now was one of Beth's phases. He handed the curtain back to Luis. "Okay, wash that, then go over this place from top to bottom and see if she's booby-trapped anything else."

"You got it."

Roy clambered up the stairs and marched down the marble hallway. There was no carpet in the house anymore. They'd all learned that lesson the hard way.

Beth's bedroom was at the end of the corridor, and his room was off to the right. Forever kept at arm's length. She hadn't let him in after twenty years of being together. He thought of them as husband and wife, but Beth didn't. He'd asked her to marry him many times over the years, but she'd always said no. Her previous marriage had scarred her figuratively and literally. He understood and had finally accepted that he'd never get the chance to put a ring on her finger. He twisted the doorknob to her room, but it was locked.

"Beth, it's me. Can I come in?" He kept his tone calm, without a hint of judgment.

No answer.

"Beth, you can lock the door, but you can't keep me out. I can kick this door in. I know it, and you know it, but I don't want to do that. I just want you to let me in. Can you do that for me?"

He heard Beth move inside the room, and he pressed his ear to the gap between the door and the jamb to get a fix on where she was in the room. "Please come to the door," he murmured to himself.

He heard shuffling. "What's wrong, Beth? Just tell me. I know you're not happy, and I don't get it. We've got clients. You and I are good. Aren't we? Have I done something to make you unhappy?"

The movement stopped.

"I know about the curtain in your office. Luis is washing it. Have you done anything else? You know I'll find it."

"Why can't you let me be happy?" Her voice sounded like it was coming from deep inside the room.

"That's not fair, Beth. Everything I've done has been for you. I've protected you. I've looked after you." *I've killed for you,* he thought.

"You've locked me up here. I never go anywhere. You smother me."

She was deflecting. He'd heard this speech a thousand times before. It was all a disguise for the real problem. "You want to go somewhere? We'll go. We'll jump in the car and go anywhere you want. We haven't gone out in years. We should do something. We deserve it."

"Where would we go?"

"Anywhere you want. Just open the door, and we'll talk."

There was more movement from inside the room, but it wasn't the sound of Beth approaching the door.

"Come on, Beth. I don't like this. There's no reason to shut me out. I love you, and I want to help."

Then he smelled it. He looked down at his feet. Smoke the color of storm clouds sneaked out from under the door and across his shoes.

Christ, I should have known. She'd been stalling him. "Luis, fire," he bellowed. "Get up here."

He bolted for his room and grabbed the fire extinguisher from his closet. Sadly, it was one of many extinguishers stashed in the house for this unfortunate situation.

"Beth, I'm coming in."

He smashed the butt of the extinguisher down on the doorknob. The knob buckled under the force and sheared off under a second blow. He kicked the door in to find the full-length drapes ablaze. The flames were scorching the ceiling, smoke spreading across it before molten swatches of it fell to the floor. The rapidly disintegrating drapes ejected slivers of burning material into the air. Some had landed on the nightstand and set it alight. More had landed on the bed and set off patches of small fires.

And where was Beth in all this carnage? Sitting expressionless in the corner of the room, watching the destruction.

Roy loved her so much, but she drove him to the edge. Why the fires? Why the destruction? There was no point in asking her anymore. Beth didn't know the answers, and even if she did, she'd never say. All he could do was love her.

He broke the safety seal and doused the drapes with the suppressant. The foam blew holes in the damaged fabric, and palm-sized rags tumbled to the floor. He let those burn themselves out while he put out the main blaze.

Luis burst into the room and smothered the bed with his extinguisher. As soon as those flames were out, he helped Roy clear the curtains and the ceiling.

"You got this?" Roy asked Luis.

"Yeah, man."

Roy placed the nearly empty extinguisher next to Luis and gathered Beth up. He rushed her into his bedroom and placed her on his bed.

"What the hell, Beth?" Despair was all the emotion he could muster. "Why? I just want to know."

"I just want to be beautiful."

He looked at her amazing green eyes through the old scarring that marred half of her face. "You are."

"Don't lie."

She might not be able to look beyond the scars, but he could. He'd fallen in love with her the day he'd met her. Nothing could change that. "I'm not."

"It doesn't matter. I'm not beautiful. Not to me. Not to anyone."

He pressed his forehead to hers. "You just have to believe it. I'll do anything to help you believe."

"Do you mean that?"

He pulled back. "Yes. You name it, and I'll do it."

"I want to see *him*."

CHAPTER NINETEEN

Andrew stopped his truck in front of the Concord Police Department. This was it—polygraph day. If Olivia failed the test, she doubted she'd ever leave the building. She took a deep breath and let it go.

"Ready for this?"

Can anyone be ready for a polygraph? Olivia wondered. "As ready as I'll ever be."

"Good. Did you do as I told you?"

"Yes. No coffee, no Coke, no caffeine."

"How's the tack in your shoe?"

"Painful." It had been digging into her big toe during the drive.

"Remember, you need to press down on it every time you answer a baseline or truthful question."

She nodded.

"Did you take the Valium?"

"Yes. About twenty minutes ago."

These were polygraph-busting techniques Andrew had found from his online research. She wasn't sure how effective eliminating stimulants and depressing any anxiety was, but even if these measures provided a placebo effect, she'd take it.

"Then you're good to go." He smiled. "Don't worry. You'll do fine."

She wasn't so sure. Despite the Valium, her heart was racing.

"I'll find somewhere to park, and I'll be waiting for you when you get out."

She'd made the right decision, confiding in him. He gave her the confidence that she'd survive this. She climbed out of the truck.

"One last thing," he said. "Did you kill your husband?"

All week, Andrew had been asking her whether she had killed Richard or knew who killed him every day and at all times of the day. He even went to the extent of calling her up just to ask her. It had worked. It desensitized her to the questions, and more importantly, it reminded her of the truth—she hadn't killed Richard, and she hadn't wanted it to happen. She was guilty, but not of murder.

"No, I did not."

He smiled. "Perfect."

Olivia checked in with the desk officer. A minute later, a secure door opened, and Finz appeared.

"Thanks for coming, Mrs. Shaw. We're all ready for you."

Olivia bottled her nervousness. She concentrated on everything she needed to do to pass the test. She reminded herself that this was a test like any other. It was hers to pass or fail. The machine possessed no mystic powers. It was simply a recording device. As long as her reactions remained like a calm sea, all was plain sailing.

Finz showed her into a cramped interview room with just enough room inside to sit around a single table. A bald-headed man sat at the far end of the table. He stood and shook hands with Olivia.

"I'm Sergeant Isaac Rivera, Mrs. Shaw," he said, smiling. "I'll be conducting today's polygraph."

That seemed a tough proposition, seeing as the polygraph machine was absent from the room. It surprised Olivia that they didn't have it on show. If Finz and company really wanted to unnerve her, what better way was there than to have it sitting across from her as a sign of impending doom? Its absence helped relax her even more. But that could also be the Valium working on her.

Rivera pulled out a chair for her, and she sat.

"I'll leave you two to it," Finz said.

"Aren't you staying?" Olivia asked.

"No, I've got a few things to follow up on. I'll check in on you when Isaac is all finished up."

Olivia didn't believe that line for a second. A video camera peered down at her from a corner in the ceiling. She assumed Finz would be watching the video feed.

Finz left, and Rivera closed the door before taking his seat at the far end of the table and opening up a folder. He glanced over it for a second before looking up.

"Okay, Mrs. Shaw. This is a pretest interview. I need to go through a few things and ask a few questions before we get down to the nitty-gritty. It helps get us an accurate result. Okay?"

Rivera's pretest took half an hour. He explained how a polygraph worked and how the test would proceed. He followed this by asking for her address, social security number, and date of birth. He also asked when she got married, Richard's full name, and about a dozen other pointless questions that the police already knew the answers to. She didn't balk at them. These were the control questions. Finally, he ran through a number of questions having to do with the murder investigation. As much as Rivera was pretending not to take any notice of her when he asked these questions, Olivia felt him following her every reaction. Just as the questioning got tedious, he closed the file.

"Okay, that concludes the interview. Let's do the test. Are you nervous?"

"A little. I get nervous taking my eye exam. I don't want to make a mistake."

"You can't make a mistake. All you have to do is tell the truth. That is what this interview was all about. Informing you how everything works removes the anxiety aspect that can skew the results. Make sense?"

Truth was no longer a simple yes/no proposition since Infidelity Limited had entered her life. "Yes. That helps. Thanks."

Rivera led her out of the interview room and into the one next door. The desk had been removed and the polygraph equipment put in its place. Instead of the usual machine pictured in countless movies, with pens and a never-ending roll of paper spilling from it, a laptop sat in its place. A cable from the laptop ran into something that looked like a computer router, and sensors that would be strapped to her dangled from a black box.

"Take a seat, Mrs. Shaw."

She sat down, and Rivera slipped a blood pressure cuff over her arm and attached all the other sensors to her.

"Comfortable?"

"As much as you'd expect."

Rivera sat behind Olivia, with the laptop turned away from her. She had nothing to look at except the wall in front of her, which meant she had nothing to focus on other than her guilt or innocence.

She noticed she'd been placed facing yet another ceiling video camera.

"If you're ready, Mrs. Shaw, then I'll begin."

"I'm ready."

"Remember to answer the questions honestly, with yes or no answers. Don't let any of this equipment put you off. Okay?"

"Okay."

Olivia zoned in on what she had to do to pass the test. She kept her breathing shallow and steady, but increased it for the baseline questions in order to hopefully match the stress she'd feel when answering the harder questions.

"Is your name Olivia Grace Shaw?"

Olivia pressed her big toe down onto the tack in her shoe. She hid the brief spike of pain before answering. "Yes."

"Is your birthday on June twelfth?"

"Yes," she said, pricking herself again with the tack. Having to do this with every answer was getting old already.

"Is your social security number 521-13-0931?"

"Yes."

"Do you have blue eyes?"

"No."

She couldn't tell how she was doing. There was no printout with pens flailing widely when she answered a question. The laptop was silent. Secretive. Just like her.

"Was your husband's name Richard Shaw?"

She felt the tide of the questioning turning. "Yes."

"Do you know who killed your husband?"

She slowed her breathing and let the Valium floating through her system dull her responses. She reminded herself to believe in her answers. She was not responsible. "No." *Infidelity Limited never told me who did it.*

"Did your husband have any enemies?"

"No."

"Were you with your sister when your husband was killed?"

"Yes."

"Had your husband gotten into a fight with anyone recently?"

"No."

"Had your husband received any threats?"

"Not that I know of."

"Yes or no, please."

She sighed. "No."

Rivera increased the pace of the questions. She struggled to keep a rhythm as she'd practiced with Andrew. She couldn't slow the questioning down by pausing, or it would look awkward. She felt her control over her breathing wane. She fought to keep it steady and hoped the Valium would keep her under the radar. She certainly felt its effects. She didn't exactly feel calm, just sluggish and slightly sedated. She'd never been much good with narcotics. She'd once been given Vicodin for post-op pain management. It left her dazed and barely able to function.

"Was your husband having an affair?"

It was a surprise question, no doubt put in there by Finz. It was a dumb move. It showed his hand more than it did hers.

"No."

"Are you an Oakland Raiders fan?"

The baseline question took her by surprise, which was surely its aim. She stepped on the tack. "No."

"Did you kill your husband?"

Slow, calm breaths, she told herself. "No." *A stranger did.*

"Did you wish your husband was dead?"

An image of Richard on their wedding day flashed into her mind. She missed his smile. "No."

"Were you involved in your husband's death?"

"No." *Roy was behind it.*

"Do you know who killed your husband?" he asked again.

"No." She felt panic clawing up inside her, trying to take over. It had seemed easy to follow the simple rules to beat the polygraph, but now that she was knee-deep in it, it seemed like an impossible task. She got a grip, remembered her breathing, and controlled it.

"Did you kill your husband?"

"No."

"Is your name Olivia Grace Shaw?"

"Yes."

"Is your birthday on June twelfth?"

"Yes."

Rivera was back on the control questions. They had to be at the end of the questioning. She felt her stress bleed out of her.

"Do you have a pet dog?"

"No."

"Okay, Mrs. Shaw. That concludes the test. You did very well."

Did well at what—passing the test or incriminating myself? she wondered.

Rivera came over and unplugged her from all the sensors. "I just need a few minutes to collate my results," he said as he exited.

A moment later, Finz let himself into the room. "How'd it go?"

"Okay, but it was a little spooky."

He smiled. "I know the feeling. Every cop submits to one before they get the job. I just have a couple of questions while Isaac finishes up. Is that okay?"

The hairs on her neck stood up. These guys were playing with her. She was sure of it. "No problem."

Finz sat down and opened up the file he'd brought with him. "I've been through your husband's financials, and I didn't see anything unusual there, but I saw a couple of things in yours that confused me. There's a check for three thousand dollars cashed by a Miles Gault two weeks ago, a thousand-dollar check to your sister, and a two-thousand-dollar cash withdrawal made a few days later. Can you explain those?"

She'd forgotten the check she'd written to the loan shark. It was unrelated, but it looked bad. What made matters worse was she couldn't imagine Gault being too forthcoming about his reason for taking the money.

"Sorry, this is a little embarrassing to admit," she said. "They're all related to my sister. I support her financially when things get tough. I gave her the two thousand in cash, and the checks covered some personal debts she owed."

Finz nodded his understanding. "We can choose our friends, but not our family, right?"

"No, we can't. Can I ask how things are going?"

"We're still piecing together your husband's last movements. It looks as if he received a call that lured him out to the spot where he was killed. Oddly, the reason he went out there was you."

Finz's gotcha remark caught her across the jaw. She opened and closed her mouth dumbly, searching for an answer. "What do you mean?"

"A witness was with your husband at the time of the call. He told this person the call was from you."

There was only one person who would have been with him—his tramp, Cassie Hill. "Who?"

"I'm not at liberty to say. Did you call your husband the night he was killed?"

"No."

"I didn't think so. I believe you were used as the lure."

It was a shitty trick, but it sounded like an Infidelity Limited tactic. "That's horrible."

"It is. Quite insidious. Unfortunately, the phone number tracks back to a burner, which doesn't help us. However, it does change things. At first glance, your husband's murder looked like a senseless killing. The fact he was lured to his death changes my theory. Your husband's death was planned. What I don't have is a reason—yet. So if there's anything you can think of that would explain why someone would want Richard dead, it would be useful. I'm convinced there's something in his background that got him killed. Any ideas?"

Olivia shook her head. She was frightened that if she spoke, her voice would crack and give her away.

"No matter. I'm actually buoyed by this. These details are helping me piece together the kind of killer I'm dealing with."

This development didn't buoy her. His step forward was a step back for her.

There was a knock, and Rivera appeared in the doorway. He smiled at Olivia before turning his attention to Finz. "Got a minute, Mike?"

Finz excused himself, leaving Olivia alone. She didn't like that they were discussing her polygraph without her, but she needed Finz out of the room so she could calm down. Seeing him find direction in his investigation was frightening. She thought she'd have more time to pull apart Infidelity Limited's threads. She had to make things happen faster now.

The door reopened, and Finz filled the doorway, with Rivera behind.

"How did I do?"

"Okay, I've reviewed the feed from the test," Rivera said, "and the result is NDI—no deception indicated."

"Great. So what happens now?" Olivia asked.

"I continue with the investigation," Finz said. "Thank you, Mrs. Shaw. I'll see you out."

Andrew was waiting for Olivia in reception. He jumped up from his seat as soon as she appeared. Finz looked a little confused to find Andrew waiting for her.

"All done?" Andrew asked.

"Yes, we are," Finz said. He put his hand out to Andrew. "And you are?"

Andrew shook Finz's hand, then Rivera's. "Andrew Macready. I'm a friend of Olivia's."

"Andrew's an old friend from high school," Olivia said.

"That's great, Mrs. Shaw," Finz said. "Thanks for coming in. This has been very helpful. I'll be in touch."

Olivia felt the heat of Finz's stare on her back as she and Andrew left the building. She hadn't made any mistakes during the test, but she still felt Finz's distrust. She'd hoped the polygraph would give her some breathing space to unmask Infidelity Limited, but it didn't seem to have worked. She couldn't tell if it was part of the standard operating procedure to always suspect the spouse until an arrest had been made or whether he was homing in on her. The affair question had scared her.

He knew something he wasn't telling. Either way, it didn't look as if the polygraph had exonerated her.

"How'd it go?" Andrew asked when they got to the street.

"I passed. Let's get out of here."

$$* \qquad * \qquad *$$

Finz and Rivera watched Olivia leave with Andrew.

"Why did you want me to tell her she had passed the poly?" Rivera asked. "It was inconclusive at best."

"I don't want Mrs. Shaw on the defensive. If she thinks she's in the clear, then she's likely to be less cautious about her activities. One of the checks Olivia had written was to Miles Gault. His primary business is loan-sharking, but he's not averse to other forms of revenue."

Madeleine Lyon emerged from a doorway and stopped next to Finz. She followed his gaze. "Who's that with Mrs. Shaw?"

"A *friend*," Finz said.

"Wow, that was fast. I didn't think she was the type."

Neither did Finz. The big question was, had Olivia found a new man to replace her dead husband, or had this guy been waiting in the wings all along? Maybe Richard Shaw wasn't the only one being unfaithful.

"This one is going weird on us," Rivera said.

"We want weird. I've got more weird for you," Lyon said. "The background check just threw up the fun fact that Olivia Shaw was previously married, and her first husband, Mark Renko, also died."

"Suspicious death?" Finz asked.

"No, DUI. Wrapped his car around a tree, but it makes you wonder now. We could have a black widow on our hands."

Finz didn't believe this potential black widow did her own killing. The coroner had determined that the force of the blows rained down on

Richard Shaw were beyond that of a small woman's capability. However, Andrew Macready appeared to be a powerful man.

Finz returned to his desk, and Lyon parked herself on the corner of it while he ran Andrew Macready through the system. The guy didn't have a criminal history or any outstanding warrants. Even his DMV record came back clean. Finz logged into CLEAR, a public information database that gave him everything from property records to wage garnishments. It would take him hours to digest it all. At first glance, the report didn't bring up anything hinky, but it did provide one interesting tidbit. He tapped the screen for Lyon to see.

"So Olivia's man friend is ex-army," she said. "He would know how to handle himself in a fight."

"The insurance investigator contacted you, didn't he?"

"Yep."

"Tell him to stall on the insurance payout. Houston, we have a problem."

CHAPTER TWENTY

Clare lit up a cigarette the moment she was outside the Target store. It had been a crappy shift. Normally, the day shift wasn't too bad. The evening and weekend shifts were the worst, guaranteed to have the highest density of assholes per hour, but someone somewhere decided it was pain-in-the-ass-customer day. She sucked in all the toxins the cigarette could provide and blew out a cloud of cleansing smoke, sending with it all the day's stress.

Maybe the customers weren't all to blame. She'd carried a lot of baggage into work today. Gault had called her three times, demanding his money. That was a good indicator of the lack of faith he had in her ability to pay him back. Olivia was the bigger issue. Threatening to turn her in had been a mistake. She knew it as soon as she'd said it, but she'd been angry about losing at the tables, for getting in hock to Gault just as she'd gotten free of his clutches, and at Olivia for cornering her with Andrew. Andrew? What the hell was she involving him for?

Clare knew why. Her sister had lost faith in her. Clare couldn't fault her. Even now, she wasn't sure if she would go to the cops. Who knew where this shit with Infidelity Limited would end up? There were no guarantees.

She'd decided to make it up to Olivia by tracking down Maxine Groves for her. It hadn't been easy. The number she had for her was dead. It took a bunch of calls among the gambling fraternity to track her down, although no one had seen her at the tables in years. All she'd gotten was a cell phone number. She'd called it during her break and left a message asking to meet up with Maxine.

Trudging across the parking lot to her car, she scanned her phone for a reply. Another voice mail from Gault. There was no voice mail from Maxine, but there was a single-word text: No.

"Shit."

She dialed the number. The call went to voice mail. She redialed. Again, the call went to voice mail.

"Maxine, we need to talk. If you don't call me, I'm just going to turn up on your doorstep. And I will. I know where you live," she said and hung up.

She didn't know where Maxine lived, but she hoped the threat would carry weight. And it did. By the time she'd reached her car, Maxine was calling.

She slid behind the wheel and answered the call.

"Why are you calling me?" Maxine growled down the phone line.

Clare took a quick drag on her cigarette and cracked the window to let the smoke out. "There's no need to be scared. Nothing's wrong. It's important though."

"Important to you, but not to me. We're done with each other."

Clare saw this call was going nowhere fast. There was no incentive for Maxine to cooperate. It was time for some emotional blackmail. "Look, Maxine, I have the right to say that—not you. I came to you, looking for help, and you screwed me. You put me in a bigger predicament than I was in in the first place. So if you need me to dress it up in some fancy language, I will—you fucking owe me."

Silence came from Maxine's end of the phone line, but no dial tone.

"My sister just wants to talk to you."

"Your sister?"

This was where Clare lost the moral high ground. "My sister is involved with—"

"Don't say their name."

"She's involved, and she's looking for a way out."

Maxine barked a derisive laugh. "Good luck with that."

"Yeah, right. Well, she needs someone to tell her the facts of life."

"How the hell did you let your sister get mixed up with them after what you went through?"

Clare heard Maxine bite off her next sentence. A long pause followed. She was putting two and two together. Clare took a quick drag on her cigarette for courage before the recriminations hit.

"You sold your sister out to them, didn't you?"

"The same way you did to me."

"Ha. At least I didn't do it to my own family. Jesus Christ, Clare."

She didn't need to feel any more like a shit than she already did. "Will you talk to her?"

Maxine sighed. "Yes. Saturday work for you?"

"Yes."

"My place. You know where?"

"No."

"You bitch. I knew you were bluffing."

Clare thought she heard admiration in Maxine's voice and smiled.

"I'll text you when and where on Saturday. Don't make me regret this, Clare."

"I won't," Clare said, but Maxine had already hung up.

She finished up her cigarette and tossed the butt out the window. Driving home, she felt good about herself for once. She was doing something for Olivia. Hopefully, it would repair some of the damage she'd done with her weak-ass attempt to extort money out of her sister.

When she reached the freeway, she called Olivia.

"Yes." Her sister's greeting couldn't be any more clipped.

"I spoke to Maxine Groves. She'll meet us on Saturday."

"Good. Thanks."

"Look, I'm sorry about the other night. I was a little desperate."

Olivia said nothing.

"It's just that money's a problem. I need it, and I don't have it. It gets to you, y'know?"

"Are you asking me for more money?"

She was. She always was. "I just need a couple grand."

"You pissed it away at the casino again, didn't you? Clare, you're a piece of work. I'll see you Saturday," Olivia said and hung up.

Clare guessed she deserved that. She'd give it a couple of days and try again. Olivia would come around. She always did.

She arrived home to find the door to her mobile home swinging open. She stopped the Honda under the carport and jumped out.

"No, no, no," she murmured as she ran up to the door.

The place had been ransacked. Cupboards opened. Sofa and chairs overturned. The bed flipped over. The closet door in the bedroom was off its track. Nothing seemed to have been taken, other than her TV in the living room. She surveyed the latest shit sandwich to be served up to her.

"What a mess, Clare."

The voice came from the doorway. She spun around to find Roy standing in the middle of it. One way in. No way out. The sight of him after all these years sent a ripple of fear through her. She took a reflexive step backward, struck the overturned lounger, and fell over.

He rushed over to her and swiftly pulled her to her feet. "Careful there." He went about flipping the sofa and lounger over and righting the furniture. "Yeah, some big guy in a pickup came by and busted the door open with a crowbar about an hour ago."

That had to have been Gault. It looked like he didn't want to wait for his money.

"He walked off with the flat screen, but I think he was looking for more, judging by all the bitching he was doing."

Normally, she kept a secret bankroll of a few hundred bucks in the mobile home, but this time she really was tapped out.

"Why didn't you do anything to stop him?"

Roy put a side table back on its feet, then turned to face her. "Not really my place. I'll tell you one thing. Your neighbors didn't do much either, other than watch, that is. You really need to move someplace with a greater sense of civic duty."

"Yeah, well . . ."

"I'm guessing it was over money, right? It was always money problems with you, Clare, if memory serves."

He dropped onto the sofa. It flexed under his weight.

She had a clear run at the doorway now. He'd never reach her in time, but how far would she get? As far as the trailer-park entrance? Possibly. But if she wanted to outrun Roy and Infidelity Limited, she needed a longer head start.

"It's been a long time since we've seen each other," Roy said. "You look good. You haven't changed much."

Flattery would get him nowhere. She knew how she looked. Every year put two on her face and body. She still had some looks, but they would have been so much more if she had been able to catch a break.

"Got a drink, Clare?"

"Coffee?"

He smiled and screwed up his face. "Something stronger."

She pulled the vodka from the fridge and two glasses from the drainer. She handed Roy his.

"Have a seat. We need to talk."

She settled into the lounger across from Roy. Her gaze went to the open door and possible escape.

"Shall I close the door, Clare? We don't really need people listening in." He crossed the room and managed to close the buckled door. She said good-bye to her freedom.

"What do we have to talk about?"

"Olivia, naturally," he said, returning to his seat.

"Hey, you told me I had to find someone to clear my debt to you guys. I did that."

He raised his hands. "Whoa. I know. I know. Slow your roll. I'm just checking in with you about her."

"The first rule of Infidelity Limited is you don't talk about Infidelity Limited."

Roy cocked his head and smiled. "Clare, don't tell me you haven't talked. The code of silence only goes so far when family is involved."

Is this a test? she wondered. She couldn't tell with Roy. Everything was geared to make sure when the shit hit the fan, it landed nowhere near him. She glanced over at him. His smile did nothing to mask the coldness in his eyes. She could lie to him, but he'd see through it. He knew his clientele too well. "We've talked."

"Like I say, only natural. How's she doing?"

Clare snorted. "How do you think? You did kill her husband, after all."

"I bet you're not so popular with her either."

"You got that right," she said and fired back the vodka. Since Richard's murder, she'd been thinking about Nick. Roy had told her Nick was dead. She hadn't believed it. Didn't want to believe it, truth be told. He hadn't been killed. He'd just taken off. It wasn't like he'd ever turned up dead. It was easier to live with the deception. But Richard was dead. That meant Nick was dead too.

"So what have you and Olivia talked about?"

"Whether you're for real. Whether you really mean what you say. Whether she can trust you."

"And what have you told her?"

"That none of it matters. That she should just do as you tell her and she'll be fine."

"That's good advice. Thank you for that."

It was the least she could do, seeing as she'd screwed her sister over.

"How much of her situation do you know?"

"Not much, but from experience, I can guess. Her husband is dead, courtesy of Infidelity Limited, so now things are moving to the next stage, where you're putting it to her."

"So you know I've told her she has to kill for me—and please don't lie to me. I can tell."

She was hiding more damning information. It was best she gave him this one. "I know."

"Is she going to go through with it?"

"Does she have a choice?"

Roy laughed. "No. Not really."

She hated how Roy was being so goddamn genial when they both knew he'd kill her if it came down to it.

"Where does she stand with the police?" he asked. "Is she a suspect?" Finally, Roy had come to the point. He wanted to know how close his ass was to the fire.

"I don't know. It's not like they advertise."

"Very true."

"Look, why don't you ask Olivia about all this? She knows far more than I do."

"I know, but it pays to have an outsider's perspective." He took a sip of his vodka. "I'll be honest, I'm worried about Olivia. She has a tough road ahead of her, and she's going to need our support if she's going to pull through."

"That's easy. Don't ask her to kill anyone. Leave her be."

Roy squeezed out a politician's plastic smile that wouldn't convince the dumbest of voters. "I wish it was that easy. I have a job for you. I'd like you to keep me updated on her progress. Do you think you can do that?"

"You want me to spy on Olivia? She's my sister."

"I know, and I'm sure you want the best for her."

Roy reached inside his sports jacket and produced a cell phone. He put it on the coffee table between them and slid it toward her. He followed this by bringing out a wad of hundred-dollar bills. He peeled off one and placed it carefully next to the phone.

"Don't think of it as spying. Think of it as guardianship. Olivia needs someone to watch over her and prevent her from doing something stupid. It wouldn't do either of us any good if she did. Naturally, I want to pay you for your time and expenses."

Clare's gaze was on the money. Roy kept adding hundred-dollar bills to the pile. He stopped at $1,000. The money represented so many things. It was enough to get Gault off her back. Better still, it was fresh stake money. If she gave Gault $200 now, it would keep him quiet for a week. That left her the remaining $800 to play at the tables. It all looked pretty good from where she was sitting. She put her hand on the untidy pile of bills.

Roy pressed his hand on top of hers. "Does that seem satisfactory to you?"

The money was. Informing on Olivia wasn't. Olivia was a bitch sometimes, but she'd always been there for her. Of course, Clare could take Roy's money and just toss him a bone from time to time about what Olivia was doing. It's not like it was a secret or anything, and the bonus was she'd get paid for doing it. The arrangement would work as long as he kept the cash coming. And he would. It was obvious that Richard's death had put him in damage-control mode.

"Yeah, it's good with me."

CHAPTER TWENTY-ONE

Clare came through for Olivia for once. She'd gotten Maxine Groves to agree to speak about Infidelity Limited. Maxine had set the time and place—two o'clock Saturday afternoon at her home.

The mood between Olivia and her sister had remained tense since Clare had tried to shake her down for more money. They'd only spoken to each other twice since that night at Clare's mobile home, and that was to set up this meeting.

The frostiness between them carried over to their car ride. They rode in silence in Olivia's car. Olivia didn't like the ever-widening distance that had opened up between them. It meant that Clare had the potential to do something dumb. She'd go for a short-term solution to a long-term issue, and that would only serve to pour gasoline on an already-raging fire. When she was at her most desperate, she was at her most dangerous. They'd entered desperation mode a long time ago.

Thankfully, it didn't take long to reach their destination. Oakley was literally a backwater, with its close proximity to the sloughs peeling off from the Sacramento River. It was a farming community in the no-man's-land between the East Bay and Stockton.

Olivia's GPS brought her to the rusted gates of an aged-looking property where Maxine Groves lived. A ranch house dating back to the fifties, judging by the unimaginative styling, sat at the end of a long driveway. Walnut trees lined either side of the drive, although they didn't seem to be part of a grove for harvesting—just the remnant of what once was. There was a lot of what once was going on here. A handful of pigs and goats combed their pens for food. A barn in need of fresh shingles was home to a Toyota pickup and nothing else. All of it failed to raise Olivia's hopes.

She and Clare climbed from the car and walked up to the gate. It was locked with a chain thick enough to hold an anchor and a heavy-duty padlock suitable for protecting pirates' treasure.

Olivia didn't like this. This woman was hiding herself away, but from whom—Infidelity Limited?

Olivia hefted the padlock. "She doesn't like visitors, that's for sure. How do you know her?"

"She was a Cache Creek regular."

A casino friend. That was an endorsement for reliability.

Clare pulled out her cell and dialed a number. "We're here, Maxine. Can you let us in?"

A minute later, a woman emerged from the house carrying a shotgun, but the charging Rottweiler was the bigger concern.

As the dog chewed up the distance to the gate, both Olivia and Clare backed up until they bumped into the Audi's hood. Olivia was ready to dive into the car if the dog made a leap for the gate, but it stopped short and just paced back and forth. Its huffing and puffing drew a glance from the goats, but not the pigs.

It took Maxine a minute to catch up. Olivia put Maxine in her fifties, average height, but slight. Her waist-length hair was mud brown, with silver streaks running through it. With no makeup on, her sun-damaged skin was exposed.

"Quit it, Jack," Maxine said, and the dog dropped to a sitting position.

Maxine swung the shotgun at Olivia's chest.

Olivia raised her hands. Maxine didn't frighten her; she was just being careful. If she'd gone through the Infidelity Limited wringer, then she was a woman worth listening to. The only thing that frightened Olivia was that this woman lived in fear.

"Jesus, Maxine, that's my sister," Clare protested.

"Is it? I don't know that."

"Trust is an earned commodity," Olivia said. "Will a driver's license help?"

"Yeah, but she gets it," Maxine said and nodded at Clare.

Clare grabbed Olivia's purse from the car and pulled out her sister's wallet.

"That'll do. I'll take that," Maxine said.

Clare tossed it, and Maxine caught it one-handed, all without losing her aim on Olivia.

"Jack, up," Maxine commanded.

The dog popped back up to his feet and resumed his pacing.

Maxine backed up two steps and lowered the shotgun. She rifled through Olivia's wallet, pulling out her license, credit cards, membership cards, and cash.

"Satisfied?" Olivia asked. She injected authority into her question, but not contempt. She just needed Maxine to know she was no mouse.

"For now." She stuffed everything back into the wallet and tossed it over the gate between Olivia and Clare so it landed in the dirt.

Just like the Rottweiler, Maxine was showing her dominance. Olivia accepted it and picked up her wallet.

"Okay, you can come in, but you stay outside," Maxine said, pointing to Clare.

"What?" Clare said. "You know me, Maxine."

"I don't like being outnumbered."

Olivia handed her wallet off to Clare. "It'll be okay."

Olivia unlocked the gate with keys Maxine threw to her. Jack sidled up to her when she let herself in, but he dropped to his belly at Maxine's instruction. Olivia repadlocked the gate and handed the keys back.

The security was unnecessary. The chain and padlock might stop a cannonball, but the gate could be taken down with a good push. But safety had more to do with perception than actual security measures. If this pantomime made Maxine more talkative, then that was fine with Olivia.

Maxine waved the gun up toward the house, and Olivia took the hint.

They walked side by side. Maxine carried the shotgun across her chest, with the barrel casually aimed at Olivia, while Jack trailed behind them.

"Do you really need the gun?"

"Why don't you let me worry about the gun and tell me why you're here?"

"I need information about Infidelity Limited."

"What phase are you at with them?"

Tell or don't tell? Olivia wondered. Maxine didn't trust her, and she didn't trust Maxine. She didn't know what deal this woman had made with Infidelity Limited. She could rat Olivia out the second she left. Then again, hadn't Olivia announced her intentions by being here?

"Spit it out. I don't have all day."

"My husband's dead, and Roy has told me the facts of life about Infidelity Limited."

Maxine cut Olivia a sideways look. "I thought you must be in deep to come asking questions. Do you know who you have to kill yet?"

"No."

"It doesn't mean he'll want you to kill someone tomorrow. It was over a year before he asked me."

While it would be nice if Roy didn't call in his kill marker for a year or ten, she really didn't want the threat hanging over her that long, never knowing when the phone might ring and he'd tell her it was time.

"Did Clare get you into all this?"

"How many people did you recommend to them?"

"Don't get snippy. It doesn't suit you. I'm just saying I'm a little surprised she'd throw her sister to the wolves."

"I could say the same about you doing this to Clare."

"Clare and I aren't family. We weren't even all that friendly. At least, that's what I tell myself. To be honest, you might say you wouldn't wish Infidelity Limited on your worst enemy, but when there's a gun pointed at your head, you'll sell out just about anyone . . . even family."

Olivia wasn't buying Maxine's tough-gal act. "Is that why you didn't invite Clare along—because you feel guilty about what you did to her?"

Maxine laughed. "I could ask you why you haven't put your sister's head on a spike for dropping you down Infidelity Limited's rabbit hole. I'm guessing she didn't tell you what you were letting yourself in for. That's got to sting. I dare you to tell me it doesn't still stick in your throat."

Olivia didn't argue the point. "Clare is helping me. That goes a long way toward making up for this."

Maxine's expression said she didn't quite believe her. Olivia wasn't sure she believed herself either.

"Look, I'm way past shame and embarrassment, but your sister gave me up," Maxine said. "She broke the golden rule—you live with the lie. I don't like that. It means I can't trust her. It means she can stay out there."

"Still, you let me come here."

"I thought I could help you."

They reached the house, but Maxine didn't let Olivia inside. Instead, they sat down at a picnic table in the shade of the walnut trees.

Maxine rested the shotgun against the side of the table, out of Olivia's reach. Jack sat next to Maxine, and she petted the dog's bulbous head.

The air was still. Every sound carried on it, from the chirrup of crickets to the drone of distant traffic. Sitting here, Olivia felt at peace and understood why Maxine would choose to live out here. Olivia's familiar surroundings had taken on a claustrophobic feel. Here, she felt free.

"Okay," said Olivia. "Tell me how you got involved."

"Much like you did. I was having problems with a husband that drank too much. A friend told me about Infidelity Limited. They were supposed to knock a little sense into him. Instead, I got a call to come out to the marshes not far from here to come get my husband. His neck was broken." Maxine palmed away a tear. "Roy told me Infidelity Limited doesn't rehabilitate, they eliminate. He handed me a shovel and told me to dig. I dug a grave and buried my husband."

Olivia reached out a comforting hand, but Maxine pulled back. "So Infidelity Limited killed your husband. Was there a police investigation?"

"Of sorts. I reported Brian missing. He's still a missing person's case." Maxine shook her head. "Roy told me Infidelity Limited is a cooperative and I would never know who killed Brian. He also told me I'd need to kill someone else's spouse. I wouldn't know who or when until the call came. It's the anonymity that makes the system work."

But not perfectly, Olivia thought. Maxine's story hadn't been quite the same as hers, but she guessed that in her case, the botched killing had brought out the police. Maxine had been lucky in that respect. She never had to feel the squeeze of the police.

"Did you get that call?" Olivia asked.

Maxine dropped her gaze. "Yes."

"When?"

"Two years ago."

"Did you do it?"

Maxine grabbed the picnic table. "Yes, I did it. I killed someone."

Jack howled, and Maxine backhanded him into silence. The dog dropped to his belly with shame on his face.

"What is it you want to know?" Maxine barked.

"I'm just trying to figure out how this chain works."

"Do you think you're the first person to think you can get to Infidelity Limited if you backtrack far enough? Wise up, girl. It's not a chain. Haven't you worked that out yet? There's no sequence to this. The person who introduces you isn't the person who kills your spouse. It doesn't work like that. It's random. Client J introduces Client K, and Client K kills Client R's spouse and so on. There's no chain. No circle. No pattern. And even if you could work out the connections, how long has this been going on for—years? There are dozens of victims, if not hundreds. You'll never get to someone who knows how to get to these people. I know, because I've tried, just like every other sucker. My advice is simple: do as you're told. Kill the person Roy tells you to kill, and don't get caught doing it. That's the only way you'll survive this nightmare."

CHAPTER TWENTY-TWO

Olivia was at home, working on arrangements for Richard's funeral, when the Infidelity Limited cell phone rang. Her stomach turned at the sound of its ring echoing through the house. Every call was bad news, dragging her deeper into Roy's abyss. As much as she didn't want to answer his call, she needed to. Roy was a blank sheet. She couldn't beat him without knowing something about him. Though he tried to distance himself from his victims, every interaction with him afforded her the chance to add another detail to that blank sheet. The more she knew, the easier it would be to bring him and Infidelity Limited down. She pulled the cell from her purse and answered it.

"You alone?" he asked.

Her heart was pounding. "Yes."

"Good. Where are you?"

"At home."

"Do you know where the Tilden merry-go-round is?"

It was interesting that he called it the "merry-go-round." He wasn't wrong, but locals called the Berkeley landmark the "carousel." So Roy was an out-of-towner. She banked that nugget of information. "Yes."

"Go there now," he said and hung up.

No preamble. Not even a threat. Just an instruction to keep her on her toes, the Infidelity Limited way. No time to think or turn to someone for help. But that was the point, wasn't it? Keep the victim in the moment. It was Roy's way of keeping control. All she could do was follow.

She didn't bother with a purse. She just jammed cash, a credit card, and her ID into her pockets. Before she got behind the wheel of her car, she called Andrew on her cell.

"He called. He wants to meet now." She hated the shakiness in her voice.

"Okay, we were expecting this. Where?"

"The Tilden carousel."

"Shit. I'm in Antioch. I can't back you up."

"You shouldn't anyway. He'll put me through the wringer like he's done every other time."

"You're probably right. Nervous?"

"Yes."

"Good. He'll be expecting that. Just remember the plan—agree to everything, and learn all that you can."

"I'll do my best."

"Call me afterward."

She promised she would and hung up. She couldn't afford to stay on the phone. Roy would have no doubt calculated the time it would take for her to get from her house to the carousel. She'd set his suspicion detector off if she was late.

The sight of Richard's car parked next to hers in the garage reminded her of her crime. She wanted to sell it, but she couldn't. Not yet. She needed to be reminded of her mistake. The car would go when Roy was finished.

She pulled out and checked the street for one of Roy's people—or worse, one of Finz's. All she needed was the police following her. She took comfort in the fact that Roy would blow off the meeting if he got a whiff of the cops.

Tilden Park was a thirty-minute drive, which was another indicator of Roy's control. The lack of notice and the close proximity robbed her of the chance to set something up from her side. All she could do was comply with his demands. The balance of power sat with him. She couldn't wait until the arrangement got reversed.

She arrived to find the carousel parking lot deserted, which wasn't surprising on a school day. She called Roy. The call went to voice mail.

"I'm here."

She was used to Roy's moves now. Just like with the meetings at the mall and Mount Diablo, this stop would be the first in a series of hoops for her to jump through. The first hoop was the waiting game. An hour dragged its feet, and nothing happened. Each minute she sat there was infuriating, but she kept her cool like a good little victim. No doubt Roy had his eyes on her. Calling Andrew would just play into Roy's hands.

It was two hours before a black van rolled into the parking lot and pulled up next to her driver's side door. The side door slid open, and Dolores from the ladies' room at the mall filled the space. Olivia climbed from her car. The second she was out, Dolores grabbed her and dragged her inside the van. She entered with so much force that she bounced off the panels on the opposite side of the vehicle.

"Hey, Roy said not to hurt her," the driver said.

Olivia could only see a fragment through the partition between the cab and cargo area, but from his voice, the driver wasn't Roy.

"Fuck Roy," Dolores said as she slammed the side door shut. "I'm not letting this bitch screw me. Get her legs."

Olivia had missed the figure at the rear of the van, until his hands grabbed her ankles and yanked her across the floor. He wore a ski mask. He was slight, but Olivia felt his strength in the grip he had on her ankles.

"Let's go," Dolores barked.

The driver put the van in reverse, and it leaped backward.

Dolores clamped a hand over Olivia's throat. "Who have you told? Cops? Your sister? Who?"

Did they know about Andrew? Panic seized her, but loosened its grip just as fast. If Roy was keeping close tabs on her, it wouldn't be hard for him to see how much time they were spending with each other. If Roy knew anything or even feared anything, he would have made true on his threats and served her up to Finz. This was a bluff.

The van lurched forward, and Dolores's grip lessened as she adjusted her balance.

"I haven't told anyone."

"I don't believe you. You told your sister. You told her everything."

"Of course she knows. She told me about Infidelity Limited."

Dolores shook her head in disgust. "Once people start talking, it never stops. What about the cops? Did you tell them too? They've been circling you like flies on shit."

Olivia slapped the woman's hand away. "Only because of the mess you people made."

Dolores slammed a fist into Olivia's stomach. Olivia doubled up. The pain knifed through her, manifesting itself as white noise in her brain.

"Don't you ever touch me again," Dolores hissed. "Have I made myself clear?"

Olivia managed a nod.

"Good."

"Take it easy back there for Christ's sake," the driver said.

"You worry about the driving," Dolores snarled back before releasing her grip on Olivia. "You know the drill. Strip."

The masked figure released her ankles.

Fighting the van's changing speed and cornering, Olivia clumsily stripped down to her underwear. Dolores inspected every piece of discarded clothing.

Once Dolores was finished with her search, she called out to the driver. "Tell Roy she's clean."

Olivia redressed under Dolores's sneering smile. She peppered Olivia with gibes, but Olivia let them bounce off her. She wouldn't be rattled. Eventually, Dolores gave up but underscored her satisfaction by muttering "bitch" under her breath.

The van drew to a halt after twenty minutes. Roy drew the side door open and smiled.

Roy helped Olivia out. His now-familiar Chrysler 300 was waiting for her. He opened the door for her to get in.

They'd brought her to the Golden Gate Fields horse-racing track. It was a nonrace day, so the parking lot was desolate.

As Olivia sat in the passenger seat, the van pulled a one-eighty and roared off, its job done. It was all very slick.

Roy got into the driver's seat and turned the car around. "How are you holding up?"

"Like you care."

"Hey, don't be mean. We have a lot of work ahead of us, and I need you to be cool."

"How can I be cool? I've got the cops breathing down my neck, and you want me to kill someone."

Roy turned to her. "You're tough, Olivia. You can handle the situation. And more."

Roy wasn't ridiculing her. He meant what he said, but the "and more" remark worried her. What other jobs did he have lined up for her?

Roy guided his car onto I-580, heading toward Oakland and San Francisco. He pulled an unsealed, letter-sized envelope from his door pocket and handed it to her. She knew what she'd find inside, because she'd produced the same documentation only weeks earlier. Somewhere, someone had fallen into the same trap she had. Out there was some sorry person, totally unaware that he or she had just set his or her own downfall in motion by signing the death warrant of someone he or she once loved. She poured the contents of the envelope into her lap. Clipped to a sheaf of paperwork was a head shot of a woman in her late thirties. From the formality of the picture, it had to be one of those office-wall pictures of staff members. Underneath the head shot was a daily diary of Amy Moore-Marbach's movements. Whoever this person was, she was a homebody, spending most of her time at her house in Morro Bay. It explained why a door key was included in the package. Someone was obviously thinking of a home invasion–style intervention.

"Amy lost her job at an LA-based law firm and has also lost her lust for life. She has spent the last year watching daytime TV, eating Cheetos, and obsessively buying junk from the Home Shopping Network, much to the disappointment of her wife, Heather," Roy said. "Heather Moore-Marbach owns a small chain of high-end gyms in Southern California, and she's sick of underwriting her wife's slacker lifestyle of the rich and feckless."

There was more information beyond the daily movements, including a head shot of Heather, but Olivia couldn't look at it, so she shoved everything back into the envelope. This was all a little too real, even though she knew she was only gathering information in order to set a trap for Roy, just the way he had for her.

"How am I supposed to do this?" she asked.

"Find a way in, corner Amy, do the deed, and get out clean."

Roy made it sound beyond simple. Maybe it was to him. Kill enough times and it becomes second nature. Maybe simplicity was the best way of thinking about killing. Complexity gave the cops too many opportunities to catch you. She shook her head at the thought.

"You can do this."

How many times had Roy had this conversation with his clients? Ten times? A hundred? And had one of those conversations ever been with Clare?

"What do I do about a weapon?" she asked.

"That's for you to work out. I set the assignment, but you're responsible for the execution of it."

Execution? Is that Infidelity Limited humor? "You're not helping me here. I don't know the first thing about killing someone."

"You'd be surprised what we're capable of when we have no choice."

That wasn't the answer she wanted to hear. She needed him to show himself. "If I get caught, you get caught."

"That won't happen. Infidelity Limited is very well insulated from our clients' mistakes."

"You bastard."

Roy shrugged off the name-calling. "Look, you didn't ask for this, but you find yourself in this position. Harsh, but you have to deal with it, because if you don't, you will suffer the consequences."

She shuddered. "What's that supposed to mean?"

"If you can't keep your shit together, then it stands to reason that the police will catch up to you. Should that happen, I have no option other than to protect myself."

"By killing me?"

Roy laughed. "No. I have Richard's murder weapon. I know the killer's identity. All I have to do is provide the cops with the connective tissue to bind you two together."

So Roy had the murder weapon. That probably made sense to him. Control the evidence; control the game. But holding on to the murder weapon also made him vulnerable. If the cops found it in his possession, he wouldn't be able to explain it away, regardless of how well insulated he believed himself to be. At last, she saw a flaw in Roy's game. All she needed to do was find out where he kept the evidence against her.

"When it comes to a weapon," Roy said, "don't use anything that can be tied back to you. So nothing from your house, like a gun that is registered to you. And whatever way you decide to do it, make damn sure you're confident with it. No point in you playing with guns if you don't know how to use them. Take your time with this. Don't rush into it."

"How long do I have to do this?"

"A month. Sooner is better because doubt will creep in. Any longer and you'll never get around to doing it. As soon as I get the feeling you're stalling, I start connecting the dots for the cops."

There it was. The carrot to keep the donkey walking.

"You can do this, Olivia. Not only that, but you can come out the other side in one piece. I truly believe that. I can't say that about everyone, but I can about you."

"Why? Do I look like a cold-blooded killer?"

"No, you look like a survivor."

It was a compliment, but it felt like an insult.

Roy pulled over to the side of the road. He leaned across her and opened the door. No ride home for her, then.

"I want to know something," Olivia said.

"What is it?"

"Has Clare killed for you?"

"That's not a question to ask."

"Just answer the question. It costs you nothing."

Roy nodded. "No, she hasn't."

At least Clare hadn't lied to her.

"Happy now?"

"Not really. Why haven't you used her?"

"Some people are best left with the threat that I will use them, while others prefer to get that monkey off their back. Clare's a coward. She doesn't face up to her responsibilities. You do."

"And that makes me a killer?"

"Olivia, I don't think you're aware of your capabilities. Let's just say I believe that killer is in your skill set."

Olivia stepped from the car.

Roy smiled at her. "I look forward to seeing what you come up with."

I bet you do, she thought.

CHAPTER TWENTY-THREE

Finz walked into the Old Spaghetti Factory in Concord for his lunchtime appointment.

"How many in your party?" the hostess asked.

She looked like she was barely out of high school. Seeing someone that young with responsibility always made him feel old. "I'm meeting someone. Bertholf."

Every cop picked up an unofficial mentor during his or her career, and Detective Bob Bertholf was Finz's. When Finz made it to detective, Bob was the one he listened to. His guidance made Finz the cop he was today. Bob was a cop for all seasons. He was what he needed to be at any given time. He could be hard and uncompromising with a belligerent suspect and kind and sensitive with a distressed witness. The greatest lesson he'd taught Finz was to just get the facts, record them, and let them build a case. Finz had worked with Bob for ten years before he retired.

The girl smiled. "Mr. Bertholf is here. This way, sir, and I'll show you to your table."

As restaurants went, the Old Spaghetti Factory always confused him. The chain touted itself as a family-friendly place, but its decor reminded him of a Wild West bordello. The restaurant was just under half-full, with the majority of its clientele consisting of young families. That put the level of table talk somewhere between whining and crying. The girl brought him to a booth toward the rear of the place.

Detective Bertholf slipped out from behind the table and crushed Finz's hand in a handshake. "Mikey, it's been a long time."

"Too long," Finz said, sitting down. "Damn, you look good. Where do you get a tan like that?"

"On the golf course and in Maui." He patted his belly. "I'm carrying a few extra pounds, but that comes with not chasing assholes all day. Maybe you need to do the same. You look like an emaciated rat."

"Enjoy your meals, gentlemen," the hostess said.

Finz waited until the girl was out of earshot. "I see that you still like to have your sit-downs here."

Whenever Bob had wanted to thrash out a case, he brought his team here. It became so commonplace that the manager had given him his own table. Finz remembered blowing entire evenings in here.

"Hey, I like this place," said Bob. "It feels like home."

The waiter introduced himself, and they ordered. Bob ordered spaghetti in clam sauce, while Finz went with a Cobb salad. He wouldn't survive the afternoon with a bellyful of pasta sloshing around in his gut.

"You said you wanted to talk about an old case," Bob said.

Finz handed Mark Renko's file to him. "This was a case you responded to twenty years ago. It's a fatal DUI. The driver killed himself after wrapping his vehicle around a power pole on Ygnacio Valley Road."

Bob thumbed through the file. "Jesus, blood alcohol of .32? This guy was seriously shit-faced."

Finz had the file practically memorized. Unlike Richard Shaw's case, Mark Renko's death hadn't been suspicious, just moronic. With a 0.32 blood-alcohol level, he shouldn't have been able to drive. In fact, he should have been barely upright. That detail scratched at Finz. Maybe Renko hadn't been driving.

"Do you remember the case?" Finz asked.

Bob nodded with a frown. "Yeah. The jerk might have survived if he'd been wearing a seat belt, but physics took over when he hit that pole. Christ, he was a mess. He was doing seventy when he went through the windshield. First responders didn't even find him for the first ten minutes. He was that far away from the car." Bob closed the file and slid it across the table, back to Finz. "Why the interest in a traffic fatality?"

"Renko's wife, Olivia. Do you remember her?"

Bob shook his head. "Vaguely. I remember her being young, not long out of high school. The two of them were living in some fleapit apartment. She seemed sweet, while Renko's rap sheet intimated he was a bit of douche, but that's about it. What's so special about her?"

"Her second husband, Richard Shaw, was recently murdered. He was bludgeoned to death after being lured out to a quiet location."

"And she's a suspect?"

"Yes. While Olivia certainly married up when it came to Shaw, it doesn't look as if she married well on the nice-guy front. He was cheating on her with someone from work."

"And you're thinking she got her licks in as payback."

Finz shrugged. "It's a possibility."

"A little excessive though."

And that was where things fell down for Finz. It was hard to believe she'd kill her husband for cheating on her. Not to say it wasn't possible; it was just hard to swallow.

The waiter returned with bread and drinks.

"I'm a little confused as to why you're so interested in Renko," Bob said.

"I have one wife with two husbands who died violently."

"But one of those deaths was self-inflicted."

"Was it, though?"

Bob cut off a piece of bread and took a bite out of it. "You're wondering whether this wreck was staged."

"Any chance?"

"If it was, I would have seen it and investigated. It was what it was—a fatal DUI."

Bob's answer didn't disappoint him. He wasn't hoping Olivia was a two-time killer or even a one-timer killer for that matter. He just wanted the truth, and if Olivia was responsible, so be it. The only disappointment he had was not having anything solid he could grasp. So far, everything was just vapor, giving him only a glimpse at the possible truth.

"I've read the report, and it gives me the facts, but not the details. Can you talk me through the investigation?" asked Finz.

"Jesus, this happened twenty years ago."

"And you've got a rattrap of a memory. Nothing gets away from you."

Bob smiled. "Not quite ready to let go of that bone, huh?"

"Not quite."

"Okay. Give me that file back."

Finz handed Bob the case file, and he flipped through it.

"For the stubborn people in the room, it went down like this. Renko met with buddies at the Flying Horse bar. It should have been called Flypaper for all the barflies it drew. Thankfully, it's long gone now. He met them at eight and drank nonstop until throwing-up time. He said he was leaving and got into his car. The Flying Horse, being the conscientious place that it was, didn't give two shits that they let one of their patrons play automotive Russian roulette on the streets. However, according to Renko's buddies, they did try to get his keys from him and get him a cab, but he wasn't having any of it, and the rest is tragic history. Questions?"

"Where was Olivia that night?"

"Night school and then home. Home alone, I should add. If I were to break down a timeline, she could have intercepted him at the bar, but it didn't seem likely. I do remember that she wasn't all that cut up about Renko being dead. That said, Renko was an asshole—passing rubber checks, some credit card fraud. His death did her a world of good." Bob then realized what he'd said. "Don't get any ideas. I'm just saying she was better off without him."

Finz smiled. "I didn't say a word."

"Good. I'd say that question was a swing and miss. What else do you want to know?"

"Did Olivia gain financially from Renko's death?"

Bob choked out a laugh. "I don't think so. The poor bitch ended up out-of-pocket. The Trans Am he destroyed wasn't insured, and Olivia got the bill for the damage to the power pole. Is she set to gain anything from Shaw's murder?"

"Four hundred and fifty grand in insurance."

"Hmm. Not to be sneezed at. But that's a second strike against you. Last chance to knock it out of the park."

Finz had missed this back and forth with his old supervisor. It had been a long time since he'd had his investigation tested in this way. It made him feel like a rookie, but that wasn't a bad thing from time to time. "The blood-alcohol level. The guy should have been catatonic. Any chance he wasn't driving the car?"

"Witnesses in the bar saw him drive away, and you've seen the pictures of the wreck. If someone else was driving, there'd be two dead bodies. Third strike. That means you're out."

"Not quite. I'm calling a mulligan on that one."

"You're mixing your sports, but okay. Do over."

"Anyone go after him to stop him?"

"Yeah, one of his buddies chased after him in his car to flag him down, but got nowhere. The kid took a chance too. He was .07 himself. If he'd finished his drink he left behind, he would have been over. That would have fucked his army career."

"What?"

"Not all Renko's pals were losers. One of them was an army grunt. On leave, by all accounts. His name is in here."

Finz knew the name before Bob found it in the file.

"Yeah, here it is. Andrew Macready."

"This is where I get back in the game. Guess who's hanging around Olivia after twenty years?"

"Macready?"

"Yep. What can you tell me about him?"

CHAPTER TWENTY-FOUR

Olivia arrived at Andrew's house a few minutes late. He lived at the end of a cul-de-sac in a nice San Ramon neighborhood not far from the golf course. She pulled up next to his truck in the driveway. The house, a midcentury ranch, was cute. Some might think the style was dated, but it felt warm and nostalgic. The setting sun casting a golden halo over the street had little to do with that feeling. A lot of it had to do with her age and the fact that these houses were the ultimate middle-class living when she was a kid. Growing up, it was a place she would have killed to have called home.

Andrew answered the door and hugged her. "Sorry I couldn't be there for you last night."

"It's okay."

He led her through the house into the dining room, across from the kitchen. For a divorced man, he kept the place feeling like a home and not a man cave. The place was nicely decorated. No sign of a gaming console or the widest of wide-screen TVs on display. She'd witnessed some sights during her time as a Realtor.

He pulled out two chairs at the dining table for them to sit. "What have we got?"

She handed over the envelope Roy had given her. He emptied the contents onto the table and sifted through it. He separated out the photographs of the two women before going through their profiles.

They spent all night, into the early hours, poring over the information Roy had gathered. She liked Andrew's methodical approach. It was something she couldn't achieve because it all seemed too familiar. Looking at the breakdowns of the lives of these women was like looking into a mirror. Somewhere there was a dossier on Richard and her, just like this one, their lives deconstructed into habits and haunts, strengths and weaknesses, opportunities and threats. She felt like a rat in a maze with the scientists watching.

"What do you think?" she asked.

Andrew looked up. "It's thorough, and it's a start. I want to get a couple of maps and see where everything is. We really need to see these people up close before we can make a move. We'll blow it if our timing's wrong. How long did he give you to get this done?"

"No longer than a month, although he didn't want me rushing it."

"I think quicker is better if we can manage it. Staying ahead of his schedule works to our advantage."

"How do we go about this, then—just approach them?"

"No. We treat this exactly how Roy expects you to. We observe first, come up with a plan, then move in. Roy's scammed you once. I don't want him doing it again."

That thought did little to allay Olivia's fears. For all she knew, this was just a test to keep her in check or put her even deeper under Roy's control.

"Are you working at the moment?" Andrew asked.

"Not really. I check in with the office, and I take calls. That's about it. I do have Richard's funeral coming up. Not to mention Finz's shadow."

"It might be better if I do the legwork. It'll give you deniability. I can take a few days off to watch Heather and Amy Moore-Marbach.

My guys don't need me around at the new house. They know what they're doing."

Confiding in Andrew was proving to be a lifesaver. "That could be good."

The doorbell rang.

Olivia stiffened. She couldn't be found here. Not with Roy's Infidelity Limited client file around. She reached for the paperwork.

"It's okay. I'm expecting this," Andrew said. "Don't look so worried. It's a surprise."

"A surprise?"

"Don't worry. You'll like it."

He went to the door. She remained out of sight in the dining room and couldn't quite hear the conversation.

Suddenly, she remembered her car. She'd left it out front for everyone to see. She should have parked a couple of streets over so no one at Infidelity Limited could connect her to Andrew.

A minute later, Andrew came back carrying a pizza box and wearing a big grin.

The panic she'd felt evaporated. "You got Royston's?"

"Only the best deep-dish pizza this side of Chicago."

He placed the pizza box on the countertop in the kitchen. He reached inside the fridge and brought out two bottles of RC Cola.

A Royston's pizza and an RC Cola was their thing when they were dating. "RC Cola too? Where the hell did you find that? What's going on?"

"Call it a celebration."

A celebration of what? She couldn't see anything worth celebrating.

"The San Pablo house closed escrow today. The Delgados have their home, and I have the fruits of my labors."

"Congratulations."

As Andrew got a couple of plates and hefted a slice onto each of them, Olivia unscrewed the caps on the RCs. He slid a plate over to her.

"Also," he said, "the key to getting through this thing with Infidelity Limited isn't just beating them at their own game. Morale is a big part of this too. That means remembering to smile. Royston's always made you smile."

Royston's did make her smile. She couldn't remember the last time she'd had a Royston's special. A few years at least. Certainly a couple of inches off her waistline ago.

She smiled. "Thanks."

He placed a hand over hers. His touch reached back twenty years. It felt familiar. It felt good. It felt right. A life not lived ran through her mind. It threw up an alternate history—one where Roy never crossed her path.

"How did we ever lose touch?" she asked.

"I made a mistake."

"And I should have forgiven you."

"Do over?"

She nodded.

Andrew leaned over. He was going to kiss her. She didn't pull away. Then her cell rang, and the moment was gone.

"I should get that." She fished her cell out of her purse. She didn't recognize the number. "Hello?"

"You want to know about Nick?" a harsh male voice barked.

The question threw her for a minute. Mandy had lied. She'd talked to someone. "Er . . . yes."

"There's a Handyman home-improvement store in Stockton. Meet me there in an hour. And come alone."

*   *   *

Olivia turned into the Handyman's parking lot as instructed. The store was deserted since it had gone out of business. Signs pronounced that it was now the site for a new housing development. Chain link surrounded the building, but the parking lot was still open.

No other vehicles were waiting for her, so she parked in the middle. If anyone approached, she'd see them coming.

"Are you *okay* back there?" she asked.

"Don't worry about me. Just keep your eyes open," Andrew said from the trunk.

The final instruction she'd received was to come alone. Andrew had told her, "No way," and insisted on coming along. He didn't want to scare the caller off, so he'd climbed into the trunk after they pulled off I-5. For a big guy, he had fit into the trunk nicely.

"Pop the trunk for me in case I need to jump out."

She did, and Andrew held the trunk on the latch.

"What do you see?" he asked.

"Nothing. We're alone. No other cars. The building's in darkness."

"Any hiding spots—dumpsters, trash enclosures, loading docks?"

"Nothing from where we are. It's just the building and the parking lot. We're alone."

"I doubt that. I'm sure we're being watched."

Olivia was glad Andrew had come with her. She needed him these days. How had life gotten so dangerous so quick? In a matter of weeks, she'd gone from normalcy to insanity.

"I'm going to try calling him," she said.

"Okay."

Her mystery caller hadn't given her his details, but that didn't matter. She pulled out her cell and pulled up her incoming-call log. Modern technology made it hard to hide your information. She dialed the number, but the call went straight to voice mail. The caller had switched his phone off.

"Any luck?"

"Nope."

"Then he's here. I'm sure we're in for a long wait."

And Andrew was right. Thirty minutes dragged by. Then forty. After an hour, the air turned stale inside the car, and Olivia cracked a window. The night air drifted in, with traces of the day's heat still in it. Its touch on her skin revived her, but there was no such respite for Andrew.

"How are you doing back there?"

"Fine. No cramps."

A splash of light caught Olivia across the back of the neck. She whipped her head around. A car was turning into the parking lot.

"There's a car," she announced.

"What's it doing?"

"It's turning around by the entrance. Now it's stopped. I don't know if they're expecting me to follow."

"Just hang tight."

Olivia stared at the car's ruby-red taillights burning in the darkness. From their glow, she could make out two figures. Then the car pulled away.

Just as she was about to tell Andrew, her door flew open. A pair of hands grabbed her by the shoulders and yanked. Her seat belt kept her pinned in place, but the belt dug deep into her neck, reducing her cry to a gurgle. She elbowed her attacker and hit the seat belt release with her other hand. She and her attacker went sprawling to the ground, with her on top.

In the faint starlight, she recognized her attacker. It was Nick. Mandy had proved to be a good liar. Olivia had believed her when she said she hadn't seen her brother.

He flipped her over and used his body weight to pin her to the asphalt. "What do you want?"

Before she could answer, Andrew was on him. He grabbed Nick and tore him off her, then disabled him with a couple of swift punches to the kidneys. Nick dropped to his knees, sucking in ugly breaths. Andrew shoved him onto his belly with his foot before pressing his knee into Nick's back and cuffing his hands behind him with a plastic cable tie.

"You okay?" Andrew asked.

Despite the minor nature of the tussle, her bones were ringing from the impact. She'd probably have a few sore spots in the morning. "I'm fine."

"Are we going to have problems with your friends in the car?" Andrew asked Nick.

"They're not with me. I'm alone. I just used that car as a distraction so I could get to Olivia," Nick whined. "If you're going to kill me, just fucking do it."

Andrew hauled Nick up to his knees. "What are you talking about?"

"I'm not stupid. You're here to kill me. Clare sent you. I didn't think she'd get her sister to do it."

"We're not here to kill you."

Nick looked from Andrew to Olivia. "You're not?"

"No," Olivia said. "We just want to talk."

"About what?"

"Why you think Clare is trying to kill you for a start," Olivia said.

"But I think we should discuss that somewhere with a little more light," Andrew said.

Andrew shoved Nick into the backseat and slid in next to him. Olivia closed the trunk, got behind the wheel, and turned the car around.

Nick stared at Andrew for a long moment before saying, "Andrew Macready, right? The last I heard, you joined the army."

"The last I'd heard of you, you were an asshole, and I don't think a lot's changed."

"Screw you, army boy."

"Hey, quit it, the both of you," Olivia said. "Leave the testosterone elsewhere."

They stopped at a Jack in the Box. As a gesture of goodwill, Andrew cut the cable tie binding Nick's wrists, and they went inside.

Following the guys into the burger joint sent Olivia back twenty years. How many times in high school had she come to a place like this with Andrew and Nick? Only Clare and Mark were missing.

Nick hadn't changed much. He was still the scrawny kid she'd grown up with. But that wasn't quite true. Back then, he'd always looked like he'd slept in his clothes and his hair never seemed to have met a comb. Now he sported a sensible haircut—number three, short with a side part—and was dressed in a freshly ironed polo shirt over dress pants. Those weren't the best clothes for a clandestine adventure. He'd picked up a tear on the right leg from the scuffle.

A handful of people were having a late-night meal in the fast-food joint, so Andrew claimed a corner booth. In case Nick had any ideas about bolting, Andrew pressed him into a seat against the wall and sat next to him to pin him in.

Olivia got the food and brought it back to the table.

Nick tore into the burger and fries. "I need this. It'll be hours before I get home."

Olivia and Andrew exchanged a look. Nick hadn't brought them to his home turf. Olivia found that curious. "Where do you live?"

"That's something you don't need to know," he squeezed out between bites.

"Answer her," Andrew said.

"No, that's okay," Olivia said. Nick was right; she didn't need to know. But more importantly, a little give-and-take was a good thing. Nick wouldn't talk if he didn't feel his safety was intact.

"So why have you been poking around, looking for me, Liv? And don't tell me it's because Clare wants me to come to a funeral. You wouldn't have had army boy hiding in the trunk if that was it."

Andrew bridled at being called "army boy," but he kept it bottled.

"My husband was murdered."

"To lose one husband, Liv, may be regarded as a misfortune; to lose both looks like carelessness," Nick said, paraphrasing Oscar Wilde.

Nick had never been much of a student, but English was the only thing Olivia remembered him ever being good at.

"Let's forget about my husbands and talk about why you ran out on my sister and why you think she's trying to kill you."

The questioning didn't agree with Nick. He struggled to get the mouthful of food down. "I'm not bullshitting you, and as much as you might not want to hear this, Clare tried to have me killed." He sat back in his seat, waiting for recriminations. When they didn't come, his expression tightened. "You knew about this?"

"Keep your voice down," Andrew said. "We're all friends here."

"Clare didn't try to kill you," Olivia said. "She hired someone to slap you around a little."

"She did what?"

"You can't say you didn't deserve it," Olivia said.

She wasn't sure Nick had heard her. He was riding a private roller coaster of emotions. After a minute, the tension went out of his body.

"You're right," he admitted. "It wasn't like I didn't need the straightening out. I was a jackass back then. But your sister was no angel either."

"I know. So what happened?"

"I was in Fairfield, driving back home to Clare. It was late, and I'd been drinking, so I kept off the main roads. I stopped at a four-way, and I got tapped from the rear. I didn't care about fault and insurance. I knew I was over the limit, so I kept going, but this chick kept following me. I tried to lose her, and I ended up dead-ending at some park. She blocked me in. I got out to tell her to forget it, and she pulled a gun. I bolted for the park, but I wasn't too good on my feet, and I went down. She was on me before I could get back up. She aimed the gun at me and told me she was sorry, she wished she didn't have to do this, but I should have been a better husband to Clare, and she didn't have a choice, she was only following orders. They made her do this. Blah, blah, blah. Not that I really gave a shit. I just didn't want to die."

"She said 'they.' That implies more than one person," Olivia said.

"Yeah, right. I wasn't worrying too much about that at the time. If I had to consider additional parties involved, I'd assume it was you. Clare doesn't do anything without your backing."

That stung, but Olivia wasn't about to get sidetracked. "How'd you get away?"

"She was having a hard time pulling the trigger. She got real close. Too close. I kicked her in the ankle. Got some real weight behind it, y'know? I scrambled away, but she shot me."

"Where?"

Nick rolled up his right sleeve. The bullet had left a blunt-looking three-inch slash that distorted the natural line of his triceps on the side of his arm. "It was just a flesh wound, but it hurt like a bitch. I went down when she hit me, and I hid. She searched for me, but eventually gave up. She was in tears when she wandered off."

"Didn't you think it was weird that the person sent to kill you was an amateur?" Andrew asked.

But that's what Infidelity Limited thrives on, Olivia thought. She didn't have to imagine too hard to understand the turmoil this woman had gone through by the time she'd reached the point of aiming a gun at Nick.

"Who said she was an amateur?" Nick asked. "Less than a month later, I saw that she was arrested for killing her husband."

"Bullshit," Andrew said.

"I shit you not. She went down for it."

And so ended the cycle of doom, Infidelity Limited–style. The ugly future facing Olivia turned her stomach. "Do you remember her name?"

"Of course I do. You don't forget the bitch who put a gun in your face. Her name is Karen Innes. Look it up."

Nick's excitement left him suddenly. "As much as I wanted to shove that gun up her ass at the time, I'd thank her now. I sorted out my shit after that night. I started over, and now I'm in a good place. I have a wife I care about and a job I'm proud of."

"That was something you could have had with Clare."

Nick dropped the smile he'd had. "No, I couldn't have. We brought out the worst in each other. As dumb as it sounds, I owe Karen and Clare for my fresh start."

"So why hide?" Andrew said. "Everybody thinks you're on the lam."

"Clare tried to kill me once. I didn't want there to be a second time."

Olivia had heard enough and got up from her seat.

"Hey, where are you going?" Nick asked. "I've answered your questions. It's time to answer a few of mine."

"Another time," Andrew said, pulling Nick from his seat.

Olivia drove Nick back to his car, which he'd parked a block away from the Handyman's lot. Despite the negotiated peace between them all, Andrew had still chosen to ride in the back with Nick. The three of them got out and stood between the cars.

"Are you going to tell Clare about our get-together?" Nick asked.

"No," Olivia said.

"So what's all this been about? You're in trouble, aren't you?"

Olivia nodded. "It's better if you don't know. You've got your secrets, and I've got mine."

CHAPTER TWENTY-FIVE

Olivia released a pent-up breath when the minister thanked everyone for coming and wished them well. Richard's service was over, and she'd held it together. The toughest part had been giving the eulogy. She'd spent a night alone with a pen and paper, coming up with one, but it all went by the wayside when it came time for her to speak. She wasn't sure what she'd actually said, but she knew she had talked about how she had loved Richard and wished he was still alive. What everyone took for a heartfelt and impassioned love note for a spouse was really the admission of a penitent who had made a terrible mistake.

As people left, a seemingly endless line of friends, coworkers, and acquaintances took turns giving their condolences and wishing Olivia well on their way out. She listened to their reminiscences with a forced smile and a polite thank-you.

Clare moved in for a hug when it got down to the stragglers. "How are you holding up?"

"Flagging."

Clare had surprised Olivia in recent days. After her attempted shakedown for money, Olivia had expected her sister to distance herself for a while, but she'd been a surprising godsend. She'd helped out with funeral arrangements and been a good sister for once. Maybe cutting Clare off had woken her up to the responsibilities of modern life.

"Did the bitch come?" Clare asked.

"Yep, and went," Olivia said. When the service had ended, Richard's mistress had been one of the first to shoot out the door. Olivia had spotted her arrival just before the proceedings began. She'd chosen to sit at the back. At least she hadn't made a scene.

Richard's dad came over and hugged Olivia. "You did great."

It wasn't a compliment she was going to receive from her mother-in-law. To avoid any and all family drama, she'd put Richard's parents up in a hotel. Richard's dad had been wonderful at running interference with his wife to keep sparks to a minimum. Olivia and Richard's mother had barely said a word to each other, which was fine with Olivia.

"Thanks, Tom."

"Louise and I are going back to the house, as it looks as if a lot of people are heading there for the wake."

"Thank you. I think I'm needed here for a little while to tie things up. The caterers are there, so you can let yourselves in. If the house gets packed, just open up the doors to the backyard."

Tom raised his hands. "It's okay. Don't worry about it. I'll deal with whatever happens."

She hugged him and kissed him on the cheek. He caught up with Louise, who was in conversation with Richard's boss at the ad agency. She fixed Olivia with a cold glare before moving on.

Leo Steele waited for another mourner to have his say before moving in. "Lovely service, Mrs. Shaw."

"Thank you."

"With your permission, I'd like to remove your husband for cremation."

"Please," Olivia said.

"Would you like to make your final good-bye?"

Olivia shook her head. "I already have."

Clare took Olivia's hand in a tight grip.

Steele nodded his approval and left.

"I haven't seen Andrew. Where is he?" Clare asked.

"He thought it was better if he didn't come," Olivia lied. Andrew was in LA, shadowing Heather and Amy Moore-Marbach.

"Good decision," Clare said. "I notice Finz is hanging around."

Olivia hadn't invited him, although she supposed it wouldn't have been hard for him to find out about the service. The detective was standing at the church's entrance. He exchanged nods with passing mourners but never entered into conversation with anyone. His presence had thrown her when her gaze fell upon him during the eulogy. She'd stumbled over her words for a moment before gathering herself. She didn't have to ask why he was there. It was pure intimidation. He wanted to see if she was cracking. It shouldn't have been a surprise to see him in attendance.

"Yeah, Finz always seems to be around," Olivia replied.

"Do you think Roy's here?"

It would be just like him to show his face to make her squirm, but she hadn't spotted him in or outside the church. She guessed the situation was a little too hot for him to put in an appearance. With cops circling, looking to pin a murder charge on someone, he would likely steer well clear of his mess.

Finz made a move toward them.

"Shit. Here comes Finz. I don't want to deal with his crap right now."

"It's okay," Clare said. "I'll put him in his place."

*   *   *

Finz let Clare cover the remaining distance between them. Her expression said she was ready to do battle. He put out his hand. "Nice to see you again, Ms. Lyndon."

"Detective, is this an appropriate time for a visit?"

That was an interesting opening salvo. Innocent people didn't greet the police this way. The appropriate response should have been, "Do you have news?" Something stank with this investigation.

"I'm just paying my respects," he replied. "I find it helpful to put a human face with the name. It's easy to forget there's a real person behind the witness statements, autopsy report, and whatnot. Apologies for any offense caused."

"Oh," she said, the fight gone from her. "I'm sorry. Thank you for coming."

The best way to win a fight was not to have it at all. "Think nothing of it. But while I have you, I wonder if you'd be okay answering some questions."

"Me?"

"I don't want to bother your sister. I can see she has a lot on her plate at the moment."

Clare whipped her head around to look for her sister.

Olivia can't help you, Clare, he thought. *You have to deal with me now.*

"The wake is starting at Olivia's house now. Can't this wait? I can come see you tomorrow."

He never made appointments. Appointments gave people time to rehearse what they would say. The impromptu approach forced people to think on their feet, and not many could keep their balance. "This won't take long."

Clare shook her head doubtfully.

"How about this? I'll drive you back to your sister's place, and we can chat during the drive. How's that sound?"

Panic and frustration played out across Clare's face before she said, "Okay, but this can't drag on. My sister needs me."

"I promise not to be a burden."

While Clare scurried off to explain to Olivia, Finz brought his car around to the front of the church. Finz liked carrying out interviews in cars. The tight confines turned up the intensity. It meant no escape.

Clare emerged a couple of minutes later. Watching her descend the church's steps, Finz thought Clare and Olivia might have been sisters by blood, but they weren't by lifestyle. Olivia had certainly found the good life. It was easy to see that Clare's black dress was a cheap cocktail dress, no doubt picked up at a discount store. He'd been to her home at the trailer park. Oh yes, Olivia had certainly discovered the good life in comparison to her older sister.

Clare opened the car door and climbed in. Finz put the car in drive and pulled away. "Has your sister shared any thoughts on potential suspects for Richard's murder?"

"No. You any closer to finding one?"

Finz could do without the antagonism. He decided to kill it before it became a problem and turned on the officialese. "I need to get your statement for the night of Mr. Shaw's death. That okay?"

"I don't know anything."

"Even if you know nothing, I have to get a record of it." He smiled. "But I'm sure you know some things."

He stopped for a light and glanced over at Clare. She sat hunched forward, with her hands clasped together, bouncing her right knee up and down.

"Nervous?"

"Huh?"

"You seem nervous."

Clare shook her head. "No. This is all just a little overwhelming. I haven't come to terms with Richard's murder. That's the type of thing that happens to other people, not us."

Finz nodded. "No one ever expects bad things to happen."

The light changed, and he eased the car forward.

At first glance, Clare seemed to be the tougher of the two sisters. She looked like she'd weathered adversity on a regular basis. The lines on her face and her broken fingernails told a story of a life hard lived. Whereas Olivia looked as if she lived a charmed life, with the well-manicured nails, the designer-label clothes, the nice cars, and the expensive home. After putting these women under the microscope, a different story emerged. Olivia was the strong one. He wouldn't learn the truth from going after Olivia. His route was through Clare.

Clare pulled a pack of cigarettes from her purse. "Do you mind if I smoke?"

Regulations said no, but when working with witnesses, you did whatever you could to make them happy. "Sure. No problem."

She lit up and blew a cloud of smoke that filled the car.

"Could you tell me where you were between seven and ten the night Richard was killed?"

"I was at home. Olivia came over, and she left at nine thirty or so."

"Can you be more precise?"

"Not really. It's not like I was clock-watching." She took a drag on her cigarette. "Do you suspect Olivia?"

Finz smiled. "No. I just need to rule her out. It's good for the DA's office that they can show family members have an ironclad alibi. Why was Olivia with you?"

"We were just hanging out."

"So you're close?"

"Yeah."

"Do you know of any troubles between Richard and Olivia?"

"No, things were good."

"So they didn't have financial troubles or personal problems?"

Clare snorted. "Richard and Olivia? No. Me, I'm a different story."

Finz smiled again. He'd pocket that remark. It could prove useful. "How about grudges or enemies?"

"Not that I know of."

Clare had passed the initial audition. It was time to make things a little tougher for her. "How's Olivia doing?"

"How well does anyone do under these circumstances?"

"Especially considering this is her second husband to die violently."

Clare had her cigarette halfway to her mouth when Finz dropped that brick on her. She sat frozen, with her mouth open, the cigarette inches from her lips. "What's that supposed to mean?"

"Just that her previous husband, Mark Renko, died in a car crash and her current husband was murdered. That's pretty unlucky."

"Well, that . . . that's exactly what it is—bad luck. I don't know what else you expect me to say."

He said nothing, leaving Clare to fill the dead air.

"Are you trying to say the deaths are connected? How could they be? You think Liv killed them? You honestly think she beat Richard to death and crashed Mark's car for him? You're crazy."

"You know what's crazier? That your husband disappeared too."

Clare took a long pull from her cigarette and blew the smoke into Finz's face. She stubbed the butt out in his pristine, unused ashtray. "If you've got a point to make, why don't you just come out and say it?"

"I'm just saying your family is no stranger to tragedy."

Again, he chose silence to give Clare the space to fill the void. This time, she didn't bite.

"What happened to your husband, Clare?"

"Nick was a deadbeat. He ran up debts and grudges. Eventually they caught up with him, so he took off, leaving me to pay them off for him, and I haven't seen him since. He was a deadbeat, so I didn't go looking for his sorry ass. Excuse me for marrying a jerk."

"I noticed you went back to your maiden name after Nick disappeared. Like you knew he wasn't coming back."

"I didn't want him back, didn't want his name or anything to do with him. But what's this got to do with anything? I thought you were supposed to be finding Richard's killer. Harassing us doesn't get you any closer to doing that. Christ, you cops are all the fucking same. You don't want to do your job. You're like piss running down a gutter. You take the easiest path to the sewer."

When it came to slams, that one was a doozy, and Finz fought to keep in a smile. "I didn't mean any offense."

"Didn't you?"

"No. When we catch Richard's killer, the defense team is going to throw mud in all directions. What I have to do is make sure none of it sticks to Olivia. That means asking the nasty, dirty, and embarrassing questions now."

Clare was silent for a second. Finz wasn't sure if she was buying his line. "Yeah, well, you don't have to be a dick about it."

"It's what puts the 'dick' in 'detective.'"

"Ha, ha."

He was closing in on Olivia's home. He had to keep pushing. "I don't think you're going to like my next question much either."

"You stun me."

"Olivia wrote a check to Miles Gault for three thousand dollars the day of Richard's murder."

"So?"

"Among other things, Miles Gault is a loan shark. Olivia doesn't seem like the type of person to need a loan shark. Then again, Gault has been known to break a few skulls. Maybe he went a little far this time. Care to comment?"

Clare fidgeted in her seat and fished out a second cigarette from the pack. Finz waited. He was an expert at waiting. She rolled the cigarette around in her fingers a few times before lighting it.

"I'm broke, okay?" she said. "My credit rating is shit. I needed money, and I got it from Gault. I got behind on payments, and Olivia, being the sister that she is, bailed me out. Satisfied?"

Well, that correlated with what Gault and Olivia had said. "Can I ask what the money was for?"

"No."

Finz let that go. He didn't need to know right at this moment.

"My brother-in-law is dead, and you're treating me and my sister like suspects."

"Sorry, this line of questioning is just routine."

Their journey came to an end. Cars lined the street in front of Olivia's home. He had no option but to double-park.

"One last question before you go. Who is Andrew Macready?"

Clare smiled, but it was a cold smile. "You really are a jerk, Detective Finz. I almost believed your bullshit line about asking the tough questions before the defense attorneys do."

He ignored her insult. He wanted to get something from this interview. He needed someone to start opening up to him. "The thing is, you're right. Olivia wasn't around when either of her husbands died, but Andrew Macready was. He was there when Mark Renko died, and he's around now. So I ask you again, who is Andrew Macready?"

"He's a high school friend of Liv's. We grew up together. He and Olivia were a couple once."

"And now?"

"Friends."

"Just friends?"

"Just friends." Clare wasn't smoking anymore. Her gaze remained on Olivia's house, the cigarette just burning between her fingers.

He let Clare stew in her own thoughts for a moment or two before pressing her harder. "I know I'm not getting the truth from you guys, and it's holding me back. Holding justice back. If you want to be on the right side of it, you'll tell me what's going on."

Clare turned to him. "Do you pay for information?"

The question blindsided him. He'd expected a lot of things from Clare's mouth but not that. "What?"

"Confidential informants, CIs, whatever you call them. How much do you people pay?"

He couldn't believe what he was hearing. "It doesn't work that way."

"Well, it does if you want anything from me."

It was her turn to play the silence game and wait for an answer. Was Clare bullshitting him? Paying him back for riding her? He couldn't tell. A car honked at them for blocking the road. They both ignored it.

"When you have a better answer, give me a call," she said and climbed from the car.

Watching her enter Olivia's house, he felt for the first time like he was getting somewhere.

CHAPTER TWENTY-SIX

Roy didn't need directions to find the spot. You never forget where you buried a body, even at Topanga State Park.

The Chrysler's wheels tore at the fire road's surface with little success. The loose red dirt provided no grip. They'd gotten as far as they were getting. He stopped the Chrysler and switched off the engine. He could leave the car on the trail. No one would be around at this time of day. The park was large and undermanned enough to pretty much ensure privacy, especially since it was close to closing time. It was the reason he'd chosen this spot in the first place.

He looked over at Beth. She gazed out the passenger-side window at the hillside. The intensity of her gaze burned a hole through the trees. Even she knew exactly where Jeff Maxwell's body was rotting in the ground.

It had been three years since Beth had last asked him to bring her out here. She only ever wanted to come when she was at her darkest.

"You sure you want to do this?" he asked.

"Yes."

The sun was falling toward the Pacific Ocean as he helped Beth from the car. He felt its heat on his back. It would be good for her skin, though he repositioned her veil to keep the sun off her damaged face.

"We've got a hike ahead of us. You sure you're up for it?" he asked.

"Yes," she snapped.

"Okay, then."

Beth was so fragile these days, both physically and mentally, but not when she was on a mission. Then nothing stopped her. Roy watched her stride ahead of him. He didn't know if she knew the spot the way he did. She hadn't been with him the night he'd buried Maxwell. She was being treated for her wounds after the fire.

He followed her to the trailhead. He thought he'd kept himself in good shape, but trudging up the stiff slope and into the shade of the trees, he felt his age. He moved with leaden legs while sucking in long, ragged breaths. It hadn't been a problem a decade ago. Then again, maybe this new weariness came from literally going over old ground. Either way, he wanted to get this over and done with. Maxwell's grasp over Beth, even from the grave, disturbed him. Maxwell had never seen her as anything more than a nice piece of ass. All she and Roy had achieved with Infidelity Limited proved she was much more than that. Still, he indulged her obsession for one simple reason; it soothed her. He hoped this was the start of an upswing for her. He needed it as much as she did.

After a mile, they left the trail. They crossed a ridgeline before dropping down into a meadow. It was a beautiful spot. It rose and dipped, rose and dipped. It was encircled by trees, giving it a secluded feel. Maxwell didn't deserve such an idyllic resting place.

Beth kept up her determined pace, but she was veering off course. He took her hand and steered her back on the true path, toward the edge of the tree line. The tallest of the bunch served as his North Star.

Roy stopped when he reached the spot. He looked down at the ground.

"Are we over him?" Beth asked.

They were. He didn't need a map or a GPS to pinpoint the grave. The lie of the ground and the faint bump in the dirt radiated familiarity, even after all these years. He nodded.

"Tell me what you did that night."

"You know what I did."

"I want to hear it again."

Beth was staring at the ground at her feet, and she didn't see him frown.

"Again."

The story was easy to remember, its details close at hand, but it was always hard to recount. He started the tale at the moment Beth had killed Maxwell and started the fire to destroy the evidence. Their futures had hinged on the minutes that followed Maxwell's last breath, so Roy had acted fast. The fire had gotten away from Beth, so he attended to her burns as best he could, then dealt with Maxwell. He'd dodged the patches of smoke and flames and wrapped Maxwell's corpse in plastic, then in a blanket before bundling it into the back of his SUV. He had dropped Beth off at an off-the-grid doctor he knew, then drove out to Topanga. He'd parked the car and spent an hour scouting the area for a suitable grave site. Once he'd found it, he grabbed his tools and Maxwell's body. How the hell he'd managed to lug Maxwell over one shoulder up the trail while carrying his toolbox and shovel, he'd never know. Blind panic and fear were the superhuman fuel of choice, he surmised. He'd dug. Even with his strength, it had been exhausting, cutting through the dirt. It was hard and unyielding, as if it didn't want to accept Maxwell's body. It had taken him more than two hours to dig a hole chest deep. It wasn't the regulation six feet under, but it was deep enough.

He'd tossed Maxwell in, but there was still work to do. All identification had to be removed. That meant fingers and teeth. He snipped Maxwell's fingers off with sheet-metal shears and smashed his teeth out with pliers before filling the grave back up with dirt. The teeth he'd dumped in various trash cans on the way back to Beth. The fingers he'd had to keep until he could burn them. The story was done.

The events had played out in 4K Ultra HD with surround sound in his head, but he'd only given Beth the bare bones in his retelling, consisting of stick-figure outlines and colorless details. He could tell she didn't like it. Her hands balled into fists, and she fidgeted in place, shifting her weight from one foot to another, like a child in need of the bathroom. He didn't care. He wouldn't let her revel in this memory.

"Tell it right."

"No."

"Do it."

He didn't want to, but he knew Beth well enough to know that she wouldn't settle down and move past this moment until she got what she wanted. He couldn't work out why she'd gotten so agitated with the world recently. Was it because Infidelity Limited was going through a tricky time, with too many screwups of late? There had been a recent rash of clients tossed to the lions to ensure Infidelity Limited's buffer to the cops remained intact, with Olivia being the most current and trickiest. Was it Olivia? Something about her case rubbed Beth the wrong way. Was it jealousy? Beth had sensed he had a soft spot for Olivia.

"Okay," he said and told it again.

When he was finished, she spat on the ground. "You should have treated me right, Jeff."

"He should have," Roy added.

Beth turned to him. She faced him with her good side—the unmarred, beautiful side—but when she spoke again, that side was no less ugly than the fire-ravaged side.

"Now, dig. I want to see his face."

CHAPTER TWENTY-SEVEN

Clare was trying her luck at Thunder Valley. She needed something to buoy her spirits after Richard's funeral. The casino was out past Sacramento and a little farther to travel to than she liked, but it had been expanding and offering some nice enticements. Besides, Cache Creek had been dealing her cold cards lately. The grand she'd gotten from Roy had only ended up lasting about two hours, and now she was in to Gault for $2,500 plus interest.

Maybe she deserved to lose Roy's money. It was tainted by the fact she was informing on her sister. She blamed her decision on the heat of the moment. Roy had caught her at a time when she was desperate for money and was willing to take it from the devil himself.

Roy called every day or so to ask her what she knew. She fed him a line of bullshit he expected to hear—Olivia was frightened, the police were asking questions, she was making preparations to fulfill her assignment. She told him nothing about Olivia trying to destroy Infidelity Limited. She didn't feel bad about this deception, considering everything the prick had put her through.

Olivia was crazy in that respect. She didn't stand a chance of bringing them down, but Clare guessed she wouldn't learn that lesson until she had exhausted every avenue and realized complying was her only escape.

Clare's cards came flying across the blackjack table at her. Eighteen. An awkward number. Too high to gamble on another card. Too low to guarantee beating the dealer.

The dealer flipped his cards over—a queen and a jack. Enough to beat everyone sitting at the table. He whisked away all the cards and chips on the table, including Clare's twenty-five-dollar bet.

She'd only gotten paid yesterday, and all she had left was two hundred bucks. It wasn't enough to get her through to her next paycheck, and certainly not enough to pay her rent. She could keep going in the hope of turning it around, but she was relying on luck and not design. How many times had Olivia berated her over her gambling? God only knew. She did remember one thing Olivia had said: "When are you going to learn that you can't win?" Well, she was learning now. She knew if she laid down another bet, she'd lose. It was time to call it a night, while she could still afford the ride home. She picked up her short stack of chips, her drink, and her purse and walked away from the table.

Olivia might even be proud of her for this show of restraint. Or maybe not, considering she had lost almost everything before she had stopped.

Clare cashed out, and on the way to the parking structure, she lit a cigarette. She'd reached the aisle where her Honda was parked, when someone called her name. She knew better than to turn around, but she did out of reflex.

It was Gault.

"Shit," she murmured under her breath.

He broke into a jog.

She had a fifty-yard head start on him, but she knew better than to run.

Despite his size, he wasn't out of breath when he caught up to her. He glanced at her cigarette. He hated smoking, so she dropped the cigarette and ground it out.

"You've been ducking my calls, Clare."

"I know. I'm sorry."

"If you know, then you're purposely avoiding me. And to make matters worse, you're here, gambling with money you've borrowed from me instead of paying me back."

Clare said nothing. Apologizing would only serve to piss off Gault even more, as would pleading.

"How much do you have left?"

"I'm all out."

"All out? I saw you go up to the cashier. They don't let you cash out nothing."

"Gault, all I have is gas money."

"That'll do. I just need a payment, not the whole thing."

"But Gault, I'll have nothing."

He snaked out an arm and grabbed her wrist, forcing her to spin back to him in order to prevent him from breaking it. He moved in close. "I think you're screwing with me, Clare."

"No, I'm not. I swear."

"I don't believe you. You take my money, blow it, borrow more, blow that, then hide from me. That's disrespectful, and I don't like it. Do I make myself clear?"

"Yes."

"After you make your payment today, what are the chances that I'll get the rest of what you owe?"

"I'll pay you back with my next paycheck."

"Really? Do I have to take your sister up on her offer and visit her?"

The last thing she needed was that. "No, no, no. You leave her out of this. I'll get you your money back."

"It only seems fair that I pay her a visit after what she did to me."

"What are you talking about?"

"The visit I got from the cops. They wanted to know why she'd paid me three grand. What was her little game—write the check, then get the cops to get it back?"

Gault twisted her arm. She felt the pain all the way up into her neck. "It's nothing like that. Her husband was killed. They were going through her finances."

Gault went quiet for a long moment. "Is your sister in trouble?"

Clare closed her eyes. She'd said the wrong thing, and now Gault was plotting. "No. It's routine. They always check out the spouse. Look, I'll get your money. Just leave my sister out of this."

"You always say that, and you do pay, but not before you dick me around. I think it's time I gave you an incentive."

He snapped back her pinkie, breaking it. She yelled out, her shriek bouncing off the walls.

He released his grip on her, and she crumpled to the ground, cradling her busted hand in her good one. For a brief moment, she saw white light.

He snatched her purse off the ground and rifled through it until he found her wallet. He sneered at the pitifully thin wad of bills. "Is this all that's left of my money? You've barely got more than a hundred. Christ, Clare, you need to deep-six the cards. You suck." He shook his head in disgust and pocketed the cash.

She didn't bother telling him that he'd missed the hundred bucks she'd tucked in her shoe. She'd learned a long time ago to break up her roll. You never knew who might take it from you.

"Start making regular payments, Clare, or I'll do worse next time."

CHAPTER TWENTY-EIGHT

The Moore-Marbachs' weekend beach house was a palatial affair, overlooking the ocean on the outskirts of Morro Bay. The architect must have had a field day, since the place was a mess of sharp angles. The roof was a series of wood-shake slashes that created sharp peaks and valleys. It rose up, church-like, on the ocean side, sporting a fabulous wall of glass offering a million-dollar view of the sea. That was in sharp contrast to the property's street-side view. An understated front entrance with a large paved turnaround for cars was shuttered in by a six-foot wooden fence with a wrought iron gate. Trees surrounded the house, giving it a sense of seclusion.

Olivia and Andrew viewed the place from the beach. They walked hand in hand, giving the impression they were a couple enjoying their Saturday afternoon instead of two people spying on the owners.

"What do you think?" Olivia asked.

"It looks good," Andrew said. "They're alone. I don't think we'll get a better opportunity."

They'd brainstormed the plan the night before. The simplest solution won out. They would simply go up to the front door and try to get invited inside. It would work as long as Heather or Amy didn't slam the door in their faces. Olivia was banking on the theory that she possessed the key that opened all doors.

"You up for this?" Andrew asked.

"I don't have much of a choice."

He squeezed her hand a little tighter. "You've got this. You know you do."

His faith lifted her.

"Now, let's kill Amy Moore-Marbach," Andrew said.

They returned to where they'd left Olivia's Audi. She got behind the wheel and drove to the private beach road. She let the car roll down the road and stopped in front of Heather and Amy's gate. She climbed from the car, went up to the squawk box, and pressed the button.

"Hello?" a voice said. Olivia didn't know if it was Heather or Amy. She'd never heard either of them speak.

"Hi, I'd like to speak to Heather Moore-Marbach, please."

"What's it regarding?"

Olivia still didn't know if she was talking to Heather or Amy. "A business matter. She'll want to see me."

"Sorry, we don't accept solicitors."

Olivia was afraid of this. The gated entry ensured unwanted parties didn't even reach the front door. It was time to get nasty and use her magic key. "I'm from Infidelity Limited."

"Infidelity what?"

That answer meant she was talking to Amy. "Infidelity Limited. Please pass that message to Heather. She'll want to talk to me."

Olivia heard Amy yell out Infidelity Limited's name, followed by some back and forth that she couldn't make out due to the squawk box's poor sound system, then silence. Amy must have taken a finger off the intercom's button.

"Come on, Heather. Be smart. You can't hide."

Before Olivia's anxiety could sink its teeth into her, the electric gate swung effortlessly open. As she guided the Audi inside, Heather emerged from the house. She looked how Olivia expected—a walking advertisement for her health and fitness business. She was tall, blonde, athletic, and attractive. The yoga leggings and sports tank top showed off all the assets that made her an in-demand trainer. She headed straight for them, her face knotted into a grimace.

Sorry, girl, Olivia thought, *this is going to get uglier than you could ever imagine.*

Olivia stopped the car, and she and Andrew managed to get out before Heather got in their faces.

"What the hell are you doing here? Are you trying to blow this for me? Do I need to call Roy? Well, do I?"

Olivia expected Heather's bluster. The woman was in a moment of blissful naïveté. She didn't know what Infidelity Limited was capable of. At least she wouldn't suffer the nightmare Olivia was going through.

"Believe me, Roy is the last person you want to call," Andrew said.

Heather eyed them with suspicion. "Who are you guys?"

"Friends. What I have to tell you is going to save you a lifetime of misery. We need to go inside," Olivia said.

Amy was standing in the doorway, watching the drama play out. She was short and soft. Whereas Heather looked ready for a photo shoot, Amy looked like she needed a couple of hours in the makeup room. She was pretty, but it was hard to tell under her tangle of hair and the dark rings around her gray eyes. Olivia figured those were symptoms of the problem Heather had hired Infidelity Limited to solve.

Olivia rounded Heather and walked toward the house.

The fitness mogul grabbed Olivia's arm at the bicep. She held up a cell phone in her other hand, no doubt one of Roy's burners. "I'm calling Roy."

Panic and fear were in the woman's expression. That was good. Those two emotions gave Olivia hope that this plan would work. "You call him and I'll be dead before the week is out, and so will you and Amy."

Heather jerked back from the revelation.

"I'm here to save our lives. You need to listen to me. I can't pretend there isn't going to be pain, but I mean you no harm. I promise you."

Heather's grip fell away, and Olivia headed toward the house, with Andrew close behind. She waved to Amy. "You're Amy, right?"

Amy nodded.

"I'm Olivia, and this is Andrew. We've got a lot to talk about."

Olivia slipped past Amy and into the house. Heather chased after her.

"We need to discuss this privately," Heather said.

Olivia shook her head. "It's too late for that."

"What's going on?" Amy said.

"It's regarding a company called Infidelity Limited. I'm one of their clients, and so is Heather. I've got some difficult news for you both." She smiled. "Let's go somewhere comfortable."

Heather looked too shell-shocked to object, and Amy was flat-out confused. Olivia used her advantage to move through the house. Everything was open plan. A sunken living room was the central feature, with a clear view of the ocean and the beach. A dining area connected off to one side, and a kitchen wrapped around the back side, so as not to block the view. A substantial deck sat outside the floor-to-ceiling glass panes. It was all gorgeous.

They sat opposite each other on a vast U-shaped sectional sofa, with Amy and Heather on one side and Olivia and Andrew on the other. The view of the Pacific went ignored. Heather glared at Olivia, while Amy looked baffled at the intrusion. Olivia willed the women to trust her. Amy took Heather's hand. That small display of affection would probably be the last between the couple once Olivia spilled the beans.

"You've got two minutes to explain yourself, then I'm throwing you out," Heather said.

It was bluster. Heather might not know what was going on, but she had to know her secret was about to blow up in her face.

"Heather hired a company called Infidelity Limited," Olivia began. "They offer a service where they will beat up a cheating spouse or an abusive lover. If someone is stepping out of line in your life, they will knock some sense into them, literally."

"Bullshit," Amy said. "Get out before I call the cops."

Heather put her hand on Amy's forearm. "Don't."

"Is what they're saying true?"

"Yes." The admission came out as a shame-filled whisper.

"Why?"

"Why do you think? You've given up on yourself since you lost your job. You constantly max out your credit cards by buying junk you don't need and leave me to clear them. You don't care about you, and you don't care about us. My telling you wasn't working, so I thought it was time for some tough love."

Something broke inside Amy, and she sank back into the sofa. "How could you pay someone to hurt me? Jesus, Heather, how could you?"

"I couldn't deal with it anymore."

"But hurt me?"

"Words weren't working."

"Not that you tried very hard."

"Okay, okay," Andrew said. "You can fight later. Right now you have to listen to us. This isn't over."

"Why should I listen to you?" Amy chided. "You work for these people."

"No," Olivia said. "I'm a client, just like Heather. Can I show you something?"

Amy nodded.

Olivia opened her purse and brought out an edition of the *Contra Costa Times* with Richard's murder on the front page. "Infidelity Limited is a scam. They're not interested in protecting abused women or helping angry spouses get a little revenge. They're about one thing—murder—and they blackmail their existing clients into doing the dirty work for them."

The women picked up the newspaper to read.

"That's my husband. I found out he was cheating on me, and I hired Infidelity Limited to rough him up. Instead, they killed him, blackmailed me, and told me that one day I would get a call and I would have to kill someone to pay back my debt. Well, I got that call, and your name came up." Olivia produced the dossier on Amy from her purse and gave it to her. "If you don't believe me, tell me how accurate this is and who would have been the only person who could have provided the information."

Amy flicked through the pages. She looked at Heather. "This is my whole life in here. How could you?"

Heather managed only a shake of her head.

"If you were hoping for some sort of reconciliation, let this be it," Andrew said.

"I don't understand what you're doing here," Amy said.

"Breaking the cycle," Olivia said. "These people have been successful because the clients have been put in a desperate situation. It stops with us."

"I'll tell them I've changed my mind," Heather said.

"It's too late," Andrew said. "Roy set everything in motion the second you hired him. If Olivia doesn't kill Amy, he'll send someone else to do it. If that happens, Amy ends up dead, Olivia goes to jail, and Roy puts the squeeze on you to kill someone for him the same way he has with Olivia. No one wins. But if you work with us, we all stand a chance of getting out of this."

"What happens now?" Heather asked.

"We have to fake Amy's murder," Olivia said. "I'm going to tell Roy that I killed you and that I did such a seamless job that no one will ever find the body."

"How are you going to say Amy died?" Heather said.

"It's best we don't tell you," Andrew said. "Everything you learn about Amy's death has to come across as a complete shock to you; otherwise, Roy will smell a rat. You can't afford to make any slipups."

"That means you have to disappear," Olivia said to Amy. "You need to go somewhere no one knows you and stay there."

"For how long?" Amy asked.

That was hard to say. Olivia was in unknown territory. Who knew what Roy's next steps would be? "It could be weeks or possibly months. We're going to have to play it by ear."

"Jesus, you're asking a lot," Amy said.

"It's nothing compared to the alternative."

"Okay, but what about me?" Heather said. "If Roy follows through as per his protocol, he's going to tell me Amy's dead and insist that I pay up. Then, a few weeks later, he's going to assign me to kill someone. I can't do that."

You'd be surprised what you can do, Olivia thought.

"I don't think so," Andrew said. "From what we've found out so far, Roy seems to hold off for a period of time before assigning you to kill someone. We think Olivia is being fast-tracked because the person who killed her husband made a mess. There's a police investigation, and they are zeroing in on her. Your case will be different. As far as anyone is concerned, Amy walked out on you. Roy will likely bide his time before telling you to kill someone."

"Do you know that for sure?" Heather said.

"Not for sure."

"This is all so risky."

"We've dug ourselves a deep, dark hole, and it's not going to be easy to climb our way out," Olivia said.

Amy ran her hands through her hair. "Okay, I disappear, but what happens next? You're going to bring this Roy down?"

"Once I fulfill my obligation to Roy and pay his blackmail money, I'm done," Olivia said. "He won't be focusing on me anymore. He'll move on to the next client."

"That would be me," Heather said, waving a hand.

"With the pressure off me, we can focus on Roy. We'll track down the evidence he has on my husband's death, turn the tables on him, and incriminate him. Once he goes down, the hold he has over everyone will be gone."

"How exactly are you going to do that?" Amy asked.

"It's a work in progress," Andrew said.

"In other words, you don't know."

Andrew didn't answer.

"As much as you're grasping at straws, I don't see how you can do anything different," Heather said.

Amy nodded in agreement. "So we'd better kill me, then."

For Amy, the solution was simple—disappear. Heather had the heavy lifting to do. While Amy and Olivia made dinner for everyone, Andrew coached Heather on how to deal with Roy—what to say, what not to say, what to expect from him. Just as he had with Olivia and the polygraph, he role-played her encounters with Roy again and again, each time shaking up the questions and scenarios. Heather got frustrated every time Andrew called her out on her mistakes, which were numerous, but by the time dinner was ready, she was rolling with the verbal punches he threw at her.

While they ate, Amy said, "So when do I die?"

"Now," Olivia said. "On Monday, I'll tell Roy that you're dead, so you need to be gone. I would leave tonight if I were you."

"Remember, you're dead," Andrew said. "That means your belongings and car stay, as do your credit cards. You use cash from now on."

"We can do that," Heather said.

Amy got up and grabbed a bottle of wine and four glasses. "I'd like to propose a toast. To the dearly departed Amy Moore-Marbach. May she rest in peace."

CHAPTER TWENTY-NINE

As planned, Olivia waited until Monday to call Roy to tell him she'd completed her assignment. As a first-time killer, she would need time to process what she'd done before talking to the person who'd forced her to kill. That was her thinking anyway.

"It's done," she said. "Amy Moore-Marbach is dead."

"Really?"

"Yes, really. What did you expect? You told me to do it, so I did it, okay?"

"Okay, okay, Olivia. Calm down."

"Didn't think I could do it?"

"No, I've always had faith in you. I just hadn't expected you to do it so quickly."

He thought she had the makings of a capable killer. She didn't find that a comforting thought. "There was no point in letting it drag on. I saw an opportunity, and I took it."

"Well, we need to walk through this. Meet me at China Cove on Angel Island tomorrow at one o'clock."

The next day, she took the ferry from Tiburon. The boat rolled with the waves. The lazy, rolling motion did nothing for Olivia's already-sensitive stomach. She took in long, slow breaths to quell her rising nausea. It wasn't working. She tried an old trick by focusing on the horizon and not the water. She locked her stare on Angel Island, dead ahead, where Roy was waiting to meet her. Passengers were few in number, which wasn't surprising for a weekday. She expected Roy's precheck crew to shake her down, but no one tailed her during the journey or showed up when she arrived at the ferry pier. Was Roy's trust in her growing, or was it the fact that Angel Island was so isolated that bringing anyone would have been easily noticed?

In its past, Angel Island had been a military garrison and an immigration station, but now it was a state park. Sitting in the middle of the San Francisco Bay, it was only accessible by boat and barred all vehicles except for bicycles and Segways. It was another isolated spot for one of Roy's meetings.

Olivia got an island map from the visitor's center and found that China Cove was less than a mile from the ferry pier, so she walked it. She didn't trust her balance on a bike at the moment. She followed the island road that hugged the island's perimeter.

Olivia had to put on the performance of her life, and she was a wreck. Her hands were cold, her stomach was churning, and she was sweating. She guessed her condition would help sell her story to Roy. She doubted he'd expect her to be calm and collected after what she'd done.

"You can do this," she told herself and wished Andrew were close. She could have done with the support of someone who believed in her.

She reached China Cove, which had been home to the old immigration station. She ignored the historical site and walked out onto the beach. Roy wasn't there to meet her. No doubt he was watching her from some vantage point. She kicked off her shoes and stepped into the water, letting the waves lap over her feet. The water was cold, but she enjoyed the sensation.

Just as she reached the water's edge, she heard her name being called. She turned to see Roy emerging from one of the barracks. He joined her on the beach.

C'mon, Olivia, she thought, *do the sales job of your life.*

He smiled at her, but his eyes weren't so jovial. Olivia felt his gaze appraising her as if he were searching for something. *For a lie, maybe?* She didn't think so. Roy was all about preserving himself. He was making sure she wasn't coming apart at the seams. Hopefully a few frayed edges would convince him.

"Have you been here before?" Roy jerked a thumb at the building behind him. "Amazing history."

"I'm not here for the cultural benefits."

"I suppose not," he said. "How are you doing?"

"How do you think? I feel like shit. I killed someone for you."

"And I'm grateful and impressed."

"Like that counts for anything."

"Olivia, you're acting like a child, and you're better than that."

"Sorry if I'm disappointing you, but if we're being honest with each other, I don't really give a shit what you think about me. All I want is to be free of you, and that's why I'm here. Are we done?"

Olivia's heart was pounding, but she liked her performance. It didn't sound fake. Mainly because it wasn't. A good lie was 80 percent truth, and there was no deception when it came to how she felt about the hole she was in.

"We still have a ways to go before we're done," Roy replied. "C'mon, let's walk and talk."

They followed the path back to the road. Olivia wasn't surprised by Roy's answer. There'd always be a reason why they weren't done. Infidelity Limited would always want her chasing after that carrot.

"Okay," Roy asked. "How'd you do it?"

"You really need to know?"

"Yes, I need to know how clean the kill was. I can do without a mess like Richard's death."

Or is he checking to see whether I'm a liar or not? Her greatest fear was that he'd suspect that she'd tried to deceive him. She surely wasn't the first to try that tactic. "Amy was staying at her beach house in Morro Bay. I gave myself a flat tire and knocked on the door, saying I needed to call AAA."

Roy laughed. "Very slick."

"I got Amy into the house, and I pulled a gun. I bound her hands, and I shot her."

"Wow, that must have been quite a moment."

"It was, and one I hope to never repeat." She couldn't keep the contempt out of her voice.

"Was there a mess?"

"Not as much as you'd think. I did it in the bathtub. It kept the mess contained. I washed the tub down with enough Clorox to destroy the blood evidence."

"Where'd the gun come from?"

"I have friends, but don't worry. It's not registered."

Roy smiled. "Do you have it?"

"No, I disposed of it."

"Shame, I would have liked to have kept ahold of it for safekeeping."

I bet you would, she thought. She wouldn't let him hang her twice.

"What did you do with the body?"

"I rented a van with a hand truck. The hand truck made it easy to move the body. I found a spot north of Cayucos and dumped the body off the cliffs. According to the tide charts, the body should be drawn out to sea. There's a chance that it'll be washed back up, but if it is, it should be a couple of hundred miles up the coast, and by then there'll be little to recognize."

"Anything go wrong? And be honest. You know how I don't like surprises."

"Nothing went wrong. No one saw me. There's no record or trail of receipts that will link me to this."

"The perfect murder."

"As perfect as it can be."

Roy smiled. A couple of people on bikes whipped by them. "You've impressed me, Olivia. I knew you had what it takes. It's why I put you through an accelerated schedule."

"Does this mean we're done? You don't have any more surprises for me, right?"

He laughed. "No, no more surprises, but we're not done. I still need that hundred grand you owe me. Once you've paid me, I'll be gone from your life." He saluted. "Scout's honor."

Olivia didn't believe him. There'd always be a twist. "I'll get you the money soon. I'm in the process of liquidating some assets without leaving a trail for the cops to find."

"Good." They came to a bench that looked out over the water. Roy pointed to it, and they sat. "How are you doing with the police?"

"Not well. They believe I'm involved somehow. Instead of looking for the killer, they're interviewing everyone about me. I don't think they have any proof, but they don't have any suspects either, so I'm the next best thing."

Olivia didn't see any point in lying to Roy about Finz's investigation. She had the feeling that Roy would be keeping close tabs on the proceedings and waiting in the wings to burn her at the first sign that the cops were moving in. She didn't want to give him any reason to doubt what she said.

"Is there any chance you'd help throw the cops' interest off me and onto the person who killed Richard?" she asked.

"Sadly, no chance. I have to protect all my clients the best I can, even if that means some, like you, have to go through a bad time. Like you say, if the cops only have their suspicions, there's not a lot they can do." He looked at his watch. "I have to go. No rest for the wicked and all that."

He smiled at his joke. Olivia didn't. She couldn't laugh at anything he said. She remembered Karen Innes, the woman who had tried to shoot Nick, currently rotting in prison for the alleged murder of her husband. Roy didn't protect anyone. He took his clients for everything they had and left them standing in the wreckage.

Roy stood. "I'll take the next ferry. You take the one after me."

"I have a question."

"Yes?"

"What made you think I'd follow through on this?"

Roy smiled with what looked like pride. "I like to think of myself as a good judge of talent, and I knew you had what it takes. You're a survivor, Olivia, even if that means you have to kill to achieve it."

It embarrassed her that Roy saw her as a killer. She was nothing like he imagined. She couldn't murder someone. What signal was she broadcasting that made Roy think she could? But he was right about her in one respect. She was a survivor, and she would do everything possible to survive Infidelity Limited. Roy would learn that at his expense.

*   *   *

The ferry slowed as it approached the pier in Sausalito. Roy was still smiling. He'd been smiling for the entire ride back from Angel Island. At last, something had gone right. Olivia had delivered him a clean kill. The last few Infidelity Limited kills had gotten away from him. His clients' clumsy and amateurish attempts had brought unwanted police interest and forced him to take drastic measures.

The boat docked, and he climbed off with his fellow passengers. He checked his watch as he stepped off the gangway. He had enough time to squeeze in his due diligence.

He got into his car and picked up 101, heading south. As he crossed the Golden Gate Bridge, he cast a look back at Angel Island, where Olivia was no doubt still mourning her predicament. She'd proved to be the model client, and it would be a shame when the cops finally came for her. *I guess I'll just have to take solace in the payday I'll be getting from her,* he mused.

Just as his drive started to feel mundane, his thoughts turned to Beth. He didn't like her mind-set at the moment. He didn't understand her. Yes, she was angry at the world for all it had done to her, and she'd created Infidelity Limited to take her revenge. It worked for her. It kept her level. In the last year though, it didn't seem to bring her any joy, and he didn't get that. The business was fantastic. They were making more money than they ever had. He knew that part wasn't important to her, but the lives they ruined were, and their head count was at its highest.

After that shit with digging up Maxwell the other night, he needed to bring in a professional before she really lost it. Finding the right guy was the problem.

He called Luis. "How's Beth?"

"Okay. I found a stash of empty acetone bottles in the garden. She bought off one of the housekeepers to smuggle it in for her."

"Goddamn it."

"I know. I fired the crew this morning. I'll have another in by next week. I haven't talked to Beth about the acetone, but I can."

"No, don't. I'll do it when I get home. While you're looking into housekeepers, I have another job for you."

"Shoot."

"Find me a shrink who'll get her off this downward spiral."

"You got it. Anything else?"

"No, just keep an eye on her. If she's hoarding acetone, she'll be stockpiling other materials. I don't want her doing some real damage."

"On it."

"Thanks. I'll see you when I see you," he said and hung up.

It was late afternoon when he reached Morro Bay. He drove by Heather Moore-Marbach's beach house first. The place was silent and looked unmolested. He parked his Chrysler and came back. He tried the main gate and found it locked, so he scaled a fence to get into the courtyard, then used his lock picks to get into the house. The place showed no sign of a scuffle. Olivia was good. The use of a hand truck to move the body was a stroke of genius. Maybe he should sacrifice Proctor and take Olivia on full-time. Unfortunately, he didn't get the feeling she would accept such a role. It was a shame.

He went into the bathroom, Olivia's makeshift killing room. The place was clean, but he did smell a whiff of bleach in the room. He'd leave the bathroom door open to help air it out. He brought out a black light and waved it over the bathtub and the tiled walls. It came back clean. No blood spray to find should the cops come a calling. They might squawk at the cleanliness of the bathroom, but that would be all they could do. It might be suspicious, but cleanliness wasn't a crime.

Thanks to Olivia, Heather's position was looking pretty intact.

He ran the black light over the other rooms Olivia would have had to pass through on her way out. She'd taken care of the bathroom, but she still could have tracked blood out of the house. Just as he expected, he found nothing. *Good girl.*

He saw himself out and reclaimed his car, then drove out to the spot where Olivia said she'd cast Amy's body into the water. He found the lookout point and waited for the couple making out in a car to leave before he climbed out of his vehicle.

He walked up to what remained of the wooden railing that protected him from the three-story drop to the water below. The ocean rushed in and smashed into the cliff. The term "angry water" was invented for this little spit of coastline. He imagined Olivia releasing the straps on the hand truck and Amy's body tumbling into the sea. There was no sign of her body on the beach or in the water below. He smiled. Olivia seemed to have executed a well-thought-out murder and disposal. He expected nothing less.

It was time to move this game on to the next stage. He pulled out his cell and scrolled past the multiple panicked voice mails that Heather had left for him. He called Heather's number. "Hi, Heather, it's Roy. I'm calling you about Amy. Something terrible has happened."

CHAPTER THIRTY

Olivia arrived at the Central California Women's Facility on an oppressively hot Tuesday morning to see Karen Innes. The prison stuck out against its surroundings. Farmland hemmed in the octagonal-shaped facility from all sides. Its concrete-and-razor-wire facade was the definition of institutional ugliness. Olivia's palms began to sweat when she turned into the visitors' parking lot.

Entering the state prison was a chilling reminder that if she didn't slip Infidelity Limited's stranglehold, prison life would be her life. Olivia didn't know what it was like to be an inmate, but she got the idea the moment she entered the visitors' center. She couldn't enter without complying with a specified dress code, passing through an airport-style metal detector, and being subjected to a pat-down. Her purse was searched and passed through an X-ray machine. Someone was always there to tell her what to do and when to do it. The rigmarole chilled her.

The men, women, and children waiting in line with her all shared the same look of melancholy resentment. This place held someone they loved, and there was nothing any of them could do about it. At least if her future brought her here, there'd be no one to burden with the pain of losing her.

Prison officers ushered her into a room of individual booths with bulletproof glass between her and the inmates. Karen Innes was already waiting for her when she reached her designated booth. She looked nothing like the pictures Olivia had seen in the online news coverage of her trial. In those, she'd been an attractive thirty-one-year-old, with long auburn hair and a pale complexion. Now her hair was shorter, with no discernible style, and the lack of makeup robbed her of her femininity. Five years into her twenty-five-years-to-life sentence, it wasn't that she looked older but that she looked hardened. It was clear in her harsh stare and the set of her jaw. She could cut you down with a look. She eyed Olivia with contempt.

Olivia took the phone off the wall to her right. Karen did likewise.

"Thanks for seeing me," Olivia began.

"When someone says they're from the Victims of Infidelity Limited Support Group, how can I say no?"

The support group was the line Olivia had used on Karen's lawyer to get her a visitation appointment. The name wouldn't mean anything to anyone else, but Olivia knew Karen would read between the widely drawn lines.

"How secure is this line?" Olivia asked.

"No one can listen in. These handsets are connected to each other and nothing else. They're magnetic or something."

That gave Olivia some comfort. This wasn't the most secure location for this discussion. The burble of conversation did more for privacy than the wooden partitions between the booths. She decided it was safe to talk because the visitors around her were more interested in talking to their loved ones than listening to anybody else's conversation.

"I didn't think I'd hear from you people again," Karen snapped. "I don't know why you're here. You've gotten all you're getting from me."

"I'm not with them. I'm what you'd call a kindred spirit."

The remark caught Karen's attention, but Olivia didn't think it bought her trust, judging from her piercing stare.

Karen leaned forward in her chair. "Is that right? How deep are they into you?"

Olivia knew she was taking a risk admitting anything to Karen. There'd be nothing stopping Karen from selling the knowledge for a reduced sentence. But Olivia was past the point of safe solutions. Everything she did held a risk. Even doing nothing was a risk. She'd prefer to go down fighting. "I'm at the point where you were when you tried to kill my brother-in-law, Nick Bonanni."

That cracked Karen's prison-hardened shell. A flicker of fear shot across her face. "How did you find out about him?"

"I've been doing a little backtracking. It led me back to him, and he led me to you. He remembers how frightened you were." *The way you look now,* Olivia thought. "You want to tell me about it?"

Karen licked her lips. "If you're where I was, you know the story."

"But I want to know your story."

Karen just stared at Olivia. She appeared to be weighing the pros and cons of telling Olivia anything. After a long moment, she said, "Screw it. What does it matter anymore? Roy came to me after my husband was killed. I used to be an interior designer. I went to a property for a consultation, and Roy was there. He told me I had to kill Nick Bonanni. When I told him I couldn't do it, he told me he'd frame me for my husband's murder. It was a him-or-me situation, so I went through with it."

"But you didn't."

Karen barked a bitter laugh. "I wanted to, needed to, but when it came to the squeeze of the trigger, I couldn't do it. Just like you."

Olivia's body tingled. "What makes you say that?"

"Something dark like that sticks to you, and it can't be washed off, regardless of how much soap and lies you use. You're still clean. Not for long though."

Karen was trying to frighten her. Olivia wouldn't let her. "What happened when you didn't follow through?"

"I pleaded with Roy for a second chance, but there are no second chances when it comes to Roy."

Olivia got that impression. He was the definition of self-preservation. It didn't matter what happened to anyone else as long as his security remained intact. Maybe that was a weakness she could exploit.

"What happened then?" Olivia asked.

"Roy wanted money. I paid him off. Have you paid him?"

"Not yet. How much did he get from you?"

"Fifty grand."

She got off cheap. Roy wants twice that much from me, Olivia thought.

"My advice is to delay the payment for as long as you can, because the second he's got it, he's gone. After I paid, he cut me off. He stopped answering his phone, but he found a new way of communicating. Evidence from my husband's murder started turning up. Eventually, the cops had enough to charge me, and the rest is history."

"So Roy framed you?"

"Of course he did. I was a liability. If I'd killed Nick, maybe things would have been different, but I doubt it. He would have screwed me regardless."

"Why?"

"My husband's murder was a public one. The cops were all over it, and someone had to go down for the crime. If Roy hadn't set me up for it, it would have tracked back to someone close to him. He had to give them a scapegoat. If the cops hadn't gotten involved, Roy might have taken the money and left me alone."

Karen's tale mirrored her own so closely that it left her cold. Roy was going to screw her. He was probably working on framing her as they spoke.

Karen smiled. "Don't tell me. Yours is a messy one too, isn't it?"

Olivia said nothing.

"You're fucked. Whatever Roy tells you, don't believe him. No matter what you do, it'll never be enough. You're a liability. He will burn you to save himself."

Olivia refused to accept her fate. She wouldn't be another of Roy's victims. There was still time. She hung up the phone.

Karen knocked on the glass and pointed to the phone. Olivia put the receiver back to her ear.

"I'm sorry. I didn't mean to be cruel. I got a little carried away. You want a way out, right?"

Olivia nodded.

"Roy likes to boast that he leaves no trail. That's bullshit. He might not blaze a trail to his door, but he leaves one. Roy burns his clients. Whatever happens, you're going to end up like me, so my advice to you is to burn him before he burns you."

CHAPTER THIRTY-ONE

"Refill?" the waitress asked Roy.

He smiled and held up his cup. "Please."

As she poured coffee into his cup, she glanced over at the diner's owner at the register. Roy could feel the guy willing him to leave. The place was cramped with a dozen tables. He had a four-top to himself, and he'd been nursing a cup of coffee and reading the newspaper for over an hour while hungry people stood waiting on the Long Beach streets.

"Is the food okay?" the waitress asked.

He'd hardly touched his eggs. There wasn't anything wrong with them. He just needed somewhere to hole up while he waited on a call from Carrington. He and Dolores were in the process of picking up and frisking Heather Moore-Marbach before he dropped his facts of life, Infidelity Limited–style, on her. "Yeah, it's good. I'm just taking it slow."

That answer earned another shared glance between owner and waitress. He'd make it up to them by leaving fifty bucks for the inconvenience and their foresight in not fucking with him.

The waitress left for the next table, and he returned to his paper. Not that he was truly reading it. His thoughts kept turning to Olivia.

She continued to astound him. The woman had some real grit. She followed through and did what had to be done. As soon as he'd gotten a string of calls from Heather saying that Amy had gone missing, he'd known Olivia had followed through. He didn't know too many people who killed without a fuss. He wished he didn't have to burn her at the end. She deserved a win.

His cell rang. Carrington's familiar number appeared on the display with no identifier. *Always numbers. Never names.*

He picked up the phone. "Yeah?"

"She's on the boat, primed and ready for you," Carrington said.

"Be there in ten."

He dropped a fifty-dollar bill on the table and left before the check could be presented.

During the drive, he refined his pitch. He was playing things a little differently with Heather Moore-Marbach. She represented a different class of client. He estimated he could take her for a million, as she was by far his highest-earning client. He didn't have to take her for everything all at once. Olivia had presented him with a clean kill. His plan was for a two-part payoff. The first stage was to hit her with the story that there'd been a terrible accident and he'd require a fee to cover it up. Then, he'd follow up again in a year's time with the truth about Infidelity Limited and explain that if she wanted to avoid killing someone, she'd have to pay her way out. He liked this double play because Heather didn't come off as the type who could keep her powder dry in a clinch.

He arrived at the boat ramp across from Mothers Beach on the east side of the city and parked on the street. The cabin cruiser Carrington had chartered for the morning with a fake ID wasn't much, just a twenty-footer with an enclosed pilothouse, but it was good enough for what he needed. He didn't want anything that stuck out. Anonymous worked fine.

Carrington stood on the jetty next to the stern line. Dolores stood over Heather in the pilothouse. The boat's engine chugged lazily, all ready for him.

Roy put on his game face as he stepped aboard, saying, "A glorious morning."

"What's going on?" Heather said with fear in her voice.

"Just going out on the water for a private chat."

He nodded to Dolores, and she left without acknowledging him. She tossed Carrington the bow and stern lines before she stepped off the boat. Roy took the controls, eased the throttle forward, and took the boat out onto the water.

"Why haven't you been answering my calls, Roy? I went out the other night, and I haven't seen Amy since. I thought that maybe your people had gotten to her and she'd run off, but she didn't take anything with her. She's not at our home or at the beach house. She's not with her friends. I've tried her cell, and it goes straight to voice mail. What's going on, Roy?"

"Take a breath, Heather."

"But—"

He raised a hand. "Take a breath."

She looked ahead at the water and did as she was told, inhaling and exhaling a few times. Each breath was ragged and untidy. For someone who ran a burgeoning gym empire, she seemed to know little about breath control. Roy noticed her grip on the handrail. It was white-knuckle tight, a little too tight for the motion over the water. A nervous sailor? He didn't think so. The fear was in her, and that was a good thing. Fear kept clients on the straight and narrow.

What do her fears whisper to her? he wondered. *What delusions will she respond with to keep her fears in check?*

"What's happened?" she asked. "Please tell me. I haven't seen Amy since the weekend. Your people did their thing, didn't they?"

He got the boat out past the breakwater and cut the power. The noise level dropped, and it became stunningly quiet on the boat. All he could hear was the slap, slap of the water against the hull and the distant murmur of the road noise from the city. He didn't drop anchor, choosing to let the tide take the cruiser wherever it decided.

"Yes, my people did their thing," he replied.

"Oh God, she's angry, isn't she? Shit. This was a mistake. I overreacted."

This was the kind of self-recrimination Roy had heard dozens of times, and he was okay with it. He needed a little panic in the bloodstream to get the best effect from his clients.

He placed a comforting hand on Heather's shoulder. "Now, I've got something serious to tell you. It's important. I need you to prepare yourself for this. I just want you to know it wasn't meant to go down like this."

Heather chewed at her lip until a pinprick of blood appeared.

"There was a problem."

"Oh my God."

"I'll be honest. We underestimated Amy. She fought back. It turned into a struggle. My people were forced to defend themselves, and I'm afraid to say in that struggle Amy was killed."

"What?"

"This is an unpredictable business, and sometimes things like this happen. It's the risk that we all have to accept."

"Amy's dead?"

"Yes. I'm sorry."

The slap took him by surprise. It wasn't the first time someone had lashed out at him when he dropped the bomb. He hadn't quite expected it from Heather. He would have put his money on a crying jag.

She swung at him again. He caught her wrist, twisted her arm around, and pinned it against her back. He wrapped his free arm across her chest. She squirmed under his grasp, but he pulled her tight against him, bringing the fight to an end.

"I know, I know," he cooed. "It hurts, but you have to be smart now if you don't want to go to jail."

"If I don't want to go to jail?"

He released her and took a step back.

She whirled around. "What are you talking about?"

"You hired Infidelity Limited to hurt Amy."

"Yes, to hurt her. Not to kill her."

"There's premeditation here. That's murder in the first degree. That's a life sentence for you."

"But you killed her."

"On your orders. That's all the cops will see."

"But I . . . I . . . I didn't."

"The cops won't believe you."

"No . . . no . . . no, this can't be happening. What have you done?"

He rubbed a reassuring hand over her shoulders and told her it was going to be okay. She tensed under his touch. He wasn't offended under the circumstances. He was the bogeyman, after all.

"What happened? Where is she?"

"This is where we have to be smart. Now, Amy doesn't have to be found. We can make it look as if she simply disappeared. You can spin whatever tale you like. You guys had a tiff over her out-of-control spending, and she cleaned you out and ran off with whatever she could carry. We know she's dead, but the rest of the world doesn't have to know."

"You can do that?"

"Yes, I can take care of the crime scene and take some of her stuff to make it look like she ran out. I can leave a dummy electronic trail of her movements, and no one will ever suspect she's dead." He paused for effect. Actually, he quite liked this twist on his usual pitch. "Naturally, there will be an expense to you."

"Me? Why am I paying you? This is your mistake. Not mine."

He thought she was going to ask for a refund. He put that down to her CEO status, her business instincts taking over her emotions. He could dig that, so he responded in kind.

"We might not have a written contract, but I was very clear at the beginning. All the risk is yours. Nothing is ever Infidelity Limited's problem. We are not liable for any mistakes."

She stared at him openmouthed.

"Right now, we're at a crucial juncture. The situation is in stasis. It can go either way. I can make it go away for you, but if you don't pay for it to go away, then I will lead a bloody trail of bread crumbs to your door, starting with Amy's body."

He couldn't actually make good on that threat since Olivia had disposed of the body so efficiently, but he knew without a doubt Heather would pay.

"If you take me down, I take you down," Heather replied.

Of all the threats slung his way, this was the chart topper. He parried it aside with a laugh. Then he hit her with "the speech," outlining how Infidelity Limited was an untouchable entity that possessed the power to implicate its clients. Although he'd spoken the same words time and time again, he didn't tire of them, because they never lost their impact, and they didn't this time.

"Have I made myself clear?" he asked when he was done.

Heather was silent for a long moment before she spoke. "How much?"

"Four hundred thousand to sanitize the situation."

"You're crazy. I only paid you five grand to take care of the situation. Now you want four hundred?"

That wasn't the response he was expecting. Normally, people feigned poverty. They never complained about overcharging. Heather was a hard-nosed businesswoman all right.

"Arranging a beating isn't the same as covering up a murder," he said. "The price is nonnegotiable."

"You really are a son of a bitch."

"I'll take that as a yes."

"Get me out of here."

He fired up the boat's engine and steered it back toward the marina. They rode back in silence. As he eased the cruiser back into the slip, Carrington stepped forward, grabbing the stern line.

"When you have the money ready, get in touch," Roy said, "but be quick about it. Take too long and I will make sure Amy is found. Okay?"

She nodded.

"My people will take you back to your car."

Heather said nothing and brushed by him. He grabbed her wrist. She tried to shake him off, but he tightened his hold.

"Be smart."

"It's a little late for that."

Isn't that the truth, he thought.

Heather stepped off the boat, and Dolores escorted her back to the van. As Roy watched them go, Carrington fell in next to him.

"How'd it go?"

"Not sure. We need to keep an eye on her."

CHAPTER THIRTY-TWO

Roy lagged a few blocks behind the van Carrington was driving with Heather Moore-Marbach and Dolores in the back. The moments after telling a client that Infidelity Limited had exceeded its remit and killed his or her loved one were crucial. Clients went one of two ways—they either manned up to the situation or fell apart and ran to the cops. That meant around-the-clock surveillance for a day or two, less if the clients could hold their shit together. His gut said it would be longer in Heather's case. She was a privileged person, and he was gouging her for big money. She might think that privilege would work in her favor with the cops, considering the amount of money on the line. At this point, the situation was abstract for her, and she wouldn't truly comprehend what was at stake. There was no blood, no body, and no detective to help her understand the black hole she was falling through. Olivia had gotten it in a snap. She had a corpse, a murder investigation, and the guilt to scare her straight. He might have to do something similar to Heather to help her come to the same realization.

Carrington stopped the van in La Brea, and Roy pulled over half a block behind them. It was over a minute before Heather emerged, staggering away from the van. The second her feet hit the sidewalk, the van lurched back into traffic with a screech of tires.

She watched the van speed off, looking bewildered and confused. Dealing with Infidelity Limited did that to a person.

Roy's cell rang. He answered.

"She's all yours," Carrington said.

"I've got eyes on her."

Heather staggered over to her Porsche Boxster and fell in behind the wheel.

"You want us to stick around?" Carrington asked.

"No," Roy said. "I'm good. Just return the boat."

"Will do."

"Get some rest. We're going around the clock for the next forty-eight. Rolling eight-hour shifts. The rotation is me, then Dolores, then you."

"Sounds good. Let me know if you need anything."

"I will," Roy said and hung up.

Heather continued to sit behind the wheel of her car. She didn't call anyone. She just sat with her hands on the wheel and her head down.

Looks as if it's just sunk in, Roy thought.

Finally, she got going, and Roy followed her to her flagship gym and head office in Beverly Hills. Moore Fitness had the corner lot, and it was a glass-fronted two-story billboard. Inside, dozens of people were getting fitter from the bench press and jumping jacks—and all thanks to Heather Moore-Marbach.

She pulled into the private underground parking garage, forcing him to find street parking. He found a spot with plenty of shade that gave him a clear view of the garage exit and Heather's corner office.

He adjusted his seat and bedded in for a long wait. He had all he needed for a surveillance shift—water and soda for hydration, an empty soda bottle for dehydration, snacks, and change for the meter.

After a couple of hours, it was pretty obvious that Heather was going to stick it out at work. He took this as a good sign. If she planned to run to the cops, she would have done it by now. So far, the only people to come to the gym were clientele. No cops and no lawyers.

"Keep playing it smart, Heather," he said to himself.

He pulled out a small set of binoculars, which looked childlike in his hands, from the Chrysler's door pocket and aimed them at Heather's office window. He dug out the burner phone and called her. He watched her stiffen at what had to be the sound of the phone ringing. She pulled the phone from her purse and answered.

"Yes?"

"Hello, Heather."

"What do you want?" she barked at him.

"It's been an emotional day. Just checking in."

"Just leave me alone."

"Can't do that. We're on the clock. Do you have an update on that money?" He chose to say "that money" and not "my money." It gave the perception they were discussing an expense and not a payoff. "I can take cash, or we can set up a wire transfer."

"I can't come up with that kind of money just like that. I don't have that much cash on hand."

"Sell some things. Take out a loan. Do whatever you have to do. I can't sit on Amy's body forever. I may have to leave it somewhere it can be found."

"All right, you've made your point. You'll get paid," she said and hung up.

Through the binoculars, he watched her make four phone calls. He hoped the calls were to her bankers. He wondered if Infidelity Limited should invest in a hacker or a telecommunications expert. It would be useful for him to be able to tap phone lines and monitor computer activity. He hadn't needed to so far, but the world was always changing and upgrading.

He noted down the time of the calls in his logbook. The logbook might seem like overkill—it did to Beth—but it helped him see changes in behavior should a client deviate from the path.

At four, Heather grabbed her things and headed out of the gym. She was on the move. He quickly wrote down the time and put everything away.

A few minutes later, she emerged from the underground garage with a smile on her face. Whatever she'd discussed in those phone calls had left her in a good mood. He started the Chrysler and slipped into traffic behind her.

He expected her to drive home, but instead of picking up the I-10 west to her home in Santa Monica, she took it heading east.

"Where are you going, Heather?" he said to himself.

She could be on her way to meet a client for a private session. Reportedly, she still made house calls if you were willing to drop five hundred bucks an hour. But that grin told him otherwise. It was the wrong signal, and it just added to his disquiet about Heather. He had expected more emotion on the boat. What he'd first taken as shock could be read as indifference. Then there'd been the reluctant acceptance of the $400,000 payment instead of rushing to pay to make the problem go away. Finally, there was her snippiness on the phone. All of it just didn't quite ring true for him. He'd dealt with enough clients over the years to know every one of them was different, but there were certain patterns of behavior. Even his strongest clients lost their rhythm when he clobbered them with the news that their loved one was dead. But not Heather. She had seemingly taken the news on the chin and carried on like normal, which made Roy nervous.

Running an around-the-clock watch on Heather for an extended period of time would be a resource drain. He could force the issue by ordering her kill assignment now and watching how she reacted to that. Right now, she was living the life she wanted—without her leech of a wife. Her behavior might change if she had to get her hands dirty, though he wasn't so sure about that. Besides, he still had Olivia in play. He made it a rule to manage client kills one at a time. To do otherwise was a risk he wasn't willing to take. No, he'd have to ride this one out until he could draw a line through Olivia.

Traffic was heavy going through LA, and he stayed tucked in behind her as they kept limping east. He kept expecting her to pull off, but she kept going, eventually switching to I-605 north. When she took the Foothill Freeway toward San Bernardino, it looked as if she was heading somewhere serious.

He pulled out his cell and called Heather's office.

"Hi, this is Jeff Marshal from Nautilus," he lied. "I've been talking to Heather all this week, and I was wondering if she could squeeze me in this afternoon. I know it's short notice."

"Sorry, she's out for the rest of the day."

"Damn. I was hoping to catch her. Is she in over the weekend?"

"No, she doesn't work weekends, but she's back on Monday. I can squeeze you in on Monday afternoon."

Roy sucked air through his teeth. "That won't work. I'm in Arizona all next week. You know what? I'll touch base with her when I'm back in town. Thanks so much for your help," he said and hung up.

So Heather was going away for the weekend. That was interesting. She normally spent her weekends in Morro Bay. Going somewhere new didn't make sense. Neither did her grin. Something was definitely wrong.

He punched Carrington's number into his cell. "You busy?" he asked when Carrington answered.

"Nope. What do you need?"

"Backup. Heather is heading out of town. I'm on the Foothill Freeway, heading east."

"I'll be on the road in thirty."

"Good. I'll keep you posted."

He hung up and settled into the drive.

Heather's car ate up the miles. She stayed on the freeway, bypassing San Bernardino and heading toward Highland. The way she drove, she was blissfully unaware of him following her. Roy was glad he made it a policy to start any surveillance with a full tank of gas. It was a lesson he'd learned the hard way a long time ago.

When she turned off the freeway and took Highway 330 into the mountains, Roy knew exactly where she was going—Big Bear Lake. That was interesting, because she didn't own any property there. He didn't like not knowing things about his clients.

The traffic got thick as Roy followed Heather into Big Bear Lake. Even so, he ended up with only a two-car buffer between himself and her. She was on her cell, laughing at the conversation she was having. He really needed to work out a way of tapping his clients' phones.

The traffic eased up when she took the road toward Big Bear Mountain and the resort area. There wasn't much on this route other than vacation homes and the occasional shop or restaurant. After a mile, she turned left onto a private road that climbed into a forested area with a number of high-end rental properties.

He couldn't follow after her. With no other traffic, he'd stick out, so he kept going until he reached a scenic overlook. He got his gun from the glove box and pocketed it.

He jogged back to the turnoff Heather had taken and walked up the road. It dead-ended half a mile ahead, but two roads intersected it before it did. Half a dozen widely spaced homes sat on either side of the road. Less than half the homes looked to be occupied, with no cars parked in front and no movement inside.

Secluded and deserted, he thought.

He didn't see Heather's Porsche parked on the street at the first intersecting road, but he spotted it on the next. It was parked in front of a two-story Swiss-style chalet. It had a great view of the lake and the street.

He followed the road to the end, where a barrier blocked any farther passage with a sign that proclaimed "Fire Road—No Authorized Personnel Beyond This Point." He clambered over the barrier and disappeared into the tree line, then traced a path to the rear of the chalet. Despite the expensive homes, there weren't any fences separating the properties. He could simply walk up to the back door.

When the chalet came into view, he descended the slope, traversing as far as he could while the trees still hid him. Using his pocket binoculars, he looked into the house and saw movement. Not just the movement of one person, but two. The other person was Amy Moore-Marbach.

Rage boiled up in him in seconds. So much was at the heart of that rage. He'd known something was off, but he wasn't expecting a deception as extensive as this. Worse, Olivia had played him when he thought he had her in the palm of his hand. Goddamn, he knew she was different from his other clients, but he never thought she had the balls to take him on. Part of him wanted to congratulate her, but a much more seething part of him wanted to kill her. He punched the tree trunk next to his head.

He yanked out his phone and called Carrington.

"People have been lying to us," he told Carrington. "Amy is alive."

"What do you want to do?"

"Take those bitches back home to Morro Bay."

"Then what?"

"Make a mess."

CHAPTER THIRTY-THREE

Finz was on his way back to his desk from lunch when Madeleine Lyon phoned him to let him know Olivia Shaw had arrived for her interview. He could have hurried back to the department, but he took his time. He wanted Olivia to sweat a little.

He'd wanted to call her in straight after Richard Shaw's funeral. Her sister offering to be a confidential informant set off the biggest warning flare in police history. The sisters were involved. But rushing to bring them in wasn't the smart play. Police work was all about the long game. He made sure he had everything in place before he made the big push. He had approval to give Clare a deal, but he wanted that as backup. He wanted a shot at Olivia first. He thought he could break her, and if he couldn't, he had Clare as insurance.

He drove into the police lot and parked. He walked through the lobby to see if Olivia had brought any company in the guise of Andrew Macready or even Clare herself, but the lobby was empty.

"Olivia Shaw?" he asked the officer working the reception area.

"In an interview room," he said.

He grabbed the case file off his desk and stopped at the video-observation suite. Lyon was watching video feed from the interview room.

"How's she doing?" he asked.

"She's spooked."

That was where he wanted her. He'd hoped leaving her alone would make her sweat. There was something about putting suspects in a small room with no windows that always shook them up.

He winked at Lyon. "Make sure you get all of this recorded."

*   *   *

Finz let himself into the interview room. "Sorry to have kept you waiting, Mrs. Shaw. Can I get you something to drink? We'll be here for some time."

A prickle of fear ran through Olivia. This wasn't a friendly chat. It was an interrogation. "How long?"

"That depends on your answers. We do have a lot to talk about. Would you like coffee or soda?"

She shook her head.

He slipped into the chair opposite Olivia, pulled his seat forward, and nudged the table that sat between them. Since the flooring was slick, the table slid into her. He didn't bother pulling it back. Olivia shifted her seat backward a couple of inches in response. The back of her chair hit the wall.

Is this a little trick of yours? she thought. *Are you trying to make me feel cornered?* The cheap psychological ploy wasn't going to work on her.

"Do you mind if I call you Olivia?"

"No, I don't mind."

He opened his file and made a pretense of looking for something. He had something on her, or he thought he did. Had she made a mistake? She didn't think so. Had Roy leaked something? He'd threatened to, but she couldn't see him doing that until she'd paid him. *Don't panic,* she told herself. *Don't volunteer anything. Let him do the talking.*

"Okay, just a couple of things to confirm first," he began. "You were with your sister the night your husband was killed, correct?"

"Yes."

"Hmm."

What did "hmm" mean? There was no disputing that she was with Clare at the time Richard was murdered. "Is there a problem?"

"Cassie Hill, are you sure you don't know her?"

"No."

"You sure about that? She was at your husband's funeral."

Play dumb, she told herself. "Yes. Who is she?"

Finz turned to a page in his file and tapped it. "That's interesting, because a woman matching your description and driving a black Audi sedan matching yours was seen outside Miss Hill's home on the evening of your husband's murder, pounding on the door and shouting. Care to explain that?"

Olivia felt her face flush. She willed it not to show and failed. Finz smiled. He'd scored a point, and he knew it. *Damn,* she thought.

"Care to comment, Olivia?"

He obviously had a witness who might be able to ID her.

"Why were you outside Miss Hill's home, Olivia?" He injected a heavy note of empathy into the question.

"I didn't know her name was Cassie Hill."

"But you were outside her home."

She said nothing because Finz didn't have anything. She wasn't about to do his job for him by volunteering information.

"Olivia, if you think your Fifth Amendment rights are going to save you, they aren't. Your silence will only drag this out." He leaned back in his chair. "Okay, let's come at this from a different angle. Your husband was having an affair and was using his athletic club as a cover. Did you know?"

Olivia broke eye contact and stared at the table. *So Finz knows about Cassie and the affair,* she thought, *but does his knowledge extend to Infidelity Limited?* She didn't see how it could.

"I'm assuming you did because you went to his mistress's house to have it out with them. I know you know. Look, this is embarrassing, but it's just you and me. Why don't you tell me about it?"

He waited for her answer, letting the silence work against her. The room seemed to shrink. She didn't see a way out of answering his question. She could ask for a lawyer, but that would send up a red flag, inviting more scrutiny.

Olivia looked up at him. "Yes, I knew Richard was having an affair."

Finz smiled a consolatory smile. "I'm sorry. How long had it been going on?"

She shook her head. "I don't know. I just found out about it. It could have been going on months or years for all I know. I didn't even know her name until you told me. How lame is that?"

"Not that lame. So that was you banging on Miss Hill's door?"

She nodded.

"How'd you find out about the affair?"

"Through the athletic club. He'd forgotten his gym bag, so I stopped by to deliver it, and he wasn't there. He came home claiming he'd had a great game. After that, I followed him one night, and it led me to her door." Suddenly, tears were rolling down her face. She hadn't meant to cry. She palmed them away.

"Did you confront them?"

"I never got the chance. They weren't at home the night I banged on the door. That's why I went to Clare's. After we talked it out, I went home, and that's when I ran into you."

Finz frowned. She thought that answer would please him, but it seemed to be a disappointment. Had she punched a hole in his theory? Maybe being seen banging on Cassie's door gave her an unexpected alibi. It screwed with his timeline. There was no way she could be in

Concord, beating Richard to death, if she was at Cassie Hill's house at the same time.

"Tell Miss Hill I'm sorry if I caused her any embarrassment with the disturbance."

"I will. And I'm sorry your husband was cheating on you. That must have really hurt. You haven't had much luck with husbands, have you?"

"What's that supposed to mean?"

"You have two dead husbands, both of whom died violently."

"What are you implying?" Olivia asked through clenched teeth. "That I had something to do with that? Mark was killed in a car crash, and Richard was murdered. They aren't even connected."

"Aren't they?"

"Not even remotely."

"I'll thicken the plot a little more. It's not just two husbands, but three. Your sister's husband disappeared and has never been found, isn't that right?"

Finz was putting some of the pieces together. He couldn't know about Infidelity Limited, but she still had to be careful. "So what are you saying? That I killed him too? He ran off. If you look for him, I'm sure you'll find him fit and well."

"You're ignoring one common denominator."

"I am?"

"Andrew Macready."

Finz let his big reveal hang in the air. If it was supposed to scare her, it worked, but not for the reason he thought. She could see how Andrew would fit Finz's cop-minded narrative, but she had to get him off that track. She couldn't pull Andrew into her crosshairs.

"Let's look at the facts," Finz said. "Andrew was with Mark the night he died, and here he is again at your side shortly after Richard's murder. I also believe he was in the vicinity when Nick 'disappeared.'"

Olivia shook her head. "I'd seen Andrew once in twenty years. We've only been in contact since Richard died."

"And he hasn't left your side since."

"He's a good friend."

"Just a *good friend*? Was your husband cheating because you were cheating?"

"How dare you. Stop accusing me just because you haven't managed to come up with a single suspect."

That remark seemed to wound him, and he sat back in his seat. "Look, I know it's getting warm in here. Sure I can't get you something to drink?"

Olivia sighed heavily. "Water, please."

"Coming right up."

Finz left the interview room and returned with a bottle of water. He uncapped it for her and put it in front of her.

Retaking his seat, he said, "Can I ask why you have two cell phones?"

Olivia jerked back from the question. Roy had really screwed her when he'd called her the night Finz came to inform her of Richard's death. She knew that would come back to bite her. "One's for work, and one's personal."

"May we see them?"

"No. Not without a warrant."

"Why? Is there something on them you don't want us to see?"

"Because they have nothing to do with you or your investigation. There's client information on my work phone, and my private information on my personal phone."

"I can get a warrant."

She hoped he wouldn't. If he did, it would prove she was a liar about having a "personal" phone. While examining Roy's burner wouldn't prove anything, it would raise suspicions, since it would have almost no information on it. The burner might have to meet with an unfortunate accident in the near future. "Then get one."

"Do you know why I find your phones of interest? According to your husband's phone records the night of his death, he received a call at nine fifteen. Miss Hill says the call came from you and that was why he left her. Care to comment?"

"As I told you before, I didn't call him."

"Do you have your phones on you?"

She didn't like where this was going. "Yes, but I'm not giving them to you."

"I don't need them. Are they on?"

"Yes."

He pulled out his cell and dialed the number Richard had received the call from at nine fifteen. Neither of Olivia's phones rang. Whatever number he was calling, it wasn't hers. Finz's confident expression evaporated.

"Not the result you were hoping for?" Olivia said. "I told you the call didn't come from me."

He pocketed his phone and said, "Look, Olivia. Can I be frank with you? We've reached the point where we need to stop playing games and be honest with each other because it's the only way we're going to end this."

You have nothing; you have nothing, she kept telling herself. She wasn't sure if that was true or a lie she told herself to help her keep it together.

"Here's what I think happened, Olivia. Your husband was cheating on you, and you found out about it. Your high school buddy is a former soldier with the strength and skill to beat a man to death. I think you two lured him out to a remote location, and you let Andrew treat Richard like a piñata. That let you get your pound of flesh and also get out of the marriage with a pretty nice insurance settlement. That's premeditated murder."

It was a reasonable theory, but Finz was wrong about most of it. It did sound a damn sight more believable than the truth, but everything

Finz had was circumstantial at best. He couldn't prove any of it. But could he convince a jury?

"If someone else orchestrated this plot, tell me, Olivia, because as far as I can see, it's the only way you're going to avoid a life sentence."

Her chances of untangling herself from this mess with Infidelity Limited were dwindling. Finz might not have the hard evidence, but he was getting closer.

"Time to tell the truth, Olivia. It's your only way."

The truth will set you free, she thought. How naive those words sounded in her mind. Maybe it was time to come clean with Finz. Roy and Finz were squeezing her from both sides, and she had no leverage with Roy. Maybe she could get some with Finz. What if she made a deal with him and traded her knowledge to trap Roy? She wouldn't come out of it clean, but at least she'd take Roy down with her. She didn't want to do it, but she didn't see another option. She closed her eyes.

"C'mon, Olivia. You know you want to do the right thing," Finz said.

A cell phone interrupted the conversation. The harsh ringtone made both of them jump.

Olivia was so in the moment with Finz she didn't immediately realize whose phone was ringing. It took her a second to recognize the standard ringtone of Roy's burner phone.

"Ignore it."

"I have to take it."

"It can wait."

"It's my lawyer."

Her response startled him, and he leaned back. She took that as an opportunity and grabbed her phone from her purse.

"Hello?"

"Olivia, you betrayed me," Roy said. "You lied to me, and you didn't do your job."

Oh my God, she thought. *He knows about Amy and Heather. How did he find out about them? What went wrong?* Her stomach churned. She gripped the table for support.

"So I had no choice but to do it for you. You need to clean up your mess," Roy said and hung up.

Olivia dropped the phone.

"Everything okay?" Finz asked.

She jumped to her feet, pushing the table into Finz. "I have to go."

"We're not finished."

"We are." She snatched up her purse to leave. She got two steps toward the door before Finz blocked her path with his body.

"What was that call about?"

"Please step aside."

"Olivia."

"Am I under arrest?"

Finz was silent for a second. "No."

"Then get out of my way."

Finz stepped aside, and she bolted for the street.

CHAPTER THIRTY-FOUR

In her distress, Olivia rushed out of the police station and headlong into traffic. A car locked its brakes to avoid slamming into her. She ignored the cursing and jumped behind the wheel of her car.

She glanced back at the police station. Finz stood at the entrance with a bewildered look on his face. He took a step toward her. She couldn't let him interrogate her, not when it was all falling apart. He was too close to working it out. She gunned the Audi's engine and lurched into traffic.

She drove. It didn't matter where. She just needed to get away from Finz. She made sure she was out of Concord and Finz's grip before stamping on the brake pedal, sending her car lurching over to the side of the road.

She called Roy. He didn't pick up.

"Shit."

Was it a bluff? She dearly hoped so. There was no doubt Roy had unearthed their deception, but would he really hurt Heather and Amy? He never got his hands dirty. That was his rule. But every rule got broken eventually.

She called Heather on the burner phone she'd bought after she and Andrew had coached them on what to do when they set up the deception. The call went to voice mail. She wasn't sure if she should leave a message. The smart money said don't, but the fear said do it.

"It's me. Call me."

She called Amy's burner phone next. The phone rang and rang.

"Come on. Come on. Come on."

Her heart sank when it clicked through to voice mail.

"Call me. He's onto you."

She hoped that message would shock Amy into responding, but Roy's tone had scared her. He'd always played the benevolent intimidator, but this time he sounded like a stone-cold killer.

She stared at the phone in her hand. The plan had been to never make contact through regular, traceable lines of communication, but that didn't matter anymore. She called Heather's office number.

"Moore Fitness, how may I direct your call?"

"Heather Moore-Marbach, please." Olivia's mouth was so dry that the words scraped her as they came out.

"Mrs. Moore-Marbach isn't in the office today."

"When do you expect her back?" *Please say soon,* she thought.

"Not until after the weekend. Would you like her voice mail?"

"No, I'll call back later," she said and killed the call.

The phone slipped from her grasp, landing in the foot well between her feet. *What have you done, Roy?* she thought. Her imagination tried to look ahead, but her fear blacked it out. She'd made a terrible, terrible mistake.

She wanted to wait to see if Heather or Amy called her back, but she didn't have that luxury. Roy was a shark, and he never stopped moving. After he chased down one prey, he moved on to another. Her survival instinct, as battered as it was, kicked in. If Roy was coming for her, she had to keep moving too.

She pulled out her cell phone and called Andrew.

"What's up?" he asked. The rapid pneumatic pop of a nail gun in full operation punctuated the background.

"Everything. Finz cornered me. He said it was for a chat, but he hauled me in for an interrogation."

"That's okay. Finz has no suspects. He's going to focus on you."

"At the end, Roy called," she said, cutting him off. "He knows I didn't kill Amy."

Silence.

"I've called Heather and Amy, and I can't get an answer. Roy said that he's done something to them. I think he has. He's done it to punish me and them." She felt a wave of tears well up, threatening to break through.

"Where are you?" he asked.

"I don't know. I tore out of the police station. I'm in Pleasant Hill somewhere."

"What do you want to do?"

Go back one month, she thought. Go back to a time where she could exist in ignorance of Richard's cheating and the knowledge that Infidelity Limited existed.

Roy wanted to punish her and make her choke on her lies, so how would he do that? The answer came to her.

"I want to go to their house in Morro Bay. If Roy's done anything, it'll be there."

"We'll do that. Go home, and I'll meet you there."

She thought of Finz. "No, Finz knows something is wrong. I can see him waiting for me."

"Then meet me here at the new house." He gave her an address in Hercules. "We'll go from here."

She found Andrew's job site easily enough, although the drive had been difficult. She didn't know if it was shock kicking in, but she'd lost control over her body. The strength had left her legs, her grip on the wheel was weak, and her focus was shot. As soon as she arrived at the site, she handed him the keys.

They tore along the freeway, with Andrew at the wheel of the Audi. Her plan had backfired, and Roy was taking his revenge. He'd warned her of what he was capable of, and now he was making good on his promise. *How far has he taken it? What did he do?* She stared into the black pool of possibility and closed her mind to the emerging answer. She didn't want to face it.

Road signs counted down the miles to Morro Bay. They didn't stop for anything other than gas, and Andrew kept his foot down. They didn't talk during most of the drive. What was there to say? They'd screwed up, and Roy had found out about their deception. If they didn't talk about it, Olivia could delude herself that nothing bad had happened.

She glanced over at Andrew, his focus solidly on the road ahead. His knuckles shone white from his grip on the wheel. She took comfort in the fact that she wasn't the only one who was scared.

Fifty miles out, she called Heather and Amy again. Once more, the calls went to voice mail.

"They're still not answering," Olivia said. "Should I call the house number?"

"No. There can't be any link between us."

"But what if they can't call?"

"We'll deal with it when we get there. Whatever has happened . . ." Andrew didn't finish his sentence, seemingly losing faith in his words.

"Finish what you were going to say."

"Olivia."

"Finish it."

"Whatever has happened has happened." He looked over at her. "Roy's done whatever he's set out to do."

It was early evening by the time they drove up to the beach house. The gate was ajar.

Andrew stopped the Audi short of the gate. Olivia glanced over at him. The color had drained from his face.

"This could be a trap," she said.

"It is," he said. "No doubt about it."

"Maybe we shouldn't go in."

"The problem is that we don't know what kind of trap it is. It might be worse for us if we don't go in. What do you want to do?"

"We go in."

Andrew climbed from the car and pushed the gate open using the back of his hand to avoid leaving fingerprints. After a short trip down the driveway, he parked the Audi next to Heather's Porsche in front of the garage. As they climbed from the car, he looked around to see if they were being watched.

Like the gate, the front door was partly open. This was definitely a trap. Roy was tossing down bread crumbs, and they were gobbling them up. Olivia reached for the door handle.

Andrew grabbed her hand. "No fingerprints, remember? There can be no trace of us ever being here, because we've never met these people." He reached into his jacket and pulled out a handkerchief, which he used to push open the door.

From the doorway, the house was still. Nothing came back at them. No noise or movement. Neither were good signs.

Andrew sniffed the air. Olivia did the same, but smelled nothing beyond air freshener. She didn't remember the scent from their last visit.

"What's wrong?" she asked.

He frowned and shook his head.

"Heather . . . Amy, are you there? It's Olivia."

No one answered.

"Stay behind me," Andrew said.

He moved down the long corridor with efficient grace, stopping where it connected with the bedroom hallway to check all the angles for a potential intruder. He obviously hadn't forgotten his army train-ing. When they reached the threshold to the living room, he stopped.

"Stay there. Don't come any farther."

Olivia ignored him and charged past him. He grabbed her before she could get too far. The sight in the living room was as she'd feared. Heather and Amy were both dead.

At the center of the sunken living room, Heather lay on her back, slumped against the sofa, blood covering her from a wound in her chest. Her head was tipped back, her gaze pointed up at the ceiling. Across from her, Amy lay sprawled on her side on the floor, with a halo of blood surrounding her head where her throat had been cut.

Olivia's legs went out from under her, and Andrew guided both of them to the floor. She sucked in a breath to scream or cry; she wasn't sure which, but her throat closed up on her and nothing came out.

It was easy to see what had happened. They'd been forced to face each other before they were killed. Olivia wondered who'd been attacked first. *Who got to see who die?* It was so cruel. It was so Infidelity Limited.

She'd been saved this sight with Richard, but now she saw Roy's vindictive might. Her fear of Roy turned into hatred.

She closed her eyes to shut out the sight, but it was etched into her mind already. Andrew pulled her close.

"This is my fault."

"No, it's not." His words were hard and unflinching.

"More people are dead because of me. I should have come clean to Finz. At least Heather and Amy would be alive."

She'd tried to save Amy's life and prevent Heather from suffering the same fate she had at the hands of Infidelity Limited. Instead, both women were dead. She couldn't help feeling Roy's killing spree had more to do with her betrayal than Heather's. She knew he'd continue to make her suffer at his hands until he tired of toying with her.

"Hey, cut that out right now." He stood, pulling her to her feet. "Heather got herself into this, dragging Amy into it with her. They knew the risk they were running. There were no guarantees. We told them what they could do to protect themselves, and either they didn't listen or something went wrong. They got caught, and it cost them their lives. Turning yourself in would have changed nothing. You aren't responsible for this. Say it."

"I'm not responsible for this . . . but I am responsible for anything that happens to you."

"Jesus, Olivia."

"Now, you listen to me. Roy knows I betrayed him, and he's coming for me. If he finds out about you, then you're going to end up the same way, and I can't have that on my conscience."

Andrew was silent for a long moment. "If you're thinking about falling on your sword and turning yourself in to Finz, don't. Roy wants to destroy you. If you sacrifice yourself, he wins."

"Serving up Roy might change things."

"You're risking a lot. Infidelity Limited is bigger than the Concord PD. Finz doesn't have the clout to handle this. Roy knows that. He's going to drop the hammer on you before you can cut a deal."

"Then what do we do?"

"We go. There's nothing to be gained by being here."

She nodded.

"First, we have to cover our tracks."

She followed Andrew over to the bodies. She had to fight the urge to vomit at the sight of the two corpses. She dropped to a crouch at Heather's side. She wanted so much to hold her hand and tell her she was sorry. Instead, she clasped her own hands together and gripped them until they hurt. A sob leaked from her.

"Don't touch them. Don't step on anything. We can't leave a mark."

"I know." Olivia hated the indignity of just leaving their bodies for someone else to find. How long would they have to wait? It was so sad.

"We were never here, and we have to make sure of it. Did you touch anything when we were here last time?"

"I don't know."

Andrew took her back to the front door and walked her through their previous visit. He told her to talk him through everything she'd said and done. She hadn't touched the door, Heather had held it open for her, but she had touched the "Call" button on the squawk box. Andrew went back outside and wiped it clean. They'd both handled wineglasses when they'd talked, and not knowing which ones, they loaded the dishwasher with all the glasses and switched it on.

Andrew repeated the exercise for himself. The only thing of note he'd touched was the glass door on the deck, the sculpture, and the hardwood floors.

"Do you think Roy did this, or did he have someone like me do it?"

Andrew appraised the carnage. "He did this. It's too ruthless to be a client."

"What do we do about the burner phones?"

"We take them."

Olivia dialed Heather's number. The phone burst into song in the kitchen. It was coming from her purse. Andrew removed it using his handkerchief. She called Amy's number, and the plain ringtone came from Amy herself. It took her a moment to realize the phone was in the back pocket of her jeans. Andrew made a move to get it.

"No, I'll do it."

She took Andrew's handkerchief from him and went to Amy. She couldn't tear her gaze away from Amy's face. Slack and unmoving, it was frozen in her final moment. If Olivia wasn't careful, this was how she would end up. That potential had to be the fuel that kept her going. Carefully, she reached inside Amy's jeans pocket. No body heat radiated from the dead woman. They'd been dead some time. Whatever Roy had planned was in motion. She removed the cell phone and pocketed it.

Something occurred to her. She stared at the carnage again. Heather and Amy had been stabbed, but where was the knife? Andrew had said this was a trap. Planting the knife on her would be the perfect way for Roy to get his revenge.

"The knife is missing."

"Shit," Andrew said. "We need to find it."

They searched the house. Every knife appeared to be accounted for. Roy must have taken it with him.

"We've been here too long," Andrew said.

She nodded. They left, leaving the house as they'd found it, with the door ajar. She hoped the women would be found soon. As Andrew reversed her car back onto the street, an image of the women filled her head. "I'm sorry," she said to them.

CHAPTER THIRTY-FIVE

One break was all it took to make a case, and Finz had just gotten his. He was in the process of getting a warrant for Olivia's cell phones when he received the call from Madeleine Lyon.

"I think we've got a break in the Richard Shaw case. You need to come see something," she said.

"Where?"

Twenty minutes later, Finz pulled up on Atlantic Street across from the Concord BART station. The scene was less than a mile from where Shaw had been murdered. Lyon was marshaling two uniforms and a crime tech in a cordoned-off area over a storm drain. She turned around at Finz's arrival and broke away from the group.

"What have we got?" he asked.

"A tire iron with blood and tissue on it found in the storm drain."

Lyon didn't have to say anymore. They both thought the same thing—this could be the weapon used to kill Richard Shaw.

They ducked under the crime scene tape.

Henry Freitas, the crime tech, removed the last bolt holding the storm-drain grate in place and lifted it out of the way. The tire iron lay on a bed of silt and trash. Freitas took shots of the iron in situ before removing it and placing it on a sheet of paper he'd laid out on the ground.

"I can't believe someone tossed this down a storm drain," Lyon said.

"Maybe they thought the rains would wash it away," one of the uniforms suggested.

"In late May, they'd be waiting a long time," Finz said.

"One killer's screwup is our good fortune," Lyon said.

But Finz knew they were getting ahead of themselves. The tire iron still had to be fingerprinted and matched to the wounds on Richard Shaw's head, as did the tissue found on it.

"Henry, tell me you've got something good for me to work with," he said.

Freitas peered at the tire iron, keeping his hands off the evidence. "We've got tissue and lots of it. I should be able to match blood and DNA if it is the murder weapon."

Lyon whooped. Finz reserved his whooping until the science was in.

"Henry, I want this booked in, and I want to know whether this is the murder weapon as soon as possible," Finz said. "How did we come across this good fortune anyway?"

One of the uniforms pointed at a dejected-looking man leaning against the hood of a blue Ford Explorer. "Mr. Carrington dropped his keys down the storm drain, saw the tire iron, and called it in."

Freitas reached down into the storm drain, plucked out the keys, and waggled them.

Finz ducked under the crime scene tape and walked up to Carrington. He straightened at Finz's arrival. The detective put out his hand, and the two men shook.

"Thanks for calling this in, sir. Could you tell me how you came to find the tire iron?" Finz purposefully didn't mention evidence or a murder weapon. He could do without any premature excitement being attached to the find.

"Like I told your other guys, I parked my car here. I was on my phone, walking back up the street. I locked my car, went to pocket my keys, and dropped the damn things. Murphy's law being what it is, they bounced straight down the storm drain. Of course I've got my house keys and everything on there, so I wasn't just going to leave them. I tried to see if I could hook them out, and that's when I saw the tire iron with the blood on it. I know there was that guy killed around here recently, so I called you guys. I mean, I wasn't touching anything, just in case."

"Why'd you happen to park here? Did you have business here?"

Carrington looked down at his shoes. "No, not really."

This wasn't the reaction Finz was expecting. "You want to explain that?"

"Look, I know you'll think I'm cheap, but I didn't want to pay for BART parking, so I parked on the streets for free. But hey, me being a cheapskate has kicked up something good, right?"

"Speculation is a dangerous trait in my business. Thank you for your time."

Carrington shrugged. "Can I get my keys back?"

"I'll have an officer take a statement and get your contact details, then we'll give you your keys, and you'll be free to go. Thank you for your time."

Finz crossed back to the scene. He told one of the officers to get a statement.

"Henry's got some interesting information for you," Lyon said with a grin.

"What's that?" Finz said.

"I just called Audi and asked them to send me a picture of the tire iron that comes with an Audi A4." Freitas held up his phone. "It's a match."

Finz felt the buzz around him. He quelled his own excitement. He couldn't get carried away. Olivia Shaw was proving to be tricky. She'd run out on him during the interview, and he didn't want to leave any gaps for her to escape through again.

He compared the tire iron in the evidence bag to the image on Freitas's phone. It was a match, but it wasn't distinctive. It looked like any other tire iron he'd ever seen.

"Is this tire iron proprietary to Audi or something they buy from the ACME Tire Iron Company of Timbuktu?"

"I have no idea, but I'll check," Freitas said.

"Does it matter?" Lyon said. "It's the same type, and we're not looking for any other bloody tire irons at the moment."

"Okay, then," Finz said. "Get me a warrant to search Olivia Shaw's car. I think we've got her."

*　　*　　*

Olivia's stomach dropped when she turned onto her street. Four police cruisers and an unmarked police car lined the street. Finz and Lyon were among the officers milling around in front of her house. Neighbors stood on their porches, watching the police presence.

"Oh shit," Andrew said.

Olivia didn't have the energy to go another twelve rounds with Finz. The last eighteen hours, driving to Morro Bay and back and erasing their existence from the beach house, had drained her. Two women were dead because she'd tried to save them. The emotional toll was just as consuming as the physical. They'd tried driving through the night, but the fatigue and shock were too much, and they'd slept in the car, not risking a record of a hotel stay.

Olivia looked over at Andrew. "I don't like the look of this."

He shifted in his seat. "Just be cool."

That was easier said than done. The question was: Why was Finz here? Was it connected to Richard's murder? Or was it because of Heather's and Amy's murders? Of course, it didn't really matter which one if Finz was here to arrest her.

The uniformed cops standing on the driveway parted as Olivia guided her Audi into the garage. Finz and Lyon strode toward her the moment she stopped the car. The first time they'd come, they'd had bad news. Olivia guessed this occasion would be no different, except the bad news would mean even more trouble for her.

Finz opened her door for her. She didn't get any sense of chivalry from him.

Climbing from the car, she became aware of the sour-smelling panic sweat radiating from her body and day-old clothes. She was a bad advertisement for innocence.

"Hello, Mrs. Shaw," Finz said. "Nice to see that you're home."

Something had happened with Finz. He was being too formal with her after his "let me call you Olivia" routine during her interrogation.

"Looks like you've had a long night." He turned to Andrew. "Good seeing you again, Mr. Macready. You always seem to be around Mrs. Shaw these days."

"Is that a crime?" Andrew said. Finz really had a knack of getting under the skin.

Finz took in her appearance. "Where have you been? I was hoping to find you home. We've been waiting quite a while for you."

She wasn't about to answer that question. "Detective Finz, what's going on?"

"I have a warrant to search your car," he said and handed her the paperwork.

Olivia stared at the legalese written on the paper and didn't understand a word of it. "What are you looking for?"

Finz held out his hand. "Your car keys, please?"

Olivia handed them over.

Finz tossed them to Lyon, who caught them in her latex-gloved hands. She went to the Audi and popped the trunk. When Olivia tried to follow the female detective, Finz blocked her path.

"You need to stay out of our way. We can't have you hampering our efforts. I promise you we won't damage anything."

She hated the arrogance in Finz's tone. It was the tone the police used when they thought they had something.

"What have you got, Maddy?"

Lyon was shoulders deep in the Audi's trunk. She reemerged with nothing. She held up her hands and waggled her fingers and smiled. "It's not here."

"What's not here?" Olivia asked.

"Mrs. Shaw, where's your tire iron?" Finz asked.

"I don't know. It should be in there. I've never used it."

"That's not a satisfactory answer," Lyon said.

"It's the only one I've got. I've never had a reason to use it, so I've never checked for it."

Lyon smirked.

Olivia scanned the expressions of all the cops in attendance and read their attitude. There was definitely no benefit of the doubt in their minds. They were convinced that she was involved.

"How many times have you used your tire iron, Detective?" Andrew asked. "Twice? Once? Never?"

Lyon didn't answer.

"Didn't think so."

"We don't have to justify ourselves to you, Mr. Macready," Finz said.

"I beg to differ."

While Andrew bickered with Finz and Lyon, the reason for the search warrant fell into place for Olivia. The tire iron was the murder weapon.

A sense of dread settled over her, its cold touch pressing down on her. This was Roy's doing. He'd said he'd punish her for her betrayal. The son of a bitch had stolen her tire iron from her and tipped off the police.

It should have been time for her to come clean with Finz, but two things stopped her. First, Finz was beyond making deals. He wanted her head on a spike. Second was the advice she had received from Karen Innes.

She'd warned her Roy would do this for crossing him. "Burn him before he burns you," she'd said. There was no option now. She had to destroy Roy.

"Mrs. Shaw, I want you to come with me," Finz said.

"Don't go, Liv."

"I'm not." She couldn't take Roy down from a jail cell.

"Excuse me?" Finz asked.

Olivia scanned the warrant. "You were hoping to find the tire iron missing, which means you have a tire iron. So, you were trying to prove a negative. You didn't find my tire iron—so what? Can you prove my car ever had a tire iron? Do you have proof that the tire iron you have is from my car?"

She waited for an answer that didn't come.

"Until you do, we have nothing to talk about. And furthermore, I don't want you coming to my home, my place of work, or anywhere else with these thinly veiled attempts to embarrass me in front of my friends, coworkers, and neighbors. It's harassment. I suggest you focus your energies on finding my husband's murderer and stay away from me."

Lyon's expression was ugly as she seethed at the dressing-down. Finz just looked disappointed. His expression said that he knew he'd lost any cooperation with her. Despite the situation, Olivia almost felt sorry for them.

"C'mon, let's go," Finz said.

He took the keys from Lyon and handed them back to Olivia. "I'll be back soon . . . and it will be with proof."

"That would be good."

Olivia and Andrew watched Finz and his team pack up from the garage's threshold. They worked in silence. Olivia's neighbors moved back inside their homes.

As Finz headed back to his car, he stopped and turned around. "Just before I go, I thought I'd let you know about an interesting development. Your sister offered to become my confidential informant. Apparently, she has something to get off her chest."

CHAPTER THIRTY-SIX

When Concord's finest pulled away, Andrew said, "He's bullshitting, right? Clare wouldn't sell you out, not her own sister."

Olivia didn't think so, but a lifetime of Clare's antics said anything was possible, especially if her back was against the wall. Somehow she didn't think Clare was talking—yet. If she were, Finz wouldn't be wasting his time with a search warrant. He would have arrested her by now. But that was subject to change. Just because Clare wasn't talking today didn't mean she wouldn't tomorrow.

"I'll talk to her," Olivia said, "but she's the least of my problems. This tire-iron crap was a message from Roy. He's coming for me."

"What can we do?"

Using Karen Innes's words, she said, "We burn him before he can burn me."

Olivia called Roy. She could guarantee he had his phone on. He'd be eagerly awaiting her reaction to Heather's and Amy's murders and, no doubt, the discovery of the murder weapon that killed Richard. Despite her belief, the call went to voice mail.

"I found them," she said, leaving a message, and hung up.

Now began the waiting game. Playing voice-mail tag was just his way of showing who was in charge. Andrew told her it was going to be okay. She so wanted to believe that, but recent history said otherwise.

She went up to her room, peeled off her clothes, and tossed them on the tiled bathroom floor. Staring at them, she knew she wouldn't be wearing them again. They were a liability, since they'd been exposed to a crime scene. But that was a minor reason. More importantly, those clothes would be a constant reminder of Heather's and Amy's murders. Their bodies, cold and still, left in their own blood. That was the real reason she could never wear them again.

She got under the shower and scrubbed herself. Soap and water would clean her of all physical traces of the murders, but not the mental ones. She found herself weeping as she ran the soap over her body.

Three people were dead because of her. She hadn't wielded the tire iron that killed Richard or brandished the knife that took Heather's and Amy's lives, but she was involved. She'd set the wheels in motion. She'd hired Infidelity Limited, and she'd told Heather and Amy to trust her. Her actions had gotten all three of them killed. Bringing down Roy and Infidelity Limited was her only penance. It would be justice for all the dead people and all the ruined lives. She turned off the faucet and stepped from the shower.

She wrapped a towel around herself and dried her hair off with another. As she returned to her bedroom to grab fresh clothes, she found Andrew standing in the doorway, holding her burner phone. It was ringing.

"It's Roy," he said.

Any self-consciousness she had felt about finding Andrew in her bedroom was set aside. She took the phone from him.

"Come in," she said, "but be quiet."

Andrew came in and sat on the corner of the bed. His gaze flashed to her body, hidden by the towel, before he fixed it on her face.

"Yes," she said into the phone.

"So you found them?" Roy snarled.

An image of Heather and Amy flashed into her mind's eye. "Yes. Did you have to kill them?"

"Did you have to lie, Olivia?"

"I didn't want to be another of your victims. I had to try something." She walked to the window overlooking her street, leaned against the sill, and looked out to see if he was out there. She felt Andrew's gaze on her.

"I thought you were smarter than that. You can't game the system. It's perfect. You lose if you don't follow instructions."

No, Infidelity Limited clients lose regardless, she thought. "You'll be pleased to hear that the police were here. They've found the murder weapon used to kill Richard. It's a tire iron, and it just so happens that the one from my car is missing. Does that have anything to do with you?"

Roy barked a derisive laugh. "I told you there'd be consequences, Olivia. Why aren't the cops sweating you?"

"Because they can't prove the one they have is the one from my car."

"Yet."

"And will they?" This was an important point. If Finz was going to connect that tire iron to her in a matter of days, she stood no chance of ending Infidelity Limited.

"The police will have an uphill struggle proving it's yours."

She wanted to believe Roy's intimation that putting the tire iron in Finz's hands was nothing more than a warning shot, but she knew better. Roy was likely holding back a piece of evidence that would definitively tie her to that tire iron. The good news was he wouldn't burn her yet. He was still talking to her, which meant he wanted something from her.

"I've learned my lesson. How can I make it up to you, Roy?"

"What makes you think you can?"

You're still talking to me, she thought. If he didn't want to put her through the wringer one more time, he wouldn't be calling. He would have disappeared back into the shadows. "I'm hoping you'll let me."

"That's what makes you smarter than everyone I've dealt with. And that's why you aren't in a jail cell. You're right; you can make it up to me. Meet me at Los Vaqueros Reservoir. Come via the Morgan Territory Road. Leave now," he said before the line went dead.

She tossed the phone on the bed.

"What's he want?"

"To meet now at Los Vaqueros Reservoir."

"Shit. He'll see me if I shadow you."

"I know. That's why I don't want you following me. He doesn't trust me anymore. His guard is going to be up, and his people won't be taking any chances. You can't back me up."

She went into the walk-in closet and closed the door. She grabbed fresh clothes, dropped the towel, and started dressing.

"I don't like it," Andrew said from the other side of the door.

"It'll be okay. He won't do anything drastic. I haven't paid him his hundred grand yet," she said, pulling on a pair of jeans.

When she opened the closet door, Andrew was standing there.

"What do I do?" he asked.

She hugged him and felt safe. In a world of shifting sands, he felt like a rock. "Go home. Get changed. Wait for me. I'll call you when it's over."

*   *   *

Fifteen minutes later, she was on the road. Maybe that was a good thing. With her Audi on the move, Finz couldn't swoop in for a second shot at examining the car.

She called Clare. She hadn't wanted to do it in front of Andrew. This was something between sisters only. Her call went to voice mail. Clare was no doubt screening her calls.

"Clare, it's me. Finz says you're offering to inform on me. You'd better not be. Call me."

After half an hour, she found herself in Roy country. The roads had narrowed to two lanes, and farmland replaced civilization. She hadn't come across another vehicle in the last five miles, and she still had another ten miles to go. She was sure it would get good and isolated by then.

What's Roy's next play? she wondered. She hadn't killed for him. What was the punishment for that—to kill two people? Making her an accessory to Richard's murder was only the tip of the iceberg. He'd want something that indebted her to him further to ensure she didn't cross him again. In the same way she'd known she couldn't kill Amy, she also knew she couldn't follow through on anything he instructed. She'd agreed to this meeting to buy time, find an angle, and sink *Infidelity Limited* and all who sailed on her. Maybe he wouldn't have a new task for her. Perhaps Roy was done with her and was bringing her out here to put a bullet in her head. She pushed that thought into the recesses of her mind.

The road rose and curved to the left. As she crested the rise, a dull explosion sounded under the car, and the steering wheel bucked in her hands. The Audi held the corner, but the steering lost its solid feel. The all-too-familiar thud-thud-thud of a deflating tire followed. She didn't want to stop on a blind corner, so she let the sedan run on around the corner and eased it to the side of the road, half on the road and half on the dirt.

She climbed out of the car to check the wheels, and lo and behold, her front right tire was flat. And because Roy had taken her tire iron, she couldn't change it. Life was really playing a cruel joke on her.

She debated calling Andrew for help, but decided it was too risky. She tracked back up the road to see what had punctured her tire. In the road sat a spike strip, the expanding kind police used on *COPS* and other reality cop shows.

"What the hell?"

She counted herself lucky it had only taken out one of her tires. Whoever the asshole was who left it out there thought he was pretty funny. As she bent down to yank the thing off the road, she heard rustling in the pasture behind her.

Reflexively, she straightened and swung around. Her first move should have been to run back to the car. That fraction-of-a-second delay was all her attacker needed. Head covered with a ski mask, he pounced, driving a shoulder into her stomach and blasting the air from her lungs. The impact sent her flying. She hit the ground hard, just managing to keep her head from connecting with the asphalt. She scrabbled to her hands and feet but gave him the perfect opening to kick her in the stomach. Again, the blow robbed her of her breath.

"You thought you could fuck with us, Olivia," he snarled. "You're going to learn the price of betrayal."

Olivia curled into a fetal ball as pain radiated throughout her body. This was it. Roy was really going to kill her. One of his lackeys would do the deed and dump her at the side of the road. Well, she wasn't going to go quietly. She shot out a donkey kick, which barely missed when he jumped clear.

She used that momentary edge to jump to her feet. Every stomach muscle screeched in pain when she stood. She lurched for her car and reached it, but not before he caught up with her. He slammed her against the Audi's side, then drove his heel into the back of one of her knees, which dropped her to the ground. He swiftly looped a pair of flex cuffs around her wrists and cinched them tight.

"Got her," he barked into a phone.

A van she was all too familiar with roared around the corner a minute later, with Dolores driving. She brought the van to a stop in front of Olivia's sedan and jumped out.

"Let's get this bitch boxed up," she said, yanking open the rear doors.

"Time to learn your fate, Olivia," Ski Mask said.

He produced a hood from his pocket and pulled it over Olivia's head. The two of them hauled her to her feet and tossed her in the back of the van, where one of them bound her feet.

"You got this?" Ski Mask asked Dolores.

"Yeah, you stay and clean this up."

"Will do."

The tires spun when Dolores drove away. The van surged forward, sending Olivia sliding across the van's metal bed and crashing into the doors.

A thousand options raced through her head to make sure this ride wasn't her last, but she decided against them all. Roy wouldn't kill her. He wouldn't be that merciful.

*　　　*　　　*

Olivia guessed they'd been driving for fifteen minutes when Dolores stopped the van. In that time, Dolores had tossed her around on the twisting roads. She estimated that they couldn't have traveled more than ten miles.

The doors burst open, and a pair of hands snatched her ankles and yanked her onto the bumper. A moment later she was weightless as she was hoisted into the air before landing on someone's shoulder. Although she couldn't see, she knew she was being carried over rough ground from the uneven steps her carrier took.

The noonday sun blazed against her back, but cool air soon replaced the heat. Wherever she was, it was dank and musty smelling.

"I'm lowering you down." It was Roy's voice. "Stand still, and I'll cut your ties."

There was little emotion in his voice, other than disappointment. He was acting like she'd really hurt his feelings. *Poor lamb*, she thought, *someone not playing by your little rules?*

He carefully lowered her to her feet. She wobbled, but he steadied her.

He pulled the sack free of her head before going behind and snipping the cuffs off her wrists and ankles. The sudden blood rush to her extremities rode the line between pleasure and pain. She massaged her wrists and rolled her shoulders, relishing the freedom.

Roy had brought her to what appeared to be a farm. They were standing at the center of a cavernous prefab structure close to three hundred feet long. It was open at both ends, with aluminum siding and clear plastic panels for lighting. There was no floor, just dirt and wood shavings. It smelled fairly fresh, except for the undercurrent of industrial cleaner.

He noticed her taking in her surroundings. "This was a poultry farm until the USDA shut them down a few months ago. This was a broiler house for raising chickens for eating, but there's also a battery farm and a hatchery here. Now it's up for sale."

She wondered if she was supposed to read some meaning into this location. Was Roy saying he was fattening her up for the kill?

Dolores stood next to the van at one end of the broiler house, blocking Olivia's potential escape route. No one guarded the other doorway. She might be able to outrun Roy, but then what? She was miles from anywhere.

"You went a little overboard with the security check," she snapped. "Hijacking me at the side of the road was a bit excessive, don't you think?"

Roy put his hands behind his back, grasping his right wrist with his left hand, and meandered in the direction of the unguarded entrance. Olivia had no choice but to follow.

"You deceived us, Olivia. I can no longer trust you. That means I have to incorporate more stringent security checks. Getting a little rough with you is our way of showing how upset we are with you."

"Killing Heather and Amy, was that your way of showing them your displeasure with their actions?"

"I've told you how Infidelity Limited works. Amy was destined to die as soon as Heather hired us. Heather gave us no option. We had to kill her too. She was a liability."

"And me?" She did her best to sound like she wasn't intimidated.

"You have to pay a price for trying to mislead us. You've personally insulted me. That's hard to forget."

She bit her tongue. Roy had scammed her, killed her husband, and tried to get her to kill a stranger—and he was the aggrieved party? He was either delusional or playing a cruel joke.

"So how do I make it up to you?" she asked. "Do I kill someone else for you? I still owe you a life. Isn't that the debt I owe you?"

He stopped walking and circled around to face her. "As much as I would like you to do that, because I think you'd do a very good job, I think that ship has sailed. You won't kill for us. It doesn't matter what I threaten you with. You won't do it."

The hair went up on the back of her neck. That was bullet-to-head talk. "What can I do, then?"

"Pay a fine."

"A fine?"

"Yes, a onetime payment to get us out of your life and vice versa."

It sounded too good to be true. "How much?"

"You cost us a lot of money. Heather was due to pay us a significant sum. There are people that need to be paid for their work on the double killing we had to do on your part. There has to be a punitive element too. You did betray us after all. I would say one to two million."

"You're crazy. I don't have that kind of money."

"I know. I'm just letting you know how much you've cost the organization. Richard had life insurance, correct? What's it worth?"

"Four hundred and fifty thousand."

"Instead of the one hundred thousand that you owe me, I will take that, and I'll call it quits between us."

She was going to tell him he was crazy again, but cut herself short. She'd worked it all out. It had always been about the money. Roy had intended to milk her for cash. She laughed and shook her head for her lack of foresight.

"What?" he asked.

"Infidelity Limited has never been about setting scores and killing people. It's just an extortion racket."

"It's many things. Money is just one element."

Bullshit, she thought.

"I would like the money in a week. Less would be better. I'd like to conclude our association as soon as humanly possible."

Richard's insurance money meant little to her. They'd taken out policies to cover the mortgage should one of them die, but she didn't need the insurance to cover the mortgage. Her job more than covered it. But the idea of handing the money to Roy made her sick. "What if I don't pay? You don't have a hold over me. The cops have the tire iron, but they can't tie it to me. There's no incentive for me to pay."

Roy smiled again. "I'll be honest; I underestimated you, but I caution you not to underestimate me. The tire iron is only one item at my disposal. You're forgetting Heather's and Amy's deaths."

Her stomach tightened. "There's nothing connecting me to them. I made sure of it."

Roy's smile turned into a smirk. "Really? Nothing?"

She and Andrew had been careful. They hadn't left a trace of themselves at the beach house. She replayed everything in her mind and couldn't see a mistake. Even if they'd left a strand of hair or a fingerprint, the police had no way of tracing it back to her. She wasn't in any database.

"No," she said, injecting as much confidence into her answer as possible.

"Bet you never found a murder weapon at the house, did you?"

She tasted bile at the back of her throat.

"Have you checked your knife block in your kitchen lately?" Roy turned from her and headed back to Dolores. "Take her back. We're done."

Roy's warning had come true. She had underestimated him, and now she was cornered.

"Call me when you have the money, Olivia."

CHAPTER THIRTY-SEVEN

Olivia barreled along the winding road. She had to get home. The Audi held the road as best it could with the space-saver wheel on the front. With only half the width of the rest of the wheels, it wanted to wash out on the left-hand turns, but the car's fancy electronics and four-wheel drive kept her on the road.

At least Infidelity Limited hadn't left her stranded. When Dolores dragged her from the van and tossed her to the ground, her car had four fully functioning wheels. She guessed she had her ski-masked friend to thank for that.

Once she left the rural roads behind and picked up the freeway, traffic and the threat of picking up a ticket slowed her. She couldn't afford unnecessary police attention.

She called Andrew and briefly told him what had happened. He was at his job site, but he agreed to meet her at her house as soon as possible so they could go over the details.

Finally, she made it home. This time, Finz and company weren't lining the street outside her house. She turned into her garage and stopped just short of slamming the car into the wall.

Inside the house, she went straight to the kitchen. The six-inch chef's knife was missing from the knife block.

Was it though? With everything that had happened in recent weeks, she couldn't remember the last time she'd used it. At the wake? Last night? She just didn't know.

Just because it wasn't in the knife block didn't mean Roy had taken it. It might be wishful thinking, but she had to be sure. Roy's job, like all terrorists, was to leave her doubting her safety and fearing the what-if. She had to know fact from fiction.

She went through the dishwasher and the kitchen, then the house. The knife was gone.

Panic rose within her. Its rising tide threatened to overwhelm her, but she calmed herself with one thought—the knife meant nothing. Whoever was investigating Heather's and Amy's deaths would have no reason to connect them to Olivia. Roy had to have something else to connect her to the knife. He would though. He always did.

All she could do was protect herself. She'd dump the knives and buy another set. If anyone came asking about the knives, she'd tell them she sold them in a yard sale or gave them to Goodwill. Reasonable doubt was her only friend.

Again, Roy could put her in the crosshairs of a police investigation, but he'd need to leave her room to duck out of its way if he expected her to pay.

She dug out the life insurance paperwork she'd left in her home office. She sat behind the desk and called the number. She jumped through all the automated-phone-line selections before finally reaching a human being.

"I'd like to check on the status of a life insurance policy claim," she said.

"Do you have the policy number?" the claims agent asked.

She provided the information and answered a bunch of security questions.

"I have all the details here, and . . . and . . . can I put you on hold for a second?"

"Is there a problem?"

"Just have to put you on hold while I check something. I won't be a minute."

He was right. He wasn't a minute. He was ten, and she was forced to listen to hold music punctuated by factoids about the insurance company. Just as the message was in the middle of congratulating the company for its responsiveness, someone came back on the line.

"Mrs. Shaw, I'm Rick Casey."

This was a different person than she'd just been talking to. Something was wrong.

"I work in the investigations department for life insurance policies, and I have to inform you that your claim is on hold."

Olivia's stomach clenched. "Why?"

"Because your husband was the victim of homicide and the case is open with no suspect under arrest."

This couldn't be right. "Is this normal procedure?"

"I can assure you it is."

She couldn't imagine it was. There were hundreds of murders in California alone, and it couldn't be normal for insurance companies to withhold payment. What would happen in all the cold cases? "This doesn't feel right. I would like to speak to a supervisor."

An awkward note entered Casey's voice. "In cases of unnatural death, holding a claim is a matter of course when one of the beneficiaries is a suspect in the death."

She was the only beneficiary on Richard's life insurance. She guessed Casey was either being polite or fearful he was talking to a potential murderer. She imagined the little ripple of excitement and fear that ran through the call center when they realized a murder suspect was calling about his or her payout. Either way, Casey deserved to be commended on his diplomacy.

"I'm sorry, Mrs. Shaw. I can only imagine how distressing this must be. I hope matters will be cleared up soon."

"Thank you," she said.

This was Finz's doing. He was squeezing her, hoping to break her. Unbeknownst to him, this single act to block her life insurance payout would set off a chain of events with Roy that would get Finz the arrest he so dearly wanted. She needed that insurance money to pay Roy. As soon as she told Roy she didn't have the cash, he'd sell her out. Infidelity Limited wasn't a patient organization. They were a slash-and-burn outfit; they'd get what they could and burn what was left. She'd given them nothing. Burning her and disappearing in the smoke was their only course of action.

The doorbell rang. She answered it.

"You okay?" Andrew asked, his face a mask of concern.

She let him in, but he kept looking at her. She'd forgotten her appearance. Her jeans and top were covered in dirt from where she'd been tossed around. The right shoulder of her top was torn.

"Let me see where they kicked you."

"It's okay."

"You might have internal bleeding. We need to check."

His concern warmed and comforted her. He reached in to lift her top so he could examine her bruises. She grabbed his wrists to stop him.

"It can wait," she said. "I have bigger problems. Roy killed Heather and Amy with a chef's knife from my kitchen. He's demanded Richard's life insurance payout, all four hundred and fifty thousand of it, but there's a problem. The payout is on hold because I'm a suspect in Richard's murder. I'm sure Finz put that thought in their heads. I'm done. They've got me. It's over."

She broke down. The tears came fast and seemingly without end. She hated herself for crying. She was the one who kept it together for everyone else's sake, but Roy had beaten her down, and she just couldn't do it anymore.

Andrew pulled her to him. He enveloped her with his broad chest and strong arms. It was nice to have someone else to hold her up instead of having to do it all herself.

"It's not over," he told her.

"It is. You should distance yourself from me now. It'll all happen fast once Roy finds out I don't have the money."

"You have the money."

She pulled away from him. "What?"

"The money from the San Pablo house sale will cover it."

She backed away from him, shaking her head. "No, I can't let you do that. I can't let you give me all your money."

"I'm not giving it to you. I'm loaning it to you."

"How can you loan it to me? There's no guarantee the insurance company will pay me."

He crossed over to her and took her hands. "They will."

"And you're forgetting that as soon as I pay Roy, he'll sell me out the same way he sold out Karen Innes. It's better for me not to pay. That way I'll screw him out of his money."

Andrew shook his head. "You're going to tell that son of a bitch you have his money, and when we pay him, we're going to take that son of a bitch and all his cronies down at the same time."

"You think we can do it?"

"I know we can. You okay with that?"

"I am more than okay."

CHAPTER THIRTY-EIGHT

It was happening, a streak. Clare hated to think of the word, in case it jinxed things, but it was what it was—a goddamn streak. She was up four grand in two hours of playing blackjack and estimated she was winning two hands for every one she lost. She was considering upping her fifty-dollar hands to a hundred, but a cautious voice inside her head whispered, "Don't blow it." She wanted to agree with the voice, but when luck was on your side, you rode that pony until it died under you.

Her luck had attracted attention. A dozen or so people had gathered around her table just to watch, as if her luck would rub off on them. She'd witnessed this phenomenon before, but she'd never had it happen to her.

An Asian woman dressed in a Cache Creek blazer slipped between the gawkers and leaned in close to Clare. "Hi, my name's Melinda, and I'm from hospitality. As a token of our appreciation, we'd like to present you with a complimentary gift certificate for a night's stay here at the casino."

Clare wanted to know where their appreciation had been all the times she'd lost money here. She never understood why casinos showered winners with gifts. Winners didn't need an incentive to stay. Losers did. She knew what the casino was up to, and it had nothing to do with appreciation. All casinos employed the tactic of gifting hotel rooms, meals, and other VIP trinkets for one simple reason—to keep the gambler in the casino long enough to lose the money back.

She accepted the superficial gesture and took the gift certificate with a small round of applause from the peanut gallery. Melinda left as silently as she'd arrived.

She thought it was interesting that during their token-of-appreciation ceremony, the pit boss had switched out the dealer for Chuck, along with a new shoe of cards. Her streak was making them nervous. And that made her nervous. They were watching her. She just wanted to win, win big if possible, and get out before anything could screw it up for her.

"You're riding a wave tonight, Clare," Chuck said. "Let's see how I can continue that wave."

"That would be nice."

"What happened to the hand?"

She examined the finger Gault had broken, now splinted to her ring finger. "Officially, an on-the-job accident."

"Unofficially?"

She winked. "It's my lucky charm."

He wished everyone good luck and dealt a hand to the players. Clare checked her cards, smiled, and flipped over a blackjack to a cheer.

"Can we all get one of those next time around?" the guy sitting next to Clare said affably.

"I'll see what I can do," Chuck said.

Clare's smile dropped when she spotted Gault eyeballing her from a three-card poker table. She knew what he was thinking. He was getting paid tonight. And she could make it happen. If she walked away from the table now, she could pay him back, interest and all, and still have money left over. While that no doubt sounded good to Gault, it didn't to her. Tonight was her night to get ahead. If she could keep the streak going, she could walk away with enough to not only pay off Gault but also, for the first time in as long as she could remember, have a bankroll to cover her bills, upgrade from the Honda, or move out of the trailer. She knew she was getting a little ahead of herself, but she had to dream. She bottled the dream for the moment, blocked out Gault, and focused on the cards. She had to play smart. She had to play like a winner.

She upped her bets to a hundred bucks a hand and was rewarded for her audacity. She played a consistent strategy and did not get carried away. Her winnings swelled to ten grand by eleven thirty, even after the cards turned a little cool on her. When they warmed up again, she upped her bets to $125, then $150.

Clare kept on winning and enjoyed the attention that came with it. Every time she won, people cheered and chanted her name. She loved the adulation, but she didn't let it distract her. It became obvious to a few players that this was her table tonight, and they switched to greener pastures.

When Clare reached the twelve-grand stage, Melinda dropped by to tell Clare dinner at their steak house was on her. While dinner sounded good and she was in desperate need of a pee, she couldn't leave the table. There was no way she was going to abandon this streak of hot cards, and on top of that, Gault was still watching her. He hadn't moved from his table. She'd noticed him paying more attention to her than to his own cards. The second she moved from the table, he'd be on her to grab his cut.

So Clare was faced with a dilemma—when to walk away? How much was enough? She was twelve grand to the good. That was the biggest haul she'd ever pulled at a table. Twelve grand was life changing for her, but she wasn't losing. She could feel there was more money at this table. She made a bargain with herself. If she crashed back down to $10,000, she was walking away. If she didn't, she'd keep going and adjust her "pull the pin" number.

Her luck turned at two in the morning. At one point, she'd gotten to the heady height of twenty-three grand, but her stack had shrunk to the $20,000 mark. It was time to go.

Her supporters had dwindled to a small but dedicated twosome. They moaned when she pushed her seat away from the table.

"Sorry, that's it for me."

She felt the heat of Gault's gaze on her back. He'd switched from three card to the slots. She didn't want to deal with him tonight, not when she had this much money.

Melinda appeared as soon as Clare called it quits. "It's late, and you must be tired. Can I get you a room?"

"No, I'd like to cash out. Could I get a security escort?"

"Certainly."

While Melinda put in a call, Clare passed a $100 chip to the dealer. She'd tipped every dealer who'd worked her table.

Two monster guys who stretched their suits to the bursting point arrived. Melinda led the way to the cashier's cage. The bouncers walked on either side of Clare.

Gault jumped up from his seat, but all he could do was follow. Clare felt safe. She knew he couldn't chance anything in the casino. Outside was a different matter.

Thinking of the outside world, with all its problems, killed this moment of joy. Protection and safety ended the second she stepped outside the building. Roy was out there, but Finz worried her more than Roy and Gault put together. She couldn't believe the son of a bitch had ratted her out to Olivia. What part of "confidential informant" didn't he understand? The cop didn't care though. He was closing in on Olivia and was all about doing what he had to do to make an arrest. And if he took Olivia in, he'd take her in too. She felt it as strongly as she'd felt the cards were on her side tonight.

Clare eyed the stack of chips in Melinda's hands. She saw a clean slate where fresh options were open to her. But those options would only last as long as she stayed out of Finz's grasp. Twenty grand and change wasn't much, but it was enough to reinvent herself. With it she could disappear to a different part of the country and reemerge with a different name. Just the thought of starting over without the lead weights she'd accumulated throughout her life filled her with hope, which was something she hadn't felt in years.

She glanced back at Gault, waiting in the wings. She could square her debt with him, but it would cut into her escape money. As much as she should, she wouldn't. She'd just have to owe him.

They reached the cage. Melinda slid Clare's chips over to the cashier.

"Is a cashier's check okay?" Melinda's question sounded more like an assertion.

If she was going to run, a check was no good. "No, I'd prefer cash."

Melinda frowned. "A check would be safer."

"But cash is more convenient."

Melinda nodded to the cashier, and they all watched him count the money in hundreds. He inserted the thick wad of bills into an envelope, then sealed it and handed it to Clare.

"Are you sure I can't offer you a room, Clare?" Melinda asked.

Clare looked past her at Gault, who was getting antsy. Maybe she should take Melinda's offer of a room, as long as it was for more than one night. "No, I need to get home tonight."

"I understand. Well, I hope you'll be back again soon."

"I will."

"Wonderful. I'll have Baptiste and Maurice escort you to your car."

Clare grinned. "I'd really appreciate that."

The bouncers walked her out to the parking lot, and she pointed out her Honda. The guys engaged her in small talk as they enveloped her in their protective shield.

She knew Gault was following without even looking back. She was protected until she drove off their lot, but what she needed was a head start.

"There's a man following us," she said. "He's been watching me all night."

"Do you know him?" Maurice asked.

"I'm here a lot, and I've seen him around."

Baptiste looked back. "We'll take care of him."

"I don't want him getting into trouble. I could be wrong. This money might be making me a little paranoid."

"Don't you worry," Maurice said. "We'll use good judgment. We have a number of protocols at our disposal."

Protocols. The word had an infinite meaning in their powerful hands.

They reached Clare's Honda. Baptiste held her door open for her as she got in.

"Enjoy your winnings, Clare, and try not to lose too much of it back to us," he said before closing her door.

Clare pulled away with a smile on her face as Maurice and Baptiste blocked Gault from getting into his car. The last sight of him she had was being escorted back into the casino.

"Reinvention," she said to herself.

But for reinvention to happen, there had to be change, and change meant disposing of the past. She pulled her car over. The on-ramp that would take her back home to Martinez was ahead of her. If she took it, winning this money tonight meant nothing. She'd go home to the same old shit. Gault would shake her down for his money, Roy would keep expecting her to spy for him, Finz would keep twisting the blade until he got his confession, and Olivia would keep on judging her. If she truly wanted a fresh start, she had to leave all that behind. It wasn't like she would miss anything if she left. All that was waiting for her back there was that shitty trailer, her crappy Target job, and a lifetime of mistakes.

That wasn't entirely true. It wouldn't be a guilt-free escape. Running meant leaving her sister in the lurch, but that was probably for the best. She'd sold her out to the cops and Infidelity Limited. Running out on Olivia was the nearest thing to doing her a favor. Clare was certainly a liability if she stayed. She'd make it up to her someday.

She eyed the money on the passenger seat next to her. That cash could take her anywhere, so where to go? Vegas? But everyone would expect her to go there. Oregon? Washington? No one would expect that. Reno? She liked the sound of that. It was reasonably close, cheap, and would give her time to regroup and plan her next move.

She had one last thing to do before she reinvented herself. She took out the two cell phones—hers and the one Roy had given her. She pulled the battery and the SIM card out of Roy's phone. She snapped the SIM card in two and tossed the pieces out the window. She took her phone and called Olivia. While it rang, she lit a cigarette. Mercifully, the call went to voice mail, saving her the awkwardness of actually talking to her sister.

"Liv, it's me. Look, I'm sorry. I know I've been ducking your calls. I'm a bitch. I shouldn't have gone to Finz. It was stupid. Not that either of us expect me to do anything smart." A lifetime of screwups and Olivia clearing them up flashed across the back of her mind. "Look, there's too much heat right now with Roy, Finz, and some other shit I've gotten myself into, so I'm leaving. I don't know where I'm going. Call me a coward, a low-down bitch, and anything else you want, but it's the right thing to do. If I don't, either Roy or Finz will get to you through me." She took a big drag on her cigarette. "As your older and dumber sister, I want to give you some sisterly advice for once—run. The bastards are closing in. They're going to get you, so get out while you still can. You have money and smarts. They'll never catch you. Shitty advice, I know, but I have faith in you."

She went to hang up, but she had one more thing to say. "I'm really sorry for getting you into all this. I hope you can forgive me and will let me make it up to you . . . if I can. I'm ditching this phone now, but I'll be in touch later. Love you, Sis."

Tears were streaming down her face when she hung up.

"You are a fucking coward," she said to herself, "but you won't be tomorrow. You'll be someone else."

She pulled apart her phone, like she'd done with Roy's, then she put her car in drive and headed toward Reno.

CHAPTER THIRTY-NINE

Olivia stared at the cash—$450,000 in neatly bound stacks. She picked up one of the stacks of bills and ran a fingernail down its edge. Money was just numbers these days. Nearly half a million bucks didn't mean a lot until you saw it in the flesh. It didn't take up much real estate on her dining room table. Just forty-five banded bundles of one hundred $100 bills. But its value far exceeded its monetary worth. It wasn't just $450,000. It was breathing space. It was her salvation. It was her last shot at saving herself.

"I don't think I've seen so much money at one time," she remarked.

"Me either," Andrew said.

She put the cash down and took his hand. "You don't know what this means to me. Whatever happens, I will pay you back."

He blushed a little. "Let's take this one step at a time. Let's get Roy off your back and worry about the money later."

"Did the bank give you any trouble?"

"No. The money was in an escrow account. They had to give it to me in some form."

It had taken Andrew two days to get the escrow company to process his request. It worked in Olivia's favor that Andrew had provided the money. If she had withdrawn the money from her account, it would have raised questions, but a payout of escrow funds wouldn't set off any alarms.

They didn't sit on their hands for those two days. They came up with a plan for taking Infidelity Limited down. Roy liked to think of himself as being off the radar. He wasn't. He lived somewhere and had a place where he kept every one of Infidelity Limited's clients' secrets. For his system to work, there'd have to be something that amounted to a little black book, whether it was a file on a computer or paper files. It would contain all the dirt on his clients and who they had killed, including Richard's killer and her. When Olivia gave Roy the cash, he'd take it either home or to his storage place. Either way, he was taking it somewhere that was real. The mission was simple—break in and get everything he had on her. Once she had that, the hold Roy had over her would be broken and she'd have something to give Finz.

The weakness in this plan was that it relied on Roy leading them to the place he kept his records, which might not be the case. At the very least, Roy would take them to a physical location that would possess a public record. They could use that information to track down his true identity. Once they had Roy's real name, public records would move Infidelity Limited from the shadows into the light.

The plan was easy in theory but harder in practice. Roy wasn't stupid. He'd been getting away with this for years. Olivia couldn't be the first person to think she could follow him back to his lair. That was why he had his little helpers on call to run interference for him. She imagined Roy himself would run all sorts of countersurveillance maneuvers to ensure he wasn't being followed. The chances of Olivia and Andrew beating Infidelity Limited at its own game were slim. But technology provided the solution. Infidelity Limited was supposed to be about finding cheaters. They weren't the only ones in that business. There were dozens of phone apps designed for catching cheating spouses. One type was a phone-finder app. It would use the GPS capabilities of a phone to locate where the phone was in the world. All they had to do was slip a phone to Roy and let him lead them to his home. That was the tricky part. He'd search Olivia, especially now that he didn't trust her. The solution was for Andrew to do it.

Roy liked his isolated meeting spots, usually with one road in and the same one out. It made surveillance easy, but it also meant picking up Roy's tail after he left was just as easy. Andrew planned to use his construction crew to rig an accident so he could slip Roy the phone in all the confusion. It wasn't the slickest of plans, but it was the best they had.

They had the cash. They had the plan. Now they just had to wait for Roy's call.

Olivia checked her watch again. "When do you think he'll call back?" She'd left a message for Roy this morning that she had the money. It was now midafternoon.

"Today, or maybe tomorrow. He needs time to get everything in place."

"I hope this works."

"Chances are it will."

"Chances? You don't sound too confident."

"I don't want to blow smoke. This may not work."

It had to. It was their only shot. Once she handed the money over to Roy, she wouldn't see or hear from him again.

"It's not like I have any other options," she said.

"You do." He patted the money. "You can do what Clare said and run. There's more than enough cash here to take off to some nonextradition country and start over. It's okay. If you want to run, I'll support your decision."

This morning, she'd picked up Clare's message and played it for Andrew. It was heartwarming to hear Clare be so honest but concerning that she believed she could solve the situation by running away. True to her word, she must have ditched the phone. Olivia's calls had dead-ended with "the subscriber you are calling isn't available."

Olivia eyed the cash. Skipping the country made sense, but she wouldn't just be skipping out on Finz and Roy; she'd be skipping out on her life, everything she'd made of it—and Andrew. He'd become more than a friend, and she felt if she went, he would come with her, destroying his life too. But the number one reason why running wasn't an option was she'd be damned if she'd let Roy get away with this. He was going down, or she was. It didn't matter which, but it ended today.

"No, I want to get my life back, and that means sticking it out."

He grinned. He pulled her to him and hugged her tight. "That's my girl. An attitude like that and we can't fail."

$$*\qquad*\qquad*$$

Roy called at three. "Chabot Space and Science Center. Now," he said and hung up.

She looked at Andrew. "We're on."

"Where?"

"The Chabot observatory."

They packed the cash into a paper Trader Joe's grocery bag and covered it with a sweater. It was less conspicuous than a briefcase or sports duffel.

"I'm scared," she said.

"That's fine. Scared is good. Scared is natural."

Andrew was probably right, but she'd been living in a state of fear and paranoia for weeks. It would be nice to feel a different emotion for a change. "Tell me this is going to work."

"There are no promises."

"Just say it."

He hugged her. "This is going to work."

He put her in her car, then went to his truck, parked on the street. As they both drove off, she felt as though she were going into battle. She'd never felt as alone as she did when she made the turn at the end of the street. Andrew might have her back, but it was just her versus Roy now. What she did in the next hour would shape the rest of her life.

"Don't screw up, Olivia," she said to herself.

The Chabot Space and Science Center was in the middle of the Redwood Regional Park in the Oakland Hills. Olivia took Highway 24, then Highway 13. Normally, this scenic route surrounded by tree-covered hills gave the area a restful, alpine feel. Today, it was more insidious. Roy and his people were hiding among the trees.

She took Skyline Boulevard from the highway and followed the long, winding road that climbed into the hills. True to form, Roy had picked a secluded place with limited access. Skyline provided the only access to Chabot. Dolores or her ski-masked sidekick would no doubt be watching to make sure she was coming alone.

It wasn't the perfect location for Roy. Skyline didn't dead-end at Chabot. It went past the space center. That meant the center could be accessed from a southerly or northerly direction, so Roy's people would have to watch two approaches. It also meant that Andrew had to cover both exits when Roy left.

"This is going to work," she reminded herself.

She turned into the center and parked the Audi in the parking structure instead of the open lot. Somehow it seemed fitting for a payoff to take place in the shadows.

Roy wasn't waiting for her inside the entrance of the center like an eager docent. She paid the entrance fee and walked in, then called him on the burner cell.

"I'm here," she said.

"I'm hanging out with Nellie, Rachel, and Leah. Come meet us. Ask for the girls if you don't know where to find us."

Roy humor, she thought. Nellie, Rachel, and Leah were Chabot's three telescopes, housed inside their own observatories outside of the main museum.

He was standing in the middle of the deck that connected the three observatories. Dozens of fifth graders from some school party zoomed in and out. He was helping a couple of kids use a filter to stare at the sun.

He looked so normal there with those kids. Despite his size and shaved head, he could be mistaken for a dad, a husband, or a teacher. Instead, he was a man who extorted money, blackmailed, and killed. It was funny how easily people could be deceived. He spotted her, handed the filter to the kids, and waved.

He was in a better mood than the one he'd been in during their meeting at the poultry farm. Maybe he'd forgiven her transgression. Then again, extorting nearly half a million bucks would likely lift a person's spirits. She cut through the kids to join him.

"Isn't this place great?" he said. "I haven't been here in a while, but I love it. Look at the kids sucking up all this science and knowledge. These are the kinds of places that change the world."

She didn't understand why he kept up with this pretense as the happy-go-lucky friend. He'd removed the mask to reveal his true face. Why pretend anymore?

"I thought we had business," she said.

He frowned. "Can't you take a minute to enjoy the moment?"

"No."

"Okay, let's take it inside."

He waved good-bye to the kids, and they returned to the relative quiet of the museum. Only a handful of kids were chasing each other back and forth past the exhibits, and there were even fewer adults.

"Let's go in here," he said and took her into the planetarium.

A docent stopped them to tell them the show was midway through and suggested they could catch the next show in half an hour.

"That's okay," Roy said.

The prerecorded show was playing to a couple of dozen people dotted around the auditorium. It wasn't hard to find an empty section of seats. He guided her to a section at the back. They settled into their seats, and she stared up at a representation of the night's sky.

Roy leaned in. "Sorry about this, but I have to do it."

She nodded. She knew what was coming. It was hunt-the-wire time.

Like they were teenagers at a movie, he reached over and ran his hand across her chest and stomach. He told her to roll onto her side so he could check the back of her neck and her back. Finally, he ran a hand between her legs.

"Enjoy yourself?" she said when he was done.

"Bitchiness is beneath you," he said, taking her purse. After he rummaged through it, he said, "Let's go."

The docent cocked her head when they walked back out.

Roy held up his hands. "You were right. We really need to see the show from the beginning."

"Starts at the top of the hour," she said.

Roy took Olivia's hand and led her back by the exhibits. Olivia wondered if it was the same hand that had held the knife that took Heather's and Amy's lives.

He made the pretense of looking at an old space capsule. "Where's my money, Olivia? I thought you said you had it."

"It's in my car."

He exhaled. "You better not be fucking with me. You tried once and failed. I won't tolerate a second time."

Her heart fluttered a note of unrest, and she shuddered. He didn't see it with his head buried in the capsule. "I thought bringing in all that cash would be weird if this place searched my bag."

The answer seemed to satisfy him. "Where'd you park?"

Olivia walked him to her car. The parking structure was long and narrow, making it cramped. It didn't offer much in the way of privacy, but with so few visitors on a weekday, she'd found a quiet spot on the top level. She popped the Audi's trunk and removed the Trader Joe's bag.

Roy smirked at the bag, but he took it. He removed the sweater and peered inside.

"It's all there. You can count it," she told him.

"I will."

She and Andrew had loaded three disposable phones with an app to track Roy. She had one in her purse, Andrew had one, and so did one of his guys. It didn't matter which of them planted the phone, as long as someone did. She got the first crack at this. There was no way she could have put it in with the money or slipped it into his pocket without him noticing. Her best option was to plant it in his car, but she needed access to it.

"You want to take it back to your car and count it there?" she asked.

"Why my car? You seem nervous. What's going on, Olivia?"

"Nothing's going on. We've got nearly half a million out in the open, and we don't need the attention. We can do it in my car if you like, but let's not do it where anyone can see."

His look was probing. She could feel him picking apart her words. After a moment, he nodded. "Okay, okay, don't fret. We can use your car."

They climbed into her car, and she saw her chance to plant the phone disappear.

She was forced to sit there and watch Roy check every bundle of bills. When he was done, he repacked the money into the grocery bag.

"You did well, Olivia. I can't believe you pulled all this money together so quickly."

"You're not the only one."

"The banks didn't give you any trouble?"

"Yeah. They bitched, but it was my money, so what could they do?"

"And now it's my money." Roy opened the door to leave.

"Is that it?"

"Yes," he said and climbed from the car.

Olivia jumped out of the car and blocked his path. "What happens now?"

"Nothing. We go our separate ways. Our business relationship is at an end."

Just as she feared. As soon as he walked off with that money, he was gone, and so was her chance at sneaking him the phone. It was down to Andrew and his guys now.

"We're not done," she protested. "You have the knife. That money buys the knife."

"It doesn't, Olivia. You cost me a lot of money. Far more than I have here. What you've bought is my silence."

"That's not right."

"You can take the money back, but then you'll take the risks that go along with that. Let me keep it, and I will protect you as best I can. Your choice."

Olivia said nothing. There was nothing to say. Roy was lying. She'd spoken to too many of his victims to believe there was protection. There was only ruin. But she couldn't force the issue. It was down to Andrew now.

"Thought not." Roy sidestepped her and kept on walking. "Don't leave for twenty minutes."

Olivia waited until Roy was out of sight before using her high ground to her advantage. The third-story vantage point meant she had a bird's-eye view of the comings and goings in and out of the science center. She tracked Roy's progress out of the parking structure and over to his familiar Chrysler, parked around the corner from the main entrance.

She pulled out her phone and dialed Andrew. He picked up on the first ring.

"I didn't plant the phone," she told him.

"That's okay. That's what we're here for. But he took the money?"

"Yes."

"Good. Do you know what he's driving?"

Roy's car rounded the corner, heading toward Skyline. He stopped at the stop sign, then turned left.

"He's driving his silver Chrysler 300. He's coming back down Skyline toward Highway 13."

"He's coming straight toward me. I've got this, Liv. And remember . . ."

"What?"

"This is going to work."

She smiled and hung up.

CHAPTER FORTY

Keep it together, Andrew thought. *It's all falling into place.* He'd had to pull a plan together on the fly once Roy called. It worked out in his and Olivia's favor that Roy had kept this meeting local. It took no time to mobilize his guys and just five minutes to come up with a plan once he'd checked out the area on Google Earth. And now that Roy was coming back down Skyline to pick up Highway 13, his plan was a lock.

But he only had one shot at it. He had to rig the fake accident before Roy turned off Skyline for Joaquin Miller Road. Once Roy was on Joaquin Miller, there were too many variables to control. Too much traffic. Too many side streets. The situation wouldn't be Andrew's to determine. The best place to take Roy out was at the intersection where Joaquin Miller intersected with Skyline. It was the only spot he could control.

Andrew had parked his truck facing uphill on a turnout on the last bend before the intersection. Around the corner, in another of his construction trucks, was Manny Reyes and his son, Alex. Manny had been with him since he'd started Macready Construction. Together they'd assembled a no-nonsense, hardworking crew that put up good-looking houses. Five years older than Andrew, Manny was both a brother and father to him. When he asked for help, Manny was there. Yesterday, when he told Manny he needed to rig a car accident in the next couple of days because it was important, Manny didn't ask why . . . he asked when. He wrangled the crew together, and they were on standby.

The other half of his crew was staked out on Pinehurst with a similar setup, should Roy have chosen that route. He called them and told them to go home for the day. Then he called Manny.

"Our guy is on the way. He's driving a silver Chrysler 300. He should be coming by in the next five, six minutes. I'll give you the heads-up as soon as I see him. Stay on the line."

"You got it. You want this to go down like you said?"

"Yes. Just sideswipe him. Superficial damage only. I want this guy mobile. But you can go heavy on the theatrics."

"You know us hotheaded Mexicans. We don't know any other way."

Andrew laughed. "I owe you, man."

"Yes, you do. Now watch the road."

Andrew focused on the road. He played over and over again the various ways he could slip the cell phone into Roy's car. He liked a couple of his ideas, if Manny and Alex could provide enough of a distraction while the occasional vehicle went by.

After a couple of minutes, he got antsy and started the truck's engine. He didn't expect Roy quite yet, but he didn't want to be caught napping if Roy was a lead foot.

His hands began sweating. The anticipation was getting to him. He wiped his palms on his jeans.

"Be cool," he said to himself.

"Say again," Manny said over the phone.

He'd forgotten the phone line was still open.

Roy's silver sedan appeared, rounding the left-hand curve four hundred yards ahead.

"Our man is here. He'll be with you in thirty seconds tops. Be ready to pull out."

"We're ready."

"He's coming toward me. Now he's slowing for the bend. He'll be with you in five seconds. He's rounding the bend now. Get him! Get him!"

It all happened out of Andrew's sight, but he heard it. The crash happened in stereo. The thud and scrape of metal on metal spilled through his open window as well as over the phone line.

"Gotcha, you prick."

He jammed the gearshift into drive and pulled a wild U-turn that almost caused a wreck when he cut off a Prius coming uphill. He raced around the corner and slithered to a halt before he added to the damage.

Manny had done a good job. Their vehicles were almost parallel to each other. Manny had clipped Roy's Chrysler at a sharp angle, starting at the front passenger door, down the rear passenger door, and finally driving into the rear fender. It looked like what it was. Manny had pulled out into the side of Roy's sedan.

Roy, Manny, and Alex were already out of their vehicles, examining the damage. Roy was a big guy with a bouncer's build to go with it, and he towered over Manny and Alex. Despite the height difference, Manny and Alex were screaming at Roy and each other in Spanish. Roy looked ready to flatten the both of them as he tried to squeeze a word in.

Part 1 of the act complete, Andrew thought. *Now on to part 2.* He snatched the cell phone they'd be tracing off the charger and jumped from his truck.

"What the hell, Manny?" he yelled as he rolled up on the trio. "Again? How many more times are you going to wreck one of my vehicles? You're a goddamn liability."

Manny rounded on Andrew and told him he was a "no good fucking piece of shit" in Spanish. They'd joked about whether they should carry the argument on in Spanish in order to chat among themselves about what to do next, but Andrew decided against it. He didn't know if Roy spoke Spanish, and what if a Spanish-speaking bystander overheard?

"English," Andrew fired back. "You're in America, buddy."

This set off Alex, who ran up to Andrew and jabbed his finger in his face while spouting what he was going to do to him.

"Will you three shut the fuck up?!" Roy bellowed.

They did.

Andrew held up his hands. "I'm so sorry. These clowns work for me. I'm insured. You won't be out-of-pocket because I'll be taking it out of these assholes' pockets."

"That's fine. I'm covered. Don't worry about it. I'm in a hurry."

Andrew was worried he wouldn't want the fuss. He had to plant that phone in the car.

"Look at this damage," Andrew said. "I can't let you do that."

"I'm good. Seriously."

Andrew ignored Roy. He circled around Manny's truck to get close to the damage. He needed to get inside the car. Roy tried to follow, but Manny and Alex got in his face.

"You speeding," Manny said in heavily accented English. "Crazy speed. Very dangerous."

"You could have killed us, man," Alex added.

"And you weren't watching the road," Roy said.

Andrew ran a hand over the damaged passenger door. "I don't know. This looks pretty fucked up. We need to check these doors."

"You say my dad wasn't watching the road. He was. He's a good driver. It's you *cochinos* who don't look." Alex leaned in, forcing Roy to take a step back.

Andrew used this moment to pull open the front passenger door. "This one's okay," he called.

A driver coming down the hill passed the wreckage and yelled, "Move that shit off the road!"

"Trying to!" Andrew yelled back.

"You know what? You're right," Roy said. "I was speeding, but you shouldn't have pulled out. Let's call it even. That's what our insurance companies will do."

Andrew moved to the rear passenger door. He had to yank on it hard to get it open. "This one's working too."

"Great," Roy said. "Then why don't we get back on the road?"

Manny and Alex maintained their protests, but Roy was pushing them aside. Andrew had seconds. He palmed the cell phone into his hand and shoved it into the gap where the seat cushion and the seat back met. "Yeah, I don't see any major damage here."

"Then I don't see that we have any business," Roy said.

Andrew slammed the passenger door. "You sure?"

Roy opened the driver's door. "I am."

"Thanks, man. I really appreciate it. Now I just have to get these assholes to pay me back for the damage to my vehicle."

Manny and Alex started up with Andrew again. Roy simply got behind the wheel and drove off. They waited until he was truly out of sight before they dropped the charade.

"Did you do it?" Manny asked.

Andrew held up empty hands. "I did. Do you think he bought it?"

"Yeah, because of our fine-ass Mexican acting," Alex said.

"Thanks, guys. You don't know what this means. Now round up the crew. Hit whatever spot you want to. It's on the company credit card."

Alex high-fived Andrew.

Manny told his son to get behind the wheel. When they were alone, he said, "Is everything cool? You've got me worried."

The elation Andrew felt ebbed away. "A friend is in a tricky spot. It's going to be okay though. Don't worry."

"I'm going to hold you to that."

"Go. Have fun. Don't get too shit-faced. I expect everyone back on the job site tomorrow."

Manny managed a smile. "And I expect the same of you."

They got into their trucks and cleared the ruse off the road.

As soon as Andrew was moving, he called Olivia.

"It's done," he told her.

"It is?"

"Yes. I'll meet you back at your place."

He liked the sound of relief in her voice.

*　　　*　　　*

At last, something's going right, Olivia thought. She was far from being out of the woods, but for once she felt like the odds of surviving this nightmare had swung just a bit in her favor.

She checked the time. Roy had had his twenty minutes. She drove the Audi out of the parking structure and got on Skyline. She let the car coast down the winding road, allowing gravity to dictate the speed.

Roy was leading them home. It would be interesting to see where he lived. What kind of lifestyle had the victims of Infidelity Limited afforded him? She hoped it wasn't lavish. It would be horrible to think he'd built a kingdom based on misery and deception. The only comfort she could take was that with a little luck, whatever standard of living he had would be gone soon.

She thought of Andrew's money. He'd worked so hard for it. He'd handed her the proceeds of a house he'd built from the dirt up without a moment's thought. She had to get it back for him.

She prayed Roy was leading them to his little black book. Once they had that, she could sic Finz on Roy. It would solve two problems by letting her aggressors neutralize each other. That would be perfect.

A sharp impact from the rear snapped her head back into the headrest. The force sent her Audi surging forward as it went into a tight bend. The car slithered on the road, but it made the curve. Olivia checked her rearview mirror. An aged Crown Victoria had just rear-ended her.

It looked like it had been a police car in a previous life, judging by the cowcatcher over the front bumper and the spotlights still on the door. From the sedan's poor outward condition, she guessed the brakes had probably gone out on it.

She really didn't have the time for this. Roy was what counted. She'd just swap insurance details and get back on the road. There wasn't much room to pull over on the narrow, descending road, but she slowed her car on the straight before the next hairpin ahead.

The Crown Victoria didn't slow. It accelerated. The Ford's big engine roared, and she looked in her rearview as it bore down on her. She hit the gas, but it was too late. The old cop car slammed into the back of her again, this time with enough force to send the Audi into a slide. She'd been up to Tahoe enough times in the snow to know how to steer into the slide. She caught it, but the rear passenger-side wheel slipped off the roadway onto the dirt. She blessed the car's four-wheel-drive system for keeping it all together. It was an extra Richard had insisted on. Now she could have kissed him for it.

The Crown Victoria came at her again. Olivia out-accelerated him.

The hairpin loomed. She was a dead duck going into the switch-back. As soon as she braked for it, the Ford driver would simply torpedo her. But if she kept it tight to the corner, she'd at least give the son of a bitch as little to hit as possible.

She stamped on the brakes. The Crown Victoria locked its brakes a second before it smashed into the back of her sedan. The impact sent Olivia's car spinning around, which only served to help her around the bend, while it forced the Ford driver to overshoot the corner and slow down.

She took her small advantage and mashed the gas pedal to the floor. The Audi leaped forward, helped by the steep downward gradient.

One thought filled her mind—*why?* But she already knew the answer. This was no case of road rage. This was Roy's doing. He wasn't content to take her money. He wanted her life too. While he'd left the likes of Karen Innes to rot in prison, Olivia wasn't getting off that lightly. She was too much of a liability since she knew about Heather and Amy. She had to die too. All police investigations stopped at the grave. Roy's words came back at her. "Our business relationship is at an end."

The Crown Victoria gathered pace behind her. A tight left-hander was coming up, but she had enough of a gap to make that turn and not have him ram her off the road. The next bend, she wasn't so sure.

The ex-cop car closed in over the next two curves. She glanced at her would-be assassin, and she recognized him. It was the man she'd chewed out for following her after she'd visited Nick's sister, Mandy. Roy had had his employees following her. Had any part of her life been her own since hiring Infidelity Limited?

The Crown Victoria nudged her again, then again. Her trunk lid popped open. Cocooned inside her car, she'd been somewhat insulated from the violence and danger trying to get at her. With the trunk lid open, the Crown Victoria's engine's roar filled her car's cabin, its angry snarl at her neck.

Another hairpin bend approached. Beyond it was just sky. Only one car was making it around that corner. The other was taking a faster route down. It wouldn't be her.

The Crown Victoria zeroed in on her bumper. It nudged it twice, with the sound of buckling metal and splitting plastic. He was teeing her up so he could drive her straight over the edge, but she had other ideas.

"C'mon, c'mon, keep it coming, buddy," she murmured.

The Ford driver backed off, letting a fifty-foot gap open up. She didn't panic. He was just getting breathing space before he rammed her again. She maintained her speed.

"C'mon, c'mon, ram me. You know you want to." She hoped to God her idea worked.

As if the Ford driver had heard her, the Crown Victoria surged forward. The engine growled. The switchback was two hundred feet away, but her gaze was on her rearview mirror. The sedan's reflection filled the mirror. When the car was just feet from smashing into her, she spun the wheel hard to the left, then stamped hard on the brakes. When the Crown Victoria struck her, it slammed into the rear corner of the Audi, sending it into a fast, tight spin. The Ford driver wasn't so lucky. The Crown Victoria had made only a glancing blow to Olivia's sedan. The Ford, large and heavy, plowed on. Its brakes locked up, smoke peeling off the tires, but they did nothing to slow the car's progress. The Audi spun back around in time for Olivia to see her attacker, still at the wheel of his car, fly off the edge of the road. The car clipped a tree as it went, sending it into a flat spin.

Olivia's Audi finally came to an untidy stop in the middle of the switchback, after clipping a dirt verge. She couldn't believe it. It had worked. She was alive. It took a moment for the realization to sink in.

She climbed from the car and staggered over to the edge of the road. The Crown Victoria lay on its roof nearly two hundred feet below. It had been a brutal fall that caved the roof in. If Roy's man was still alive, he'd be crippled. The son of a bitch deserved it.

She walked back to her car. The adrenaline coursing through her body suddenly turned off its tap. Her neck was stiff. Her left elbow and knee ached. She got behind the wheel and maneuvered her car onto the turnout at the edge of the road, then called Andrew.

"Roy just tried to have me killed." Her voice sounded a million miles away.

CHAPTER FORTY-ONE

Olivia was a mess once she got back behind the wheel. Somehow she'd lost the ability to drive. Her feet were clumsy on the pedals, and her arms were weak on the steering wheel. She guessed she was going into shock.

"I can't drive."

"You can," Andrew said and talked her down Skyline. He told her to find somewhere to park and he'd come for her. When she reached the bottom of the hill, she hauled up in a church parking lot to wait for him.

The Audi was trashed. The rear was completely caved in, the trunk half its size. With no lights and the license plate unreadable, there was no way she could drive it without a cop stopping her. She couldn't afford that. They didn't have time for questions.

Andrew held her when he saw the wrecked car. "It's okay. You're safe. Are you okay?"

"I think so."

Andrew spent five minutes checking her out for broken bones or a concussion.

"He's getting away," she protested.

"He's not. We know his location. We can catch up with him any-time." He eyed her Audi. "We need another car. The Audi's out, and he's seen my truck."

"Richard's car."

Andrew paused for a beat. "You okay using it?"

"Yes."

"Good. We have to get your car out of here though. It's too much of a red flag to leave it here, and we don't want anyone putting two and two together when they find Roy's guy."

He pulled out his phone. "Manny, it's me. You know anyone with a tow truck? I need to get a car off the road for a couple of days. Tell your guy he can find it at that Greek Orthodox Church on Lincoln. It's a black Audi A4. You can't miss it. The rear end is totally caved in. I'll leave the keys under the driver's seat."

They cleared out the car and left the keys under the seat. Andrew drove her home, where they switched cars for Richard's Mercedes. She hadn't touched it since she'd driven it home from the impound yard after Finz's people had cleared it from their investigation.

Andrew drove. She couldn't. The image of her would-be killer flying off the edge of the road filled her mind. It shouldn't have surprised her that Roy wanted her dead. Killing was his business, so why would he treat her any differently? She'd outlived her usefulness.

Olivia's gaze was on her phone in its holder. Roy's name appeared in a digitized thumbtack on a map display. Every few seconds, the map under the thumbtack jumped a fraction. Their cell phone homing beacon was working.

The "Find My Sweetie" phone-finding app made tailing Roy sim-ple, but having to switch cars had cost them precious time. Roy had a forty-minute head start on them by the time they hit the road in Richard's Mercedes. That was a big deficit to make up. The Bay Area rush hour helped reduce Roy's escape velocity. Andrew had been chip-ping away at the gap, but Roy still had a twenty-minute lead. It was a decent margin. If Dolores or anyone was watching Roy's back, he or she would give him the all clear. Still, those twenty minutes equated to a fifteen-mile head start. A lot could happen in that distance. Roy could switch cars. He could discover the phone. The phone's battery could go flat. They could hit a black spot and lose the signal. She knew it was the paranoia screaming at her, but it didn't mean any of these outcomes were less real. All she could do was succumb to the fact that her future was in fate's hands.

While her gaze might have been on Roy's progress, the man himself filled her thoughts. He had put a bounty on her head. She couldn't get past that notion. She tried to come to terms with the concept of Roy wanting her dead. Bounties were for outlaws and government officials in banana republics. Hits weren't put out on wives and Realtors. It showed her how far she'd fallen off life's tightrope.

"Do you think he's going home?" Olivia asked.

"He got what he wanted out of you. There's no reason for him to stick around," Andrew said.

"Do you think he knows I'm still alive?"

Andrew shook his head. "Hard to say. His guy should have contacted him by now, so he must know something went awry. He'll likely send someone to check."

Since Roy's attempt on her life had failed, would he send someone else to kill her? If they didn't get him now, he would get her. It was weird to imagine there was a bullet out there for her, lurking around the corner. She couldn't live like that. Roy was a terminal disease, lurking in her system, biding his time before turning malignant. The cure was simple. This had to work. She had to take him down tonight.

She had the advantage for once. He thought he'd won, so his guard would be down. He wasn't expecting her to learn his secrets. That thought warmed her. She was about to crack Roy wide open—his true identity, where he lived, and where he stashed his blackmail evidence. He couldn't hide from her now.

She looked at where Roy was on the moving map and estimated where they were in relation to him. She guessed they were four miles behind.

"I think we need to be closer," she said.

They were traveling south on I-680, closing in on San Jose. According to the app, Roy had already passed by the city.

"Where do you think he's heading?" Olivia asked.

Andrew shook his head. "I think we still have a ways to go. If I was Roy, I wouldn't be working out of my backyard."

That answer ignited a flame of fear in her. "What if he takes a flight? The phone is in the car, not on him."

"I don't think he's flying anywhere. He's just bypassed three airports. Also, he won't want a record of him going through airport security. Wherever he's going, he's going by car. All we can do is follow and see where he leads us."

Olivia frowned.

"I know this is scary, but try not to worry. He doesn't know we're coming for him. We have the element of surprise. We're in good shape."

*   *   *

Roy checked his dashboard clock. He'd been on the road a couple of hours. Olivia was dead by now.

"Rest in peace, Olivia."

It had been a tough call to order the hit on Olivia, but she was trouble. Her tenacity was the problem. He could see her going public if the cops busted her. Not that the cops were a concern. They could never track him down. Olivia had the potential for being bad for business. Infidelity Limited worked because it was a secret. It wouldn't if Olivia spread rumors about how it operated. Now that she'd paid him off, there was no more to gain and quite a bit to lose.

Lou Carrington was supposed to check in after it was done, and he hadn't, so Roy called Carrington's cell. The call went through to voice mail, which surprised him.

"How did things go, Lou? Call me."

After an hour, Carrington still hadn't called. It wasn't like him not to report in. Roy called him again and still got voice mail.

Carrington wasn't ducking his calls. Something was wrong. Even if he'd failed to take out Olivia, he would have reported in. Had Carrington gotten hurt in the wreck with Olivia?

He called Dolores. She answered on the second ring. At least someone was taking his calls tonight.

"What's up?" she asked, above the noise of what sounded like a rowdy bar.

"I need you to work. You available?"

"Sure."

"Lou was meant to take out Olivia Shaw after she paid me off, but he isn't answering his phone. Will you check it out?"

"It'll take me a couple of hours to get over there. That okay?"

"No problem."

"I'll get back to you."

There was nothing else for him to do, so he focused on driving. As he racked up the miles, he ran through the possible scenarios. None of them would really have an impact on him, even if Olivia was alive. Whatever the outcome, he just needed to cross the t's and dot the i's with Olivia Shaw before moving on to the next client. If she wasn't dead yet, she soon would be.

He pulled up in front of the house and smiled. Coming home always felt good.

Luis, attentive as usual, came out to greet him. "What happened to the car?"

"Just a fender bender."

"How'd everything go?"

Roy popped the trunk and held up Olivia's grocery bag filled with cash. "We got paid."

Luis took Roy's overnight bag, and they both entered the house. "How's Beth?"

Luis said "okay" in a way that meant she was just shy of that. Before Roy could ask for a better explanation, his cell rang. It was Dolores.

"Carrington's dead," she informed him. "He wiped out on Skyline Boulevard."

"And Olivia?"

"Don't know. News reports are saying Carrington went off the road after colliding with another car. The cops are considering it a hit-and-run. I went by Olivia's house and her sister's place. Neither of them is there. I think she's alive."

Roy didn't know what he felt. It was a mix of admiration and irritation. "What do you want me to do?"

"Go home. I'll take care of this," he said and hung up.

"What's wrong?" Luis asked.

"Carrington's dead, and Olivia is alive."

"Shit. What are you going to do?"

"See what she does next."

*   *   *

"I think this is it," Olivia said.

Roy had pulled off Highway 101. They'd been on it since San Jose, following his progress south for hours. He'd passed through Salinas and Paso Robles. For one frightening minute, Olivia thought he was returning to Morro Bay, but he kept going south. He'd stopped for gas in Santa Maria, and they did the same, in case Roy kept going into Mexico, but Santa Barbara was his final destination.

They were a mile behind Roy when he left Highway 101, so Andrew ramped up his speed. He narrowed the gap to only a few hundred yards once they hit the surface streets. He closed the gap to the point they no longer needed the tracking app. Roy's Chrysler appeared in the distance, its brake lights glowing in the night.

"Don't get too close," Olivia said.

"I won't."

Roy cut through the city, toward the mountains. On the unfamiliar streets, they lost visual contact with Roy, but the dot on Olivia's phone kept moving. She called out the turns as Roy made them.

As they left the city for the foothills, the properties thinned out, leaving them exposed as the lone car following Roy. Andrew dropped back, making sure he was out of sight.

"He's stopped," she said with a note of panic.

"That's okay."

They closed in on the dot's location. Andrew stopped the Mercedes when they caught up with Roy's signal. This was it. They stared across at the house.

Here's what inflicting misery buys, Olivia thought. Roy's home was a two-story mansion with a view of the Pacific. It was pretty. The architecture reminded her of an Italian villa. High walls and an electric gate hemmed in the large estate. Through the wrought iron gates, they could see Roy's Chrysler sitting at the end of the driveway. They'd found the bogeyman.

"He's been at this for a long time to be able to afford this," Andrew said.

How many dead people? How many ruined lives, Roy? Olivia wondered.

Andrew pulled away.

"Where are you going?"

"We can't stick around here. Besides, I need a better lay of the land."

CHAPTER FORTY-TWO

Olivia's phone pinged. It was another text from Andrew. On my way back, it said.

She'd been sitting in the car for over half an hour while Andrew scouted out Roy's property. Neighbors were sparse on the narrow road. There were several blocks between homes, and the road dead-ended half a mile after his house. Roy lived on the uphill side of the street and didn't have any neighbors to spoil his view of the ocean on the downhill side. That meant they had all the privacy they needed to break into his house.

But the remoteness and seclusion also worked against them. This was a ritzy neighborhood, so strangers stuck out. This wasn't the kind of neighborhood where people parked on the street, not that anyone could. It was narrow, barely wide enough for two cars to pass each other without trading door paint. Cops would likely get called for a suspicious vehicle.

Luckily, they'd found parking a quarter mile down the street. There were turnoffs dotted up and down these mountain roads, paved for only a few feet before turning to dirt. Olivia didn't know if they were fire roads or private access roads to someone's property. Whatever they were,

Andrew found one and parked as far off the road as he could before the Mercedes lost traction. It was good enough. A stand of trees hid them from the roadside.

Andrew opened the passenger door and slid in. "It looks good. This perimeter wall only covers the front and the sides. There are no other homes above this street, so there's no one to see us. On the uphill side, there's nothing other than a chain-link fence, and there's a ton of tree cover hemming the back side in. We can get in without being seen."

The anxiety in her chest lessened. "Did you get close to the house?"

He nodded. "I don't see any security systems or muscle patrolling the place. I only saw Roy talking to a young guy."

"Roy said he has a 'woman.'"

"So that's three."

She thought of the guy who'd tried to kill her on Skyline and of Dolores. "There could be more. He does have people working for him."

"Possibly, but I don't think so. I only saw two vehicles other than Roy's Chrysler. We won't know until we get in there, but I don't think the place is teeming with people."

It made sense. Until now, Roy had ensured an impenetrable buffer between himself and his victims. No one knew where he lived, so there was no need for a heavy security presence.

"Let's go," he said.

Andrew grabbed his tool bag off the backseat. They walked together on the road. She slipped her arm around Andrew's.

"What are you doing?"

"Keeping up appearances. We're two people on a night walk, not two burglars casing multimillion-dollar homes."

"Good idea."

They followed a trail up into the mountains. It was a steep enough calf workout that Olivia would feel it in the morning, but it was manageable. The night gave them plenty of cover, and the moon provided enough light to see where they were going without tripping. It took them about twenty minutes to loop around behind Roy's property. When they reached the chain-link fence, Andrew asked her about her climbing skills.

"It's been a while."

He smiled and gave her a boost. With his guidance, she managed to make it over the side without breaking her neck. He tossed his tool bag over before climbing over himself.

"This way," Andrew said.

She followed him through the trees until they reached an opening. He dropped to a knee, and she did likewise.

There were two hundred feet between the tree line and the house. The back side of the house seemed to consist of a living room and a kitchen, which opened out onto a large covered patio. The patio connected to an ornate swimming pool, complete with cabana. Then it was all lawn between that and the tree line.

The lights were off in the living room but not the kitchen, although no one seemed to be in there. The lights were also off on the second floor. The only other illumination came from the pool.

Andrew pointed to the corner of the house to the right of the living room. "We're heading for there. That side of the house is in total darkness. We're aiming for a set of French doors. Stay directly behind me. If those security lights on this side of the house have motion sensors, we need to stay clear of them."

"Got it."

And she did. In the last few weeks, she'd lied to the police, helped two people go into hiding, fled a murder scene, stood up to interrogation, and fought for her life. Compared to all that, what was a bit of housebreaking?

They darted across the lawn. Olivia mimicked Andrew's every move. She kept low and took the same arcing curve around to the side of the house, all without being seen. She pressed herself against the wall next to the French doors.

Andrew pulled out a small penlight and flashed it into the darkened room. It was a den or office. Then he ran the light around the French doors. Each door was made up of individual panes of glass.

"Single pane. Nice," he said.

He handed Olivia the light and pulled out a glass cutter, which he used to cut one of the sectional panes next to the door handle. He carefully removed the glass and laid it on the ground before reaching through the hole and opening the door.

They spent a couple of minutes going through the room. The contents belonged to someone named Luis. It didn't surprise her. Everything Roy had on Infidelity Limited's victims would be in a far more secure place.

It was time to go through the rest of the house.

"We go room by room," Andrew whispered. "Find anything, text me, and I'll do the same. First sign of trouble, run. Get out through this door. Got it?"

"Got it."

"Upstairs or downstairs?"

"Upstairs."

Andrew cracked the door to the hall. No one was outside, so they slipped out.

Standing in the hallway, Olivia's anxiety skyrocketed. What they were doing was insane. They were totally exposed, with nowhere to hide. If Roy walked around the corner, it was over. He was a killer. They'd never leave this place alive. They'd been lucky to get this far without being caught. The smart thing would be to turn around and get the hell out. But the smart thing wasn't available to her. Roy had a kill order out on her, and Finz was closing in. It was only a matter of time before one of them caught up to her. "You okay?" Andrew mouthed.

She nodded.

Andrew went to the first door on his left and put his ear to it. He waved her on before opening it and disappearing inside.

She crossed to the end of the hallway and found herself in the main foyer. The front entrance was straight ahead, a pair of curving stairways to the second floor flanked the foyer, and hallways extended to her left and right. She peered down the hallways and saw no one. When she heard no voices or movement, she jogged over to the stairs, careful to make sure that her sneakers didn't squeak on the tiled floors.

She moved with deliberate pace to the top of the stairs and stopped. She listened again for people, then crossed to the first room. Like Andrew, she pressed her ear to the door and heard nothing. She cracked the door. It was dark inside. She listened for sounds of someone sleeping and heard none. She went inside and flicked on the lights.

It was a bedroom. Going through the closets and drawers, she decided it was a guest room, judging by the lack of personal belongings. She switched off the light and left the room, closing the door.

She repeated the same cautious procedure with the next room. When she got no signs of occupancy, she opened the door, and an acrid stink greeted her. She let herself in and flipped on the light. It was another bedroom, and it had been stripped bare, but that only showcased the fire damage on the floor and walls. It was recent, by the smell. She had a nasty vision of Roy torturing a client in here, and she shuddered.

She left the room and worked her way down the hallway. Every room was either a bedroom or a bathroom. There were another five doors still to open, and she'd keep going, but it was becoming clear the Infidelity Limited vault of secrets wasn't upstairs.

In the hallway, she pulled out her cell and sent a text to Andrew: It's all bedrooms up here so far. Need me down there?

As she pocketed her phone, a voice behind her said, "Who are you?"

CHAPTER FORTY-THREE

Andrew was in what looked to be Roy's personal den. It was a total man cave, with its vintage pinball machine, movie posters, and big-screen TV. The den looked like the kind of place someone would keep secret files, but the most valuable thing he'd found was an extensive vinyl-record collection. Roy seemed to have a bent for '70s American rock music.

Having found a sitting room, a laundry room, a gym, the kitchen, a dining room, and now the den, he was beginning to worry that Roy ran Infidelity Limited elsewhere. If he kept his identity and home this far from his clients, then maybe he did the same with his business records. Everything could be in a storage unit in Temecula for all he knew. If that were true, it would mean a change in plans. This would go from a break-in to a kidnapping.

The door to the den opened. Andrew dived behind the wet bar and hoped the occupant wasn't looking for a drink.

Roy crossed the room and went to his wall of vinyl. If he turned around, he'd see Andrew. Andrew shifted his position to keep out of sight.

Roy pulled out a couple of records and left the room without closing the door.

A thought formed at the back of Andrew's mind—*where's Roy been?* He had seen Roy enter the house but had not seen him since. Andrew had been doing a dance with the young guy, Luis, in order to move around the house unobserved, but Roy seemed to have fallen into a black hole until now. Olivia would have texted him if she'd seen him upstairs. Roy had himself secreted away somewhere in this house.

Andrew ran to the door in time to see Roy turn a corner. He followed, moving with a deliberate pace, ensuring his precise steps didn't make a sound.

The house was separated into three sections, a central section and two wings on either side. He followed Roy across the foyer into the other wing. Halfway down the hallway, Roy descended a set of stairs and disappeared from sight. Andrew held his position. He heard a door open, then close.

He hurried over to the stairway. The stairs led down to a basement, but it was no ordinary basement. The door to it was secured by a keypad, and an intercom was on the wall. This place was secret. This place was Infidelity Limited. Olivia's salvation was on the other side of that door, and he couldn't get in, not without the code.

At least he knew where everything was. It was time to regroup. He climbed back up the stairs, where he found Luis standing in the middle of the hallway, holding an expandable baton.

"You picked the wrong fucking house to rob, douche bag," Luis snarled.

If Andrew was alone, he would have run, but Olivia was in the house somewhere. He couldn't leave her exposed.

I don't think so, Andrew thought. He needed to get into that room, and Luis just might be his way in. He put his tool bag down.

Luis took that as his opening and charged the thirty-foot gap between them. Andrew simply held his position. Luis swung the baton back, preparing to smash it over Andrew's head. Andrew raised his forearm to block the downward blow and drove a fist into Luis's stomach.

The young man's swing went wide as his breath exploded from his mouth. He deflated, falling to the floor on his butt. Andrew moved in fast, grabbed Luis's wrist, and twisted his arm hard, forcing the baton from his grasp.

Luis smashed a fist into the back of Andrew's right knee, dropping him to the floor. The second he was on his knees, Luis was all over him. While Andrew had fifty pounds and six inches on him, the guy was fast. He smashed Andrew with rapid punches that rocked him.

Luis used the moment to untangle himself from Andrew and deliver a few swift kicks. The guy had more game than Andrew thought, but these weren't dojo moves. They were all street moves—fast, nasty, and vicious. That told Andrew something. This kid could handle himself, but he'd never been taught how to fight. His moves were designed to hurt, not to disable his opponent. He rolled away from Luis before the guy could do some real damage and also to buy himself some space.

Andrew jumped to his feet in time to just miss a foot to the head. He brought the baton down on Luis's thigh as it went by. The dense thud of metal against muscle churned Andrew's stomach. The shock wave of pain felled Luis. As he hit the ground, Andrew caught the young man, slapping a hand over his mouth before his scream could rouse anyone.

Keeping his hand across Luis's mouth, Andrew came in tight behind him and wrapped his other arm around Luis's neck so it was squeezed by the crook of his arm. Andrew removed his hand from Luis's mouth and pressed it against his other hand, increasing the pressure on either side of Luis's neck and pinching the veins. If the guy had any fight smarts, he'd know what was coming.

"I need into that room. You going to tell me the code?"

"Fuck you," Luis growled.

He bucked in Andrew's grasp, but Andrew nipped that in the bud by wrapping his legs around his quarry. He increased the pressure. "One . . . two . . . I bet you're seeing starbursts . . . three . . . four . . . you won't hear me say ten."

The guy was already going limp.

"Tell me."

Luis tried saying "fuck you" again, but his words trailed off. He was out cold in Andrew's arms. He released his hold and laid him out.

Snatching up his tool bag, Andrew pulled out the duct tape and started trussing up Luis. Sure, it would have been nice to have gotten the kid's cooperation, but he didn't need it. He'd thought of another way into the basement.

*   *   *

Olivia turned around. A diminutive woman stood at the entrance of one of the bedrooms. She was no more than five feet tall and painfully thin. She couldn't have weighed more than a hundred pounds. It was hard to tell her age from the severe burn scarring half of her face. She could have been thirty or fifty. The full-length nightdress failed to hide the disfigurement to her left hand. Olivia guessed the scarring covered half of her body. She did her best not to let her shock at the woman's appearance show. *Is this Roy's woman?*

"I said, who are you?"

Olivia had nothing. All she could do was talk her way out of this. "Olivia."

"You're a client of Roy's."

Olivia's cover was blown. Her only option was to do everything she could to stop this woman from yelling for Roy. "Yes. And you are?"

"Beth."

Olivia smiled. "So, you're Beth."

"Roy's mentioned me?"

"He calls you his lady." Banter could be her savior. Anything to keep this woman talking and not asking the obvious question—why are you in my home?

"He does." She smiled back. "Would you like to come into my room?"

"I'd love to."

Olivia followed Beth into her room. It was a little Barbie-esque in its furnishings. There were a lot of colorful pillows and draped fabrics. It was all a little too girlish for a woman of her age. One other thing was clear. This wasn't a bedroom she shared with Roy. Nothing suggested a man slept here.

She felt sad for this woman and Roy. Whatever their relationship, he was keeping Beth as comfortable and happy as possible.

"Could you close the door?" Beth asked. "I don't want to be disturbed. It's nice to have some girl time."

Beth pointed to a couple of floral-print reading chairs by the window. A circular coffee table, complete with a tea set, separated the chairs. They each took a seat.

Olivia had the horrible feeling this room was Beth's whole world.

"Tea?" Beth asked. "It's just been brewed."

"Please."

Beth poured them both a cup.

Olivia saw this meeting as her chance to learn something about Roy. He knew everything about her. It would be useful to finally learn something about him. Maybe she'd learn something that would prevent him from retaliating against her.

"So how long have you two been together?" Olivia asked.

"I thought you said Roy talked about me."

"He talks about you, but he's never talked about your relationship."

Beth laughed. "Just like him. We've been together twenty years now. He saved me from an abusive relationship."

"That's terrible. I'm sorry."

Beth ran a hand over her damaged face. "I owe him my life. Not just from the fire. In other ways too. He indulges me. He keeps me safe from harm. I know that man would kill for me."

"Has he killed for you?" She was taking a risk asking that question, but Beth seemed so out of it that Olivia didn't think it would register as weird. If she could get a name of someone he'd killed and prove that he had done it, then she'd have the ammunition she needed to bring Roy down. It would be nice to do to him what he'd been doing to others.

"No, he hasn't, but he would. I know it."

Just like Roy to be squeaky clean, Olivia thought.

"How did you meet Roy?" Beth asked.

The question made Olivia sweat, but this could be interesting. Beth could know some interesting facts about what funded her lavish lifestyle.

"Through Infidelity Limited," Olivia replied.

Beth nodded her understanding.

"Do you know what Infidelity Limited does?"

"Yes. Roy punishes people who are unfaithful to their families. Did someone wrong you?"

"Yes, my husband."

"And Roy took care of it."

And how, Olivia thought. "Yes. My husband died."

Beth nodded as if Olivia had just said her husband was waiting in the car. The woman either had checked out on reality or was overmedicated.

"My husband was killed by Infidelity Limited," Olivia said.

"Yes."

"Roy killed my husband."

Beth smiled and shook her head. "No . . . no . . . no."

"Yes, that's what he does. He might be a wonderful man to you, but he's actually a killer."

"No, he isn't. Infidelity Limited doesn't work that way. Other clients kill for him. Roy's never killed."

Beth's answer sucker punched Olivia. The woman knew what Roy did, and she was okay with it. "You know?"

"Of course I know. Roy just does as he's told. I created Infidelity Limited."

Olivia got to her feet, dropping her tea. She'd been suckered again.

Beth stood too. "I've been where you've been. I've been someone's punching bag and doormat. I wanted my pound of flesh, and it cost me." She pointed at her ruined face. "But I deserved it too. I let it happen. I deserved to be punished as much as my abuser. That's why if someone has to kill for you, you have to be willing to kill too and pay the price."

Olivia had no answer. Beth's convoluted and twisted sense of right and wrong was beyond her understanding.

Beth looked down. "Look at the mess you made. Tea all over my carpet. Do you have any matches?"

The question baffled Olivia. "Matches? No."

"That's okay. I have my own."

From under the coffee table, she produced a matchbook. She tore a match off, lit it, then touched it to the other matches in the book. A sense of wonder spread across her face as all the matches ignited at once. Then she dropped the burning matchbook to the carpeted floor.

"What are you doing?" Olivia cried.

Olivia went to stamp the matchbook out, but the second it hit the carpeting, flames spread across the floor at an alarming rate. Now she knew who was responsible for the scorched bedroom. She grabbed the teapot and threw the contents on the growing fire.

"Don't!" Beth screamed, shoving Olivia away.

The tea stemmed the fire's progress, but it continued to burn far more quickly than it should have.

"You've ruined it!" Beth screamed. She upended the coffee table and tore off a bunch of matchbooks taped to the underside.

The fire continued to spread, despite the tea dousing. Olivia snatched a pillow off the bed and beat at the flames. Beth backhanded her across the face, sending her to the ground.

Beth torched another matchbook and touched it to the sheer curtains. The flames ate through the sheer material in seconds. The curtain blackened and curled up into itself, carrying the flames up to the ceiling.

"Stop it. You'll burn the place down." Olivia jumped to her feet and grabbed a quilt from the bed. She beat at the flames as they jumped from the sheer curtains to the main curtains.

Beth charged past her, threw open the door, and ran into the hallway.

That was when Olivia witnessed the most amazing sight of her life. Beth touched the flaming matchbook to one of the hallway walls, then to the other. A shimmering flame danced up each wall to meet on the ceiling. The archway of fire turned into a tunnel as the flames chased along the length of the hallway and Beth chased after them.

CHAPTER FORTY-FOUR

Being in the Vault soothed Roy tonight. He sat with his feet up on his desk while Creedence played on the turntable. He had a nice three fingers of bourbon warming his insides. The setting was conducive to letting him think. That was why he liked the Vault so much. It was his personal space where he could lock the world out and think. And he had plenty to think about.

He stared at Olivia's money sitting on the table in front of him. He'd fly out to the Caymans to deposit it next week. Four hundred and fifty thousand dollars. It was a pretty nice haul. He usually raked in around two hundred grand per client these days. Still, he was disappointed. This job hadn't gone well. According to Dolores, Lou Carrington was dead at the bottom of Skyline Boulevard. He and Carrington had been forced to step in and kill Heather and Amy Moore-Marbach. He'd lost a million bucks when they killed Heather.

All of these things happened because Olivia Shaw had fought back. He didn't blame Olivia for that. It was only natural. The bigger takeaway from this job was things had to change. Procedure and tactics required tweaking. He needed to read his clients better. Not all of them were cut out for killing or, for that matter, competent at it. It was all about truly understanding their pressure points. To control someone, you had to know how to squeeze them. He used to know it. Maybe he'd gotten complacent.

Where are you, Olivia? he thought. *Injured or hurt?* As much as he wanted to forget her and move on, he couldn't. She'd killed Carrington. He'd have to finish what Carrington started. He didn't have a choice.

His intercom crackled. The words came through garbled and impossible to comprehend. He slung his legs off the desk and went over to the intercom.

He pressed the button. "I didn't get that. Say again."

More garbled words.

"Luis, I can't hear you. I'm busy."

Luis said something. Roy could only make out one word in three, and he couldn't get a handle on what was being said, but he didn't have to. He already knew what the problem was—Beth. It was his own fault. He'd come home and given her the CliffsNotes version of what happened, patted her on the head, and sent her off to bed. She hated it when he ignored her.

"Okay, I'm opening up," he said, unlocking the door.

As he pulled it open, a man swung a baton at his face. He cocked his head and took the blow on the side of the neck. The blond man hurled himself at Roy, and the two of them went crashing to the ground.

Roy recognized this guy. It was that construction-crew boss who'd bawled out his guys after they'd crashed into his Chrysler at the bottom of Skyline. *What the hell is going on?* The answer didn't matter right this second. What mattered was kicking this guy's ass.

Roy lunged for the blond, but he recovered fast and hit Roy with an onslaught of baton blows. One connected with the back of his hand. Another struck him across his forearm. The one to his forehead made its mark. The pain was as searing as it was disorienting.

A single thought whistled through his brain. *Who the fuck is this guy?*

Roy got his wits back just as the baton came down toward his face again. He snatched the blond's wrist and yanked his arm forward, unbalancing him. When the guy toppled forward, Roy threw him off and scrabbled to his feet.

It was time to return the favor. He rushed forward and kicked the blond in the side of the head. The impact sent the guy rolling across the floor. To his credit, the blond was down but he wasn't out. He was slow getting up, but that was okay because Roy wanted to take his time with this guy.

"You've made a very big mistake, friend," he said.

The blond held his ground. He wasn't rushing in to fight Roy, despite still having the baton. No doubt he was trying to get his bearings back. Well, if the mountain wouldn't come to Muhammad and all that . . .

Roy dropped a shoulder and rushed the blond. The blond swung the baton and managed to strike a blow across Roy's back, but Roy slammed into him, lifting him off his feet and slamming him into the concrete wall. The blond crumpled. He lost his grip on the baton and slid down the wall to the floor.

Roy picked up the baton. "You don't mind dishing it out, but can you take it?"

He grabbed the blond's foot and dragged him to the center of the room.

"You got a name, friend?"

The blond, conscious but obviously rattled, said nothing.

"Okay, then," Roy said and struck him across the knee.

The blond yelled out and clutched his knee with both hands. The second he did, Roy landed him one on the jaw. The guy clung to consciousness by a thread.

He raised the baton to hit the intruder again. "Fuck it. I'm bored with this. It's time to teach you a lesson, whether you're aware of it or not."

"Leave him."

Roy spun around. Olivia was standing at the bottom of the stairs. *How did she find me?*

"Beth is burning the house down."

He saw thin wisps of smoke behind her. Questions didn't matter. He bolted for the stairs, brushing Olivia aside.

In the hallway, he could see the smoke filtering through the house and hear the crackle of a fire consuming it. He ran for the foyer, calling out Beth's and Luis's names. Neither of them responded.

In the foyer, he could see the upstairs was already ablaze from floor to ceiling. *Why didn't the smoke detectors go off?* He knew the answer before he finished asking himself the question. Beth had sabotaged them.

The crash of something falling to the floor in the kitchen drew his attention. He raced through the house, passing small fires as he went. He reached the kitchen in time to see the gas range explode into flames. The stink of gas was everywhere. And there was Beth at the center of it, a butcher knife in one hand and throwing cookbooks at the fire she'd created with the other.

"Beth!" he yelled.

She turned. Her grin was maniacal, but she'd never looked so happy.

"What are you doing?"

Her grip on the knife tightened. "Making it burn."

*　　　*　　　*

Olivia helped Andrew up. He was pale. "You okay?"

He nodded. "Sore and nauseous but fine."

"We've got to get out of here. Beth has set the place on fire."

"Not yet. This is our chance. Look at this place. This is Infidelity Limited's nerve center. Everything on everybody is in here."

It was. There were storage and filing cabinets, two computers, and whiteboards on wheels. She helped Andrew over to one. It was covered in notes about Heather and Amy and her. It was Roy's puppet show laid out in note form. All the hoops they had to jump through so he could squeeze them for every penny.

She went over to one of the storage cabinets and opened it. It was filled with sealed bag after sealed bag. Some bags held clothes. Some held knives, guns, and other weapons. In the filing cabinets, she found client files.

"This is an evidence dump," she said.

"This place needs to burn too," Andrew said.

It did. If everything burned, Roy's magic spell over her and all his other victims disappeared. She could be free, but more importantly, everyone could be free.

Andrew sat down at one of the computers and started tapping away. "We need to find everything he's got on you and Richard's killer, but we can't leave anything to chance. We have to burn this room. There's a bunch of booze in Roy's den. It's by the gym."

"I saw it when I was looking for you."

"Bring as many bottles as you can."

Olivia raced up the stairs and tore through the house. Fires had broken out all over, and they were spreading. The smoke was building up too. She held her hand to her mouth to keep the smoke from her lungs. With the speed the fire moved through the house, either it was the world's most flammable home or Beth had rigged this place to burn.

Running through the foyer, she heard Roy and Beth arguing somewhere. She didn't bother dodging them. They had bigger problems than her now.

She found the gym, then Roy's den. She grabbed an armful of bottles of bourbon, then spotted an added bonus—a butane cigar lighter. She stuffed it into her pants and raced back to Andrew. She dropped a bottle on the way, but she had more than enough to do the job.

Back in Roy's bunker, Andrew was tearing through one of the storage cabinets. He brought out a sealed plastic bag containing a blood-stained knife.

"Look familiar?" he asked.

It was the chef's knife from her kitchen, and it had Heather's and Amy's blood on it. She couldn't speak and nodded instead.

"I have everything. The knife. The files. You've got your life back."

The malignant fear she'd been living with for weeks disappeared, its oppressive grip gone. She could breathe again, and feelings snagged on her every breath. She let out a sob.

Stuffing the knife into his pocket, Andrew limped over to her and took the bottles from her. "It's okay. Almost home-free."

They opened up all the cabinets and splashed the bourbon over the files and the evidence bags. Olivia grabbed a bunch of the liquor-soaked files and tossed them at the bottom of each of the storage cabinets. Andrew grabbed an axe from one of the evidence bags. Olivia tried not to think about whom it had been used on. He brought the axe down on each computer tower. He whaled on them until the cases splintered. He didn't stop there, and he smashed away the circuit boards and the hard drive until they were in pieces. Then he poured a bottle of bourbon over it all.

She brought out the butane lighter and touched it to the files in the cabinets. The papers ignited. Roy's expensive bourbon accelerated the speed at which the flames jumped from file to file. She could feel her life returning to her. She'd more than earned this moment.

She went from cabinet to cabinet, setting fire to the contents, while Andrew packed her files and the knife into the grocery bag that was still filled with their cash. By the time she'd set light to the computer, everything in Roy's bunker was burning pretty well. She wanted to watch his empire of deception and lies burn. But it was time to go.

She took Andrew's hand, and they climbed the stairs. The walls in the hallway were ablaze. The whole house seemed to be burning. She had no doubt that Infidelity Limited's secrets would go up with this house.

Andrew handed her the Trader Joe's bag. "This way."

He limped over to a door and opened it. He pulled out a young Hispanic guy with his wrists and ankles duct-taped together. Despite the man's attempts to fight Andrew's approach, Andrew slung the man over his shoulder.

"Grab my tool bag, please," Andrew told her.

She did, and they cut through the house, looking for the first exit. The main entrance was proving to be their best option as fire after fire cut off their escape routes. She didn't want to die here. Not after everything they'd done to escape Roy's grip.

Just as they reached the foyer, Beth ran past them. She didn't even see them. She just leaped barefoot onto the burning staircase and charged up the steps like nothing was on fire.

Roy lurched into the foyer. He was holding his stomach with one hand. Blood was pouring from a stab wound. He stopped when he saw them.

Beth wailed.

He looked up, then back to Olivia.

"Don't," she said.

He looked at her with sadness and resignation. It was probably a look he'd seen in his victims' eyes a hundred times before. He wouldn't try to stop them now. There was nothing in it for him. In that moment, she felt sorry for Roy. Almost. He deserved his fate.

"I have to," he said and lumbered up the stairs into the flames.

"Let's go," Andrew said.

They pushed their way out of the house. It felt good to be breathing clean air and to be alive.

Andrew waited until they were clear of the house before lowering the Hispanic man to the ground. He was conscious and writhing against his bonds. Andrew yanked his gag free.

"I saved your life," Andrew said.

"Fuck you," he spat back.

"Let's go," Olivia said.

They went back the way they came, over the fence and back down the hillside to the Mercedes. As they drove back down the road, they passed Roy and Beth's house. Flames poured from every window.

"Infidelity Limited is closed for business," Olivia said, as the distant wail of sirens drifted up the hillside.

CHAPTER FORTY-FIVE

Sitting behind the wheel of Richard's Mercedes at the top of Mount Diablo, Olivia was on top of the world. She'd succeeded. She'd rescued her life from Infidelity Limited. The fire at Roy and Beth's home had been a week ago. News reports out of Santa Barbara pointed no fingers at outside suspects. The fire and police investigation blamed arson, and theories abounded that Roy and Beth were responsible. Landscapers and other witnesses remarked that Beth had a pyromania problem. Olivia's safety was further assured when fire crews recovered two corpses from the fire. IDs hadn't been confirmed, but the corpses were of a man and a woman fitting the size description of Roy and Beth. There'd been no mention of the young man Andrew had fought with, so he'd likely escaped. He was a loose end, but not a worry. If he was smart, he would have made for the hills. The same would apply to Roy's entire band of helpers. They'd lost their leverage. The vice grip of incriminating evidence Infidelity Limited had held over its victims had gone up in flames. The only thing for them to do was move on to other illegal activities.

The police hadn't reported finding anything unusual, other than a bizarre cache of charred weapons in the basement. Even if they did recover records in the fire, nothing would come back to her. She and Andrew had made sure of that when they took her files and evidence with them. Within miles of leaving Santa Barbara, they had burned her file in a barbecue pit at a park and tossed the chef's knife used to kill Heather and Amy into the sea. As her mistake turned to ash, relief swept over her.

The Morro Bay police were just as lost when it came to Heather's and Amy's murder investigation. Nothing would track back to her door. As much as it pained Olivia that it would go down as an unsolved case, she took comfort in the fact that their killer was dead.

Gault had come looking for Clare, and when she told him Clare had skipped town, he demanded that Olivia cover her sister's debts. She told him Clare's debts weren't hers to settle and if he didn't like it, he could take her to court.

She'd forgiven her sister, as hard as that was. She knew it was just Clare's nature, and having seen so much human loss in the last few weeks, she didn't want to lose her sister too. So far Clare hadn't called, but Olivia knew she would, likely when she needed money. She hoped Clare would prove her wrong for once.

Two days after the fire, Finz had made an unannounced visit to her door. She thought he'd come to arrest her. It would have been the irony of all ironies if after all she'd done to find Roy, destroy Infidelity Limited, and get all their victims off the hook, Finz had finally made his case against her.

"We both know you were behind your husband's murder," he'd told her.

"So you're here to arrest me?"

"No, the district attorney doesn't think we have a strong enough case against you," he said. "The DA only prosecutes the cases he knows he can win. It's too costly to try a case unless it's a slam dunk. But you know what? That won't stop me. There's no such thing as a cold case in our department. We keep working them until we get to the truth. That's what I'm going to do with your husband's case. I'm going to make it my pet project to learn the truth. I just wanted you to know that."

The speech had sounded heavily rehearsed, like the product of some major obsessing. She guessed the DA had killed the case days ago and it had been eating the detective up.

"And when you do, Detective Finz, you'll learn that I didn't kill my husband." It was the truest thing she had ever said to Finz or ever would.

He'd left after that, but not before delivering what he thought was a final "fuck you." There'd be no insurance payout any time in the near future. He'd seen to it by sharing his theories about her involvement in Richard's death with the life insurance company. That was fine with her. She had no intention of taking the insurance payment. She didn't want it. She didn't deserve it.

Despite all she'd done to release herself from Infidelity Limited's hold, she had one last thing to do. There was still Richard's killer to deal with. Olivia knew his name, John Proctor, and his address from Roy's files. She'd taken a leaf out of Roy's book of intimidation and left a burner phone with a single number in the contacts, along with a note attached to it, in Proctor's mailbox. The message had been simple: "Infidelity Limited. Call me. Speed-dial #1."

Andrew had watched Proctor's house after dropping the phone off. Proctor had called her within minutes of picking it up.

"Infidelity Limited is dead," she told him. "It's time to get your life back."

There were no screams of hallelujah, just silence. It was understandable. She would have reacted the same way in Proctor's position. Anyone who'd gone through the Infidelity Limited wringer no longer took the world at face value.

"Did you hear me?" she'd asked.

"Who are you?"

"Someone like you. Another client. Another victim."

Olivia had hoped those credentials would be enough for Proctor to trust her, but her explanation hung in the dead air between them.

"It's really over," she added.

"It's never over."

That was true. Infidelity Limited might be ashes—Roy and Beth were dead—but its aftereffects were not. Olivia, Proctor, and everyone who'd ever employed Infidelity Limited would have to live with the guilt of setting events in motion that had resulted in the death of a loved one. The one regret Olivia had was that she couldn't help more of the other Infidelity Limited victims, like Karen Innes, who was still in prison. Olivia could have grabbed the evidence that would have helped Karen prove her innocence, but it would have only implicated another victim. Letting everything burn had been the best solution. Nobody was entirely innocent. As clients, they'd all committed crimes. Some people were just luckier than others.

"It's as over as it can be," she told him.

"How do I get my life back?"

"Meet me."

"And how much will it cost me?"

There'd been a weary tone to Proctor's speech, but a bitter edge had replaced it now. She guessed Roy must have milked him hard. "No cost."

"Where?"

Andrew wanted to go with her when she met with Proctor, but she told him no. Proctor wasn't someone to be taken lightly. He'd been battered by Infidelity Limited, which made him unpredictable, and he'd killed Richard, which made him dangerous. She and Proctor had a connection. They were both victims. Proctor would understand that.

Andrew deferred to her but insisted on looking out for her. He was positioned a couple of miles down the mountain at one of the lookout spots.

Her cell phone rang. It was Andrew.

"He's on his way up," he said. "Blue minivan."

"Alone?"

"No one in the car with him, and no one following."

That had been her only fear. Finz had been trying ceaselessly to incriminate her. There could be another Finz somewhere doing the same to Proctor. But so far, so good.

A few minutes later, the blue minivan pulled into the parking lot. Olivia climbed from her car and waved at him.

Proctor didn't smile—and neither did she.

She grabbed the backpack from the trunk and slung it over her shoulder. She approached his car but stopped short, forcing him to get out.

At the first sight of the man who'd killed her husband, Olivia didn't know what to feel. She'd expected anger and contempt. Instead, she felt only a mess of half-formed emotions that bordered on compassion. After all, Proctor hadn't killed out of spite or financial gain. Roy had coerced him. He'd been an unwilling participant under extreme duress, just like her. Victims of Infidelity Limited had to support each other, not turn on each other.

"John?"

Proctor nodded. Andrew had told her the guy was big, and the photo he'd snapped of him on his cell phone bore that out, but in the flesh he was bigger than she expected. It was easy to see why Richard had been no match for him.

"Let's go somewhere private."

"Okay. I'll drive us," he said.

She shook her head. One of Andrew's rules had been to make sure to meet in the open. She wasn't going to get into his car, and he wasn't going to get into hers. In close quarters, Proctor had the upper hand. In the open, she stood a chance of getting away.

"No need. We're not going far," she told him.

She walked him down to the overflow parking lot where Roy had dropped his Infidelity Limited bombshell on her. It was deserted, just as before. They were alone.

"Did you deal with a man calling himself Roy?" she asked.

"Yes."

She had wondered if Roy used a raft of aliases on his victims. It didn't appear so.

"He's dead, and so is his partner." She'd decided not to provide the nitty-gritty details, just the raw facts. She didn't want anyone tracing anything back to her involvement in Infidelity Limited's downfall. "All that Infidelity Limited is and ever was has been destroyed in a fire. Any hold they had over you is gone."

Proctor put a fist to his mouth. His breathing turned ragged. Tears welled up, and he turned away from her.

Olivia realized this man was barely holding it together. She understood that feeling all too well, but it must have been even worse for him. He'd gone much further than she had, and he'd done it alone. At least she'd had Andrew to support her.

It was a good minute before he turned back to her. "I never thought it would be over. Not like this. Not getting my life back."

"Well, it is."

"Did you kill Roy?"

"No."

"Who are you?"

It was time to be cruel. "I'm the wife of the man you killed."

Whatever fragile shell that had been keeping Proctor together fractured. He came apart in front of her, shrinking away from her and collapsing to his knees before bursting into tears.

Proctor grabbed her hand and yanked it to him, jerking her forward. "Forgive me."

Forgiveness. She wasn't sure she had that in her to give. He'd been used by Roy like all of Infidelity Limited's victims. In some ways, he was nothing more than a weapon. But like her, he had a choice. She'd given in to her anger at Richard, and that had gotten him killed. She would have to live with that mistake for the rest of her life. But she'd also chosen to resist Infidelity Limited. When Roy had ordered her to kill, she'd fought to bring him down. Proctor hadn't. She didn't know if she could forgive him for that, but she wasn't going to turn him in to Finz either. He'd been punished enough and would continue to be punished. He'd have to live with Richard's death on his conscience.

"Forgive me," he repeated.

The words wouldn't come. Richard was dead because of him. Because of Roy. Because of her.

He looked up at her. "I need to hear you say it."

"I forgive you," she said, her words barely audible.

"Thank you. Thank you." The rest of what he said was lost to more sobbing.

Her own tears ran then. The bond between them was unique—both guilty and innocent at the same time. True justice would never be seen for their loved ones, but in an Infidelity Limited universe, this was as close as it got. She pulled her hand free of his, then shrugged the backpack off her shoulders and held it out to him.

"What's this?"

"Everything Roy had on you."

Still on his knees, he took the backpack from her. He unzipped it, then peered in and ran a thumb over the exposed papers. "Have you read it?"

"Only briefly. Just to make sure it was yours."

"Does it say who killed my wife?"

"Yes."

Proctor zipped the backpack shut. Olivia guessed he didn't need to know the identity of his wife's killer.

"I suggest you destroy that."

Proctor nodded as he got to his feet.

"What do we do now?" he asked.

"Try and live our lives," she said.

Olivia left Proctor standing there with the backpack and tried to imagine how she was going to do that.

Andrew was waiting for her at his lookout point. She stopped the car and walked over to him. He pulled her into a tight embrace, and she reached up and kissed him. After standing there in each other's arms for a few minutes, they got into the car.

"You're finally free," he said.

That wasn't entirely true, not while Finz continued to beaver away at the case, but she was as free as she could be under the circumstances, and that was okay with her. She'd take it. That was the price of freedom in a post–Infidelity Limited world.

ACKNOWLEDGMENTS

In many of my books, the supporting characters are named after some of my readers who have volunteered their identities. This book is a little different. At the request of a reader, several of the supporting characters are named after deceased friends and family members. I'd like to thank Mike Finz (nominated by Janet Finz), Robert Bertholf (nominated by Julie Wood), Mark Renko (nominated by Carole Javaux), Leo Steele (nominated by Rhonda Holley Ray), Isaac Rivera (nominated by Meagan Beaumont), Henry Freitas (nominated by Annette Mahon), Rick Casey (nominated by Colleen Casey), Nicholas Bonanni (nominated by Nikki Bonanni), Allen Yager (nominated by Elise Dee Beraru), and Lou Carrington (nominated by Kari Wainwright). I'd also like to thank Madeleine Lyon, Maxine Groves, Amy K. Marbach, Cassie Hill, and Heather Brown Moore for donating their names.

ABOUT THE AUTHOR

A former race-car driver, licensed pilot, endurance cyclist, and private investigator, Simon Wood is the author of more than a dozen novels, including *The One That Got Away*, *Accidents Waiting to Happen*, and *Paying the Piper*. He has also penned more than 150 short stories. Wood has won the Anthony Award for his mystery fiction and was nominated for a CWA Dagger Award. A native of the United Kingdom, he lives with his wife, Julie, in California. Learn more at www.simonwood.net.